The Complete WAR of the WORLDS

The Complete WAR of the WORLDS

Mars' Invasion of Earth from H.G. Wells to Orson Welles

Brian Holmsten & Alex Lubertozzi • **Ray Bradbury** • **Ben Bova** • **John Callaway**

Editors   Foreword   Afterword   Narration

SOURCEBOOKS MEDIAFUSION™
AN IMPRINT OF SOURCEBOOKS, INC.®
NAPERVILLE, ILLINOIS

Published by Sourcebooks, Inc.
P.O. Box 4410, Naperville, Illinois 60567-4410
(630) 961-3900
FAX: (630) 961-2168

Library of Congress Cataloging-in-Publication Data

The complete war of the worlds: Mars' invasion of Earth from H.G. Wells to Orson Welles / edited by Brian Holmsten and Alex Lubertozzi.
          p. cm.
     Includes bibliographical references.
     ISBN 1-57071-714-1 (alk. paper)
     1. Wells, H.G. (Herbert George), 1866–1946. War of the worlds. 2. Wells, H.G. (Herbert George), 1866–1946—Adaptations. 3. Welles, Orson, 1915–1985—Criticism and interpretation. 4. Science fiction, English—History and criticism. 5. Imaginary wars and battles in literature. 6. War of the worlds (Radio program). 7. Science fiction radio programs. 8. Mars (Planet)—In literature. I. Holmsten, Brian. II. Lubertozzi, Alex.

PR5774.W33 C66 2001
823'.912—dc21

00-066166

Printed and bound in the United States of America
DO   10 9 8 7 6 5 4 3 2 1

To H.G. and Orson,
whose unique genius each
helped shape the twentieth century
in remarkable and wonderful ways

I felt the first inkling of a thing that presently grew quite clear in my mind, that oppressed me for many days, a sense of dethronement, a persuasion that I was no longer a master, but an animal among the animals, under the Martian heel.

—H.G. Wells
The War of the Worlds

...Remember, please, for the next day or so, the terrible lesson you learned here tonight. That grinning, glowing, globular invader of your living room is an inhabitant of the pumpkin patch, and if your doorbell rings and nobody's there, that was no Martian...it's Hallowe'en.

—Orson Welles
"The War of the Worlds"

Contents

CD This symbol, throughout the book, denotes which track of the audio CD corresponds to the text.

THE WAR of
the WORLDS

H. G. Wells

Foreword by Ray Bradbury

H.G. Wells, Master of Paranoia

Now consider *The War of the Worlds*, which induces paranoia in its hapless readers and causes listeners a similar madness when Orson changes Wells to Welles, while clamoring ten million radios with invasions.

I witnessed both, I discovered my own fears of far planets and terrible aliens in the August 1927 *Amazing Stories* reprint of *The War of the Worlds*. Fresh out of high school years later, I heard the United States under siege by radio Martians.

Both were delights.

There is nothing like a wholesale statewide destruction to make a boy sit up and eat his spinach.

Delight was mine when I heard half-seen mobs tear passions to tatters the night Orson Welles was truly born.

The Wells novels and the Welles ear-candy beckon the seedling paranoias in most men and boys born needful for power, accomplishments, or destruction.

Women, on the other hand, mind their knitting and say, "Get on with it. While you're being invaded, I'll just make another child to freshen the paranoid stock."

Wells and Welles prepared us for the delusional madness of the past fifty years. In fact, the entire history of the United States in the last half of the twentieth century is exemplified beautifully in Wells' work. Starting with the so-called arrival of flying saucers in the 1950s, we've had a continuation of our mild panic at being invaded by creatures from some other part of the universe. It started with that alien professor who sold hot dogs with saucers of Invaders at the foot of Mt. Palomar. It then ravened up the years with half-baked sightings to end in Roswell and wild true believers who claimed they never met a bug-eyed monster they didn't love.

Dr. Hynek disagreed, and he was the expert on flying saucers hitting the fan, having started the Center for UFO Studies.

People said yes to his truths but snuck off the next day to Bide-a-Wee Martian Shoals in California, Arizona, and New Mexico.

The myths proliferated, all the way from the friendly beasts that invaded Meteor Crater in my *It Came from Outer Space* to the incredible Mother Ship landing in firework illuminations in *Close Encounters of the Third Kind*. God reaching down to touch Adam's upstretched hand.

So the invasions will never cease. Or, not until we landfall Mars, build towns, and become friendly invaders to the universe. We will arrive in peace and, hopefully, go with God.

We are still playing "The War of the Worlds" on our audiotape machines and imagining it is Halloween 1938 and Nothing Can Save Us except a convenient earthbourn germ.

When we read H.G. Wells' *The Man Who Could Work Miracles*, the story's lunatic hero, Fotheringay, cries, "By God, I will run the world or by God, destroy every man, woman, and child of it." Wells' *Invisible Man* sees himself run amok among stupid non-thinkers to correct their behaviors and longs to destroy dumb things and people who live by stupid laws.

This is the attraction of some of Wells' most famous pieces. We wish we were invisible, we wish we could command the world to pull up its socks or know annihilation. There is grim satisfaction in being a Martian fresh out of its spaceship, come to rule the world or die trying.

So we are all closet paranoids preached to by a paranoid.

Now consider the other outstanding author of science fiction at the turn of the twentieth century. Jules Verne created a mad scientist also, but when you consider Captain Nemo on board his *Nautilus*, out to conquer the world, or his secret self, you are confronted by an amiable lunatic compared to the madmen who inhabit many of H.G. Wells' stories. H.G. Wells' heroes are true villains and dangerous.

But there are no villains in *The War of the Worlds*, only our panics and night dreams, the dark lopside of our numbskull invading the half that stands in full sun. There is no paranoid lunatic at the center of *The War of the Worlds*. Instead, the reader is the one who becomes filled with paranoia. *The War of the Worlds* is a nightmare vision of humanity's conquest—one that inspired paranoia in all its forms throughout the twentieth century. Wells was reacting to the injustice and ignorance of man in his work, while Verne envisioned the wonder of technology. We enjoy them both for different reasons, but they both capture truths about the world, good and bad. It speaks volumes about us that Wells' vision caused the more spectacular impact. And, truth be told, ever since the novel and the broadcast, we are still in the throes of believing that we've been invaded by creatures from somewhere else.

Introduction

"There are no Martians. There are no intelligences on Mars superior to our own in any way comparable. It seems quite likely that there never have been. In fact, the evidence we now have makes it seem likely that there is no life of any kind on Mars and there may not even have been any life on the planet in the past."
—*Isaac Asimov, in an afterword to* The War of the Worlds

On October 30, 1938, Orson Welles took Howard Koch's adaptation of H.G. Wells' classic, *The War of the Worlds*, and convinced more than a million Americans that a Martian army had come to Earth to annihilate the human race. Orson Welles' Mercury Theatre, broadcast coast-to-coast on CBS Radio, simulated a program of dance music ("Ramón Raquello and his orchestra") being interrupted by increasingly alarming and unbelievable newsflashes from Grovers Mill, New Jersey. By the time it became clear what was being reported, men, women, and children in dozens of towns and cities all over the nation fled their homes in terror from objects that existed only in their imagination.

"The War of the Worlds" was a short-lived conflict. The invaders, shot like cannonballs from Mars to remote regions around the globe, decimated most of New Jersey and set half the planet on fire all before the first scheduled program break (about forty minutes). A suspiciously short time frame, one would think. Conspicuous also was CBS News' exclusive on the story.

A number of conditions may help explain America's susceptibility to the hoax—the continuing economic hardships of the Great Depression, Hitler pushing Europe to the brink of war, the Hindenburg explosion of 1937 (the first disaster to be broadcast live), and news of the devastating hurricane that hit the East Coast earlier in the year. People had grown accustomed to hearing bad news, especially, in recent months, in the form of late-breaking newsflashes.

The panic broadcast, as it came to be known, was an experiment in mass delusion set not in a university, but in America's living room. What was it about H.G. Wells' tale that caused so many people to act so irrationally? And what is it about *The War of the Worlds* story that continues to fascinate us?

H.G. Wells published his classic story in 1898, when many in England eyed Germany's growing war machine with the same trepidation that preceded World War II. His book, which predated the Boer War and World War I, foresaw a warfare more mechanized and brutal than any seen before. The idea of refugees fleeing a devastated London must have seemed incredible in that Victorian age; so too would the notion of flying machines and poison gas used as instruments of war. Since its initial publication, publishers around the world have released numerous editions of *The War of the Worlds*, pulp comics serialized it, Hollywood made a movie of it, and in 1978, Jeff Wayne even staged his *Musical Version of The War of the Worlds*, starring Richard Burton. Other radio performances, inspired by the Orson Welles broadcast, have aired at various times and on various stations in the U.S. and abroad. In response to the 1949 "War of the Worlds" broadcast from Quito, Ecuador, enraged townsfolk rioted, ultimately torching the radio studio building and killing several station employees.

Countless others, inspired by H.G.'s book and Orson's broadcast, have created their own take on Earth's invasion from outer space. In the 1940s and

50s, as the Cold War heated up, science fiction came to the fore as a popular movie genre, particularly stories of alien invasion, with films such as *The Day the Earth Stood Still, The Thing, Invasion of the Body Snatchers,* and the 1953 screen version of *The War of the Worlds.* Those movies were the at the fore of the monsters-from-space crop; other fare included *Purple Death from Outer Space, Invaders from Mars, Killers from Space, Flying Disc Man from Mars, Zombies of the Stratosphere, Devil Girl from Mars, Santa Claus Conquers the Martians, I Married a Monster from Outer Space, Teenagers from Outer Space, Mars Needs Women,* and the movie many consider the worst of all time, Ed Wood's *Plan 9 from Outer Space.* In 1962, Topps released their "Mars Attacks!" trading cards, which later inspired the Tim Burton film, *Mars Attacks!*

They all owed a debt to the original monsters-from-outer-space epic, H.G. Wells' *The War of the Worlds.*

And for most of the twentieth century, beings from outer space were cast as villains—bent on destroying our civilization, taking over the planet, and, if possible, having their way with Earth women. Although the science fiction literature was way ahead of Hollywood—Ray Bradbury's *The Martian Chronicles,* which depicted Earthmen as "invaders" of Mars, came out in 1950, and Robert A. Heinlein's *Stranger in a Strange Land,* about a human raised by enlightened Martians who returns to earth, was published in 1961—it wasn't until the 1970s and 80s that empathetic extraterrestrials were introduced to audiences in movies like *Close Encounters of the Third Kind, E.T.,* and *Starman.* This more enlightened or hopeful view, however, has not eradicated the paranoid view we hold of the outsiders, the malevolent and mysterious *them.*

Arthur C. Clarke, who in 1952 envisioned a race of benevolent aliens in *Childhood's End,* said in a 1969 interview with Howard Koch, "I think that the sort of unmotivated malevolence which is typical of many science fiction stories is unlikely because some of the invaders in space that we've encountered in fiction would simply have destroyed themselves before they got anywhere else." But he went on to say, "...at the same time, one must admit that in a practically infinite universe almost anything is theoretically possible to happen somewhere."

The expectation that aliens would be hostile seems irrational. And it reveals our tendency to xenophobia, our fear of anything alien or different. We tend to project our own fears and hostilities on those who are different until those imaginings become real to us. Which raises an important question: Would anyone have believed the broadcast if the Martians were said to have come in peace?

★ ★ ★

In *The War of the Worlds,* the Martians are ultimately defeated by "the humblest thing that God in His wisdom put upon this earth," the bacterium. But seventy-one years later, in Michael Crichton's *The Andromeda Strain,* we learn that this cuts both ways, as an extraterrestrial virus, brought to earth by an unmanned satellite, wipes out a small Arizona town in a matter of hours, threatening humankind's very existence. In 1996, when NASA scientist David McKay uncovered fossil evidence of possible bacterial life forms on Mars, the idea of deadly space microbes suddenly seemed less like science fiction. The more technologically adept we become, and the more possibilities we are able to imagine, the more we find to be scared of. We've learned to laugh at our fears, of course, as the movie parody of *Mars Attacks!* and shows like *Third Rock from the Sun* prove. But popular entertainments like *Invasion Earth, V, The X-Files, Roswell, Alien Autopsy,* and *Independence Day* remind us that we are still, at heart, paranoid creatures.

Science has advanced at an astounding pace since 1898, a time when the scientific community—unable to imagine relativity or quantum theory—believed there was little left to discover. Breakthroughs in transportation, communications, medicine, biotechnology, computer science, and nuclear physics have changed every aspect of our daily lives. We've shrunken the globe with satellite broadcasting and wireless communications; we've explored space, landing men on the moon and unmanned vehicles on Mars; we've enhanced, automated, and sped up countless processes with ever-smaller and more powerful computers; we've cloned animals; and we've split the atom, unleashing the power of the sun.

We've only begun to question our place in the universe within the last hundred years and have arrived at no great insight but this: we are either the only intelligent life in the cosmos or we are not. Either scenario is mind-boggling. If we're not alone, that means that someday we may actually have to deal with it. Like relativity or quantum physics, extraterrestrial intelligence is a concept we've only recently become able to imagine. That knowledge forces us to question some long-held assumptions about our place and our purpose. For one, if we're not the masters of the universe, then who is?

THE
PANIC
BROADCAST

The Eve of Halloween

"We have so much faith in broadcasting. In a crisis it has to reach all people. That's what radio is here for."

The night before Halloween, known as Mischief Night, or Devil's Night, is the night you might expect the neighborhood kids to soap your windows or T.P. your silver maple. But that's about it. October 30, 1938, was a peaceful Sunday evening, a little foggy in the East, partially obscuring the night skies over the farmlands of New Jersey. This outward calm, however, belied a nation tense with apprehension. The country, still struggling out of the Great Depression, feared the worst in Europe, where Neville Chamberlain and Edouard Daladier were attempting to appease Hitler, as the Nazis annexed the Sudetenland and greedily eyed the rest of Europe. The Munich Pact of September 30, in which Britain and France gave away a substantial chunk of Czechoslovakia to Hitler, had averted a war, but only for so long. One news commentator summed up America's fears best:

> *…It is the opinion of this commentator, that, in spite of all our hopes and our prayers, this new accord, this Munich agreement, will not, no matter how many times and with what apparent sincerity he assures us otherwise, I repeat, will not satisfy the ambitions of Adolf Hitler.…I tell you that this man is drunk with success. And I tell you that his government is barbaric and inhuman. And that he will never rest until all of Europe, and perhaps more, is under that government…*

President Roosevelt had sent a telegram to Hitler and the president of Czechoslovakia three days prior to the Munich settlement, begging them to continue negotiations rather than resort to arms. In the end, the Czechs were not consulted on their country's dismemberment. While America's role remained uncertain, Americans grew worried as radio news flashes about the situation in Europe regularly interrupted programming.

For more than thirty million of these radio listeners, the top-rated *Chase and Sanborn Hour*, starring Edgar Bergen and Charlie McCarthy, was the lighthearted distraction they needed.

A ventriloquist act. On the radio.

The Mercury Theatre on the Air, produced by twenty-three-year-old Orson Welles and the elder, Bucharest-born, former grain merchant John Houseman, posted a miserable 3.6 Crossley rating, compared to *Chase and Sanborn*'s 34.7 rating. But, about twelve minutes after eight, Edgar Bergen and Charlie McCarthy's act broke for a musical interlude with Nelson Eddy singing the "Neopolitan Love Song," and a large chunk of the audience switched stations to hear what else was on (the first noteworthy instance of zapping, or "channel-surfing"), only to find a CBS news correspondent announcing on WABC in New York:

Hitler and Hermann Göring lead a victory procession into Czechoslovakia, after the Sudetenland was ceded to the Nazis, October 10, 1938.

Ladies and gentlemen, this is Carl Phillips again, at the Wilmuth farm, Grovers Mill, New Jersey.... Well, I...hardly know where to begin, to paint for you a word picture of the strange scene before my eyes, like something out of a modern Arabian Nights. *Well, I just got here. I haven't had a chance to look around yet. I guess that's it. Yes, I guess that's the...thing, directly in front of me, half buried in a vast pit. Must have struck with terrific force. The ground is covered with splinters of a tree it must have struck on its way down. What I can see of the...object itself doesn't look very much like a meteor, at least not the meteors I've seen. It looks more like a huge cylinder....* **CD 1**

Neville Chamberlain, Edouard Daladier, Adolf Hitler, and Benito Mussolini at the Munich Conference, September 30, 1938

This curious but arresting description kept many a listener's rapt attention. (It was later estimated by the Hooper ratings service that about 12 percent of those who had been listening to Edgar Bergen and Charlie McCarthy, about four million listeners, switched to CBS at the break.) The "reporter," Carl Phillips, accompanied by the fictional Princeton astronomer, Professor Pierson, went on to describe the tentacled, squid-like Martian as it emerged from the capsule. "It's as large as a bear and it glistens like wet leather....I can hardly force myself to keep looking at it. The eyes are black and gleam like a serpent. The mouth is V-shaped with saliva dripping from its rimless lips that seem to quiver and pulsate."

And then it got worse.

Phillips called the play-by-play as the Martians unleashed their horrible heat ray on the crowd that had gathered, and eventually on Phillips himself, as the signal went dead for what must have seemed a very long time. There was apparent confusion back at the station, while they filled the dead air with a short, but ominous piano interlude of "Claire de Lune." Bulletins followed detailing the death toll at Grovers Mill. "Brigadier General Montgomery Smith" placed half of New Jersey under martial law. Units of Red Cross emergency workers were said to be dispatched to the area. Ironically, in hindsight, "Harry McDonald," the fictitious vice president of operations, announced: "In view of the gravity of the situation, and believing that radio has a definite responsibility to serve in the public interest at all times, we are turning over our facilities to the state militia at Trenton." Finally, from the New York studio, came the unequivocal announcement that encapsulated the lie at the heart of the show:

Orson Welles broadcasting on CBS radio

Ladies and gentlemen, I have a grave announcement to make. Incredible as it may seem, both the observations of science and the evidence of our eyes lead to the inescapable assumption that those strange beings who landed in the Jersey farmlands tonight are the vanguard of an invading army from the planet Mars....

On the night of October 30, 1938, more than thirty-two million people tuned in to hear what was on the radio.

Surprisingly, or perhaps *not* surprisingly given the realism of the reportage, a large portion of the radio audience never bothered to switch back to Charlie McCarthy to check the authenticity of CBS' broadcast.

As the Martians marched toward New York, easily defeating the Army, destroying lines of communication, and releasing black clouds of deadly gas over the countryside, people who hadn't been to church that morning prayed with the fervor of the born-again. When an unnamed "Secretary of the Interior" came on the air to urge Americans to remain calm and "in the meantime placing our faith in God...so that we may confront this destructive adversary with a nation united, courageous, and consecrated to the preservation of human supremacy on this earth," it was impossible not to notice the uncanny resemblance of the speaker's voice to that of President Franklin Delano Roosevelt.

Women wept in front of their radios; so did their husbands. Everywhere, people ran into the streets, unsure where to go or what to do. Many took to their cars, speeding around like mad and covering their faces with wet towels to protect themselves from the gas. In Newark, traffic cops watched dumbfounded as dozens of automobiles careened through intersections, heedless of stoplights, pedestrians, or other motorists. Panicked listeners tied up phone lines, calling their loved ones to warn them or just to say good-bye, and jamming the switchboards of radio stations, newspapers, and police headquarters. Those who didn't get through reasoned that it was the Martians who were responsible.

Grovers Mill in 1938, ground zero for the Martian invasion

An Alvin Correco drawing illustrating the devastating effect of the Martian heat ray

Of the more than six million estimated listeners, 1.7 million were believed to take the radio play as fact, and 1.2 million panicked, according to a study conducted by a *real* Princeton professor, Hadley Cantril, and published in his 1940 book, *Invasion from Mars*. Most failed to check the veracity of the Martian invasion by either checking the radio program listings in the paper or switching channels. All somehow missed the announcement at the beginning of the show that it was a dramatization of "The War of the Worlds." By the first break and second announcement, most had stopped listening to the radio and were off panicking somewhere out of earshot.

Near Grovers Mill, ground zero for the Martian invasion, the panic was probably most immediate. The fire chief of Cranbury, five miles from Grovers Mill, received dozens of calls reporting fires in the woods set by the Martian heat rays. He spent most of the night responding to nonexistent fires set by nonexistent alien invaders. In the course of chasing down these imaginary conflagrations, he was able to observe farmers, armed with shotguns, roaming the countryside looking for Martians or for the militia, which was supposed to have

The water tower once mistaken for a Martian, as it looks today

of a peaceful slumber, and take him on a wild, drunken ride, which ended when Welles came on to say that it was all just a play. What the brother then did to the man was not reported.

Some of the Grovers Mill locals actually fired shots at what they believed to be one of the Martians rising up on its giant metal legs. It turned out to be a tall, fanless, and most likely unarmed water tower and windmill. This "Martian" still stands today in the backyard of a house, across the street from the grist Mill that gave the community its name. The present-day owner of the Martian water tower (it overlooks a swimming pool now), Catherine Shrope-Mok, reported that the ones who were primarily shooting at the water tower in 1938 were in fact the neighbors from across the road, "who you'd think would know better," she said, "since they saw it every day." The famous water tower actually receives visitors from around the country and as far away as Scandinavia and Japan every Halloween, according to Ms. Shrope-Mok.

been deployed to the area to fend off the "intruders." Later, more than a hundred state troopers descended on the area to calm the local residents and disarm the "volunteers" before anybody got hurt.

Another local to the Grovers Mill area was in such a hurry to drive off to reach his wife's family in Pennsylvania, he neglected to open the garage door first and, despite his wife's screamed warning, drove right through the door with a crunch, saying back to his wife, "Well, we won't be needing it anymore."

Another neighbor, who had emptied a bottle of whiskey while listening to the broadcast, decided that his chow dog would be much safer in its kennel at the side of the house. Grabbing the animal, he rushed outside and attempted to fling the chow over the fence into the kennel. Terrified and confused at his master's strange behavior, the dog clamped down on the man's sleeve with his jaw and held on for dear life. The man swung the dog over his head several times until the sleeve, with chow attached, ripped off. The man then proceeded to drive to his brother's house, yank him out

The day after the panic, a New York Daily News *photographer got seventy-six-year-old William Dock to recreate his armed resistance to the Martian invaders in a staged pose.*

New York Daily News *front page*

That same night, a few miles away, a couple of other real Princeton professors, Arthur Buddington, chairman of the geology department, and geologist Harry H. Hess, spent the better part of the evening searching for the object reported on the broadcast—"something of an unusual nature, possibly a meteorite"—which had supposedly landed in Grovers Mill. According to the *Trenton Evening Times*, "Armed with a geologist's hammer and a flashlight, they began a systematic tapping of rocks to determine if they were of earthly or heavenly origin." The two no doubt endured quite a bit of razzing from their colleagues for their expedition.

In Newark, those who weren't racing their cars around the streets with their faces covered by wet rags were busy spilling out into the streets, taking their wordly possessions with them, or having conniption fits. One hospital in Newark treated fifteen men and women for shock and hysteria; the parents of three children called the hospital to say they were coming to take their kids and leaving the city. New Jersey national guardsmen flooded the armories of Essex and Sussex counties

with calls asking when and where to report. Hundreds of doctors and nurses offered their services to the Newark police to aid the "injured," while city officials made emergency plans. The governor of Pennsylvania even offered to send troops to New Jersey to help quell the Martian insurgency.

In New York, the source of the broadcast, the *New York Times* reported that the Dixie Bus Terminal was ready to change its schedule upon confirmation of "news reports" on an "accident" near Princeton on their New Jersey route. When Dorothy Brown at the terminal sought verification, she was refused by the person on the other end of the line, who said, "The world is coming to an end, and I have a lot to do."

At the wedding reception of Rocco and Connie Cassamassina in uptown Manhattan, a group of latecomers arrived, visibly shaken by something. One of them took the microphone from the singer in the dance band and announced to the party that the city was being invaded by creatures from outer space. After the initial bewildered reaction, panic set in and guests started running for their coats and leaving. Connie begged the few people who were left not to leave with tears in her eyes. Rocco grabbed the microphone and started singing hymns to the handful of stunned guests who remained.

A young college student reported to radio play scriptwriter Howard Koch:

My girlfriend and I were at a party in the Village. Someone turned on the radio. It was just when the Martians were spraying the people at Grovers Mill with the heat ray. At first we couldn't believe it was happening, but it was so real we stayed glued to the radio, getting more scared every minute. My girl began to cry. She wanted to be with her family. The party broke up in a hurry, our friends scattering in all directions. I drove like crazy up Sixth Avenue. I don't know how fast—fifty, maybe sixty miles an hour. The traffic cops at the street crossings just stared at us, they couldn't believe their eyes, whizzing right past them going through the red lights. I didn't care if I got a ticket. It was all over anyway. Funny thing, none of the cops chased us. I guess they were too flabbergasted. My apartment was on the way, so I stopped just long enough to rush in and shout up to my father that the Martians had landed and we were all going to be killed and I was taking my girl home. When we got to her place, her parents were waiting for us. My father had called them. Told them to hold me there until he could send a doctor as I'd gone out of my mind.

A senior in a large eastern college, returning from a date with his girlfriend, heard the broadcast in his car and returned to save her. "One of the first things I did was to try to phone my girl in Poughkeepsie, but the lines were all busy, so that just confirmed my impression that the thing was true. We started driving back to Poughkeepsie. We had heard that Princeton was wiped out and gas and fire were spreading over New Jersey, so I figured there wasn't anything to do—we figured our friends and families were all dead. I made the forty-five miles in thirty-five minutes and didn't even realize it. I drove right through Newburgh and never even knew I went through it. I don't know why we weren't killed….The gas was supposed to be spreading up north. I didn't have any idea exactly what I was fleeing from, and that made me all the more afraid….I thought the whole human race was going to be wiped out—that seemed more important than the fact that we were going to die."

The authorities were often of little help to panicked listeners. In some cases, as one listener reported, they probably made things worse:

I immediately called up the Maplewood police and asked if there was anything wrong. They answered, "We know as much as you do. Keep your radio tuned in and follow the announcer's advice. There is no immediate danger in Maplewood." Naturally, after that I was more scared than ever.

New Jersey State Police had to reassure its officers: "WABC broadcast as drama re: this section being attacked by residents of Mars. Imaginary affair." And New York police eventually sent out the following message to its force: "Station WABC informs us that the broadcast just concluded over that station was a dramatization of a play. No cause for alarm."

The terror was not confined to New Jersey and New York, however. One man in Pittsburgh came home just in time to save his wife, who was in the bathroom holding a bottle of poison in her hand and screaming, "I'd rather die this way than like that!"

Joseph Hendley, a small-town Midwesterner, recounted his evening:

That Halloween Boo sure had our family on its knees before the program was half over. God knows but we prayed to Him last Sunday. It was a lesson in more than one thing to us. My mother went out and looked for Mars. Dad was hard to convince or skeptical or sumpin', but he even got to believing it….Aunt Grace, a good Catholic, began to pray with Uncle Henry. Lily got sick to her stomach. I don't know what I did exactly, but I know I prayed harder and more earnestly than ever before. Just as soon as we were convinced that this thing was real, how pretty all things on Earth seemed; how soon we put our trust in God.

The New York Times.

Copyright, 1938, by The New York Times Company.

NEW YORK, MONDAY, OCTOBER 31, 1938.

Radio Listeners in Panic, Taking War Drama as Fact

Many Flee Homes to Escape 'Gas Raid From Mars'—Phone Calls Swamp Police at Broadcast of Wells Fantasy

A wave of mass hysteria seized thousands of radio listeners throughout the nation between 8:15 and 9:30 o'clock last night when a broadcast of a dramatization of H. G. Wells's fantasy, "The War of the Worlds," led thousands to believe that an interplanetary conflict had started with invading Martians spreading wide death and destruction in New Jersey and New York.

and radio stations here and in other cities of the United States and Canada seeking advice on protective measures against the raids.

The program was produced by Mr. Welles and the Mercury Theatre on the Air over station WABC and the Columbia Broadcasting System's coast-to-coast network, from 8 to 9 o'clock.

The radio play, as presented, was to simulate a regular radio pro-

The panic soon spread all over the United States. A Warner Brothers studio executive later confided to Koch his reaction:

> *My wife and I were driving through the redwood forest when the broadcast came over our car radio. At first it was just New Jersey, but soon the things were landing all over, even in California. There was no escape. All we could think of was to try to get back to L.A. to see our children once more and be with them when it happened. We went right by gas stations, but I forgot we were low in gas. In the middle of the forest, our gas ran out. There was nothing to do. We just sat there holding hands expecting any minute to see those Martian monsters appear over the tops of the trees. When Orson said it was a Halloween prank, it was like being reprieved on the way to the gas chamber.*

One small Southwestern college reported the following:

> *The girls in the sorority houses and dormitories huddled around their radios trembling and weeping in each other's arms. They separated themselves from their friends only to take their turn at the telephones to make long distance calls to their parents, saying good-bye for what they thought might be the last time. This horror was shared by older and more experienced people—instructors and supervisors in the university. Terror-stricken girls, hoping to escape from the Mars invaders, rushed to the basement of the dormitory. A fraternity boy, frantic with fear, threw off dormitory regulations when he sought out his girlfriend and started for home. Another boy rushed into the street to warn the town of the invasion.*

In the small town of Concrete, Washington, the local power failed at the exact moment when the Martians in the play were disabling communication and power lines around the U.S. The result, of course, was mass hysteria as people fled into the darkened streets, cut off from any news source that might calm their fears.

Chicago newspapers and radio stations were flooded with calls from worried listeners; in St. Louis, people gathered outside to discuss what to do about the "invaders"; in San Francisco and New Orleans, the general impression was that New Jersey had been laid waste by the Martians and that their machines were heading west. In Providence, Rhode Island, the office of the *Providence Journal* was swamped with hysterical phone calls asking for information about the "invasion," and many called the power company to urge them to shut off power so that the city would not be seen by the Martians. Similar reports of panic reactions came from Baltimore, Atlanta, Birmingham, Indianapolis, Richmond, Memphis, Minneapolis, Kansas City, and Salt Lake City. In Hollywood, in a story Orson Welles loved to repeat often, actor John Barrymore, in a fit of panic, released his ten beloved Great Danes, bellowing to the poor creatures, "The world is finished, fend for yourselves!" **CD 5**

In churches around the country, evening services became "end of the world" prayer meetings. In the South, where fundamental Christianity and apocalyptic

THE CHICAGO DAILY NEWS, MONDAY, OCTOBER 31, 1938.

U. S. Probing Radio Fantasy Which Terrorized Listeners

RADIO DRAMA SPREADS PANIC

Washington, Oct. 31.—(AP)—The Federal Communications Commission began an investigation today of a dramatic radio broadcast which led some people to believe last night that men from Mars had attacked the United States.

Chairman Frank P. McNinch asked the Columbia Broadcasting System to turn over to the commission an electrical transcription of the broadcast, a dramatized version of H. G. Wells' imaginative story, "War of the Worlds."

Some woman listeners to the broadcast fainted. Others became hysterical. Thousands believed the drama to be authentic news reports.

Calls Broadcast Regrettable.

McNinch told reporters that he had received many telephone calls last night about the broadcast, but that the commission had received only 10 telegrams, all protesting it. He issued this statement:

"I nave this morning requested the Columbia Broadcasting Company by telegraph to forward to the commission at once a copy of the script and also an electrical transcription of the 'War of the Worlds' which was broadcast last night and which the press indicates caused widespread excitement, terror and fright. I shall request prompt consideration of this matter by the commission.

"I withhold final judgment until later, but any broadcast that creates such general panic and fear as this one is reported to have done is, to say the least, regrettable.

"The widespread public reaction to this broadcast, as indicated by the press, is another demonstration of the power and force of radio and points out again the serious public responsibility of those who are licensed to operate stations."

Thousands Flee from Homes.

New York, Oct. 31.—(AP)—Thousands of terror-stricken radio listeners throughout the country fled from their homes last night when they tuned in on a series of synthetic news broadcasts which depicted the beginning of an interplanetary war.

The simulated news bulletins, which accompanied a CBS dramatization of H. G. Wells' fantasy, "War of the Worlds," became so realistic that they sent a wave of mass hysteria across the continent. The broadcast was intended only as fiction.

Explanatory announcements during the program, between 8 and 9 p. m., were overlooked by thousands who were led to believe that a poison gas expedition had arrived from Mars and was spreading death and destruction over the New York

his wife bromide as result of the broadcast; several wanted to know to whom to protest.

Five College Boys Faint.

Asheville, N. C.—Times says five boys at Brevard College, Brevard, N. C., fainted as pandemonium reigned on campus for half hour when students were convinced that the world was coming to an end. Many fought for telephones to inform parents to come and get them. Students were finally quieted by a few who know the program was dramatization.

Indianapolis—Woman ran into the Indianapolis Methodist Church screaming: "New York destroyed. It's the end of the world. You might as well go home to die. I just heard it on the radio." Services dismissed immediately.

Milwaukee — Newspaper switchboard operator got several calls saying "it was thrilling; there ought to be more programs like that." She reported most men liked the program; most women didn't.

Auto Party in Flight.

Louisville, Ky.—Filling station operator reports carload of tourists, bound for California, stopped quickly for a tankful of gas and drove away with a roar, saying they had heard about meteors on the radio and wanted to get "as far away from the destruction as possible."

Detroit—a Pennsylvania motorist who heard the program stopped at Ann Arbor police station to ask whether it was true that New York and New Jersey had been conquered and hordes were marching on Pennsylvania; said two daughters in back seat had fainted during the broadcast.

Changes Unauthorized, Says Wells.

London, Oct. 31.—H. G. Wells, whose "War of the Worlds" furnished the basis of the broadcast which spread alarm in the United States last night, said today that it was "implicit" in the agreement for selling the radio rights that any broadcast would clearly "be fiction and not news."

The novelist added that he gave no permission whatever for alterations which might lead to the belief that the broadcast material was real news.

7 IN DAYTON CITED FOR CONTEMPT IN SCHOOL CLOSING

Dayton, Ohio, Oct. 31.—(UP)—Five members of the Dayton board of education and two school officials were cited today for contempt of court because they violated a

Orson Welles, 23-year-old Broadway theatrical prodigy, after he had dramatized and enacted over the Columbia Broadcasting System a pre-Halloween fantasy of war waged on the United States by fearsome space-conquering men from Mars.

H. G. Wells, author of the fantasy, dramatization of which caused panic among radio listeners in the United States and Canada. Wells' story hypotheticated invasion of England. "I gave no permission for changes," said Wells today.

Caroline Cantlon, WPA actress, sits beside the radio in New York over which she heard the announcement of "smoke in Times Square" in the dramatization of H. G. Wells' "War of the Worlds" broadcast last night. Panic-stricken, she rushed to the street, falling and breaking her arm.

theology made an end-of-the-world scenario less out-landish, the panic tended to be more pronounced than in other regions. "I knew the forces of God were over-whelming us," said Miss Jane Dean, a fifty-seven-year-old spinster with firm religious convictions, "and we were being given punishment at last for our evil ways."

Other reactions culled by the Hadley Cantril study and published in *Invasion From Mars* revealed the depth of some people's faith in the face of death:

> *The Bible says that the first time the end of the world was by flood and the next time it will be by fire, and that went through my mind.*

> *We tuned in to another station and heard some church music. I was sure a lot of people were worship-ing God while waiting for their death.*

The power of suggestion to inspire hallucinations in otherwise sane people cannot be underestimated.

Orson Welles, youthful director of the Mercury Theater group, expresses his bewilderment at the mass hysteria produced last night as a result of his graphic radio dramatization of "The War of the Worlds."

Residents of Riverside reported to baffled police seeing Martian machines poised on the Jersey Palisades, prepar-ing to cross the Hudson on their way to attack New York City. "I stuck my head out of the window and thought I could smell the gas," said one interviewee afterward. "And it felt as though it was getting hot, like fire was coming."

"I looked out of my window and saw a greenish-eerie light which I was sure came from a monster," admitted another. "Later on it proved to be the lights in the maid's car."

The *New York Times* reported on patrolman John Morrison, who was on duty at Bronx Police headquar-ters when all of the phone lines lit up. The first call he answered started with a man who informed him, "They're bombing New Jersey!" "How do you know?" Morrison asked. "I heard it on the radio," the man replied, "then I went to the roof and I could see the smoke from the bombs, drifting over toward New York. What shall I do?"

A woman in Boston said she could actually see the fire as described on the radio; other families in Boston congregated on rooftops and imagined they could see a red glow against the southern night sky, as the Martians burned New York; some people told of hearing machine gun fire or the "swish" sound of the Martians. A man even climbed atop a Manhattan building with binoculars and claimed seeing "the flames of battle."

Other listeners found a variety of reasons to believe what they were hearing:

I believed the broadcast as soon as I heard the professor from Princeton and the officials in Washington. I knew it was an awfully dangerous situation when all those military men were there and the secretary of state spoke.

If so many of those astronomers saw the explosions, they must have been real. They ought to know.

I was most inclined to believe the broadcast when they mentioned places like South Street and the Pulaski Highway.

I looked out of the window and everything looked the same as usual, so I thought it hadn't reached our section yet.

12 X   THE NEW YORK TIMES, SUNDAY, OCTOBER 30, 1938.

RADIO CHALLENGES PLAYWRIGHTS TO TRY NEW TRICKS

EXPLORING IN DRAMA

MacLeish, Poetic Dramatist, Talks About
The Task of Writing a Broadcast Play

A New York Times *story on radio drama, which ran on the day of the broadcast, clearly announces that evening's program.*

Even some regular listeners to Orson Welles were fooled. Sarah Jacob, from Illinois, complained:

They should have announced that it was a play. We listened to the whole thing and they never did [they did, of course, four times—once at the beginning, twice during the commercial break, and then again at the end]. I was very much afraid. When it was over, we ran to the doctor's to see if he could help us get away. Everybody was out in the street, and somebody told my husband it was just a play. We always listen to Orson Welles, but we didn't imagine this was it. If we hadn't found out it was a play almost as soon as it was over, I don't know what we'd have done.

The Mercury Theatre broadcast was well advertised and announced in the radio program listings. The *New York Times* even ran a full-page story that day on radio drama, featuring a photograph of Orson Welles and the other Mercury actors in rehearsal: "…tonight's show is 'The War of the Worlds,' by H.G. Wells," it points out. Perhaps it says something about the relative impact of print media to broadcast. Then again, as another listener admitted, "I listened from the very beginning. I always listen to the Mercury Theatre. But when the flashes came, I thought they were really interrupting the play."

Some who took the broadcast as fact found a silver lining:

My only thought involving myself as a person in connection with it was a delight that if it spread to Stelton I would not have to pay the butcher's bill.

The broadcast had us all worried, but I knew it would at least scare ten years' life out of my mother-in-law.

My girlfriend pointed out to me that I had passed a couple of red lights, and I answered, "What's the difference? If I get a ticket, it will only be burned anyway."

It was the thrill of a lifetime—to hear something like that and think it's real.

Many believed the Martians were actually either Germans or Japanese, a more plausible interpretation of the broadcast, in retrospect. Sylvia Holmes, a Newark housewife, said, "We listened, getting more and more excited. We all felt that the world was coming to an end....I wanted to be together with my husband and nephew so we could all die together. So I ran out of the house. I guess I didn't know what I was doing. I stood on the corner waiting for a bus, and I ran out to get it. People saw how excited I was and tried to quiet me, but I kept on saying over and over again to everybody I met: 'Don't you know New Jersey is destroyed by the Germans—it's on the radio.' I was all excited, and I knew that Hitler didn't appreciate President Roosevelt's telegram a couple of weeks ago. While the U.S. thought everything was settled, they came down unexpected. The Germans are so wise, they were in something like a balloon, and when the balloon landed—that's when they announced the explosion—the Germans landed. When I got home, my husband wasn't there so I rushed in next door and warned the neighbors that the world was coming to an end."

Her neighbors eventually persuaded her to calm down and go home. She wasn't convinced they were out of danger, though, but still found an excuse to raid the fridge. "I found my nephew had come home and gone to bed," she said. "I woke him up. I looked in the icebox and saw some chicken left from Sunday dinner that I was saving for Monday night dinner. I said to my nephew, 'We may as well eat this chicken—we won't be here in the morning.'"

Other listeners also translated what they were hearing into something that made sense in the context of looming war:

I knew it was the Germans trying to gas all of us. When the announcer kept calling them people from Mars, I just thought he was ignorant and didn't know yet that Hitler had sent them all.

The announcer said a meteor had fallen from Mars, and I was sure he thought that, but in the back of my head I had the idea that the meteor was just a

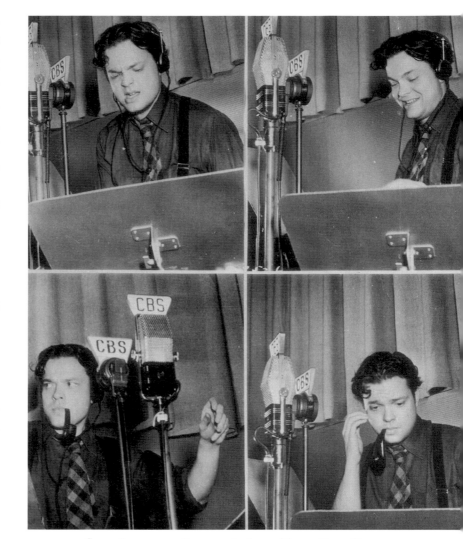

camouflage. It was really an airplane like a Zeppelin that looked like a meteor, and the Germans were attacking us with gas bombs. The airplane was built to look like a meteor just to fool people.

The Jews are being treated so terribly in some parts of the world, I was sure something had come to destroy them in this country.

I felt it might be the Japanese—they are so crafty.

One person actually welcomed annihilation from Mars rather than suffer existence under fascism: "I was looking forward with some pleasure to the destruction of the entire human race and the end of the world. If we have fascist domination of the world, there is no purpose in living anyway."

While Rome Burned

Ray Collins, the Mercury actor playing the last CBS reporter, described the Martian machines crossing the Hudson river, "like a man wading through a brook." The poison black cloud advanced on Manhattan, engulfing Times Square, then Fifth Avenue, until a terrible silence again interrupted the horror show. The last voice heard was the pathetic plea of a shortwave operator coming through the air from some remote outpost: "2X2L calling CQ…2X2L calling CQ…New York. Isn't there anyone on the air? Isn't there anyone…"

Several minutes earlier, CBS broadcasting supervisor Davidson Taylor had received a phone call in the control room and hurriedly left the studio. By the time he returned, "pale as death," according to producer John Houseman, the damage was done, and the players in the studio, Houseman, and Welles were about to learn just what kind of mischief they'd perpetrated. Taylor entered the booth with orders to interrupt the show immediately and announce that the program was fiction. Houseman refused to let him stop the broadcast before the break, insinuating himself between Welles and Taylor. Within five minutes, they reached the first scheduled program break, anyway. Civilization's last gasp was followed by Dan Seymour reminding the portion of the audience that hadn't fled in terror with towels on their heads that this was in fact a Mercury Theatre presentation of "The War of the Worlds."

The panic had begun in New Jersey, spread north and west, and finally throughout the country. Taylor had heard horror stories about affiliate reactions to the show. In an appropriate reverse-hoax, Welles and Houseman were informed that casualties were mounting across the nation. Mobs trampled people under foot in their haste to escape the Martians; people were committing suicide rather than suffer the death ray or black cloud.

The show continued. But the rest of the play was straight drama, with Welles portraying a ragged Professor Pierson, roaming the desolate New Jersey countryside and describing the human wreckage. From his journal, now relating the tale in flashback, he told how the Martians succumbed to everyday bacteria to which their bodies had no resistance. Welles closed the

Welles after the broadcast, as if to say, "I had no idea."

show with a prepared sign-off/apology that gives a hint as to what effect he thought the broadcast might have:

This is Orson Welles, ladies and gentlemen, out of character to assure you that "The War of the Worlds" has no further significance than as the holiday offering it was intended to be. The Mercury Theatre's own radio version of dressing up in a sheet and jumping out of a bush and saying "Boo!" Starting now, we couldn't soap all your windows and steal all your garden gates by tomorrow night…so we did the next best thing. We annihilated the world before your very ears, and utterly destroyed the Columbia Broadcasting System. You will be relieved, I hope, to learn that we didn't mean it, and that both institutions are still open for business. So good-bye everybody, and remember, please, for the next day or so, the terrible lesson you learned tonight. That grinning, glowing, globular invader of your living room is an inhabitant of the pumpkin patch, and if your doorbell rings and nobody's there, that was no Martian…it's Hallowe'en.

The Aftermath

The Mercury Theatre signed off the air. But the terror was just beginning for Welles and Houseman. As the final theme was playing, the phone in the control room rang. It turned out to be the mayor of a large Midwestern city. "He is screaming for Welles," recalled Houseman. "Choking with fury, he reports mobs in the streets of the city, women and children huddled in churches, violence and looting…" Welles quickly hung up as police burst into the studio, confiscating scripts and segregating the actors. Kept alone in a room for a time, the police eventually threw Welles and Houseman to the press. The print reporters, resentful of the business radio had taken away from their papers, were out for blood. How many deaths have you heard of? they asked, implying, as Houseman told it, "that they knew of thousands." Had they heard of the fatal stampede in the New Jersey hall? Did they know about all of the traffic deaths and suicides? The way the reporters put their questions, Houseman assumed that the ditches were choked with corpses.

When they were later released by a back exit into mid-town Manhattan, Houseman found it "suprising to see life going on as usual in the midnight streets." Of course, no one had died because of the broadcast. There were a few bumps and bruises. But most of the bruises were to the egos of the embarrassed and sheepish listeners who had been taken in by the story.

Welles surrounded by reporters, photographers, and film cameras at a press conference the day after the broadcast

Howard Koch had listened to the broadcast in his apartment, unaware of the panic it was causing. Exhausted from another hectic week of writing scripts for Welles and Houseman, he slept so soundly that he didn't hear the phone ring later that night when Houseman called him to break the news. Monday morning, he walked down Seventy-second Street on his way to get his hair cut:

> *Catching ominous snatches of conversation with words like "invasion" and "panic," I jumped to the conclusion that Hitler had invaded some new territory and that the war we all dreaded had finally broken out.*
>
> *When I anxiously questioned the barber, he broke into a broad grin, "Haven't you heard?" and he held up the front page of a morning newspaper with the headline "Nation in Panic from Martian Broadcast."*

So Koch, who had written the radio play, became in a way a victim himself of Welles' "Hallowe'en prank."

Welles, "looking like an early Christian saint"

At a press conference later that day, **CD 2** Welles denied knowing about the panic during the broadcast. "Looking like an early Christian saint," **CD 5** as he later described himself, he held the roomful of reporters in the palm of his hand as he claimed utter amazement that the show could be taken as fact by anyone. What the doe-eyed, innocent Welles failed to mention was that it was he who urged Mercury player Kenny Delmar to play the part of the Secretary of the Interior as Roosevelt. "I was not supposed to impersonate the president," recalled Delmar, "that order came down from the network brass. When Orson came in to direct the dress rehearsal, he said, 'Oh Kenny, you know what I want.' So every fifth word was done as FDR so it gave a very strong impression of the president." John Houseman, who later denied that they intentionally did this (Houseman, like Welles, gave conflicting versions of the story depending on whom he was talking to and when), once admitted in an interview, "That was the only naughty thing we did that night. Everything else was just good radio."

One of the reporters asked Welles, "Were you aware of the terror such a broadcast would stir up?"

Welles answers a reporter's question at the press conference on October 31, 1938

"Definitely not," he answered. "The technique I used was not original with me. It was not even new. I anticipated nothing unusual." Welles was correct about the technique having been used before. On January 17, 1926, in a BBC radio broadcast from Edinburgh, Scotland, Father Ronald Knox described in a false news report how a fictitious unemployed mob in London had sacked the National Gallery, blown up Big Ben, hanged the Minister of Traffic to a tramway post, and demolished the Houses of Parliament. The "newscast" ended with the destruction of the BBC's London headquarters. Occurring during a period of unusual labor strife, days before the general strike, panicked listeners called the radio station, newspapers, and police to find out what was happening and what, if anything, they could do.

If Welles knew about the BBC panic, it strains credulity to think that he wouldn't have expected a similar reaction to his own broadcast. In fact, according to Joseph Bulgatz in *Ponzi Schemes, Invaders from Mars & More Extraordinary Popular Delusions and the Madness of Crowds*, Welles had led up to the realistic

Welles directs the Mercury Theatre on the Air *actors.*

newsflash style of "The War of the Worlds." He had used a narrator, the well-known political commentator H.V. Kaltenborn, in the first *Mercury Theatre on the Air* fall broadcast, "Julius Caesar." Kaltenborn's recognizable style and voice added a dimension of realism and immediacy to Shakespeare's drama. In addition, says Bulgatz, Welles listened to Archibald MacLeish's *Air Raid* on the Columbia Workshop just days prior to the panic broadcast. In it, an announcer stood on the roof of a tenement describing an everyday peaceful scene when, suddenly, the sounds of bombing aircraft, explosions, and screams interrupted the calm. Another meaningful coincidence happened a month earlier, on September 25, when a news bulletin on the crisis in Europe actually interrupted *The Mercury Theatre on the Air* presentation of "Sherlock Holmes." Welles took these realistic elements and created a powerfully effective technique.

If Welles guessed at the effect his broadcast would have, he later hinted at his motives for doing it in 1955 on a BBC television special, *Orson Welles Sketchbook*, when he said:

> We weren't as innocent as we meant to be when we did the Martian broadcast. We were fed up with the way in which everything that came over this new magic box, the radio, was being swallowed....So, in a

Welles on the phone the day after the broadcast, his desk covered by newspapers reporting the panic it created

An aerial view of Wilson farm, Grovers Mill, New Jersey, in 1938

"There were headlines about lawsuits totaling some $12 million," Welles later recalled. "Most of them, as it turned out, existed in the fevered imagination of the newspapers. They'd been losing all that advertising to radio, so here, they reckoned, was a lovely chance to strike back. For a few days, I was a combination Benedict Arnold and John Wilkes Booth. But people were laughing much too hard, thank God—and pretty soon the papers had to quit."

CBS issued a public apology and promised not to "use the technique of a simulated news broadcast within a dramatization when the circumstances of the broadcast could cause immediate alarm to numbers of listeners." Of the claims against CBS and Orson Welles, none was substantiated or settled save one, made by George Bates, an unskilled laborer from Massachusetts, who wrote a letter to Welles shortly after the broadcast:

When those things landed, I thought the best thing to do was go away, so I took $3.25 out of my savings and bought a ticket. After I had gone sixty miles I heard it was a play. Now I don't have any money left for the shoes I was saving up for. Would you please have someone send me a pair of black shoes, size 9-B.

way, our broadcast was an assault on the credibility of that machine. We wanted people to understand that they shouldn't take any opinion predigested and they shouldn't swallow everything that came through the tap, whether it was radio or not.

Media Confusion

For three days, the future of *The Mercury Theatre on the Air* was up in the air. CBS couldn't figure out whether they were scoundrels or heroes. The broadcast dominated the newspapers for days, with stories of panic, editorials alternately condemning and praising Welles, and even cartoons satirizing the whole affair.

The day after the broadcast, reporters descended on Grovers Mill, the scene of the "landing." Although the fictional farmer who was interviewed in the radio play, whose farm received the first Martian capsule, was named Wilmuth, the reporters did find a real Wilson farm that was close enough. Changing it from Wilmuth to Wilson conveniently gave them a site to photograph "where the Martians landed."

Grovers Mill townsfolk discuss the previous night's broadcast.

It Seems to Me — By Heywood Broun

I'm still scared. I didn't hear the broadcast, and I doubt that I would have called up the police to complain merely because I heard that men from a strange machine were knocking the daylights out of Princeton. That doesn't happen to be news this season. My first reaction would have been, "That's no Martian but merely McDonald, of Harvard, carrying the ball on what the coaches call a 'naked reverse' or Sally Rand shift."

Just the same, I live in terror that almost any time now a metal cylinder will come to earth, and out of it will step fearsome creatures carrying death ray guns. And their faces will be forbidding, because the next radio invasion is likely to be an expedition of the censors.

Obviously, Orson Welles put too much curdle on the radio ways, but there isn't a chance on earth that any chain will sanction such a stunt again. In fact, I think it would be an excellent rule to make

sort to which the imagination of H. G. Wells turned when he was very young.

But Mr. Wells, of late, has faced more factual subjects. I have not recently caught up with his current economic and political views, for he sets them down on paper at a pace which leaves the willing reader breathless. When last my eye encountered his words he was liberal rather than radical. But he possessed so lively a concern for the world and so deep a faith that it can be changed for the better that there is no telling what theory he may spring suddenly.

Up to last Sunday night the State Department seemed to be unruffled as to visits from Martians. There is no record that any stranger from that inhabited planet had ever been detained at Ellis Island for questioning or had his visa canceled. Of course, the line of questioning would be obvious.

• • •

Maybe a Socialist State.

According to such astronomy as I have picked up

Over the objections of his lawyers, Welles honored the request.

Among those who praised Welles was influential *New York Tribune* columnist Dorothy Thompson, who wrote, "…far from blaming Mr. Orson Welles, he ought to be given a Congressional medal and a national prize for having made the most amazing and important contributions to the social sciences." She added, "They have cast a brilliant and cruel light upon the failure of popular education. They have shown up the incredible stupidity, lack of nerve, and ignorance of thousands."

Hugh S. Johnson wrote, "There are no men on Mars. If there were there would be no occasion for their attack on earth. If there were such an occasion, there is

no reason to believe that in Mars, or anywhere else, there are weapons that could devastate a state or two in fifteen minutes." H.G. Wells foresaw a Martian technology centuries ahead of our own, but Johnson couldn't imagine human technology a mere seven years off.

Heywood Broun, echoing the sentiments of many in the media, warned, "I live in terror that almost any time now a metal cylinder will come to earth, and out of it will step fearsome creatures carrying death ray guns. And their faces will be forbidding, because the next radio invasion is likely to be an expedition of the censors."

Censorship and government control of what content was broadcast over the airwaves was a hallmark of

"Mars Panic" Useful — By Hugh S. Johnson

WASHINGTON, Nov. 2.—One of the most remarkable demonstrations of modern times was the startling effect of the absurd radio scenario of Orson Welles based on an old Jules Verne type of novel by H. G. Wells—"The War of the Worlds."

Simulated Columbia broadcast radio flashes of a pretended attack, with mysterious new aerial weapons, on New Jersey from the planet Mars, put many people into such a panic that the witch-burning Mr. McNinch, chairman of the Federal Communications Commission, has a new excuse to extend the creeping hand of government restriction of free speech by way of radio censorship.

When the hysterical echoes of an initial hysterical explosion die down the whole incident will assay out as about the silliest teapot tempest in human history.

There are no men on Mars. If there were there would be no occasion for their attack on earth. If there were such an occasion there is no reason to believe that in Mars, or anywhere else, there are weapons that could devastate a State or two in fifteen minutes. The result of public panic was so absurd as to be

donian phalanx. Always the dope is that some magic new armament is going to change the face of war. Always events prove that invention for defense keeps abreast of invention for attack. Always it turns out that the outcome is decided by the shock of masses of men breast to breast—and in no other way.

This does not for a moment mean that this country can neglect any development of its weapons for defense. It has done that in the past. If this hysterical happening means anything it is that there is a vague restless suspicion among the people of the truth that there has been such neglect.

Many things have happened and—let us hope—in time, to wake us up to these defensive defaults. There was the Munich sell-out and the sudden disclosure of Hitler and Mussolini as masters of Europe through the neglect of their defenses by both England and France compared with the vast military preparations of the dictatorships. There are the slow leaks of some of the shocking things that Hitler suggested as his price for peace, among them German air and naval bases in the Caribbean—direct threats against us. Finally, there comes this dramatic proof of the jitters of our own people on the subject of our own defenses.

• • •

Aid to Defense Program.

LITERAL LYMAN

NEWS ITEM:—"Thousands of listeners all over the country thrown into hysteria by radio play, 'War of the Worlds.' Believe broadcast of 'devastation' is fact."

fascist regimes. This, as many were finding out, was a slippery slope to start down. "No political body must ever, under any circumstances, obtain a monopoly of radio," said Dorothy Thompson. "The power of mass suggestion is the most potent force today....If people can be frightened out of their wits by mythical men from Mars, they can be frightened into fanaticism by the fear of Reds, or convinced that America is in the hands of sixty families, or aroused to revenge against any minority, or terrorized into subservience to leadership because of any imaginable menace."

Within days, most of the alarmist reactions condemning the broadcast, as well as the serious ones praising it, gave way to parodies lampooning the gullibility of the listeners who fell for it.

Other Counties Heard From

Federal Communications Commission Chairman Frank R. McNinch received 644 pieces of mail about the broadcast, about 40 percent favorable and 60 percent unfavorable. Although the FCC studied the matter, it took no action, except to say that it was "regrettable." The responses varied from condemning Welles as some kind of sadistic monster to applauding his broadcast as if it were a heroic deed. Those who applauded enjoyed pointing their fingers at the "idiotic display of feeble-mindedness brought about by Mr. Orson Welles' very fine production..." and complained, "What a bunch of jitterbug softies the people of America have turned out to be." For those whose reaction was unfavorable, the hostility and bile brought forth for Welles seemed quite personal. This letter, addressed to Welles, came from A.G. Kennedy, a judge from South Carolina:

Your radio performance Sunday evening was a clear demonstration of your inhuman instincts, beastial [sic] sensuality and fendish [sic] joy in causing distress and suffering. Your savage ancestors, of which you are a degenerate offspring, exulted in torturing their enemies and war captives, and you doubtless revelled in feindish [sic] delight in causing death to some and great terror, anguish and suffering to thousands of helpless and unoffending victims of your hellish designs.

Your contemptable [sic], cowardly, and cruel undertaking, conceived by a demon and executed by a cowardly cur is doubtless in keeping with your sense of humor. When you are faced with the enormity of your heinous crime and are liable to prosecution for you [sic] atrocious conduct and that you are morally guilty of murder if not legally guilty, then you fawn and whimper like a cringing cowardly entrapped wolf when apprehended in its wicked acts of destruction....

I would not insult a female dog by calling you a son of such an animal. Your conduct was beneath the social standing of and what would be unbecoming and below the moral perception of a bastard son of a fatherless whore....You, if you were not a carbuncle on the rump of a degenerate theatrical performers [sic], would as an effort towards making partial amends for your consumate [sic] act of asininity, never again appear on the stage or before the radio, except for the purpose of announcing your withdrawal....

I hope suit will be brought against you individually, the Company which you represent, and also the Columbia Broadcasting Company, for your combined wrong. I also purpose [sic] to use the radio in appealing to the American people to boycott the Columbia Broadcasting System in an expression of their disapproval of your disgraceful, fraudulent, atrocious, malicious, and illegal performance....

From the front page of the New York World-Telegram, *November 2, 1938*

H.G. Wells' initial reaction to the broadcast was less than euphoric.

zation was made with a liberty that amounts to a complete rewriting and made the novel an entirely different story," said Wells. "It's a total unwarranted liberty." He went on to say, "It was my understanding with the broadcasting company that the broadcast should be presented as fiction and not as news. I gave no permission whatever for alterations which might lead to the belief that it was real news." Although H.G. Wells was at first perturbed by Orson Welles' youthful impudence, he soon mellowed, as sales of *The War of the Worlds*—one of his lesser-known novels—soared as a result of the attention generated by the broadcast. (When H.G. met Orson two years later in a San Antonio radio studio [see part III, "H.G. Wells" **CD 3**], he took an immediate liking to the younger Welles.)

Welles received this message in a telegram from his friend, *New York Times* drama critic Alexander Wolcott (although sometimes it was from President Roosevelt, depending on whom Welles was telling the story to): "This only goes to prove, my beamish boy, that all the intelligent people were listening to the dummy [Charlie McCarthy], and that all the dummies were listening to you."

Interestingly, Harry Wright Jr. wrote of his nine-year-old son's reaction upon learning that some people took the broadcast literally: "…his comment was that those people must have been 'dumb-bells' to have been scared by such a program. Perhaps, a person of mature age might have put it differently." One such mature adult wrote that the broadcast "caused a number of sub-morons to become panic stricken. This is no reason why intelligent people should be deprived of virile entertainment." Perhaps, as one letter-writer suggests, those who were fooled and lashed out at Welles and CBS were just over-compensating. "It seems to me obvious," wrote Lydel Sims to McNinch, "that, realizing their stupidity and desiring to save their faces, they are taking it out on Mr. Welles and the CBS."

Meanwhile, in England, H.G. Wells was not amused. According to correspondence between Wells and CBS prior to and after the broadcast, an "adaptation" of his work was never mentioned. Wells thought they were simply going to read his book on the air. "The dramati-

Mercury's Legacy

The night of the broadcast, according to Koch, the switchboard supervisor at CBS overheard one of her

John Houseman collaborated with Orson Welles until parting ways in 1940.

operators say, very politely, "I'm sorry, we haven't that information here." The supervisor, responsible for instituting a new policy to provide more courteous customer service, said, "That was very nicely spoken. What did the party ask?" The operator replied, "He wanted to know if the world was coming to an end."

Besides the swarm of lawsuits against CBS, Welles, and the Mercury Theatre, the world did not come to an end. The lawsuits were dismissed (no precedent existed for which to hold them liable), and The Mercury Theatre, Welles, and Koch became instant stars. *The Mercury Theatre on the Air* got the one thing it never managed to before—a sponsor. "The sponsor had turned us down two weeks before because we tended to too much violence and sensationalism," said Welles. "[They] picked us up the week after 'The War of the Worlds.' Thanks to the Martians, we got us a radio sponsor, and suddenly we were a big commercial program, right up there with Benny, Burns and Allen, and Lux Radio Theatre with Cecil B. DeMille. The next stop was Hollywood." As John

Houseman so succinctly put it years later, "They [Edgar Bergen and Charlie McCarthy] may have had the thirty-four rating, but *we* caused the panic."

Mercury, with its new sponsor, Campbell's, became *The Campbell Playhouse* on December 9, 1938, debuting with an adaptation of Daphne du Maurier's *Rebecca*. "I guess they figured if Orson could make 'The War of the Worlds' credible and the Martians credible," said Houseman, "he could make Campbell's chicken soup credible." *The Campbell Playhouse*, which Houseman and Welles continued to produce, put on first-rate radio dramas until 1940.

Welles, signed by RKO to a multi-picture deal and given an unprecedented amount of control, went on to direct and star in *Citizen Kane*, released in 1941. It is still regarded by film critics as one of the greatest, most innovative films ever made. It was nominated in nine categories at the 1942 Academy Awards, but won only one Oscar, thanks in no small part to the influence of

Welles continued to direct and star in The Campbell Playhouse *on CBS, even after he began shooting* Citizen Kane.

William Randolph Hearst, the film's thinly-fictionalized central figure. Welles and Herman Mankiewicz won for Best Screenplay, beating out, among others, Howard Koch for *Sergeant York*. Koch had been hired by Warner Brothers studio shortly after the "War of the Worlds" broadcast. Although his old taskmaster bested him for the gold statue in '42, Koch did earn an Oscar in 1944 for the adapted screenplay he and Julius Epstein wrote for *Casablanca*.

Welles was never happy with Koch getting credit for the script on "The War of the Worlds." In correspondence with Hadley Cantril, who was working on his famous study of the broadcast, *Invasion from Mars*, Welles complained bitterly and repeatedly that he, and not Koch, deserved credit for the radio play script. Cantril pointed out that Koch also claimed authorship and had sent affadavits to this effect. In the opening to the broadcast, Koch had written, "The Columbia Broadcasting System and its affiliated stations present Orson Welles and *The Mercury Theatre on the Air* in a

Houseman, who worked in the theater for years behind the scenes, achieved fame in his seventies, as the crusty Professor Kingsfield in The Paper Chase.

radio play by Howard Koch suggested by the H.G. Wells novel *The War of the Worlds*." By air time, however, Welles instructed announcer Dan Seymour to omit any reference to Koch in the introduction. And that's how it went out over the air. But, in the end, Koch retained copyright in the work.

John Houseman continued to work with Welles on *Citizen Kane*, but parted ways with the temperamental boy genius after an irreconcilable row. According to Mercury actress Geraldine Fitzgerald, Houseman told her, "Well, I didn't mind him throwing a table at me, but when he sets fire to the tablecloth first, and then throws it—then I mind." Houseman worked under David O. Selznick in Hollywood, but soon left to join a wartime propaganda program that would become the Voice of America, which he later headed. Of course, Houseman would gain most fame for his role as the crusty law professor, Charles Kingsfield, in the movie and television series *The Paper Chase*.

Howard Koch, in 1944, accepting an Oscar for his screenplay for Casablanca.

Grovers Mill Revisited

For years, many residents of the Grovers Mill area preferred not to talk about the events of October 30, 1938. A combination of embarrassment and just plain sick-and-tired-of-hearing-it was the prevailing attitude. By 1988, however, fifty years after the non-landing of the Martians, locals had developed a different view. A "War of the Worlds Committee" was formed by West Windsor mayor Doug Forrester, who spearheaded the four-day 50th Anniversary celebration from October 27 to 30, which included a juried art show, Martian costume contest, dinner dance, panel discussions on "Could It Happen Again?" and "Should We Go to Mars?" a reread-

Howard Koch was invited to Grovers Mill in 1987 for the forty-ninth anniversary of the broadcast, and returned in 1988 for the fiftieth.

ing of the original Koch script at Princeton's McCarter Theater, and the "Martian Panic 10K Run." Howard Koch returned to the scene of his crime, accompanied by a slew of local, national, and international media there to cover the event. A time capsule was buried, to be opened on the hundredth anniversary in 2038, and a monument was installed to mark the spot of the capsule and the place where the Martians "landed." A similar celebration took place to commemorate the sixtieth anniversary in 1998, and the Sci-Fi Channel presented its own tribute to the broadcast and the part that Grovers Mill played in it. *Martian Mania*, hosted by director James Cameron, aired on October 30, 1998. It seems the people in the Grovers Mill area have come to embrace their unique place in history, even if it is as the site of an event that never actually took place.

A monument to the broadcast, in Grovers Mill, marks the spot where a time capsule was buried in 1988.

★ ★ ★

The eve of Halloween, 1938, was one of those moments that signaled an imperceptible shift in society. The days that followed found an America a little less innocent, not quite so naïve and trusting, a little more skeptical. Like the quiz show scandal of the 1950s and, later, Watergate, Americans were forced to grow up like the child who discovers there is no tooth fairy, no Easter Bunny.

Hadley Cantril's study of the causes of the panic, published in *Invasion from Mars*, identified some predictable reasons. A lack of critical ability was perhaps the most obvious one. Another reason suggested was the presence of a set of beliefs that were consistent with what was described on the radio—apocalyptic religious beliefs, a fear of technology, or simply the expectation that the world was headed toward disaster. The widespread feeling that things were out of control, that individuals no longer had any control over what happened to them no doubt exacerbated the panic reaction.

"Particularly since the depression of 1929," wrote Cantril, "a number of people have begun to wonder whether or not they will ever regain any sense of economic security. The complexity of modern finance and government, the discrepancies shown in the economic and political proposals of the various 'experts,' the felt

Present-day Grovers Mill

threats of Fascism, Communism, prolonged unemployment among millions of Americans—these together with a thousand and one other characteristics of modern living—create an environment which the average individual is completely unable to interpret."

Technology rushes ahead of our ability to understand it; political and economic factors epitomize complexity. We understand these conditions as givens. But in 1938, people were just beginning to get it:

> *Things have happened so thick and fast since my grandfather's day that we can't hope to know what might happen now. I am all balled up.*

> *So many odd things are happening in the world. Science has progressed so far that we don't know how far it might have gone on Mars. The way the world runs ahead, anything is possible.*

Orson Welles, with his Mercury Theatre actors and writers, applied his particular genius to a prophetic work by H.G. Wells. And on October 30, 1938, the results of their efforts changed the mental landscape of America and the world for years to come.

War of the Worlds 50ᵗʰ Anniversary T-shirt

The Radio Play
"War of the Worlds"
by Howard Koch

Announcer: The Columbia Broadcasting System and its affiliated stations present Orson Welles and *The Mercury Theatre on the Air* in *The War of the Worlds* by H.G. Wells. **CD 1**

(Mercury Theatre Musical Theme)

Announcer: Ladies and gentlemen: the director of the Mercury Theatre and star of these broadcasts, Orson Welles…

Orson Welles: We know now that in the early years of the twentieth century this world was being watched closely by intelligences greater than man's and yet as mortal as his own. We know now that as human beings busied themselves about their various concerns they were scrutinized and studied, perhaps almost as narrowly as a man with a microscope might scrutinize the transient creatures that swarm and multiply

The Mercury Theatre actors who performed "Invasion from Mars" were: Orson Welles, William Alland, Ray Collins, Kenneth Delmar, Carl Frank, William Herz, Frank Readick, Stefan Schnabel, Howard Smith, Paul Stewart, and Richard Wilson.

in a drop of water. With infinite complacence people went to and fro over the earth about their little affairs, serene in the assurance of their dominion over this small spinning fragment of solar driftwood which by chance or design man has inherited out of the dark mystery of Time and Space. Yet across an immense ethereal gulf, minds that to our minds as ours are to the beasts in the jungle, intellects vast, cool and unsympathetic, regarded this earth with envious eyes and slowly and surely drew their plans against us. In the thirty-ninth year of the twentieth century came the great disillusionment.

It was near the end of October. Business was better. The war scare was over. More men were back at work. Sales were picking up. On this particular evening, October 30, the Crossley service estimated that thirty-two million people were listening in on radios.

ANNOUNCER

…for the next twenty-four hours not much change in temperature. A slight atmospheric disturbance of undetermined origin is reported over Nova Scotia, causing a low pressure area to move down rather rapidly over the northeastern states, bringing a forecast of rain, accompanied by winds of light gale force. Maximum temperature 66; minimum 48. This weather report comes to you from the Government Weather Bureau.

…We now take you to the Meridian Room in the Hotel Park Plaza in downtown New York, where you will be entertained by the music of Ramon Raquello and his orchestra.
(Spanish theme song [a tango]…fades)

ANNOUNCER THREE

Good evening, ladies and gentlemen. From the Meridian Room in the Park Plaza in New York City, we bring you the music of Ramon Raquello and his orchestra. With a touch of the Spanish. Ramon Raquello leads off with "La Cumparsita."
(Piece starts playing)

ANNOUNCER TWO

Ladies and gentlemen, we interrupt our program of dance music to bring you a special bulletin from the Intercontinental Radio News. At twenty minutes before eight, Central Time, Professor Farrell of the Mount Jennings Observatory, Chicago, Illinois, reports observing several explosions of incandescent gas, occurring at regular intervals on the planet Mars.

"It didn't sound like a play the way it interrupted the music when it started."

"The announcer would not say if it was not true. They always quote if something is a play."

The spectroscope indicates the gas to be hydrogen and moving towards the earth with enormous velocity. Professor Pierson of the Observatory at Princeton confirms Farrell's observation, and describes the phenomenon as (quote) like a jet of blue flame shot from a gun (unquote). We now return you to the music of Ramon Raquello, playing for you in the Meridian Room of the Park Plaza Hotel, situated in downtown New York.

(Music plays for a few moments until piece ends…sound of applause)

ANNOUNCER THREE

Now a tune that never loses favor, the ever-popular "Star Dust." Ramon Raquello and his orchestra…

(Music…)

ANNOUNCER TWO

Ladies and gentlemen, following on the news given in our bulletin a moment ago, the Government Meteorological Bureau has requested the large observatories of the country to keep an astronomical watch on any further disturbances occurring on the planet Mars. Due to the unusual nature of this occurrence, we have arranged an interview with a noted astronomer, Professor Pierson, who will give us his views on the event. In a few moments we will take you to the Princeton Observatory at Princeton, New Jersey. We return you until then to the music of Ramon Raquello and his orchestra.

(Music…)

ANNOUNCER TWO

We are now ready to take you to the Princeton Observatory at Princeton where Carl Phillips, our commentator, will interview Professor Richard Pierson, famous astronomer. We take you now to Princeton, New Jersey.

(Echo chamber FX: tick-tock sound)

PHILLIPS

Good evening, ladies and gentlemen. This is Carl Phillips, speaking to you from the observatory at Princeton. I am standing in a large semi-circular room, pitch black except for an oblong split in the ceiling. Through this opening I can see a sprinkling of stars that cast a kind of frosty glow over the intricate mechanism of the huge telescope. The ticking sound you hear is the vibration of the clockwork. Professor Pierson

"We had company at home and were playing cards while the radio was turned on. I heard a news commentator interrupt the program but at first did not pay much attention to him."

stands directly above me on a small platform, peering through a giant lens. I ask you to be patient, ladies and gentlemen, during any delay that may arise during our interview. Besides his ceaseless watch of the heavens, Professor Pierson may be interrupted by telephone or other communications. During this period he is in constant touch with the astronomical centers of the world…Professor, may I begin our questions?

PIERSON
At any time, Mr. Phillips.

PHILLIPS
Professor, would you please tell our radio audience exactly what you see as you observe the planet Mars through your telescope?

PIERSON
Nothing unusual at the moment, Mr. Phillips. A red disk swimming in a blue sea. Transverse stripes across the disk. Quite distinct now because Mars happens to be the point nearest the earth…in opposition, as we call it.

PHILLIPS
In your opinion, what do these transverse stripes signify, Professor Pierson?

PIERSON
Not canals, I can assure you, Mr. Phillips, although that's the popular conjecture of those who imagine Mars to be inhabited. From a scientific viewpoint the stripes are merely the result of atmospheric conditions peculiar to the planet.

PHILLIPS
Then you're quite convinced as a scientist that living intelligence as we know it does not exist on Mars?

PIERSON
I'd say the chances against it are a thousand to one.

PHILLIPS
And yet how do you account for these gas eruptions occurring on the surface of the planet at regular intervals?

"My radio had been tuned to the station several hours. I heard loud talking and excitement and became interested."

PIERSON

Mr. Phillips, I cannot account for it.

PHILLIPS

By the way, Professor, for the benefit of our listeners, how far is Mars from earth?

PIERSON

Approximately forty million miles.

PHILLIPS

Well, that seems a safe enough distance.
(Pause)

PHILLIPS

Just a moment, ladies and gentlemen, someone has just handed Professor Pierson a message. While he reads it, let me remind you that we are speaking to you from the observatory in Princeton, New Jersey, where we are interviewing the world famous astronomer, Professor Pierson…One moment, please. Professor Pierson has passed me a message which he has just received…Professor, may I read the message to the listening audience?

PIERSON

Certainly, Mr. Phillips

PHILLIPS

Ladies and gentlemen, I shall read you a wire addressed to Professor Pierson from Dr. Gray of the National History Museum, New York. "9:15 P.M. Eastern Standard Time. Seismograph registered shock of almost earthquake intensity occurring within a radius of twenty miles of Princeton. Please investigate. Signed, Lloyd Gray, Chief of Astronomical Division"…Professor Pierson, could this occurrence possibly have something to do with the disturbances observed on the planet Mars?

PIERSON

Hardly, Mr. Phillips. This is probably a meteorite of unusual size and its arrival at this particular time is merely a coincidence. However, we shall conduct a search, as soon as daylight permits.

"I turned the radio on to get Orson Welles, but the announcement that a meteor had fallen sounded so much like the usual news announcements that I never dreamt it was Welles. I thought my clock was probably fast.…When the machine started to come apart, I couldn't imagine what it was."

"Being we are in a troublesome world, anything is liable to happen. We hear so much news every day—so many things we hear are unbelievable. Like all of a sudden six hundred children burned to death in a schoolhouse, or a lot of people being thrown out of work. Everything seems to be a shock to me."

PHILLIPS

Thank you, Professor. Ladies and gentlemen, for the past ten minutes we've been speaking to you from the observatory at Princeton, bringing you a special interview with Professor Pierson, noted astronomer. This is Carl Phillips speaking. We are returning you now to our New York studio.

(Fade in piano playing)

ANNOUNCER TWO

Ladies and gentlemen, here is the latest bulletin from the Intercontinental Radio News. Toronto, Canada: Professor Morse of McGill University reports observing a total of three explosions on the planet Mars, between the hours of 7:45 P.M. and 9:20 P.M., Eastern Standard Time. This confirms earlier reports received from American observatories. Now, nearer home, comes a special bulletin from Trenton, New Jersey. It is reported that at 8:50 P.M. a huge, flaming object, believed to be a meteorite, fell on a farm in the neighborhood of Grovers Mill, New Jersey, twenty-two miles from Trenton.

The flash in the sky was visible within a radius of several hundred miles and the noise of the impact was heard as far north as Elizabeth.

We have dispatched a special mobile unit to the scene, and will have our commentator, Carl Phillips, give you a word description as soon as he can reach there from Princeton. In the meantime, we take you to the Hotel Martinet in Brooklyn, where Bobby Millette and his orchestra are offering a program of dance music.

(Swing band for twenty seconds…then cut)

ANNOUNCER TWO

We take you now to Grovers Mill, New Jersey.

(Crowd noises…police sirens)

PHILLIPS

Ladies and gentlemen, this is Carl Phillips again, out at the Wilmuth farm, Grovers Mill, New Jersey. Professor Pierson and myself made the eleven miles from Princeton in ten minutes. Well, I…I hardly know where to begin, to paint for you a word picture of the strange scene before my eyes, like something out of a modern "Arabian Nights." Well, I just got here. I haven't had a chance to look around yet. I guess that's it. Yes, I guess that's the…thing, directly in front of me, half buried in a vast pit.

Must have struck with terrific force. The ground is covered with splinters of a tree it must have struck on its way down. What I can see of the…object itself doesn't look very much like a meteor, at least not the meteors I've seen. It looks more like a huge cylinder. It has a diameter of…what would you say, Professor Pierson?

PIERSON (OFF-MIKE)
What's that?

PHILLIPS
What would you say…what is the diameter?

PIERSON
About thirty yards.

PHILLIPS
About thirty yards…The metal on the sheath is…well, I've never seen anything like it. The color is sort of yellowish-white. Curious spectators now are pressing close to the object in spite of the efforts of the police to keep them back. They're getting in front of my line of vision. Would you mind standing to one side, please?

POLICEMAN
One side, there, one side.

PHILLIPS
While the policemen are pushing the crowd back, here's Mr. Wilmuth, owner of the farm here. He may have some interesting facts to add…Mr. Wilmuth, would you please tell the radio audience as much as you remember of this rather unusual visitor that dropped in your backyard? Step closer, please. Ladies and gentlemen, this is Mr. Wilmuth.

WILMUTH
Well, I was listenin' to the radio.

PHILLIPS
Closer and louder please.

WILMUTH
Pardon me?!

> "It all sounded perfectly real until people began hopping around too fast…when people moved twenty miles in a couple of minutes, I put my tongue in my cheek and figured it was just about the smartest play I'd ever heard."

"At first I was very interested in the fall of the meteor. It isn't often that they find a big one just when it falls. But when it started to unscrew and monsters came out, I said to myself, 'They've taken one of those *Amazing Stories* and are acting it out.' It just couldn't be real. It was just like some of the stories I read in *Amazing Stories*, but it was even more exciting."

PHILLIPS
Louder, please, and closer.

WILMUTH
Yes, sir—I was listening to the radio and kinda drowsin'. That Professor fellow was talkin' about Mars, so I was half dozin' and half…

PHILLIPS
Yes, yes, Mr. Wilmuth. Then what happened?

WILMUTH
As I was sayin', I was listenin' to the radio kinda halfways…

PHILLIPS
Yes, Mr. Wilmuth, and then you saw something?

WILMUTH
Not first off. I heard something.

PHILLIPS
And what did you hear?

WILMUTH
A hissing sound. Like this: Ssssssss…kinda like a fourt' of July rocket.

PHILLIPS
Yes?

WILMUTH
Turned my head out the window and would have swore I was to sleep and dreamin.'

PHILLIPS
Then what?

WILMUTH
I seen a kinda greenish streak and then zingo! Somethin' smacked the ground. Knocked me clear out of my chair!

PHILLIPS
Well, were you frightened, Mr. Wilmuth?

WILMUTH
Well, I—I ain't quite sure. I reckon I—I was kinda riled.

PHILLIPS
Thank you, Mr. Wilmuth. Thank you very much.

WILMUTH
Want me to tell you some more?

PHILLIPS
No…That's quite all right, that's plenty.

PHILLIPS
Ladies and gentlemen, you've just heard Mr. Wilmuth, owner of the farm where this thing has fallen. I wish I could convey the atmosphere…the background of this…fantastic scene. Hundreds of cars are parked in a field in back of us. Police are trying to rope off the roadway leading into the farm. But it's no use. They're breaking right through. Cars' headlights throw an enormous spot on the pit where the object's half buried. Some of the more daring souls are now venturing near the edge. Their silhouettes stand out against the metal sheen.
(Faint humming sound)

One man wants to touch the thing…he's having an argument with a policeman. The policeman wins.…Now, ladies and gentlemen, there's something I haven't mentioned in all this excitement, but now it's becoming more distinct. Perhaps you've caught it already on your radio. Listen please: (*Long pause*) … Do you hear it? It's a curious humming sound that seems to come from inside the object. I'll move the microphone nearer. (*Pause*) Now we're not more then twenty-five feet away. Can you hear it now? Oh, Professor Pierson!

PIERSON
Yes, Mr. Phillips?

PHILLIPS
Can you tell us the meaning of that scraping noise inside the thing?

PIERSON
Possibly the unequal cooling of its surface.

"At first I thought it was a lot of Buck Rogers stuff, but when a friend telephoned me that general orders had been issued to evacuate everyone from the metropolitan area, I put the customers out, closed the place, and started to drive home."

—*Emanuel Priola, bartender from West Orange, New Jersey*

"I was alone with my two younger brothers. My parents had gone to a party in Newark. When they mentioned, 'Citizens of Newark, come to the open spaces,' I got scared. I called my mother to find out what to do, and there was no answer. I found out later that they had gone to an empty apartment so that they could dance. Nobody was left at the place I phoned. My only thought was that the flames had overcome my parents."

PHILLIPS

I see, do you still think it's a meteor, Professor?

PIERSON

I don't know what to think. The metal casing is definitely extra-terrestrial...not found on this earth. Friction with the earth's atmosphere usually tears holes in a meteorite. This thing is smooth and, as you can see, of cylindrical shape.

PHILLIPS

Just a minute! Something's happening! Ladies and gentlemen, this is terrific! This end of the thing is beginning to flake off! The top is beginning to rotate like a screw! The thing must be hollow!

VOICES

She's movin'!
Look, the darn thing's unscrewing!
Keep back, there! Keep back, I tell you!
Maybe there's men in it trying to escape!
It's red hot, they'll burn to a cinder!
Keep back there. Keep those idiots back!
(*Suddenly the clanking sound of a huge piece of falling metal*)

VOICES

She's off! The top's loose! Look out there! Stand back!

PHILLIPS

Ladies and gentlemen, this is the most terrifying thing I have ever witnessed...Wait a minute! Someone's crawling out of the hollow top. Someone or...something. I can see peering out of that black hole two luminous disks . . are they eyes? It might be a face. It might be...
(*Shout of awe from the crowd*)

PHILLIPS

Good heavens, something's wriggling out of the shadow like a gray snake. Now it's another one, and another. They look like tentacles to me. There, I can see the thing's body. It's large, large as a bear and it glistens like wet leather. But that face, it...Ladies and gentlemen, it's indescribable. I can hardly force myself to keep looking at it. The eyes are black and gleam like a serpent. The mouth is V-shaped with saliva dripping from its rimless lips that seem to quiver and pulsate. The monster or whatever it is can hardly move. It seems weighed down by…possibly gravity or something. The thing's rising up. The crowd falls back now. They've seen plenty. This is the most extraordinary experience. I can't find words…I'll pull this microphone with me as I talk. I'll have to stop the description until I can take a new position. Hold on, will you please, I'll be right back in a minute.

(Fade into piano)

ANNOUNCER

We are bringing you an eyewitness account of what's happening on the Wilmuth farm, Grovers mill, New Jersey. (*More piano*) We now return you to Carl Phillips at Grovers Mill.

PHILLIPS

Ladies and gentlemen (Am I on?). Ladies and gentlemen, here I am, back of a stone wall that adjoins Mr. Wilmuth's garden. From here I get a sweep of the whole scene. I'll give you every detail as long as I can talk. As long as I can see. More state police have arrived. They're drawing up a cordon in front of the pit, about thirty of them. No need to push the crowd back now. They're willing to keep their distance. The captain is conferring with someone. We can't quite see who. Oh yes, I believe it's Professor Pierson. Yes, it is. Now they've parted. The Professor moves around one side, studying the object, while the captain and two policemen advance with something in their hands. I can see it now. It's a white handkerchief tied to a pole…a flag of truce. If those creatures know what that means…what anything means!…Wait! Something's happening!

(Hissing sound followed by a humming
that increases in intensity)

PHILLIPS

A humped shape is rising out of the pit. I can make out a small beam of light against a mirror. What's that? There's a jet of flame springing from the mirror, and it leaps right at the advancing men. It strikes them head on! Good Lord, they're turning into flame!

(Screams and unearthly shrieks)

PHILLIPS

Now the whole field's caught fire. (*Explosion*) The woods…the barns…the gas tanks of automobiles…it's spreading everywhere. It's coming this way. About twenty yards to my right…

> "I kept translating the unbelievable parts into something I could believe until finally I reached the breaking point—I mean my mind just couldn't twist things any more, and somehow I knew it couldn't be true literally, so I just stopped believing and knew it must be a play."

"I became terribly frightened and got in the car and started for the priest so I could make peace with God before dying. Then I began to think that perhaps it might have been a story, but discounted that because of the introduction as a special news broadcast. While en route to my destination, a curve loomed up and, travelling at between seventy-five and eighty miles per hour, I knew I couldn't make it, though as I recall, it didn't greatly concern me, either. To die one way or another, it made no difference, as death was inevitable. After turning over twice, the car landed upright and I got out, looked at the car, and thought that it didn't matter that it wasn't my car or that it was wrecked, as the owner would have no more use for it."

(Dead silence)

ANNOUNCER

Ladies and gentlemen, due to circumstances beyond our control, we are unable to continue the broadcast from Grovers Mill. Evidently there's some difficulty with our field transmission. However, we will return to that point at the earliest opportunity. In the meantime, we have a late bulletin from San Diego, California. Professor Indellkoffer, speaking at a dinner of the California Astronomical Society, expressed the opinion that the explosions on Mars are undoubtedly nothing more than severe volcanic disturbances on the surface of the planet. We now continue with our piano interlude.

(Piano…then cut)

ANNOUNCER TWO

Ladies and gentlemen, I have just been handed a message that came in from Grovers Mill by telephone. Just one moment please. At least forty people, including six state troopers lie dead in a field east of the village of Grovers Mill, their bodies burned and distorted beyond all possible recognition. The next voice you hear will be that of Brigadier General Montgomery Smith, commander of the state militia at Trenton, New Jersey.

SMITH

I have been requested by the governor of New Jersey to place the counties of Mercer and Middlesex as far west as Princeton, and east to Jamesburg, under martial law. No one will be permitted to enter this area except by special pass issued by state or military authorities. Four companies of state militia are proceeding from Trenton to Grovers Mill, and will aid in the evacuation of homes within the range of military operations. Thank you.

ANNOUNCER TWO

You have just been listening to General Montgomery Smith commanding the state militia at Trenton. In the meantime, further details of the catastrophe at Grovers Mill are coming in. The strange creatures after unleashing their deadly assault, crawled back into their pit and made no attempt to prevent the efforts of the firemen to recover the bodies and extinguish the fire. The combined fire departments of Mercer County are fighting the flames which menace the entire countryside. We have been unable to establish any contact with our mobile unit at Grovers Mill, but we hope to be able to return you there at the earliest possible moment. In the meantime we take you to—uh, just one moment please.

(Long pause)

(*Whisper*) Ladies and gentlemen, I have just been informed that we have finally established communication with an eyewitness of the tragedy. Professor Pierson has been located at a farmhouse near Grovers Mill where he has established an emergency observation post. As a scientist, he will give you his explanation of the calamity. The next voice you hear will be that of Professor Pierson, brought to you by direct wire. Professor Pierson.

(Feedback, then filtered voice)

PIERSON

Of the creatures in the rocket cylinder at Grovers Mill, I can give you no authoritative information—either as to their nature, their origin, or their purposes here on Earth. Of their destructive instrument I might venture some conjectural explanation. For want of a better term, I shall refer to the mysterious weapon as a heat ray. It's all too evident that these creatures have scientific knowledge far in advance of our own. It is my guess that in some way they are able to generate an intense heat in a chamber of practically absolute nonconductivity. This intense heat they project in a parallel beam against any object they choose, by means of a polished parabolic mirror of unknown composition, much as the mirror of a lighthouse projects a beam of light. That is my conjecture of the origin of the heat ray…

ANNOUNCER TWO

Thank you, Professor Pierson. Ladies and gentlemen, here is a bulletin from Trenton. It is a brief statement informing us that the charred body of Carl Phillips has been identified in a Trenton hospital. Now here's another bulletin from Washington, D.C. The office of the director of the National Red Cross reports ten units of Red Cross emergency workers have been assigned to the headquarters of the state militia stationed outside Grovers Mill, New Jersey. Here's a bulletin from state police, Princeton Junction: The fires at Grovers Mill and vicinity are now under control. Scouts report all quiet in the pit, and there is no sign of life appearing from the mouth of the cylinder…And now, ladies and gentlemen, we have a special statement from Mr. Harry McDonald, vice president in charge of operations.

"The gas was supposed to be spreading up north. I didn't have any idea exactly what I was fleeing from, and that made me all the more afraid. All I could think of was being burned alive or being gassed."

—*A senior at a large eastern college*

"I always feel that the commentators bring the best possible news. Even after this I still will believe what I hear on the radio."

MCDONALD

We have received a request from the state militia at Trenton to place at their disposal our entire broadcasting facilities. In view of the gravity of the situation, and believing that radio has a responsibility to serve in the public interest at all times, we are turning over our facilities to the state militia at Trenton.

ANNOUNCER TWO

We take you now to the field headquarters of the state militia near Grovers Mill, New Jersey.

CAPTAIN

This is Captain Lansing of the signal corps, attached to the state militia now engaged in military operations in the vicinity of Grovers Mill. Situation arising from the reported presence of certain individuals of unidentified nature is now under complete control. The cylindrical object which lies in a pit directly below our position is surrounded on all sides by eight battalions of infantry. Without heavy field pieces, but adequately armed with rifles and machine guns. All cause for alarm, if such cause ever existed, is now entirely unjustified. The things, whatever they are, do not even venture to poke their heads above the pit. I can see their hiding place plainly in the glare of the searchlights here. With all their reported resources, these creatures can scarcely stand up against heavy machine-gun fire Anyway, it's an interesting outing for the troops. I can make out their khaki uniforms, crossing back and forth in front of the lights. It looks almost like a real war. There appears to be some slight smoke in the woods bordering the Millstone River. Probably fire started by campers. Well, we ought to see some action soon. One of the companies is deploying on the left flank. An quick thrust and it will all be over. Now wait a minute! I see something on top of the cylinder. No, it's nothing but a shadow. Now the troops are on the edge of the Wilmuth farm. Seven thousand armed men closing in on an old metal tube. Wait, that wasn't a shadow! It's something moving…solid metal…kind of shieldlike affair rising up out of the cylinder…It's going higher and higher. Why, it's standing on legs…actually rearing up on a sort of metal framework. Now it's reaching above the trees and the searchlights are on it. Hold on!

ANNOUNCER

Ladies and gentlemen, I have a grave announcement to make. Incredible as it may seem, both the observations of science and the evidence of our eyes lead to the inescapable assumption that those strange beings who landed in the Jersey farmlands tonight are the vanguard of an invading army from the planet Mars. The battle which took place tonight at Grovers Mill has ended in one of the most startling defeats ever suffered by any army in modern times; seven thousand men armed with rifles and machine guns pitted against a single fighting machine of the invaders from Mars. One hundred and twenty known survivors. The rest strewn over the battle area from Grovers Mill to Plainsboro, crushed and trampled to death under the metal feet of the monster, or burned to cinders by its heat ray. The monster is now in control of the middle section of New Jersey and has effectively cut the state through its center. Communication lines are down from Pennsylvania to the Atlantic Ocean. Railroad tracks are torn and service from New York to Philadelphia discontinued except routing some of the trains through Allentown and Phoenixville. Highways to the north, south, and west are clogged with frantic human traffic. Police and army reserves are unable to control the mad flight. By morning the fugitives will have swelled Philadelphia, Camden, and Trenton, it is estimated, to twice their normal population. Martial law prevails throughout New Jersey and eastern Pennsylvania. At this time we take you to Washington for a special broadcast on the National Emergency...the Secretary of the Interior...

SECRETARY

Citizens of the nation: I shall not try to conceal the gravity of the situation that confronts the country, nor the concern of your government in protecting the lives and property of its people. However, I wish to impress upon you—private citizens and public officials, all of you—the urgent need of calm and resourceful action. Fortunately, this formidable enemy is still confined to a comparatively small area, and we may place our faith in the military forces to keep them there. In the meantime placing our faith in God we must continue the performance of our duties each and every one of us, so that we may confront this destructive adversary with a nation united, courageous, and consecrated to the preservation of human supremacy on this earth. I thank you.

"From interviews after the broadcast, we found that the pronouncements of the scientists, the military men, and the Secretary of the Interior reassuring the listeners that everything was under control and there was no cause for alarm only succeeded in convincing them that the truth was being withheld and that the invaders were, indeed, Martians, invincible and bent on our destruction."

—*Howard Koch*

ANNOUNCER

You have just heard the secretary of the Interior speaking from Washington. Bulletins too numerous to read are piling up in the studio here. We are informed the central portion of New Jersey is blacked out from radio communication due to the effect of the heat ray upon power lines and electrical equipment. Here is a special bulletin from New York. Cables have been received from English, French, German scientific bodies offering assistance. Astronomers report continued gas outbursts at regular intervals on the planet Mars. Majority voice opinion that enemy will be reinforced by additional rocket machines. There have been several attempts made to locate Professor Pierson of Princeton, who has observed Martians at close range. It is feared he was lost in recent battle. Langham field, Virginia: Scouting planes report three Martian machines visible above treetops, moving north towards Somerville with population fleeing ahead of them. The heat ray is not in use; although advancing at express-train speed, invaders pick their way carefully. They seem to be making conscious effort to avoid destruction of cities and countryside. However, they stop to uproot power lines, bridges, and railroad tracks. Their apparent objective is to crush resistance, paralyze communication, and disorganize human society.

Here is a bulletin from Basking Ridge, New Jersey: Coon hunters have stumbled on a second cylinder similar to the first embedded in the great swamp twenty miles south of Morristown. Army fieldpieces are proceeding from Newark to blow up the second invading unit before cylinder can be opened and the fighting machine rigged. They are taking up position in the—foothills of Watchung Mountains. Another bulletin from Langham Field, Virginia: Scouting planes report enemy machines, now three in number, increasing speed northward kicking over houses and trees in their evident haste to form a conjunction with their allies south of Morristown. Machines also sighted by telephone operator east of Middlesex within ten miles of Plainfield. Here's a bulletin from Winston Field, Long Island: Fleet of army bombers carrying heavy explosives flying north in pursuit of enemy. Scouting planes act as guides. They keep the speeding enemy in sight. Just a moment please. Ladies and gentlemen, we've run special wires to the artillery line in adjacent villages to give you direct reports in the zone of the advancing enemy. First we take you to the battery of the 22nd Field Artillery, located in the Watchtung Mountains.

"I never hugged my radio so closely as I did last night. I held a crucifix in my hand and prayed while looking out of my open window for falling meteors. I also wanted to get a faint whiff of the gas so that I would know when to close my window and hermetically seal my room with waterproof cement or anything else I could get hold of. My plan was to stay in the room and hope that I would not suffocate before the gas blew away. When the monsters were wading across the Hudson River and coming into New York, I wanted to run up on my roof to see what they looked like, but I could not leave my radio while it was telling me of their whereabouts."

—*Mrs. Delaney, an ardent Catholic from a New York suburb*

OFFICER
Range, thirty-two meters.

GUNNER
Thirty-two meters.

OFFICER
Projection, thirty-nine degrees.

GUNNER
Thirty-nine degrees.

OFFICER
Fire! (*Boom of heavy gun…pause*)

OBSERVER
One hundred and forty yards to the right, sir.

OFFICER
Shift range…thirty-one meters.

GUNNER
Thirty-one meters.

OFFICER
Projection…thirty-seven degrees.

GUNNER
Thirty-seven degrees.

OFFICER
Fire! (*Boom of heavy gun…pause*)

OBSERVER
A hit, sir! We got the tripod of one of them. They've stopped.
The others are trying to repair it.

OFFICER
Quick, get the range! Shift thirty meters.

GUNNER
Thirty meters.

"I was home and my friend called and said, 'Is your radio working? Tune to WABC—the world is coming to an end.' I tuned in and heard buildings were tumbling down in the Palisades and people were fleeing from Times Square.

"At first I didn't think there was any danger. A monster in a pit had fallen from somewhere and took life and shape. Then later I heard Martians and realized the creatures were from Mars. I didn't realize at first that they were hostile—my impression was that communication with Mars was beginning. In a short time I realized that these creatures were attacking. It wasn't beyond a possibility that such things could happen, but it seemed peculiar that the announcer could be right next to it and watching it."

"[I] thought it was all up with us. I grabbed my boy and just sat and cried, and then I couldn't stand it anymore when they said they were coming this way, so I turned the radio off and ran out into the hall."

—*a mother in a crowded New Jersey tenement*

OFFICER
Projection…twenty-seven degrees.

GUNNER
Twenty-seven degrees.

OFFICER
Fire! (*Boom of heavy gun…pause*)

OBSERVER
Can't see the shell land, sir. They're letting off a smoke.

OFFICER
What is it?

OBSERVER
A black smoke, sir. Moving this way. Lying close to the ground. It's moving fast.

OFFICER
Put on gas masks. (*Pause…voices now muffled*) Get ready to fire. Shift twenty-four meters.

GUNNER
Twenty-four meters.

OFFICER
Projection, twenty-four degrees.

GUNNER
Twenty-four degrees.

OFFICER
Fire! (*Boom*)

OBSERVER
Still can't see, sir. The smoke's coming nearer.

OFFICER
Get the range. (*Coughs*)

OBSERVER

Twenty-three meters. (*Coughs*)

OFFICER

Twenty-three meters. (*Coughs*)

GUNNER

Twenty-three meters. (*Coughs*)

OBSERVER

Projection, twenty-two degrees. (*Coughing*)

OFFICER

Twenty-two degrees. (*Fade in coughing*) (*Fading in...sound of airplane motor*)

COMMANDER

Army bombing plane, V-8-43, off Bayonne, New Jersey, Lieutenant Voght, commanding eight bombers. Reporting to Commander Fairfax, Langham Field...This is Voght, reporting to Commander Fairfax, Langham Field...Enemy tripod machines now in sight. Reinforced by three machines from the Morristown cylinder...Six altogether. One machine partially crippled. Believed hit by shell from army gun in Watchung Mountains. Guns now appear silent. A heavy black fog hanging close to the earth...of extreme density, nature unknown. No sign of heat ray. Enemy now turns east, crossing Passaic River into the Jersey marshes. Another straddles the Pulaski Skyway. Evident objective is New York City. They're pushing down a high tension power station. The machines are close together now, and we're ready to attack. Planes circling, ready to strike. A thousand yards and we'll be over the first—eight hundred yards...six hundred...four hundred...two hundred...There they go! The giant arm raised...(*Sound of heat ray*) Green flash! They're spraying us with flame! Two thousand feet. Engines are giving out. No chance to release bombs. Only one thing left...drop on them, plane and all. We're diving on the first one. Now the engine's gone! Eight...(*Plane goes down*)

OPERATOR ONE

This is Bayonne, New Jersey, calling Langham Field...This is Bayonne, New Jersey, calling Langham Field...Come in, please...

"Right after we tuned in I had gone out to see my baby, when my husband called to me. I ran in and got frightened right away. I ran downstairs to the telephone and called my mother. She hadn't been listening. Then I took the little baby and my husband wrapped our seven-year-old child and we rode with friends who live on the street to the tavern where my mother works. By the time we got there my mother had the radio on and all of the people in the tavern were excited. I just sat down and cuddled my baby and shook so that I couldn't talk. I was sick in bed for three days after the broadcast."

—*a mother in a small eastern town*

"A man ran up the stairs, and when he saw us, he laughed at us and said downstairs the people were fooled too and that it was only a joke. We didn't believe him and told him to pray, but he finally convinced us. He said he had called the police, and they told him it was a play. So I went back into the apartment, and just kept crying till my husband came home because I was still upset."

—*A mother from New Jersey*

OPERATOR TWO

This is Langham Field...Go ahead...

OPERATOR ONE

Eight army bombers in engagement with enemy tripod machines over Jersey flats. Engines incapacitated by heat ray. All crashed. One enemy machine destroyed. Enemy now discharging heavy black smoke in direction of—

OPERATOR THREE

This is Newark, New Jersey...This is Newark, New Jersey...Warning! Poisonous black smoke pouring in from Jersey marshes. Reaches South Street. Gas masks useless. Urge population to move into open Spaces...automobiles use Routes 7, 23, 24...Avoid congested areas. Smoke now spreading over Raymond Boulevard...

OPERATOR FOUR

2X2L...calling CQ...
2X2L...calling CQ...
2X2L...calling 8X3R...
Come in, please...

OPERATOR FIVE

This is 8X3R...coming back at 2X2L.

OPERATOR FOUR

How's reception? How's reception? K, please. (*Pause*) Where are you, 8X3R? What's the matter? Where are you?
(*Bells ringing over city gradually diminishing*)

ANNOUNCER

I'm speaking from the roof of the Broadcasting Building, New York City. (*Pause, as if he isn't sure he's on the air*) I'm speaking from the roof of the Broadcasting Building, New York City. The bells you hear are ringing to warn the people to evacuate the city as the Martians approach. Estimated in last two hours three million people have moved out along the roads to the north, Hutchison River Parkway still kept open for motor traffic. Avoid bridges to Long Island...hopelessly jammed. All communication with Jersey shore closed ten minutes ago. No more defenses. Our army wiped out...artillery, air force, everything wiped out. This may be the last broadcast. We'll stay here to the end…People are holding service below us…in the cathedral.

(Voices singing hymn)

Now I look down the harbor. All manner of boats, overloaded with fleeing population, pulling out from docks.

(Sound of boat whistles)

Streets are all jammed. Noise in crowds like New Year's Eve in city. Wait a minute…Enemy now in sight above the Palisades. Five—five great machines. First one is crossing the river. I can see it from here, wading the Hudson like a man wading through a brook…A bulletin's handed me…Martian cylinders are falling all over the country. One outside of Buffalo, one in Chicago, St. Louis…seem to be timed and spaced…Now the first machine reaches the shore. He stands watching, looking over the city. His steel, cowlish head is even with the skyscrapers. He waits for the others. They rise like a line of new towers on the city's west side…Now they're lifting their metal hands. This is the end now. Smoke comes out…black smoke, drifting over the city. People in the streets see it now. They're running towards the East River…thousands of them, dropping in like rats. Now the smoke's spreading faster. It's reached Times Square. People trying to run away from it, but it's no use. They're falling like flies. Now the smoke's crossing Sixth Avenue…Fifth Avenue…one hundred yards away…it's fifty feet…

(Body falls)

OPERATOR FOUR
2X2L calling CQ…
2X2L calling CQ…
2X2L calling CQ…New York.
Isn't there anyone on the air?
Isn't there anyone on the air?
Isn't there anyone…?
2X2L—

Announcer: You are listening to a CBS presentation of Orson Welles and the *Mercury Theatre on the Air* in an original dramatization of *The War of the Worlds* by H.G. Wells. The performance will continue after a brief intermission.

This is the Columbia Broadcasting System

(Music)

"I was terribly frightened. I wanted to pack and take my child in my arms, gather up my friends and get in the car and just go north as far as we could. But what I did was just set by one window, prayin', listenin', and scared stiff and my husband by the other snifflin' and lookin' out to see if people were runnin'. Then when the announcer said 'evacuate the city,' I ran and called my boarder and started with my child to rush down the stairs, not waitin' to ketch my hat or anything. When I got to the foot of the stairs I just couldn't get out, I don't know why. Meantime my husband he tried other stations and found them still runnin'. He couldn't smell any gas or see people runnin', so he called me back and told me it was just a play. So I set down, still ready to go at any minute till I heard Orson Welles say, 'Folks, I hope we ain't alarmed you. This is just a play!' Then I just set!"

—*Mrs. Joslin, a woman living in a poor neighborhood of a large eastern city*

"We were at a party. Everybody was frightened. I wanted to see if other stations had the program, but the others wanted to hear the end of the broadcast."

Announcer: *The War of the Worlds* by H.G. Wells, starring Orson Welles and the Mercury Theatre on the Air.
(Music up—dramatic, lonely theme)

PIERSON

As I set down these notes on paper, I'm obsessed by the thought that I may be the last living man on earth. I have been hiding in this empty house near Grovers Mill—a small island of daylight cut off by the black smoke from the rest of the world. All that happened before the arrival of these monstrous creatures in the world now seems part of another life…a life that has no continuity with the present, furtive existence of the lonely derelict who pencils these words on the back of some astronomical notes bearing the signature of Richard Pierson. I look down at my blackened hands, my torn shoes, my tattered clothes, and I try to connect them with a professor who lives at Princeton, and who on the night of October 30, glimpsed through his telescope an orange splash of light on a distant planet. My wife, my colleagues, my students, my books, my observatory, my…my world…where are they? Did they ever exist? Am I Richard Pierson? What day is it? Do days exist without calendars? Does time pass when there are no human hands left to wind the clocks?…In writing down my daily life I tell myself I shall preserve human history between the dark covers of this little book that was meant to record the movements of the stars…But to write I must live, and to live, I must eat…I find moldy bread in the kitchen, and an orange not too spoiled to swallow. I keep watch at the window. From time to time I catch sight of a Martian above the black smoke. The smoke still holds the house in its black coil…but at length there is a hissing sound and suddenly I see a Martian mounted on his machine, spraying the air with a jet of steam, as if to dissipate the smoke. I watch in a corner as his huge metal legs nearly brush against the house. Exhausted by terror, I fall asleep…it's morning…

(Quietly) Morning! Sun streams in the window. The black cloud of gas has lifted, and the scorched meadows to the north look as though a black snowstorm has passed over them. I venture from the house. I make my way to a road. No traffic. Here and there a wrecked car, baggage overturned, a blackened skeleton. I push on north. For some reason I feel safer trailing these monsters than running away from them. And I keep a careful watch. I have seen the Martians…feed. Should one of their machines appear over the top of trees, I am ready to fling

myself flat on the earth. I come to a chestnut tree. October chestnuts are ripe. I fill my pockets. I must keep alive. Two days I wander in a vague northerly direction through a desolate world. Finally I notice a living creature…a small red squirrel in a beech tree. I stare at him, and wonder. He stares back at me. I believe at that moment the animal and I shared the same emotion…the joy of finding another living being. I push on north. I find dead cows in a brackish field. Beyond, the charred ruins of a dairy. The silo remains standing guard over the waste land like a lighthouse deserted by the sea. Astride the silo perches a weathercock. The arrow points north.

Next day I came to a city vaguely familiar in its contours, yet its buildings strangely dwarfed and leveled off, as if a giant hand sliced off its highest towers with a capricious sweep of his hand. I reached the outskirts. I found Newark, undemolished, but humbled by some whim of the advancing Martians. Presently, with an odd feeling of being watched, I caught sight of something crouching in a doorway. I made a step towards it, and it rose up and became a man!—a man, armed with a large knife.

STRANGER

(*Off mike*) Stop…(*Closer*) Where did you come from?

PIERSON

I come from…many places. A long time ago from Princeton.

STRANGER

Princeton, huh? That's near Grovers Mill!

PIERSON

Yes.

STRANGER

Grovers Mill…(*Laughs as at a great joke*) There's no food here. This is my country…all this end of town down to the river. There's only food for one…Which way are you going?

PIERSON

I don't know. I guess I'm looking for—for people.

STRANGER

(*Nervously*) What was that? Did you hear something just then?

> "I was getting worried when my friend came in and his face was ghastly white. He said, 'We're being invaded,' and his conviction impressed me."

"[I] kept on saying, 'Where are we going to go? What can we do? What difference does it make whether we get killed now or later?' I was really hysterical. My two girlfriends and I were crying and holding each other and everything seemed so unimportant in the face of death. We felt it was terrible we should die so young. I'm always nervous anyway and I guess I was getting everybody even more scared. The boy from downstairs threatened to knock me out if I didn't stop acting so hysterical. We tried another small station which had some program on that confirmed our fears. I was sure the end of the world was coming."

—Helen Anthony, a Pennsylvania
high school student

PIERSON

No. Only a bird…(*Amazed*) A live bird!

STRANGER

You get to know that birds have shadows these days…Say, we're in the open here. Let's crawl into this doorway and talk.

PIERSON

Have you seen any…Martians?

STRANGER

Naah. They've gone over to New York. At night the sky is alive with their lights. Just as if people were still livin' in it. By daylight you can't see them. Five days ago a couple of them carried somethin' big across the flats from the airport. I believe they're learning how to fly.

PIERSON

Fly!

STRANGER

Yeah, fly.

PIERSON

Then it's all over with humanity. Stranger, there's still you and I. Two of us left.

STRANGER

They got themselves in solid; they wrecked the greatest country in the world. Those green stars, they're probably falling somewhere every night. They've only lost one machine. There isn't anything to do. We're done. We're licked.

PIERSON

Where were you? You're in a uniform.

STRANGER

Yeah, what's left of it. I was in the militia—national guard…That's good! Wasn't any war any more than there's war between men and ants.

PIERSON

And we're edible ants. I found that out…What will they do with us?

STRANGER

I've thought it all out. Right now we're caught as we're wanted. The Martian only has to go a few miles to get a crowd on the run. But they won't keep doing that. They'll begin catching us systematic-like—keeping the best and storing us in cages and things. They haven't begun on us yet!

PIERSON

Not begun!

STRANGER

Not begun! All that's happened so far is because we don't have sense enough to keep quiet…botherin' them with guns and such stuff and losing our heads and rushing off in crowds. Now instead of our rushing around blind we've got to fix ourselves up—fix ourselves up according to the way things are NOW. Cities, nations, civilization, progress…

PIERSON

But if that's so, what is there to live for?

STRANGER

Well, there won't be any more concerts for a million years or so, and no nice little dinners at restaurants. If it's amusement you're after, I guess the game's up.

PIERSON

And what is there left?

STRANGER

Life…that's what! I want to live. Yeah, and so do you. We're not going to be exterminated. And I don't mean to be caught, either, and tamed, and fattened, and bred, like an ox.

PIERSON

What are you going to do?

STRANGER

I'm going on…right under their feet. I got a plan. We men as men are finished. We don't know enough. We gotta learn plenty

"Radio Dispatchers Frank Kramer and Francis Parr said they were swamped with telephone calls requesting information on antidotes for poison gas and the treatment of persons overcome by the deadly fumes. One Hamilton Township woman vowed she had stuffed all the doors and windows with paper and wet rags, but that the fumes were already seeping into her living room."

—Trenton Evening Times

before we've got a chance. And we've got to live and keep free while we learn, see? I've thought it all out, see.

PIERSON

Tell me the rest.

STRANGER

Well, it isn't all of us that were made for wild beasts, and that's what it's got to be. That's why I watched *you*. All these little office workers that used to live in these houses—they'd be no good. They haven't any stuff to 'em. They just used to run off to work. I've seen hundreds of 'em, running to catch their commuter train in the morning for fear they'd get canned if they didn't; running back at night afraid they won't be in time for dinner. Lives insured and a little invested in case of accidents. And on Sundays, worried about the hereafter. The Martians will be a godsend for those guys. Nice roomy cages, good food, careful breeding, no worries. After a week or so chasing about the fields on empty stomachs they'll come and be glad to be caught.

PIERSON

You've thought it all out, haven't you?

STRANGER

Sure, you bet I have! And that isn't all. These Martians will make pets of some of 'em, train 'em to do tricks. Who knows? Get sentimental over the pet boy who grew up and had to be killed…And some, maybe, they'll train to hunt us.

PIERSON

No, that's impossible. No human being…

STRANGER

Yes they will. There's men who'll do it gladly. If one of them ever comes after me, why…

PIERSON

In the meantime, you and I and others like us…where are we to live when the Martians own the earth?

STRANGER

I've got it all figured out. We'll live underground. I've been thinking about the sewers. Under New York are miles and miles

> "Hitler managed to scare all Europe to its knees a month ago, but he at least had an army and an air force to back up his shrieking words."
>
> —*Dorothy Thompson*, New York Tribune

of 'em. The main ones are big enough for anybody. Then there's cellars, vaults, underground storerooms, railway tunnels, subways. You begin to see, eh? And we'll get a bunch of strong men together. No weak ones; that rubbish—out.

PIERSON

And you meant me to go?

STRANGER

Well, I gave you a chance, didn't I?

PIERSON

We won't quarrel about that. Go on.

STRANGER

And we've got to make safe places for us to stay in, see, and get all the books we can—science books. That's where men like you come in, see? We'll raid the museums, we'll even spy on the Martians. It may not be so much we have to learn before—just imagine this: four or five of their own fighting machines suddenly start off—heat rays right and left and not a Martian in 'em. Not a Martian in 'em! But MEN—men who have learned the way how. It may even be in our time. Gee! Imagine having one of them lovely things with it's heat ray wide and free! We'd turn it on Martians, we'd turn it on men. We'd bring everybody down to their knees.

PIERSON

That's your plan?

STRANGER

You, and me, and a few more of us we'd own the world.

PIERSON

I see…

STRANGER

(*Fading out*) Say, what's the matter?…Where are you going?

PIERSON

Not to your world…Goodbye, stranger…

"San Francisco—An offer to volunteer in stopping an invasion from Mars came among hundreds of telephone inquiries to police and newspapers during the radio dramatization of H.G. Wells' story. One excited man called Oakland police and shouted: 'My God! Where can I volunteer my services? We've got to stop this awful thing!'"

—*Associated Press*

"Little did I suspect when I made that haphazard choice that in the days following the broadcast, an enterprising farmer in Grovers Mill would be charging a fifty-cent parking fee for the hundreds of cars that swarmed on his farm bringing tourists who wanted to see the spot 'where the Martians landed.'"

—*Howard Koch*

PIERSON

After parting with the artilleryman, I came at last to the Holland Tunnel. I entered that silent tube anxious to know the fate of the great city on the other side of the Hudson. Cautiously I came out of the tunnel and made my way up Canal Street. I reached Fourteenth Street, and there again were black powder and several bodies, and an evil ominous smell from the gratings of the cellars of some of the houses. I wandered up through the Thirties and Forties; I stood alone on Times Square. I caught sight of a lean dog running down Seventh Avenue with a piece of dark brown meat in his jaws, and a pack of starving mongrels at his heels. He made a wide circle around me, as though he feared I might prove a fresh competitor. I walked up Broadway in the direction of that strange powder—past silent shopwindows, displaying their mute wares to empty sidewalks—past the Capitol Theatre, silent, dark—past a shooting gallery, where a row of empty guns faced an arrested line of wooden ducks. Near Columbus Circle I noticed models of 1939 motorcars in the showrooms facing empty streets. From over the top of the General Motors Building, I watched a flock of black birds circling in the sky. I hurried on. Suddenly I caught sight of the hood of a Martian machine, standing somewhere in Central Park, gleaming in the late afternoon sun. An insane idea! I rushed recklessly across Columbus Circle and into the Park. I climbed a small hill above the pond at Sixtieth Street. From there I could see, standing in a silent row along the mall, nineteen of those great metal Titans, their cowls empty, their great steel arms hanging listlessly by their sides. I looked in vain for the monsters that inhabit those machines.

Suddenly, my eyes were attracted to the immense flock of black birds that hovered directly below me. They circled to the ground, and there before my eyes, stark and silent, lay the Martians, with the hungry birds pecking and tearing brown shreds of flesh from their dead bodies. Later when their bodies were examined in the laboratories, it was found that they were killed by the putrefactive and disease bacteria against which their systems were unprepared…slain, after all man's defenses had failed, by the humblest thing that God in His wisdom put upon this earth.

Before the cylinder fell there was a general persuasion that through all the deep of space no life existed beyond the petty surface of our minute sphere. Now we see further. Dim and wonderful is the vision I have conjured up in my mind of life spreading slowly from this little seedbed of the solar system throughout the inanimate vastness of sidereal space. But that is a remote dream. It may be that the destruction of the Martians is only a reprieve. To them, and not to us, is the future ordained perhaps.

Strange it now seems to sit in my peaceful study at Princeton writing down this last chapter of the record begun at a deserted farm in Grovers Mill. Strange to see from my window the university spires dim and blue through an April haze. Strange to watch children playing in the streets. Strange to see young people strolling on the green, where the new spring grass heals the last black scars of a bruised earth. Strange to watch the sightseers enter the museum where the dissembled parts of a Martian machine are kept on public view. Strange when I recall the time when I first saw it, bright and clean-cut, hard, and silent, under the dawn of that last great day.

(Music swells up and out)

Orson Welles: This is Orson Welles, ladies and gentlemen, out of character to assure you that "The War of The Worlds" has no further significance than as the holiday offering it was intended to be. The Mercury Theatre's own radio version of dressing up in a sheet and jumping out of a bush and saying Boo! Starting now, we couldn't soap all your windows and steal all your garden gates by tomorrow night…so we did the best next thing. We annihilated the world before your very ears, and utterly destroyed the C. B. S. You will be relieved, I hope, to learn that we didn't mean it, and that both institutions are still open for business. So goodbye everybody, and remember, please, the terrible lesson you learned tonight. That grinning, glowing, globular invader of your living room is an inhabitant of the pumpkin patch, and if your doorbell rings and nobody's there, that was no Martian…it's Halloween.

(Mercury Theatre Music Theme up full, then down)

Announcer: Tonight the Columbia Broadcasting System and its affiliated stations coast-to-coast have brought you *The War of the Worlds* by H.G. Wells, the seventeenth in its weekly series of dramatic broadcasts featuring Orson Welles and *The Mercury Theatre on the Air*. Next week we present a dramatization of three famous short stories.…This is the Columbia Broadcasting System.

(Theme up to finish)

> **"We expected a lunatic fringe, but we didn't know it would go all across the country."**
>
> —*Orson Welles*

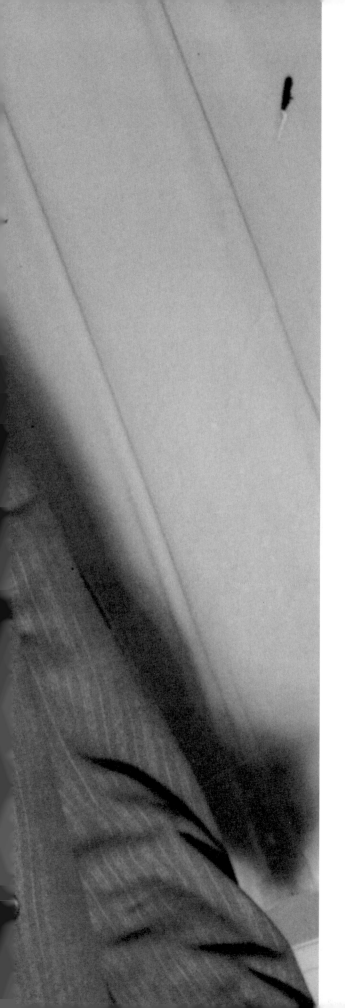

Orson Welles and the Mercury Theatre

"Orson Welles has made history, he has created masterpieces in three art forms: film, theater, and radio—but his most fascinating and enigmatic creation may be himself."

—*Barbara Leaming*

By 1938, H.G. Wells' book had been in print and available for forty years. While viewed as a classic piece of science fiction, it no longer held the collective attention of the public. All of that changed due to the vision of a precocious twenty-three-year-old performer, whose manic treatment of the material thrust the fear of Martians back into the public's eye.

Born in Kenosha, Wisconsin, on May 6, 1915, George Orson Welles was the second son of Richard and Beatrice Ives Welles, prominent Kenosha socialites. Orson's early life was marked with all the trappings of affluence; his father, wealthy from investments in wagon factories, rarely worked, while his mother, an accomplished pianist, was active in the local arts community. However, this façade of prestige hid the family's private troubles. Orson's brother Richard, of whom very little is known, was considered to be an intellectual and professional failure, eventually being diagnosed with schizophrenia and spending time in a mental institution. Meanwhile, father Dick began drinking heavily, driving a wedge between himself and Beatrice. Little Orson soon became the focus of Beatrice's life; she spent most of her time teaching him to read Shakespeare and play piano, priming him for the success she felt eluded her husband and eldest son.

At age six, Orson's parents divorced. He moved with his mother to Chicago, where she immersed him in theater and classical music. Two years later, Beatrice unexpectedly died, leaving a shaken Orson to return to the care of his father and Dr. Maurice Bernstein, a Kenosha physician who had taken an interest in young Orson's talents. Bernstein arranged for Orson's enrollment in the exclusive Todd School for Boys in Woodstock, Illinois, an atmosphere in which Orson flourished. Here, headmaster Roger Hill encouraged Orson's talents, becoming somewhat a father figure to the boy. Orson delved into the arts under Hill's direction, staging and performing in several plays, including *Julius Caesar*. When he wasn't on stage, Orson was often painting or trying out his latest magic tricks on his classmates. This idyllic childhood lasted until 1930, when Welles' father passed away due to his alcoholism.

Now, under the guidance of dual surrogate fathers in Bernstein and Hill, fifteen-year-old Orson graduated from Todd School, and under pressure from Bernstein, traveled to Ireland. Bernstein had hoped that the trip would temper Orson's love of the theater. The plan backfired, however, as Orson immediately made his way to the Gates Theatre, one of Dublin's most respected and honored theater companies. There he claimed to be a Broadway actor and auditioned for producers Hilton Edwards and Micheal MacLiammoir. In his memoir, *All for Hecuba*, MacLiammoir tells of their initial meeting:

Hilton walked into the scene dock one day and said, "Somebody strange has arrived from America; come and see what you think of it."

"What," I asked, "is it?"

"Tall, young, fat: says he's been with the Guild Theatre in New York. Don't believe a word of it, but he's interesting. I want him to give me an audition. Says he's been in Connemara with a donkey, and I don't see what that's got to do with me. Come and have a look at him."

Though able to see through Orson's obviously false and grandiose claims, the producers were taken by his talent, displayed through his brilliant audition. In fact, not only his talent, but his supreme confidence in himself. MacLiammoir later recounted that "That was his secret. He knew that he was precisely what he himself would have chosen to be had God consulted him on the subject of his birth; he fully appreciated and approved what had been bestowed, and realized that he couldn't have done the job better himself, in fact he would not have changed a single item. Whether the world felt the same—well, that was for us to decide." Orson was hired, and debuted a few weeks later to rave reviews as the Duke in *Jew Suss*. Leading roles in six subsequent productions followed, although none created the same level of excitement, and soon Orson packed his bags and headed for England. The London theater scene did little to placate Orson's dreams of stage stardom, so he soon headed home, returning to the safe haven of the Todd School.

Portrait of Orson Welles as a young man

Welles on stage as Doctor Faustus

Welles kept busy the next year writing and producing performances such as *Everybody's Shakespeare*, *Marching Song*, and *Bright Lucifer*, all done with the help of Hill. His life (and career) took a remarkable turn in the summer of 1933 when he accompanied Hill to a cocktail party in Chicago. Left alone to mingle, Orson soon struck up an awkward conversation with another shy young man. When asked by this man what he did for a living, Orson replied that he was a writer. The young man shot back, "Funny, I could have sworn you were Orson Welles." Thus began the friendship between Orson and playwright Thornton Wilder. An incredulous Orson couldn't believe that his name was known by one of the country's foremost playwrights. The conversation progressed to the point of Wilder offering to introduce Orson to Alexander Wolcott, the influential drama critic of the *New York Times*. The next day, Orson was on a superliner bound for New York.

Young Welles was warmly received by Wolcott, who wined and dined the actor and became impressed by

Orson's "effortless magnificence" of a voice. A few days later, Wolcott arranged a meeting for Welles with Guthrie McClintic, husband of America's reigning first lady of theater, Katherine Cornell. McClintic hired Welles within minutes, giving Welles his first professional acting job on American soil. Thus began Orson's tenure with Katherine Cornell's national touring company, where he was heralded for his performance as Mercutio in *Romeo and Juliet*. By late 1933, the eighteen-year-old Welles was busy creating an impressive résumé of acting credits: appearing in touring productions of *Candida* and *The Barretts of Wimpole Street*; joining mentors Edwards and MacLiammoir in a summer drama festival at the Todd School; writing, directing, and starring in his first film, the abstract *The Hearts of Age*; and making his Broadway debut as Tybalt in *Romeo and Juliet*. Shortly thereafter, Welles met John Houseman, who asked him to join in the production of the stage piece *Panic*. The performance was so well received, a radio dramatization soon followed. It marked Welles' introduction to radio.

In addition to possessing a charismatic and engaging dramatic presence, Welles was also blessed with a remarkably deep, resonant voice that made him an instant hit over the airwaves. Sounding nothing like the youth he still was, Welles quickly became a regular on many radio programs, including *Cavalcade of America*, NBC's *March of Time*, *Streamlined Shakespeare*, and *America's Hour*. These spots led to his most well-known series of performances to date, as the dark and mysterious Lamont Cranston on Mutual Radio's *The Shadow*, which aired from late 1937 until summer 1938. Millions of listeners tuned in each week breathlessly awaiting the chilling words intoned by radio's boy wonder: "Who knows what evil lurks in the hearts of men? ...The Shadow knows." In fact, Welles was in such demand as a radio performer that he came up with a creative way of commuting from studio to studio. Faced with tight time frames and constant gridlock, Orson hired out an ambulance to transport him, sirens screaming, from commitment to commitment.

Meanwhile, Welles and Houseman worked tirelessly producing theatrical performances for the Federal

*Welles eyes the next classic book he'll adapt
for an upcoming radio broadcast.*

Theatre Project. Their first project was staging an all-black *Macbeth* at the Lafayette Theatre in Harlem. The resulting performance, still remembered years later as the "Voodoo Macbeth," made theater history, eventually moving to Broadway. Other Welles-Houseman productions for the Federal Theatre Project included *Horse Eats Hat*, *Ten Million Ghosts*, *Doctor Faustus*, and the children's opera *The Second Hurricane*. These shows were a precursor to the Federal Theatre Project's most controversial production, Marc Blitzstein's pro-labor opera *The Cradle Will Rock*. Locked out of the theater by federal agents on opening night, Welles and Houseman led the performers and audience down the street to the Venice Theatre. Prevented by the union from appearing on stage, the actors performed from their seats throughout the auditorium, accompanied by Blitzstein himself playing the musical score from an old piano. The performance was a smash, and it made Welles a star.

Welles left the Federal Theatre Project soon after *The Cradle Will Rock* bowed, joined shortly after by Houseman, who was fired. Working together, and with a scant hundred dollars in the bank, they formed a new repertory company, the Mercury Theatre, named, according to James Naremore, "from a copy of *Mercury* magazine lying in a corner of an empty fireplace at Welles' home." Their first production was a modern version of *Julius Caesar*, adapted by Welles and set in fascist Italy. The play opened November 11, 1937, to much controversy, rave reviews, and capacity crowds. Four more stage shows were produced during the next year: *The Shoemaker's Holiday*, *Heartbreak House*, *Too Much Johnson*, and *Danton's Death*. Then, on July 11, 1938, Welles and Houseman took their talents to radio, as the Mercury Theatre debuted on CBS with their dramatic weekly program, *First Person Singular*.

Initially a nine-week summer series scheduled to replace Cecil B. DeMille's *Lux Presents Hollywood*, this sixty-minute program immediately set the standard for live radio drama. With a cast headed by Welles and including the formidable talents of Broadway veterans Agnes Moorehead, Alice Frost, Martin Gabel, Ray Collins, and Virginia Welles (Orson's wife), *First Person Singular* adapted literary works that were deemed to be suitable for the medium of radio. As Welles himself said in a press conference announcing the program, "I think it is time that radio came to realize the fact that, no matter how wonderful a play may be for the stage, it cannot be as wonderful for the air. The Mercury Theatre has no intention of producing its stage repertoire in these broadcasts. Instead, we plan to bring to radio the experimental techniques so successful in another medium, and so treat radio itself with the intelligence such a beautiful and powerful medium deserves." The broadcasts incorporated extensive sound effects as well as live music written and conducted by CBS staff composer Bernard Hermann, who would go on to compose the score for Welles' *Citizen Kane* and a multitude of other films such as *The Day the Earth Stood Still*, *Vertigo*, *Psycho*, *Fahrenheit 451*, and *Taxi Driver*. Welles was to act as announcer as well as assuming a major dramatic role. Their initial offering was Bram Stoker's horror drama *Dracula*, which in subsequent days was praised as "adventurous," by *Newsweek*, and heralded by the *New York Times* as "realistically broadcast, the characters living electrically." Ensuing weeks saw the production of such classics as *Treasure Island*, *A Tale of Two Cities*, and *The 39 Steps*. Each performance was selected and directed by Welles, with both Welles and Houseman creating and perfecting the script.

At the end of their nine-week "trial," CBS quickly announced that it was renewing the now-titled *Mercury Theatre on the Air*, giving it a permanent spot on the Sunday evening schedule at 8:00. With the varying stage and radio responsibilities taking their toll on both Welles and Houseman, they eventually turned over the radio writing duties to a lawyer-turned-playwright named Howard Koch. His play, "The Lonely Man," which played in Chicago and starred John Huston, had caught the attention of the two Mercury producers. For seventy-five dollars a week, they hired the thirty-three-

year-old Koch to turn a literary work of their choosing into sixty pages of radio script. Each script usually featured rewrite after rewrite, as both Welles and Houseman honed the words to their exacting specifications. Final scripts were due Sunday at noon, in order for Welles to lead the troupe through a day's worth of rehearsals before their Sunday evening live airing at eight o'clock sharp. This continued unabated throughout the late summer and autumn, until Houseman dropped a project on Koch's lap that he described as "Orson's favorite project." The project was to turn a science fiction novel, first read by Welles in 1927 in the *Amazing Stories* comic book serials, into a radio drama in the form of news bulletins. The book: H.G. Wells' classic tale, *The War of the Worlds*.

Welles talks to Agnes Moorehead while directing a rehearsal of the Mercury Theatre.

In his book, *The Panic Broadcast*, Koch relates how the task of adapting the Wells story for radio meant virtually rewriting the entire story. "Reading the story," he said, "which was laid in England and written in narrative style, I realized I could use practically nothing but the author's idea of a Martian invasion and his description of their appearance and their machines." Far from a simple adaptation, it meant the creation of an original radio play, sixty or seventy pages, written and revised in six days. Koch began his arduous task on his one day off. On the Monday prior to the broadcast, he visited his family up the Hudson in New York state. On his drive back, he realized he needed a map to establish the location of the first Martian arrivals. He stopped in a gas station on the New Jersey stretch of Route 9 and purchased a map of New Jersey. Back in his Manhattan apartment, he spread the map out, closed his eyes, and dropped his pencil point in the middle of the map. The winning location: Grovers Mill, a community possessing a quaint, authentic sounding name and located near Princeton, which would allow university scientists to become part of the play.

The following days were a nightmare to Koch, who frantically wrote scenes, sent them off to Welles and Houseman for approval, then rewrote the scenes time and time again. Koch recalled the frenetic process, saying, "Eventually I found myself enjoying the destruction I was wreaking like a drunken general. Finally, after demolishing the Columbia Broadcasting Building, perhaps a subconscious wish fulfillment, I ended the holocaust with one lonely ham radio voice on the air." Still, something was missing.

On Thursday, October 27, Welles returned to his suite at New York's St. Regis Hotel to review a recording of that day's rehearsal. He, along with cast members and sound engineers, felt that the show was weak. "This is so ghastly," complained Welles, "Nobody's going to believe a word of this." He felt that a sense of immediacy was needed, and thought that news bulletins and eyewitness accounts would add to the effect. He also suggested that the names of real people and places be used wherever and whenever possible. Koch and Houseman spent all day Friday reworking the script, adding the touches Orson suggested. By Friday afternoon, a "final" script was sent to the CBS legal department for a standard read-through. The official verdict: the script was *too believable* and would have to be softened before airing.

Protesting vehemently, Welles, Houseman, and Koch quickly began the task of making the script less believable. They made minor changes in phrasing and wording, hoping to placate the network while still involving the audience. For instance, the "Princeton University Observatory" became the "Princeton Observatory"; the "United States Weather Bureau in Washington, D.C." became the "Government Weather Bureau"; and the "New Jersey National Guard" was changed to the "State Militia." Other scenes, such as the cries of the Martians as they advanced, shouting "Ulla, ulla, ulla," were dropped, CBS feeling that it sounded too terrifying. Meanwhile, Mercury actor Frank Readick was intently studying the record of Herb Morrison's account of the Hindenburg disaster of 1937. Playing the broadcast over and over again to get a sense of the urgency in Morrison's strained voice, Readick prepared to make his role as the doomed reporter Carl Phillips as realistic as possible.

The Sunday evening broadcasts started out in an underwhelming fashion for CBS. At seven o'clock, the audience was treated to an hour of Secretary of Agriculture Henry Wallace, along with General Hugh Johnson and Professor Lyman Bryson, discussing what the country should do with its farm surpluses. It was hardly the sort of programming that was a portent of things to come. Most of the radio listening audience was planning on tuning into *The Chase and Sanborn Hour*, starring Edgar Bergen and Charlie McCarthy, on NBC at eight o'clock; in fact, that show was the highest rated radio program that aired on Sundays, reaching 34.7 percent of the audience. The only hint of things to come for the usual 3.6 percent share that listened to Welles was a quick descriptive sentence in that day's *New York Times*: "Tonight—Play: H.G. Wells' 'War of the Worlds.'" Another page of the paper featured a photo of Welles, Moorehead, and other cast members, with a caption reading, "Mercury Theatre players huddle around Orson Welles on WABC's stage Sunday nights at 8 o'clock:

tonight's show is 'War of the Worlds' by H.G. Wells.'" All in all, it was shaping up to be another Sunday evening as usual.

At 7:58 that evening, Welles ascended to the podium in the center of the studio, downed a bottle of pineapple juice (his pre-broadcast custom), cleared his throat, loosened his tie, and put on his headphones. The moment the studio clock's second hand reached exactly 8:00, Orson cued announcer Dan Seymour to start the show:

> *The Columbia Broadcasting System and its affiliated stations present Orson Welles and The Mercury Theatre on the Air in* The War of the Worlds *by H. G. Wells.* **CD1**

Bernard Hermann's orchestra followed with the program's usual introductory theme, the first twenty seconds of Tchaikovsky's "Piano Concerto No. 1 in B-flat Minor." Then, Seymour again: "The Director of the Mercury Theatre and star of these broadcasts, Mr. Orson Welles."

What followed changed forever the face of radio broadcasting.

★ ★ ★

Orson Welles had already achieved fame before the broadcast—after all, his face had graced the cover of *Time* magazine on May 9, 1938, three days after his twenty-third birthday. But in one night, Orson Welles went from being a rising star on Broadway to a world-famous radio prankster. Newspapers around the globe recounted the broadcast, and everyone wanted to know more about this boy wonder who fooled a nation. More important, they all wanted to know what he was going to do next. How does one follow up a performance so breathtaking, so culturally shocking? By doing the unexpected, of course.

He went to Hollywood.

Up to that point in his life, Orson had always deemed motion pictures as being a lesser form of performance than either live theater or radio theater. However, an unprecedented offer from RKO Pictures changed his mind. Orson would receive $100,000 per year (a sum higher than the president of the United States received on a yearly basis), would be expected to produce one film per year, and would have total and complete artistic and managerial *carte blanche*. In effect, RKO opened their doors to Orson and told him to make the movies of his choosing, and they'd simply be his bankroll.

Welles, Houseman, and the whole Mercury Theatre crew moved out to California in late 1939 to begin work on their first movie. Orson wanted to produce, as his initial film, *Cyrano de Bergerac*, but found the studio to be less than thrilled by his choice (especially since a poll indicated that only 3 percent of the public would be interested in seeing that movie). He next turned his attention to Conrad's *Heart of Darkness*, securing the rights for an adaptation and receiving RKO's blessings. Eventually this, too, fell apart, due to increasingly large cost estimates and a continually shrinking European market (England was closing many theaters in response to the burgeoning war). Faced with a looming deadline and no story, he decided to take the story *The Life of Dumas* and update it, basing it on the wealthy Hearst family, California's publishing magnates. Welles began work on the script, along with Houseman and writer Herman Mankiewicz, who had already compiled unpublished reams on Hearst. In twelve weeks, a script was completed. Titled *American*, the script was reworked over the next month, finally resurfacing under a new title: *Citizen Kane*.

It's difficult to believe now that upon its release on May 8, 1941, *Citizen Kane* was not warmly greeted by the public. In fact, due to overt pressure by the Hearst Media conglomerate, many theater owners booked the movie but didn't show it, writing the costs off as a loss. Despite the glowing reviews and universal raves, *Citizen Kane* was gone from the theaters by mid summer, and for the fiscal year, ended up showing a net loss of over $150,000. Welles felt somewhat vindicated the next spring, when *Citizen Kane* received nine Academy Award nominations including Best Picture, Best Direction, Best Screenplay, and Best Actor. Neither Orson nor *Citizen Kane* were warmly received at the Awards ceremony (a chorus of boos and hisses greeted both his name and the film's title), and *Citizen Kane*

Welles campaigning as Charles Foster Kane in his directorial debut, Citizen Kane.

won but a single award, for Best Screenplay. Welles had taken on Hollywood on his own terms; had rankled the established hierarchy; had offended perhaps the most powerful man in publishing; and had created what is generally regarded today as the greatest motion picture ever made. The experience left him financially broke, professionally condemned, and personally vilified.

Welles proceeded unaffected, diving into his next project, *The Magnificent Ambersons*, with his typical brazen sense of confidence. As soon as shooting on that film was completed, he immediately began work on his next film, *Journey Into Fear*. Schedule conflicts, delays due to the Hayes Office (censors), and his constant sixteen-hour days eventually took their tool on Welles, and he handed the directorial reigns over to Norman Foster. *Ambersons*, with its last real recut by the studio, debuted in August of 1942 to relatively empty theaters (the public choosing to spend their time outdoors in the heat of the summer), while *Journey* was halted by the studio from seeing a release until 1943. Meanwhile, Welles was also in Rio de Janiero filming a documentary titled *It's All True*. This project was filled with mishap after mishap,

lack of communication between the set and the studio, and exorbitant cost overruns. It was never completed.

During these three years, Welles completed three films for RKO. Not only did none of them show any profit, but the combined losses well exceeded one million dollars. Welles, and Mercury Productions (as the theater troop was now called), was thrown off the RKO lot on July 1, 1942, before *Journey Into Fear* was released. Welles, ever the temperamental artist, forged ahead as a genius-at-large, willing to hire out his virtuosic talents to whichever studio was smart enough to hire him. He was twenty-seven years old, viewed as both an icon and a pariah.

Welles spent the next three decades locked in a continual battle with the Hollywood establishment, intent on doing things the right way—his way. He picked up the occasional contract to direct a movie, usually producing a stunning visual spectacle that lost money and guaranteed his dismissal. These movies included *The*

Welles with his second wife, actress Rita Hayworth.

Lady from Shanghai (1948), *Macbeth* (1948), *Othello* (1952), and *Touch of Evil* (1958). He began to accept acting jobs, appearing in such films as *Jane Eyre, The Third Man, The Long Hot Summer, Moby Dick*, and *A Man for All Seasons*. He spent time on the lecture circuit, particularly in the 1940s, trying to raise money for his continued film productions. He divorced his wife, Virginia; had a very public relationship with actress Delores Del Rio; married, and then divorced, actress Rita Hayworth; and was then married a third time, to Countess Paola Mori Di Girfalco. He fathered three daughters; Christopher (with Virginia), Rebecca (with Rita), and Beatrice (with Paola).

There are very few people who would not admit that Orson Welles was a genius. There are also very few people who would not admit that he possessed a tremendous ego, one that often precluded him from working well with others. He often maintained that Hollywood was scared of him and tried to blackball him. He spent most of his later years either working in Europe or attempting to secure the funding for various films, many of which were never completed. In fact, the end for Orson came, fittingly enough, as he was writing stage directions and camera movements for *The Magic Show*, a film he'd never finish. A heart attack claimed his life sometime during the evening of October 9, 1985.

It was after his death that the acceptance and admiration Welles sought was finally given. Janet Leigh said, "We all wish we could have made more use of his genius." John Huston said, "What a shame, and I mean that literally, that one of the finest talents motion pictures has ever had was rejected out-of-hand." Charlton Heston added a thought that was echoed by many when he said, "We have lost the most talented man I ever knew." Even William Randolph Hearst Jr., felt a sense of loss. "Goddamn it," said the man whose father was depicted in *Citizen Kane*, "It makes me mad because I wanted to meet that man. I really wanted to talk about that movie." He was—and is—remembered as a supremely talented artist, someone whose profound effects on two different media cannot be matched. What makes the legend of Orson Welles all the more mystical is that he created his two masterpieces—the radio dramatization of *The War of the Worlds* and the film *Citizen Kane*—both before he reached the age of twenty-six.

Boy wonder, indeed.

1915–1985

INVASIONS
FROM
MARS

Martians, Moon Men, Close and Other Encounters

"No one would have believed in the last years of the nineteenth century that this world was being watched keenly and closely by intelligences greater than man's…minds as ours are to those of the beasts that perish, intellects vast and cool and unsympathetic, regarded this earth with envious eyes, and slowly and surely drew their plans against us."

—H.G. Wells

A fascination with our nearest celestial neighbors—the moon, Venus, and Mars—is nothing new; speculating about these worlds is, in fact, one of our oldest pastimes. Human beings have always felt a familial tie to Earth's only moon; and Venus, representing the goddess of love in Western mythology, has been regarded as Earth's sister. It is the red planet—Mars, the god of war—that gives us pause.

In 1878, long before we could have known much about Earth's nearest heavenly bodies, an Italian astronomer, Giovanni Virginio Schiaparelli, observed thin, dark lines on the surface of Mars. He described these features as channels, or "canali," in his native Italian. Mistranslated into English as "canals," these lines took on new meaning—as something created by an intelligent civilization as opposed to a natural phenomenon.

This discovery and its misinterpretation prompted much speculation as to the canals' meaning. In 1895, three years before H.G. Wells published *The War of the Worlds*, Percival Lowell released his book,

Mars. In it, he proposed an entire race of intelligent Martians. He further postulated that the Martians had built the huge canals in order to solve the problem of the planet's desiccation. The canals were to bring water from Mars' polar ice caps to the arid mainlands—no doubt a marvel of technology and engineering.

Lowell's creative nonfiction suggested that Mars was a dying planet with a highly advanced civilization. This scientific premise became Wells' basis for the Martians' motivation to invade earth—at the time, a plausible foundation upon which to build his story.

That Wells' science fiction tale was also a political allegory is made plain by both the book's timing—published at the peak of the British Empire—and Wells' own political leanings, elucidated in the introductory passage:

And before we judge of them too harshly we must remember what ruthless and utter destruction our own species has wrought, not only upon animals, such as the vanished bison and the dodo, but upon its inferior races. The Tasmanians, in spite of their human likeness, were entirely swept out of existence in a war of extermination waged by European immigrants, in the space of fifty years. Are we such apostles of mercy as to complain if the Martians warred in the same spirit?

As Isaac Asimov pointed out in the afterword to a later edition, this was a fiendish irony—that the Martians would invade and conquer England, thus turning the tables by colonizing the world's foremost colonial power. Surely, this played into a certain fear of the conqueror becoming the conquered, whether out of a subconscious guilt or insecurity. And, no doubt, Orson Welles and Howard Koch grasped the significance of changing the locale of the invasion from Woking, England, to Grovers Mill, New Jersey, in 1938, by which time the United States had demonstrated a predisposition to creating its own empire with its actions in the Caribbean, the Phillipines, and Central and South America. Tapping into a shared anxiety, the Mercury Theatre broadcast gave Americans a preview of their fall from grace. What happens to the powerful when they become powerless, subjugated by a superior force?

The 1953 film version capitalized on similar fears, with the Soviet Union taking the place that Nazi Germany had occupied in the collective subconscious. It is fear, ultimately, that drives H.G. Wells' story, an apocalyptic preview of our first encounter with alien intelligence.

The War of the Worlds was initially published in 1897 in monthly installments by *Pearson's* magazine in England and, later, by *Cosmopolitan* in the U.S. The book, with extensive revisions by Wells, was released in England in February 1898. It was a great success and helped confirm Wells' status as one of the foremost young writers in Great Britain. A prolific author, he eventually became one of the most respected novelists and social thinkers of his day, with novels like *The Invisible Man* and *The First Men in the Moon*, and works

The debut of "The War of the Worlds" in Pearson's *magazine, April 1897*

of nonfiction such as *The Outline of History* and *The Shape of Things to Come*. Yet *The War of the Worlds* was not universally acclaimed as one of H.G. Wells' finest works until after the 1938 Mercury Theatre broadcast—it was Orson Welles who secured the book's place in history as a classic. And it was radio that brought a frightening immediacy to the story that the medium of the novel never could.

In the first few decades of the twentieth century, most of the readers of *The War of the Worlds* were probably young boys, like Orson Welles, who found the story again serialized, only this time in comic books like *Weird Tales* and *Amazing Stories*. The 1938 Mercury Theatre broadcast would go on to inspire numerous new versions, adaptations, and homages. Some were well done, some were noteworthy, but few achieved the artistic merit of either H.G.'s original or Orson's adaptation.

Prior to *The War of the Worlds*, however, it was another medium—the newspaper—that gave the world its first taste of alien-inspired mass delusion, before there was such a thing as radio or such a person as H.G. Wells.

The Great Moon Hoax:
Bearded Bat-Men, Biped Beavers,
and Telepathic Unicorns

More than a hundred years before Orson Welles played his "Hallowe'en prank," a young Englishman named Richard Adams Locke, while working as a reporter for the *New York Sun*, created a hoax so elaborate and fanciful that no one, apparently, could help but believe it. Locke, who had been educated at Cambridge, knew a little about astronomy. He knew that a number of respected scientists at the time believed that there was life on the moon. So, on August 21, 1835, the inventive showman and fabulist concocted a teaser item to run in the *Sun* with the headline, "Celestial Discovery." The scant text delivered little, but promised much:

The *Edinburgh Courant* says—"We have just learnt from an eminent publisher in this city that Sir John Herschel, at the Cape of Good Hope, has made some astronomical discoveries by means of an immense telescope of an entirely new principle."

This tease was sufficiently tantalizing and, as would be seen in later hoaxes, followed the rule of easing the

audience into the deception, establishing a reasonable credibility first. John Herschel, the son of astronomer William Herschel who had discovered Uranus, was well known in his own right and had been in the news recently for establishing a significant new observatory in Cape Town, South Africa. (He remained ignorant of the ensuing canard until months after it ended, but reportedly found it quite amusing.)

The follow-up to Locke's bait came four days later, on August 25, with a story captioned, "Great Astronomical Discoveries Lately Made by Sir John Herschel, L.L.D., F.R.S.&c. at the Cape of Good Hope." Herschel's telescope was said to use a lens weighing 14,826 pounds that could magnify objects forty-two thousand times. Through an innovative new technique—described with a good deal of technical gibberish—it solved the problem of distant objects becoming fainter the more they were magnified. With this telescope, the story promised, Herschel was able to examine the moon's surface in minute detail. The story ended with the claim that Herschel "has affirmatively settled the question whether this satellite be inhabited, and by what order of beings."

The next installments chronicled a tour of a land that could only be from outer space—idyllic landscapes of brown basalt covered with red flowers, massive green forests, and a blue sea with towering waves and white sand beaches, bordered by "wild, castellated rocks, apparently of green marble." The account proceeded to the hinted-at feature attraction: the creatures.

On a wooded hillside were "herds of brown quadropeds, having all the external characteristics of the bison…but more diminutive." Another creature resembled a tailless beaver that walked on two feet. "It carries its young in its arms like a human being and moves with an easy gliding motion," it read. "Its huts are constructed better and higher than those of many tribes of human savages, and from the appearance of smoke in nearly all of them, there is no doubt of its being acquainted with the use of fire." Another group of creatures appeared as blue-gray unicorns who could sense the astronomers' observations and moved in some kind of telepathic response to the scientists' movements. More beings

The Ruby Colosseum, home of the "Vespertilio-homo," or "Bat-man"

Illustrated from an 1836 English pamphlet, detailing the "Bat-men" and "biped beavers"

were described in stunning detail: small reindeer-like animals; flocks of red and white birds; horned bears; moon elks and moose; miniature zebra; and a giraffe-like creature with a sheep's head, two long, spiral horns, and a white, bushy tail.

The scientists discovered an island with hills of orange and yellow quartz crystals, melon-bearing trees, and crevices filled with veins of pure gold. Most astonishing of all were the "flocks of large winged creatures, wholly unlike any kind of birds." They walked upright, had wings like bats, large foreheads, prominent, bearded jaws, and appeared slightly more attractive than your average orangutan. The astronomers named the creature "Vespertilio-homo," or Bat-man. They found the Bat-men to be intelligent animals capable of reason and producing works of art, perhaps more innocent than humans, though, the story hinted, much less inhibited sexually.

Locke's fantastic deception proved irresistible to readers who, by the fourth installment on August 28, had made the *Sun* the world's largest newspaper, with a circulation of 19,360 (as compared to the venerable *Times* of London, which had a readership of seventeen thousand). That this success was built entirely on a fraudulent series of six articles would not be disclosed until after Locke had sold sixty thousand copies of the articles in pamphlet form and the *Sun* had its own

pamphlet reprinted and sent to London, Edinburgh, and Paris. From there, the story spread throughout Europe to astound slack-jawed readers in Germany, Italy, Spain, and Portugal. Back in the States, throngs numbering in the thousands gathered outside the *Sun*'s offices, hoping to get an update on the moon men before the story went to press. No one in the public seemed capable of questioning the veracity of the incredible account—to sniff out the plain truth that the story was complete bunkum.

But the public weren't the only ones. The *New York Times*, the *New Yorker*, the *Daily Advertiser*, and the *U.S. Gazette*, among others, all testified as to the credence and plausibility of the "discoveries." It fell to the New York *Journal of Commerce* to reveal the hoax—and then only due to sheer dumb luck. Just before the *Journal* was about to reprint the *Sun*'s moon series, Locke confided to a friend at the paper that the story was a fake and that he was the author. The *Journal* then, rather ignominiously, exposed the hoax and Locke with it.

Although no one ever discovered the true purpose behind the moon hoax, it seems safe to assume that the *Sun* was primarily interested in the exposure and the riches it would, and did, bring. Locke, on the other hand, appears to have been satirizing something or

A vivid moonscape, with various moon creatures and a mysterious "Lunar Temple"

someone—perhaps, as Edgar Allan Poe, one of Locke's victims and admirers, suggested, that someone was Thomas Dick. Dick, a Scottish astronomer, had some fairly farfetched ideas of his own about the moon and other natural phenomena, even for 1835.

While it did not create a panic, the moon hoax does parallel the 1938 "War of the Worlds" broadcast in some respects. It brought to light the gullibility and lack of critical faculties among people, even educated people, the world over. It also made a star of its perpetrator, Richard Locke, who continued to sell new editions of his *Moon Hoax* pamphlet for the next twenty years.

Radio, Radio

Orson Welles had discovered an effective medium for scaring the wits out of mass audiences in 1938. Still, you'd think that the panic broadcast would be a warning to other radio programmers not to try airing a dramatization of *The War of the Worlds* again. On the contrary, it actually inspired a few to try and duplicate the magic.

After the panic, the recording of the Orson Welles broadcast was in high demand.

Mars 2, South America 0

On November 12, 1944, an adaptation of Koch's "Invasion from Mars," broadcast from a radio station in Santiago, Chile, caused widespread panic across the nation as citizens fled into the streets or barricaded their homes. The governor of one province mobilized troops and artillery to repel the Martian horde. A realistic show, the play included references to the Red Cross and had an actor impersonate the minister of the interior.

Quito, Ecuador, circa 1949

A little over four years later, a group of Ecuadorians in Quito, apparently having learned nothing from either Grovers Mill or Santiago, created their own take on the Welles version of *The War of the Worlds* on February 12, 1949. Radio Quito, broadcast out of the Comercio building and owned by the leading newspaper, *El Comercio*, was the most popular radio station in Quito, Ecuador's capital. In early 1949, artistic director Leonardo Paez and dramatic director Eduardo Alcaras (whose real name was Alfredo Vergara Morales) were looking for a radio program that would really grab their listeners. Aware of the 1938 Welles broadcast of "The War of the Worlds," they found a vehicle with just the level of excitement they needed…and then some.

Creating their own script, based on the newsflash style Mercury Theatre used, Paez and Alcaras crafted a story that would seem realistic to the people of the peaceful, mostly rural region at the foot of Mt. Pichincha in the Andes. They saw no reason to inform station management of their plans—they had put on plenty of dramas in the past. So on the evening of Saturday, February 12, they were ready to go.

As usual, the nightly music program followed that evening's newscast. (Unlike the 1938 broadcast, which was the regularly scheduled dramatic program, listed as such in the newspaper, this drama began unbeknownst to anyone but the actors.) Suddenly, an announcer broke in mid-song: "Here is an urgent piece of late news!" He went on to describe how Martians had landed twenty miles south of Quito, near Latacunga. Having razed Latacunga, he said, the Martians were now headed toward Quito in the shape of a cloud. Not surprisingly, many people mistook perfectly harmless clouds for Martian death clouds and reacted accordingly. The first announcement was followed by: "The air base of Mariscal Sucre has been taken by the enemy, and it is being destroyed. There are many dead and wounded. It's being wiped out!"

Radio Quito took Mercury's sound-alike secretary of the interior idea a step further by using actors to impersonate not only the interior minister, who urged citizens to stay calm and "organize the defense and evacuation of the city," but also Quito's mayor, who announced: "Let us defend our city. Our women and children must go out into the surrounding heights to leave the men free for action and combat." A priest followed, who prayed for God's mercy as church bells rang in the background. A reporter broke in atop Quito's tallest building, La Previsora Tower, to report on a monster engulfed in plumes of fire and smoke advancing on the city. Reports from the nearby village of Cotocallao, which was now "under attack," came in, describing the carnage there.

Thousands of Quito's residents filled the streets, racing in every direction, presumably away from the Martians and to safety. As one Associated Press reporter put it, they were "fleeing from their homes and running through the streets. Many were clad only in night clothing." Much like the Mercury Theatre listeners a decade before, who assumed the account must be a Nazi invasion, many of the Radio Quito audience believed that the country was being invaded by Peru; others thought it was the Soviet Union. When Radio Quito staff members overheard the noise coming from their panicked listeners running around town, they realized what they had to do. Scared helpless, the terrified mobs of Ecuadorians in the streets lacked direction for their adrenaline—that is, until Radio Quito made the announcement revealing the broadcast as a hoax. From that point on, the mob had a purpose. Having been stirred from their homes, some from their beds, they weren't about to return quietly. They made a bee-line for the Comercio Building and began to riot. Some forward-thinkers came equipped with gasoline. Some brought copies of *El Comercio*. The combination yielded all-too-predictable results. Most of the one hundred or so *El Comercio* and Radio Quito employees escaped through a back door. Others were forced to flee to the

The Comerico Building in flames after an angry mob set fire to it, killing twenty radio station employees

third floor. When rioters began tossing lit, gasoline-soaked newspapers into the building, the police and army were called to quell the uprising. Unfortunately, they were already well on their way to Cotocallao to put down the Martian insurgency there.

As fire engulfed the Comercio building, dozens of employees, still trapped on the third floor, leapt from open windows to escape the flames. Others formed a human chain to descend to safety, but when the chain broke, many fell to the sidewalk below.

By the time the police and army arrived, the fire had spread to other buildings. To make matters worse, the mob had removed the fire hydrants and blocked firefighters from extinguishing the fire. One of the policemen initially on the scene was beaten by the crowd. With armored vehicles and tear gas, they dispersed the throng of rioters, making way for fire trucks. They were able to save the surrounding buildings, but all that was left standing of the Comercio building was

'Mars Raiders' Cause Quito Panic; Mob Burns Radio Plant, Kills 15

By The Associated Press.

QUITO, Ecuador, Feb. 13—An enraged mob that hurled gasoline and flaming balls of paper took fatal vengeance here last night for a panic caused by an Orson Welles-type radio dramatization of an "invasion from Mars." The mob attacked and burned the building of the newspaper, Comercio, which housed the radio station, and killed fifteen persons and injured fifteen others.

Army troops were called out and used tanks and tear gas to restore order.

The mob wrecked the newspaper building, its equipment and the radio station. Damage was estimated at more than $350,000.

Indictments were drawn against Leonardo Paez, director of art at the station, known as Radio Quito, and Eduardo Alcaras, a Chilean who is the station's dramatic director. Heads of the station said the two men prepared and directed the dramatization without their knowledge.

Police detained ten suspects and more arrests were ordered. The Government appointed Diaz Granados, Minister of Defense, to investigate the rioting.

As in the Orson Welles broadcast that caused panic in the United States in 1938, the populace had been terrified by a radio dramatization of H. G. Wells' fantastic novel, "The War of the Worlds," localized to describe strange creatures from Mars landing near by and heading for Quito.

Hysteria drove most of the population of Quito into the streets before the program directors learned how much consternation they had caused. Frantically they appealed to the people to be calm, and assured them it was all fictional.

When the people finally were convinced, they swept upon the Comercio Building, which housed Ecuador's principal newspaper, showering it with stones and driv-

Continued on Page 7, Column 4

Front page of the New York Times *for February 14, 1949*

the façade. The newspaper presses, studio and transmission equipment, and all of the company's files were destroyed. According to the final count, twenty people died in the fire or trying to escape it. Some of the bodies were charred beyond recognition. More than a dozen others sustained injuries.

Alcaras was arrested on criminal charges and jailed. He promptly rolled over on Paez, who was also under indictment, although nowhere to be found. It was Paez, said Alcaras, who planted stories in the papers about flying saucers in the area before the broadcast; Paez insisted that the program not be announced as fiction; and Paez ordered the studio doors locked so as not to "disturb" the actors during the show, all contributing factors to the riot. The police searched for Paez, but he had already fled the country. The other survivors from Radio Quito and *El Comercio* were left to clean up the mess. In all, the rioters had caused $350,000 worth of damage, aside from the human cost. The newspaper and radio station rebuilt over time, regaining their respected positions in the community. But neither wants to remember the tragedy that "The War of the Worlds" brought Ecuador's capital city of Quito more than fifty years ago.

Bewildered in Buffalo

On October 31, 1968, after the most intensive promotional campaign in the station's history, WKBW in Buffalo, New York, broadcast its own updated version of "The War of the Worlds." **CD 4** Not wanting to have its studio burnt to the ground, WKBW ran announcements about the radio play every hour, on the hour, for twenty-one straight days prior to the broadcast. They sent press releases to TV stations, newspapers, police, even schools to warn them that they were planning a "War of the Worlds" presentation. So at 11:00 P.M. on the thirtieth anniversary plus one day of the Orson Welles broadcast, WKBW's program director, Jefferson Kaye, put on his own version of the by now classic radio play.

Being 1968, the programming was a little different than that of the late 1930s. Instead of Ramón Raquello and his orchestra soothing listeners with their rendition of "La Cumparsita," D.J. Sandy Beach spun records like

Cream's "White Room" and The Beatles' "Hey Jude." Newsflashes would periodically interrupt the songs with updates on the mysterious explosions on Mars, then the meteor crashing on Grand Island, and eventually, some real carnage as the Martians let loose with their heat rays, poison gas, and so on, killing off the station's reporters one by one. Instead of using actors, Kaye employed the station's evening D.J., Sandy Beach, and regular reporters like Joe Downey, Don Lancer, Jim Faigan, and WKBW-TV anchor Irv Weinstein, who were told to report on the invasion as though it were really happening, instead of relying on a prepared script.

After the Army blew the bridge to Grand Island, the Martians waded across the river atop their machines, releasing a deadly black cloud, killing everyone in the area, including reporters Jim Faigan and Don Lancer. As the reporters left on the air gathered themselves, listeners started jamming the station's phone lines, believing that what they were hearing was real. At this point, Jeff Kaye decided that things had gone too far. He wanted to cut into the show, but director Dan Kriegler refused, offering to duke it out with Kaye. When Kriegler realized that Kaye was going to pull the reel-to-reel tape and end the show, he relented, allowing Kaye to go on the air to remind listeners that this was indeed a drama.

The show then proceeded to its inevitable conclusion, with Irv Weinstein being incinerated by a Martian heat ray atop City Hall, Jeff Kaye succumbing to the black gas in a deserted downtown Buffalo, and the Martians themselves being killed off by a few measly germs. Despite the frequent station breaks to identify the program as "The War of the Worlds" and the huge promotional media blitz undertaken by WKBW before the broadcast, four thousand people frantically phoned Buffalo police stations, newspapers, and TV and radio stations to find out if the Martian attack was real. The Canadian national guard sent units to the Peace Bridge, Rainbow Bridge, and Queenston Bridge to repel Martian invaders. Although the local newspaper received three press releases from WKBW, they still sent a team of reporters and photographers to Grand Island to cover the invasion. One county civil defense unit went on alert and ordered men to all stations. United

Buffalo, New York, before the 1968 WKBW broadcast

Press bureaus up and down the Eastern seaboard were besieged by phone calls asking about the Martian landing in Buffalo.

At one Buffalo police station, the police chief had the bad luck to be there when a dazed man stumbled in, spouting a wild tale about Martians landing on Grand Island and attacking people with a heat ray. Figuring he was drunk, they asked where he had heard this outlandish story. When they tuned in WKBW to placate him, they heard for themselves the death and devastation unleashed by the Martians. Amid the hubbub of handing out weapons to defend the local populace from the invaders, they heard a station break interrupt the "newscast." Sheepishly, they put away their shotguns, ordered a pizza, and listened to the rest of the show.

Forty-seven newspapers around the country carried the story of the panic in Buffalo. Although it was tiny compared to the scare the 1938 broadcast inspired, the WKBW version of "The War of the Worlds" had only been broadcast locally.

Other Broadcasts

In 1964, WPEN, in Portland, Oregon, broadcast a performance of the original Koch script, "Invasion from Mars" live, but without the usual accompanying panic. In 1967, the BBC produced its own six-part adaptation that is faithful to the H.G. Wells novel, not the news-flash style of the Mercury Theatre broadcast. It was later aired on National Public Radio (NPR) in the U.S. in 1995.

On Halloween night in 1974, radio station WPRO in Providence, Rhode Island, aired a drama based on H.G. Wells' original *War of the Worlds* that began with "a meteorite falling in Jamestown, Rhode Island," and launched the Martian invasion from there. Amazingly, many in Providence were frightened by the broadcast despite the fact that the 1938 broadcast had caused quite a commotion there.

Radio Braga in Portugal caused a minor panic in the northern part of that country as recently as 1988. As in Quito almost forty years earlier, the reaction turned from terror to anger when listeners learned of the deception. A group of two hundred protesters descended upon the station to express their displeasure—in this instance, thankfully, without any arson or loss of life.

Back in the States that same year, NPR aired "The War of the Worlds 50th Anniversary Production." David Ossman of the Firesign Theatre reworked the Koch script to make it sound more like modern public radio. Actors such as Jason Robards, Steve Allen, and Hector Elizondo joined familiar NPR voices like Douglas Edwards, Terry Gross, and Scott Simon with the effect that it was difficult to tell when the regular public radio programming ended and the show began. In this case, however, no panic.

In 1994, L.A. Theaterworks did a live production of the Koch script. Several *Star Trek* actors were featured, including Brent Spiner, Will Wheaton, Armin Shimerman ("Quark"), Leonard Nimoy as Professor Pierson, and Gates McFadden (Dr. Crusher) as the reporter, "Carla" Phillips. Directed by John de Lancie ("Q"), it was performed live before an audience as part of the regular L.A. Theaterworks broadcasts in November.

Stage and Screen

War of the Worlds, the Movie

George Pal's 1953 production of Byron Haskin's film *The War of the Worlds* is probably the best-known version of Wells' book. Some consider it a science fiction classic, others a typical 1950s B horror movie. But Pal's *War of the Worlds* did earn an Oscar for its special effects. Still shown occasionally on TV, and available on VHS and DVD, the movie struck a chord with audiences then and remains a significant take on Wells' original—whether as classic or kitsch.

With World War II still fresh in the minds of movie-goers and the Cold War brewing, Americans were primed for tales of alien invasion. Science fiction movies of the 1950s tended to be about horrifying the audience with radioactive mutations, technologically superior enemies, and alien infiltrators. In this film version, the action was, naturally, transplanted to California, with the Martians trading their clumsy walking machines in for sleek, flying ships (although they still arrived in capsules—why they didn't just fly to earth in their spaceships is never adequately explained). Gene Barry, as Dr. Clayton Forrester, played the role of Wells' narrator (Orson Welles' "Professor Pierson"). He was accompanied by Sylvia Van Buren, played by Ann Robinson, who provided plenty of hysterical shrieking at inopportune moments. The film revealed humanity's impotence in

A movie poster from the 1953 George Pal film

the face of a technologically superior civilization. When the U.S. Army dropped an A-bomb on the Martians, and they emerged unscathed in their force-field–protected ships, the people of Earth had to consider other options—namely, running and hiding. The destruction wrought by the Martians was total, as they turned their shrill, green heat ray on everyone and everything. In the end, once again, Earth was saved by common, microscopic bacteria. But…for how long?

The TV Series

The answer, according to the 1988–1990 Fox television series, was about thirty-five years. Apparently, the Martians weren't dead, just hibernating. *The War of the Worlds* TV show used the 1953 film as prologue. It deviated from Wells' original story markedly in that the humans fought back and started to win. The latest "professor" was modeled more after Indiana Jones, and the female lead was a microbiologist this time, but reverted to stereotypical behavior when things got hairy. A minor cult hit (i.e., seen by almost no one), with a cast of unknowns, the series still managed to last for forty-four episodes on Fox.

The Night America Trembled

Not an adaptation of the novel or the broadcast, *Studio One*, a live weekly television playhouse on CBS hosted by Edward R. Murrow, presented a teleplay, "The Night America Trembled," dramatizing the events of October 30, 1938, twenty-nine years later, on September 9, 1957. The program featured such as-yet-unknown actors as Warren Beatty, James Coburn, and Ed Asner. Strangely, no mention was ever made of the broadcast's star and director, Orson Welles, or the play's author, Howard Koch. Perhaps this can be explained by the fact that both men were expatriates—Welles, by then an entertainment industry nonentity, was living in Italy, and Koch, who had been blacklisted in Hollywood all during the 1950s for his leftist politics, was spending his exile in London. Welles later sued CBS over the program, asserting his old claim that it was he, and not Koch, who authored the script. He lost.

The Musical

Perhaps the most terrifying version of *The War of the Worlds* was Jeff Wayne's London stage musical. Frighteningly representative of 1978, this deadly serious rock opera featured Richard Burton in the role of narrator with music written by Jeff Wayne and Gary Osborne. The Moody Blues' Justin Hayward, Phil Lynott of Thin Lizzy, and David Essex, among others, performed songs that sounded like an unholy union of Pink Floyd and ABBA. Wayne, who somehow convinced the likes of Burton and Hayward to take part in this questionable production, remained faithful to the text by Wells. The original cast double album inspired some imaginative Roger Dean–style artwork. Despite its overwhelming campiness, *Jeff Wayne's Musical Version of The War of the Worlds* entered the UK album charts and remained there for six years, achieving multi-platinum status with sales in excess of six million *double* albums. The recording is now available on CD (from CBS Records, coincidentally) and includes all of the illustrations. Hearing Thin Lizzy frontman Phil Lynott, as Pastor Nathaniel, rant and

sing about the Martian "devils" makes sitting through the rest of it nearly worthwhile.

"Jeff Wayne's War of the Worlds" is now also (perhaps inevitably) a PC computer game in which you can choose to be the humans or the Martians. Humans need to preserve their stockpiles of steel, oil, and coal. Martians need copper, heavy elements, and human blood. A techno remix of the soundtrack accompanies the action. (The game is a logical progression when you consider that the first breakthrough video arcade game in the late 1970s was, after all, Space Invaders.)

Inspired by the Book

Mars Attacks!

In 1962, Topps released their "Mars Attacks!" bubble-gum cards, a set of fifty-five lurid illustrations by Len Brown and Woody Gelman that outraged parents

Mars Attacks! trading cards

and thrilled prepubescent boys with tons of graphic violence and vivid gore, not to mention the requisite suggested Martian-Earthling sex. The story, which mirrored Wells' setup, was told on the back of the cards. Mars was about to explode; the Martians needed a new home, and they set their sights on Earth. Just one problem—those pesky Earthlings.

Depicted as little green homunculi with huge, exposed brains, the Martians were psychotic, bloodthirsty killing machines who burnt puppy dogs, molested Earth women, and sent giant insects to feast on what was left of the living. Back on Mars, they lounged around in Speedos before big-screen monitors, laughing at their hapless human victims. Earth eventually regrouped, sending manned rockets to Mars as part of its counteroffensive, and finally defeated the Martians.

The Topps trading cards were the inspiration for Tim Burton's 1996 movie parody *Mars Attacks!* in which the Martians are defeated, not by Earth space ships or bacteria, but by Slim Whitman's yodeling, which caused the Martians' giant heads to explode, splattering the insides of their helmets with green goo.

Parody for Bookworms

In June 1996, Bantam Spectra released *War of the Worlds: Global Dispatches*, an anthology of short stories edited by Kevin J. Anderson that uses Wells' book as a jumping off point. Writers pretending to be Mark Twain, Teddy Roosevelt, Jules Verne, Albert Einstein, Rudyard Kipling, Winston Churchill, Pablo Picasso, and other notables of the age give their own unique accounts of life with the Martians. One of the stories, "Paris Conquers All" by Gregory Benford and David Brin (writing as Jules Verne), features a memorable scene in which the Martian machines attempt to make love to the Eiffel Tower and are subsequently electrocuted.

La Día de la Independencia

Among recent movies about alien invasion, the big-budget blockbuster *Independence Day* was the one that made it okay to fear and loathe aliens once again. In

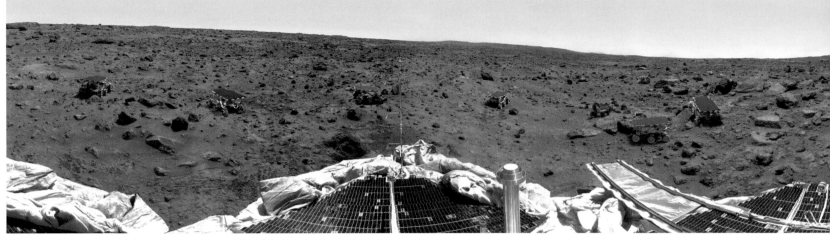

Photographic panorama from the perspective of Pathfinder on the surface of Mars

Spain, prior to the European release of *Independence Day* in 1996, the PubliEspaña ad agency ran TV ads for the movie that imitated real newsflashes. A newscaster broke in with a report showing space ships hovering over New York, a White House press conference about the invasion, and scenes of New Yorkers fleeing wildly in the streets. Hundreds of Spaniards believed the news reports, despite the warning at the bottom of the screen that read, "Advertisement," and flooded TV and radio switchboards with calls.

Martian Mania

In this modern world, in which you can download a SETI (Search for Extraterrestrial Intelligence) screensaver and scan the heavens for aliens while your computer idles, it shouldn't surprise anyone to see Martians cropping up everywhere.

After its success with the Apollo program, NASA launched Viking 1, the first of two Martian probes, on August 20, 1975, to take pictures of the Martian surface, characterize the composition of the surface and atmosphere, and search for evidence of life.

On July 25, 1976, Viking 1, while orbiting Mars, photographed a rock formation that, to the Viking investigators scrutinizing the images for likely landing sites for Viking 2, resembled a face. Taken from a distance of 1,162 miles, the face-like hill was approximately one mile across.

After the release of the photograph, some in the popular press argued that the face-like hill was an artificial formation. It captured the imagination of people ready and eager to believe that Mars must have harbored life at one time. Of course, reading that into the face-shaped hill was a little like deriving meaning from a cloud shaped like a pterodactyl or a potato that resembled Gerald Ford. The leadership at NASA was smart enough to realize that this kind of publicity

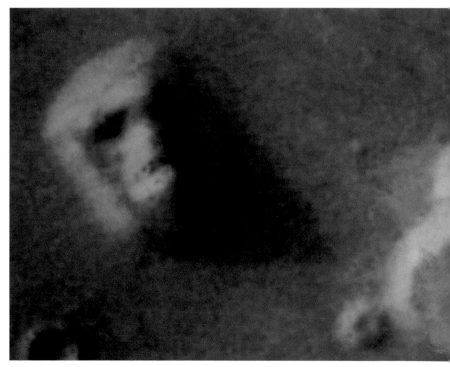

The "face" on Mars

would attract attention and interest in the Viking program, as well as future Mars expeditions.

The Viking Orbiters were powered down by August 1980 after a combined total of more than 2,106 orbits of Mars. The Viking Orbiters and Landers transmitted images of the surface, took surface samples, analyzed them for composition and signs of life, studied atmospheric composition and meteorology, and deployed seismometers. The Viking 1 Lander ended communications on November 13, 1982, after both Landers transmitted more than 1,400 images of the two sites.

The Viking experiments provided the most complete view of Mars to date. Volcanoes, lava plains, immense canyons, cratered areas, wind-formed features, and evidence of surface water were revealed in the Orbiter images. Mars is divided into two main regions, northern low plains and southern cratered highlands. Mountainous volcanic ridges, the Tharsis and Elysium bulges, and a system of giant canyons near the equator, the Valles Marineris, dominate the planet's geography. The surface soil is a kind of iron-rich clay, which contributes to Mars' red appearance, and temperatures at the landing sites ranged from –123° to –23° Celsius. Seasonal dust storms, changes in pressure, and movement of atmospheric gases between the polar ice caps were also recorded. The biology experiment, however, produced no proof of life at either landing site.

It wasn't until NASA researcher David McKay examined Martian fossils in 1996 that any persuasive evidence of life, even primitive life, was found on the red planet. NASA's Pathfinder mission, which was launched in 1997, was NASA's latest successful mission to Mars. The failed Mars Polar Lander, which lost contact with Earth on December 3, 1999, may have come at the expense of NASA's new "faster, cheaper, better" directive. Still, there is no doubt that future planned missions to Mars will feed our imagination for years to come.

Hollywood, having no shortage of imagination, continues to churn out Martian and other alien movies like *Independence Day, Mission to Mars, Red Planet*, and

Kang (or possibly Kodos) from the TV show The Simpsons

Starship Troopers, with occasional thought-provoking alien films like *Contact*. We've seen the late Ray Walston play "My Favorite Martian" on TV; Marvin the Martian appear in Looney Tunes cartoons with Bugs Bunny and Daffy Duck; Kazoo annoyed us in the 1960s as Fred Flinstone's alien sidekick; and Kang and Kodos entertain us with their return to *The Simpsons* every Halloween to abduct Homer, take over the world, or incinerate the audience of the *Jerry Springer* show. The alien as invader, friend, guide, sidekick, or foil has become so ubiquitous, you have to wonder what it will be like if we ever encounter the real thing.

Since 1898, *The War of the Worlds* has been translated into countless languages, adapted by comic books, radio, film, stage, and even computer games, and has inspired a wide range of alien invasion tales in every medium. Few ideas have captured the imagination of so many people all over the world in the last century so well. It is a tribute to H.G. Wells that his story of alien conquest was not only the first of its kind, but remains among the best.

H.G. WELLS

AND

THE WAR

OF THE

WORLDS

W H.G. ells

"Wells saw as clearly as anyone into the secret places of the heart, but he also saw the universe, with all its infinite promise and peril."
—Arthur C. Clarke

It's doubtful that in 1896, thirty-year-old H.G. Wells had any idea that his visions of Martian invasions would lead not only to public acclaim, but also to public panic and a famous (or as some would say, infamous) evening that would live in history.

Herbert George Wells was born on September 21, 1866, in a lower-middle class section of Bromley, Kent, in the southeast corner of England. His father, Joseph Wells, was a simple man, a shopkeeper specializing in sporting goods and china who also found the time to play professional cricket and chartered the Bromley Cricket Club. His mother, Sarah, was a religious woman who made extra money by keeping house on a part-time basis at the nearby estate of Up Park in Sussex. The youngest of three boys, "Bertie" was a less-than-active child, content to read and draw. His formal schooling was sporadic; at various times, he was homeschooled by his mother, attended an English dame school operated by a headmistress named Mrs. Knott, and, from 1874 to 1879, regularly attended Thomas Morley's Bromley Academy.

One experience, which Wells in later life called his "lucky moment," happened during the summer of his seventh year. A friend of his

Young H.G. Wells

gain acceptance to a college or university. Possessing limited funds, Wells eventually talked his way into a scholarship at Midhurst Grammar School, where he would not only study but assist as a student teacher. For two years, he devoured every book, paper, and nugget of information he could find, passing numerous tests and winning dozens of examinations, often finishing with the top score. His interests and strengths were in the sciences—he repeatedly took top honors in biology, astronomical physics, math, and geology.

In 1884, Wells entered the Normal School of Science at South Kensington (which eventually became part of the University of London). His teacher and mentor here was T.H. Huxley, whom Wells held in high esteem throughout his life. Of Huxley, Wells later remarked, "I believed then he was the greatest man I was ever likely to meet, and I believe that all the more firmly today." It was the teachings and theories of Huxley that Wells spent the better part of his life trying to translate and espouse in his stories and writings.

Three years later, Wells decided that it was time to move on, as he was tiring of his studies (as evidenced by a failure in a geology class) and wishing to join the ranks of the married. He took a position as teacher at the Holt Academy at Wrexham, an undistinguished school that he called "an uncongenial environment" in subsequent letters. Here he taught science and coached the school football team. During one of the practices, Wells was kicked in the kidneys by a student, an act which he later described as deliberate. Wells began to spit blood; an examination by doctors discovered not only a bruised kidney but also evidence of tuberculosis. He soon found himself to be an invalid, recuperating at the home of his mother's employer in Up Park. He passed his time by reading works from their great library, titles such as Plato's *Republic*, Winwood Reade's *The Martyrdom of Man*, and Robert Burton's *Anatomy of Melancholy*. Reade's book, in particular, was a major inspiration for Wells, and its effect can be seen in much of Wells' writing throughout his career.

His illness brought him to an important realization: he wanted to make his living writing, not teaching. As he told one of his friends at the time, "The only

father's was playing with young Bertie, throwing him in the air and catching him. They attempted this maneuver one time too many; on the final toss, Bertie twisted through the air, falling outside of the man's waiting arms. Wells landed on a tent stake, which broke his tibia. Forced to convalesce in bed for two months, Wells passed the hours reading everything he (and his no-doubt remorseful father) could get his hands on. One book in particular, Wood's *Natural History*, opened up an entire world that Wells never knew existed. In addition, Wells would later recount that this injury taught him the need to suppress pain, and that religion was of little use in this quest, two themes that eventually made their way into many of his later writings.

At age thirteen, Wells was apprenticed to a local draper in order to learn a trade. The work was long (7:30 A.M. until 8:00 P.M.), arduous, and dull, and Wells disliked every moment. His interest and attention was geared toward education, as he became determined to chance now for a living is literature....I think the groove I shall drop into will be cheap noveletteering, not with my entire approval, though. I hanker after essays and criticism—vainly." His vocation settled on, Wells then put his mind on getting the rest of his life in order. He moved to Stoke-on-Trent, looking for a better atmosphere in which to convalesce. He crammed for his final examinations. He went on a holiday with his cousin, Isabel, who later became his first wife. And he began writing short paragraphs for the news journal *Answers to Correspondents*. It was his first taste of writing for money.

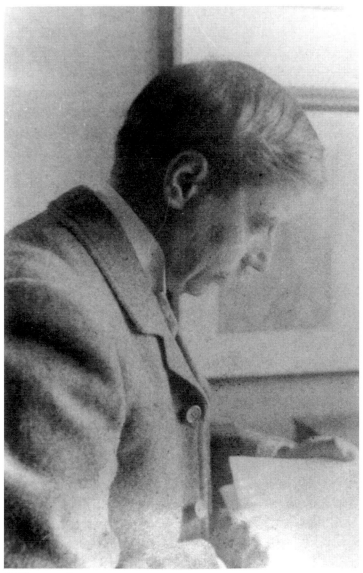

Wells at work

Wells passed his examinations in early 1890 and was subsequently offered, and accepted, a position with the University Correspondence College at Cambridge as a reader of correspondence lessons. He was paid per item read and corrected; thus, the more he read, the more he earned. He worked very hard, and by October of 1891, was able to marry his cousin Isabel with plenty of money in the bank. During this period, he also wrote pieces for science and educational journals throughout England, including the *Educational Times*, and began authoring two textbooks, *Honours Physiography* and the two-volume work *Textbook of Biology*. He also began, in 1891, a fictional story blending his love of science with his natural curiosity. It was published as an unfinished trio of shorts in the *Science Schools Journal*, of which he was the acting editor. These stories were eventually grafted together, and became his first work of fiction, *The Time Machine*.

The period between 1890 and 1910 was truly a golden age of scientific thought and science fiction writing. Darwin's landmark *The Origin of Species* was released in 1859 to tremendous critical acclaim and enthusiasm. It opened the door for the four major sciences of the day (biology, geology, astronomy, and chemistry) to be incorporated into philosophical thinking, and to be used as a basis of questioning the mystery of life itself. And it enabled those with a solid grasp of the theories of the day to be able to blend hard scientific fact into stories of the fantastic. Wells was the right person at the right time, a gifted and brilliant scientific thinker who also possessed the clarity of style and clarity of thought that made the unthinkable sound plausible. He would never have been able to write *The Time Machine* earlier; no writer would have been able to do so. The knowledge base wasn't there until the late nineteenth century. It was the perfect time for science to finally catch up to our collective imaginations. Of course, Wells didn't know any of this. He was just happy to receive compensation for his literary efforts.

His next effort was a story that asked the question, What would be the result of science without ethics? Praised by the public while vilified by scientists, *The Island of Dr. Moreau* was an instant hit, even sparking a bidding war between publishers (a war which was won by William Heinemann, who paid Wells the princely sum of £60 for the British rights to the story). Filled with images of mutant, half-animal creatures and mad scientists, *Dr. Moreau* not only made Wells famous, but it proved to him that he could, indeed, make a living with his writing. His third novel, *The Invisible Man*, further emphasized this point.

Up to this point, Wells had written of sciences that man could explore—zoology, biology, geology, and chemistry. For his next book, he'd take elements of all of those and add to them the final scientific piece: astronomy. What if you combine science with the sky, the stars—with outer space? Working from an idea given to him by his older brother Frank, Wells began to play with the idea of people from outer space coming to earth. The resulting story opened people's eyes and played on their fears. And it has never been out of print in more than one hundred years.

The War of the Worlds originally appeared as a nine-part series in the English periodical *Pearson's Magazine*, debuting in the April 1897 issue. Far from considering it a completed piece of work, Wells used the serialization as an opportunity to solicit critical reaction to the story and edited it further for later publication. Complete with custom illustrations by artist Warwick Goble, *The War of the Worlds* was a tour de force of what Wells termed "fiction about the future." So great was the response, in fact, that it was released almost simultaneously in America, with Macmillan attempting to rush the completed book to press before Wells had the chance to make his final corrections. William Heinemann released the first edition of the book in the United Kingdom in February of 1898, over five months after the book was completed. This decision was made in order to ensure that the book not be lost or ignored in the Christmas shuffle.

One facet that contributed to the book's believability was the current social climate of the era. The British Empire was under the constant threat of attack by Germany, with German troops sitting across the channel from the island. Many Englanders believed that the invasion of London by the Germans was not only

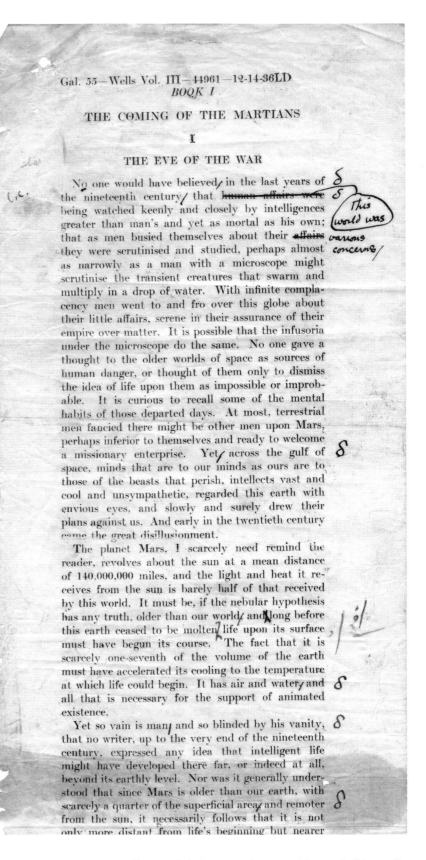

Galley proof of The War of the Worlds, *marked by Wells*

H. G. WELLS' NEW STORY.

Mr. Wm. Heinemann begs to announce that H. G. WELLS' *New Romance,*

THE WAR OF THE WORLDS,

Revised and Amplified, will be Ready To-morrow (Friday), at all Libraries, Booksellers', and Bookstalls, in 'one volume, price Six Shillings.

London : WM. HEINEMANN, 21, Bedford-street, W.C.

Newspaper ad touting Wells' new book

possible, but inevitable. It was a time of great paranoia in England, where the specter of ships dropping out of the skies was not unthinkable. It took little persuasion to make readers of that time and place believe that any attack was feasible. Wells was lucky enough to bring together his perfect marriage of science and fantasy at the exact time when the English culture was ripe with the fear of the unknown. In many ways, *The War of the Worlds* was the literary equivalent of a rainbow: all the elements had to be in place at precisely the right moment. A year or two earlier, the science and technology didn't exist that would have allowed the story to be plausible. A year or two later, the English-German hostilities were over. The story could only have made the splash it did when it was written and released.

Wells constructed *The War of the Worlds* as a book with two distinct stories. The opening portion, called Book I, dealt with the arrival of the Martians, and their hostile takeover of England. Book II told the story of Earth under the control of the Martians, and the ultimate bacterial strain that wipes out the invaders and saves the world. During this portion of the story, the reader also gets his or her first view of the Martians. Wells describes them as being mostly head with a beak and two eyes, and with sixteen tentacles near the mouth. What made the story even more gripping and frightening was the fact that Wells constructed it with the help of British Ordinance Survey maps. He made sure the action occurred in real places,

such as Horsell Common, Primrose Hill, and Maybury Hill. Previously, fictional stories took place in fictional locales. In *The War of the Worlds*, the action took place in the reader's own backyard.

The book was an immediate commercial and critical success. Wells' agent worked tirelessly, securing not only domestic rights to the book and serialization but also American book and serial rights, all of which made a handsome profit for Wells. British reviewer J.M. Barrie wrote glowing reviews of the book and even broached the subject with Wells of producing a stage adaptation of the work. After six months of discussion and negotiation, Barrie and Wells decided against the dramatic adaptation. They celebrated their joint decision by playing cricket.

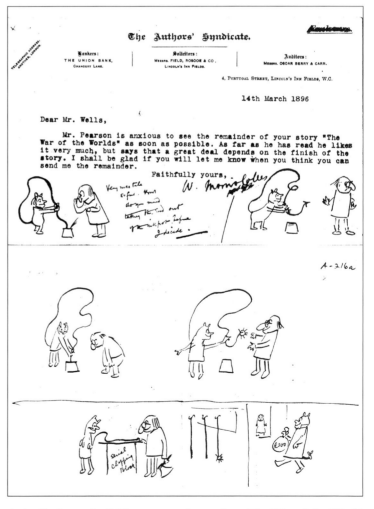

A doodle drawn by Wells satirizing his work on The War of the Worlds

The War of the Worlds helped to cement Wells' place in the literary firmament. From this point on, he was able to command sizable sums for his work. His advance for the story *Amazing Adventures of Mr. Cavor* was an unheard of £500, a tremendous amount of money for the turn of the century. His works were published and sold around the world, often appearing in numerous countries simultaneously. And he grew to enjoy a number of friendships in his wide and distinguished circle of peers—names such as G.K. Chesterton, George Bernard Shaw, and Violet Paget.

★ ★ ★

While Wells grew to enjoy great success and acclaim in his professional life, his personal life was somewhat more muddied. His marriage to Isabel collapsed in 1893, leading to their divorce in 1894. This was due in part to Wells' acquaintance with, and interest in, Amy Catherine Robbins, one of his students. Throughout his life he called her Jane, owing to his (and her) dislike of "her given Catholic name," as he referred to it. Their relationship, at first strictly intellectual, blossomed into romance, and he and Jane married in 1895. Their first child, G.P. "Gip" Wells, was born in 1901, and a second son, Frank, arrived in 1903. The family moved to a grand estate named Spade House, located in the idyllic village of Sandgate, Kent, where Wells spent most of his time writing both novels and sociological studies.

During the first decade of the twentieth century, Wells was active on many fronts. He published numerous novels including *The First Men in the Moon, Kipps, The Sea Lady, In the Days of the Comet*, and *The War in the Air*. He also turned his attention to scientific and social-political writings, publishing *Anticipations, Mankind in the Making, Socialism and the Family*, and *The Future in America*. He joined the Fabian Society, a socialist movement in Britain that dreamt of a plutocratic labor system. He became politically active, both in the UK and throughout Europe. He took ill several times, possibly recurrences of his earlier bout with tuberculosis. And he began a series of extramarital flings that continued throughout the course of his marriage.

Amy Catherine Robbins (Jane Wells) and H.G. Wells at home

Two affairs became particularly notable due to their intensity and the long-lasting effect they had on Wells.

Amber Reeves was the daughter of Pember Reeves, a wealthy New Zealander who was stationed in Great Britain as a high commissioner. Like Wells, Pember Reeves was a Fabian, and he encouraged his daughter, an intelligent young girl, to study the writings and ideals of Wells. Wells met Amber, and fell for her almost instantly. They began an intense physical relationship that lasted for many months and eventually became known to Amber's parents. One interesting aspect of their relationship was their growing willingness to let the affair become public, what with Wells being a married man with two young sons. In fact, Wells wrote a story for *The Times*, in which he speaks of a young love and their trysts in the woods (ironically published in the same issue as a scathing piece by Mrs. Humphry Ward commenting on society's declining morality). In 1909, Reeves became pregnant. A friend of Pember Reeves

Wells with, from left to right, his son Frank, wife Jane, Elizabeth Dixon, his cousin Ruth Neal, and his eldest son, Gip (lying down)

simply a part of the marriage. With Jane's death in 1927, Wells was free of the moral ambiguity that followed him in marriage and continued unabated in the sexually free lifestyle to which he was accustomed. A later relationship with Odette Keun, which began prior to Jane's death, was to bring scandal to his name and hers, as they ended bitterly amidst provocative letters, accusations, barely-hidden references in books, and tell-all stories in the newspapers. Wells' dalliances, which had been hinted at for years, were public knowledge by the mid 1930s, and his reputation and popularity suffered as a result.

was hastily brought in to marry Amber, thus "legitimizing" the child. Yet Amber and child, named Anna-Jane, continued to live near Wells, with Wells and wife Jane paying frequent visits. His novel *Ann Veronica* is often thought to be an account of Wells and Reeves.

In 1913, Wells met a charming young woman named Rebecca West. She was a writer who, like Wells, was a great supporter of the Fabian ideals of socialism. Oddly enough, she first learned of Wells and his beliefs through reading his 1912 book *Marriage*. They quickly came together in an often-stormy relationship that resulted in the birth of Anthony West in 1914. She was the great passion of his life through this decade, though they both held a remarkably ambivalent attitude about their life together. West, and their relationship, became a staple of Wells' writing over the next decade, with titles such as *The Research Magnificent*, *The Wife of Sir Isaac Harman*, and *The Secret Places of the Heart* all detailing their time together. Although the relationship ended in 1923, and West eventually married, they remained close until his death.

Additional affairs followed on a continual basis, with Wells often juggling two or three mistresses along with his wife. Jane Wells knew of many of the relationships and accepted them as a fact of life, they being

Wells at the London premier of the film, Things to Come, *based on his book,* The Shape of Things to Come, *February 12, 1936*

As his life and career progressed, the books Wells wrote tended to fall into one of two categories: scientific-based fiction and social commentary. Books from both genres became more and more autobiographical as time went on—they either had as their basis his social and political beliefs, or they were based on characters and situations that he himself was involved with. Those people who Wells had close relationships with often turned up (albeit with different names) in his books. In fact, his 1911 novel *The New Machiavelli* is generally regarded as his most autobiographical novel, populated with people, places, and events from his life, cleverly (or, as some pointed out, not so cleverly) disguised.

During World War I, and again preceding World War II, Wells became a tireless campaigner for political

Wells meeting Orson Welles in 1940

causes. He wrote articles and manifestos; he lectured, both at home and abroad; he gave radio addresses over the BBC; and he wrote numerous books that dealt with man's ability (or inability) to live with one another. Books such as *The Common Sense of World Peace*, *After Democracy*, and *The Shape of Things to Come* all positioned Wells as a major political thinker. He also wrote the book that many people at the time considered the finest book ever written, *The Outline of History*. This was a major work and is still regarded by many scholars as Wells' masterpiece. His break with the Fabians over beliefs and policy left him more centrist in thought, and he made appearances all over the world in the name of England looking for ways to promote peace.

It was during one of his American speaking tours prior to World War II that Wells had the only meeting of his life with the one person that took a Wells work and outshined Wells himself with it.

Wells was contracted in 1940 to make a series of speeches in the United States, stumping for both America's increased war support and reelection for his friend Franklin Delano Roosevelt. He found himself in San Antonio, Texas, in late October 1940, when KTSA Radio contacted him. Would he agree, they asked, to being interviewed along with Orson Welles? It would make a great story—H.G. in town, Orson in town (coincidentally, for another speaking engagement), and it all happening on the second anniversary of the famous Mercury Theatre broadcast.

Wells readily agreed. Time had healed the wound he had felt over the initial broadcast, to which he had replied with a terse letter ("Mr. Wells was not informed…that any adaptation was intended: Mr. Wells believed that he was giving permission for a reading of the novel"). In fact, any outrage harbored by Wells was quickly forgotten, due to the fact that the broadcast and resulting panic had brought greater fame to *The War of the Worlds* than it had ever achieved on its own. The increased attention drew new readers to the book, renewed critical examination, and acted as publicity for Wells, whose new novel, *Apropos of Dolores*, hit the stores a scant three days later. Wells and Welles met on October 29, 1940. They chatted briefly about the broadcast,  CD3 but spent much of the remaining interview discussing the escalating war in Europe and the presidential election that would be held during the next week.

Wells returned to England in the 1940s, living in London throughout the war, and writing his last great paper, the *Declaration of the Rights of Man*. His final novel, *You Can't Be Too Careful*, was published in 1941, although he continued to publish social, political, and scientific papers until 1945. He fell ill in late '45, and passed away quietly at his Regent's Park home on August 13, 1946. Per his request, Wells was cremated, and his ashes were scattered by sons Gip Wells and Anthony West over the English Channel, between the Isle of Wight and St. Alban's Head. A memorial service was held on October 30, 1946, at the Royal Institution in London, where several of Wells' friends, peers, and lovers paid tribute to a man whose vision and imagination touched the world. In fact, his influence was (and is) so strong that the H.G. Wells Society was founded in England with the express purpose of keeping his ideals, teachings, scholarship, and spirit alive. The Wellsians, as they're called, continue to this day to publish newsletters and research papers and hold conferences. To many people around the world, the voice of H.G. Wells continues to speak in clear tones of the world in which we live.

1866–1946

by H.G. Wells

"But who shall dwell in these Worlds if they be inhabited?...
Are we or they Lords of the World?...And how are all things made for man?"
—Kepler, quoted in *The Anatomy of Melancholy*

BOOK I
THE COMING OF THE MARTIANS

Chapter One
★ ★ ★
The Eve of the War

No one would have believed in the last years of the nineteenth century that this world was being watched keenly and closely by intelligences greater than man's and yet as mortal as his own; that as men busied themselves about their various concerns they were scrutinised and studied, perhaps almost as narrowly as a man with a microscope might scrutinise the transient creatures that swarm and multiply in a drop of water. With infinite complacency men went to and fro over this globe about their little affairs, serene in their assurance of their empire over matter. It is possible that the infusoria under the microscope do the same. No one gave a thought to the older worlds of space as sources of human danger, or thought of them only to dismiss the idea of life upon them as impossible or improbable. It is curious to recall some of the mental habits of those departed days. At most, terrestrial men fancied there might be other men upon Mars, perhaps inferior to themselves and ready to welcome a missionary enterprise. Yet across the gulf of space, minds that are to our minds as ours are to those of the beasts that perish, intellects vast and cool and unsympathetic, regarded this earth with envious eyes, and slowly and surely drew their plans against us. And early in the twentieth century came the great disillusionment.

The text illustrations, by Warwick Goble, accompanied the debut of "The War of the Worlds" on the pages of Pearson's *magazine in 1897.*
The illustrations at the opening of Book I and Book II were drawn by Alvin Correco in 1906.

The planet Mars, I scarcely need remind the reader, revolves about the sun at a mean distance of 140,000,000 miles, and the light and heat it receives from the sun is barely half of that received by this world. It must be, if the nebular hypothesis has any truth, older than our world; and long before this earth ceased to be molten, life upon its surface must have begun its course. The fact that it is scarcely one seventh of the volume of the earth must have accelerated its cooling to the temperature at which life could begin. It has air and water and all that is necessary for the support of animated existence.

Yet so vain is man, and so blinded by his vanity, that no writer, up to the very end of the nineteenth century, expressed any idea that intelligent life might have developed there far, or indeed at all, beyond its earthly level. Nor was it generally understood that since Mars is older than our earth, with scarcely a quarter of the superficial area and remoter from the sun, it necessarily follows that it is not only more distant from time's beginning but nearer its end.

The secular cooling that must someday overtake our planet has already gone far indeed with our neighbour. Its physical condition is still largely a mystery, but we know now that even in its equatorial region the midday temperature barely approaches that of our coldest winter. Its air is much more attenuated than ours, its oceans have shrunk until they cover but a third of its surface, and as its slow seasons change, huge snowcaps gather and melt about either pole and periodically inundate its temperate zones. That last stage of exhaustion, which to us is still incredibly remote, has become a present-day problem for the inhabitants of Mars. The immediate pressure of necessity has brightened their intellects,

I still remember that vigil very distinctly.

enlarged their powers, and hardened their hearts. And looking across space with instruments, and intelligences such as we have scarcely dreamed of, they see, at its nearest distance only 35,000,000 of miles sunward of them, a morning star of hope, our own warmer planet, green with vegetation and grey with water, with a cloudy atmosphere eloquent of fertility, with glimpses through its drifting cloud wisps of broad stretches of populous country and narrow, navy-crowded seas.

And we men, the creatures who inhabit this earth, must be to them at least as alien and lowly as are the monkeys and lemurs to us. The intellectual side of man already admits that life is an incessant struggle for existence, and it would seem that this too is the belief of the minds upon Mars. Their world is far gone in its cooling and this world is still crowded with life, but crowded only with what they regard as inferior animals. To carry warfare sunward is, indeed, their only escape from the destruction that, generation after generation, creeps upon them.

And before we judge of them too harshly we must remember what ruthless and utter destruction our own species has wrought, not only upon animals, such as the vanished bison and the dodo, but upon its inferior races. The Tasmanians, in spite of their human likeness, were entirely swept out of existence in a war of extermination waged by European immigrants, in the space of fifty years. Are we such apostles of mercy as to complain if the Martians warred in the same spirit?

The Martians seem to have calculated their descent with amazing subtlety—their mathematical learning is evidently far in excess of ours—and to have carried out their preparations with a well-nigh perfect unanimity.

Had our instruments permitted it, we might have seen the gathering trouble far back in the nineteenth century. Men like Schiaparelli watched the red planet—it is odd, by-the-bye, that for countless centuries Mars has been the star of war—but failed to interpret the fluctuating appearances of the markings they mapped so well. All that time the Martians must have been getting ready.

During the opposition of 1894 a great light was seen on the illuminated part of the disk, first at the Lick Observatory, then by Perrotin of Nice, and then by other observers. English readers heard of it first in the issue of *Nature* dated August 2. I am inclined to think that this blaze may have been the casting of the huge gun, in the vast pit sunk into their planet, from which their shots were fired at us. Peculiar markings, as yet unexplained, were seen near the site of that outbreak during the next two oppositions.

The storm burst upon us six years ago now. As Mars approached opposition, Lavelle of Java set the wires of the astronomical exchange palpitating with the amazing intelligence of a huge outbreak of incandescent gas upon the planet. It had occurred towards midnight of the twelfth; and the spectroscope, to which he had at once resorted, indicated a mass of flaming gas, chiefly hydrogen, moving with an enormous velocity towards this earth. This jet of fire had become invisible about a quarter past twelve. He compared it to a colossal puff of flame suddenly and violently squirted out of the planet, "as flaming gases rushed out of a gun."

A singularly appropriate phrase it proved. Yet the next day there was nothing of this in the papers except a little note in the *Daily Telegraph*, and the world went in ignorance of one of the gravest dangers that ever threatened the human race. I might not have heard of the eruption at all had I not met Ogilvy, the well-known astronomer, at Ottershaw. He was immensely excited at the news, and in the excess of his feelings invited me up to take a turn with him that night in a scrutiny of the red planet.

In spite of all that has happened since, I still remember that vigil very distinctly: the black and silent observatory, the shadowed lantern throwing a feeble glow upon the floor in the corner, the steady ticking of the clockwork of the telescope, the little slit in the roof—an oblong profundity with the stardust streaked across it. Ogilvy moved about, invisible but audible. Looking through the telescope, one saw a circle of deep blue and the little round planet swimming in the field. It seemed such a little thing, so bright and small and still, faintly marked with transverse stripes, and slightly flattened from the perfect round. But so little it was, so silvery warm—a pin's-head of light! It was as if it quivered, but really this was the telescope vibrating with the activity of the clockwork that kept the planet in view.

As I watched, the planet seemed to grow larger and smaller and to advance and recede, but that was simply that my eye was tired. Forty millions of miles it was from us—more than forty millions of miles of void. Few people realise the immensity of vacancy in which the dust of the material universe swims.

Near it in the field, I remember, were three faint points of light, three telescopic stars infinitely remote, and all around it was the unfathomable darkness of empty space. You know how that blackness looks on a frosty starlight night. In a telescope it seems far profounder. And invisible to me because it was so remote and small, flying swiftly and steadily towards me across that incredible distance, drawing nearer every minute by so many thousands of miles, came the Thing they were sending us, the Thing that was to bring so much struggle and calamity and death to the earth. I never dreamed of it then as I watched; no one on earth dreamed of that unerring missile.

That night, too, there was another jetting out of gas from the distant planet. I saw it. A reddish flash at the edge, the slightest projection of the outline just as the chronometer struck midnight; and at that I told Ogilvy and he took my place. The night was warm and I was thirsty, and I went stretching my legs clumsily and feeling my way in the darkness, to the little table where the siphon stood, while Ogilvy exclaimed at the streamer of gas that came out towards us.

That night another invisible missile started on its way to the earth from Mars, just a second or so under twenty-four hours after the first one. I remember how I sat on the table there in the blackness, with patches of green and crimson swimming before my eyes. I wished I had a light to smoke by, little suspecting the meaning of the minute gleam I had seen and all that it would presently bring me. Ogilvy watched till one, and then gave it up; and we lit the lantern and walked over to his house. Down below in the darkness were Ottershaw and Chertsey and all their hundreds of people, sleeping in peace.

He was full of speculation that night about the condition of Mars, and scoffed at the vulgar idea of its having inhabitants who were signalling us. His idea was that meteorites might be falling in a heavy shower upon the planet, or that a huge volcanic explosion was in progress. He pointed out to me how unlikely it was that organic evolution had taken the same direction in the two adjacent planets.

"The chances against anything manlike on Mars are a million to one," he said.

Hundreds of observers saw the flame that night and the night after about midnight, and again the night after; and so for ten nights, a flame each night. Why the shots ceased after the tenth no one on earth has attempted to explain. It may be the gases of the firing caused the Martians inconvenience. Dense clouds of smoke or dust, visible through a powerful telescope on earth as little grey, fluctuating patches, spread through the clearness of the planet's atmosphere and obscured its more familiar features.

Even the daily papers woke up to the disturbances at last, and popular notes appeared here, there, and everywhere concerning the volcanoes upon Mars. The seriocomic periodical *Punch*, I remember, made a happy use of it in the political cartoon. And, all unsuspected, those missiles the Martians had fired at us drew earthward, rushing now at a pace of many miles a second through the empty gulf of space, hour by hour and day by day, nearer and nearer. It seems to me now almost incredibly wonderful that, with that swift fate hanging over us, men could go about their petty concerns as they did. I remember how jubilant Markham was at securing a new photograph of the planet for the illustrated paper he edited in those days. People in these latter times scarcely realise the abundance and

enterprise of our nineteenth-century papers. For my own part, I was much occupied in learning to ride the bicycle, and busy upon a series of papers discussing the probable developments of moral ideas as civilisation progressed.

One night (the first missile then could scarcely have been 10,000,000 miles away) I went for a walk with my wife. It was starlight and I explained the Signs of the Zodiac to her, and pointed out Mars, a bright dot of light creeping zenithward, towards which so many telescopes were pointed. It was a warm night. Coming home, a party of excursionists from Chertsey or Isleworth passed us singing and playing music. There were lights in the upper windows of the houses as the people went to bed. From the railway station in the distance came the sound of shunting trains, ringing and rumbling, softened almost into melody by the distance. My wife pointed out to me the brightness of the red, green, and yellow signal lights hanging in a framework against the sky. It seemed so safe and tranquil.

Chapter Two
★ ★ ★
The Falling Star

Then came the night of the first falling star. It was seen early in the morning, rushing over Winchester eastward, a line of flame high in the atmosphere. Hundreds must have seen it, and taken it for an ordinary falling star. Albin described it as leaving a greenish streak behind it that glowed for some seconds. Denning, our greatest authority on meteorites, stated that the height of its first appearance was about ninety or one hundred miles. It seemed to him that it fell to earth about one hundred miles east of him.

I was at home at that hour and writing in my study; and although my French windows face towards Ottershaw and the blind was up (for I loved in those days to look up at the night sky), I saw nothing of it. Yet this strangest of all things that ever came to earth from outer space must have fallen while I was sitting there, visible to me had I only looked up as it passed. Some of those who saw its flight say it travelled with a hissing sound. I myself heard nothing of that. Many people in Berkshire, Surrey, and Middlesex must have seen the fall of it, and, at most, have thought that another meteorite had descended. No one seems to have troubled to look for the fallen mass that night.

But very early in the morning poor Ogilvy, who had seen the shooting star and who was persuaded that a meteorite lay somewhere on the common between Horsell, Ottershaw, and Woking, rose early with the idea of finding it. Find it he did, soon after dawn, and not far from the sand pits. An enormous hole had been made by the impact of the projectile, and the sand and gravel had been flung violently in every direction over the heath, forming heaps visible a mile and a half away. The heather was on fire eastward, and a thin blue smoke rose against the dawn.

The Thing itself lay almost entirely buried in sand, amidst the scattered splinters of a fir tree it had shivered to fragments in its descent. The uncovered part had the appearance of a huge cylinder, caked over and its outline softened by a thick scaly dun-coloured incrustation. It had a diameter of about thirty yards. He approached the mass, surprised at the size and more so at the shape, since most meteorites are rounded more or less completely. It was, however, still so hot from its flight through the air as to forbid his near approach. A stirring noise within its cylinder he ascribed to the unequal cooling of its surface; for at that time it had not occurred to him that it might be hollow.

He remained standing at the edge of the pit that the Thing had made for itself, staring at its strange appearance, astonished chiefly at its unusual shape and colour, and dimly perceiving even then some evidence of design in its arrival. The early morning was wonderfully still, and the sun, just clearing the pine trees towards Weybridge, was already warm. He did not remember hearing any birds that morning, there was certainly no breeze stirring, and the only sounds were the faint movements from within the cindery cylinder. He was all alone on the common.

Then suddenly he noticed with a start that some of the grey clinker, the ashy incrustation that covered the meteorite, was falling off the circular edge of the end. It was dropping off in flakes and raining down upon the sand. A large piece suddenly came off and fell with a sharp noise that brought his heart into his mouth.

For a minute he scarcely realised what this meant, and, although the heat was excessive, he clambered down into the pit close to the bulk to see the Thing more clearly. He fancied even then that the cooling of the body might account for this, but what disturbed that idea was the fact that the ash was falling only from the end of the cylinder.

And then he perceived that, very slowly, the circular top of the cylinder was rotating on its body. It was such a gradual movement that he discovered it only through noticing that a black mark that had been near him five minutes ago was now at the other side of the

Find it he did, soon after dawn.

circumference. Even then he scarcely understood what this indicated, until he heard a muffled grating sound and saw the black mark jerk forward an inch or so. Then the thing came upon him in a flash. The cylinder was artificial—hollow—with an end that screwed out! Something within the cylinder was unscrewing the top!

"Good heavens!" said Ogilvy. "There's a man in it—men in it! Half roasted to death! Trying to escape!"

At once, with a quick mental leap, he linked the Thing with the flash upon Mars.

The thought of the confined creature was so dreadful to him that he forgot the heat and went forward to the cylinder to help turn. But luckily the dull radiation arrested him before he could burn his hands on the still-glowing metal. At that he stood irresolute for a moment, then turned, scrambled out of the pit, and set off running wildly into Woking. The time then must have been somewhere about six o'clock. He met a waggoner and tried to make him understand, but the tale he told and his appearance were so wild—his hat had fallen off in the pit—that the man simply drove on. He was equally unsuccessful with the potman who was just unlocking the doors of the public-house by Horsell Bridge. The fellow thought he was a lunatic at large and made an unsuccessful attempt to shut him into the taproom. That sobered him a little; and when he saw Henderson, the London journalist, in his garden, he called over the palings and made himself understood.

"Henderson," he called, "you saw that shooting star last night?"

"Well?" said Henderson.

"It's out on Horsell Common now."

"Good Lord!" said Henderson. "Fallen meteorite! That's good."

"But it's something more than a meteorite. It's a cylinder —an artificial cylinder, man! And there's something inside."

Henderson stood up with his spade in his hand.

"What's that?" he said. He was deaf in one ear.

Ogilvy told him all that he had seen. Henderson was a minute or so taking it in. Then he dropped his spade, snatched up his jacket, and came out into the road. The two men hurried back at once to the common, and found the cylinder still lying in the same position. But now the sounds inside had ceased, and a thin circle of bright metal showed between the top and the body of the cylinder. Air was either entering or escaping at the rim with a thin, sizzling sound.

They listened, rapped on the scaly burnt metal with a stick, and, meeting with no response, they both concluded the man or men inside must be insensible or dead.

Of course the two were quite unable to do anything. They shouted consolation and promises, and went off back to the town again to get help. One can imagine them, covered with sand, excited and disordered, running up the little street in the bright sunlight just as the shop folks were taking down their shutters and people were

The dull radiation arrested him.

opening their bedroom windows. Henderson went into the railway station at once, in order to telegraph the news to London. The newspaper articles had prepared men's minds for the reception of the idea.

By eight o'clock a number of boys and unemployed men had already started for the common to see the "dead men from Mars." That was the form the story took. I heard of it first from my newspaper boy about a quarter to nine when I went out to get my *Daily Chronicle*. I was naturally startled, and lost no time in going out and across the Ottershaw bridge to the sand pits.

Chapter Three
★ ★ ★
On Horsell Common

I found a little crowd of perhaps twenty people surrounding the huge hole in which the cylinder lay. I have already described the appearance of that colossal bulk, embedded in the ground. The turf and gravel about it seemed charred as if by a sudden explosion. No doubt its impact had caused a flash of fire. Henderson and Ogilvy were not there. I think they perceived that nothing was to be done for the present, and had gone away to breakfast at Henderson's house.

There were four or five boys sitting on the edge of the Pit, with their feet dangling, and amusing themselves—until I stopped them—by throwing stones at the giant mass. After I had spoken to them about it, they began playing at "touch" in and out of the group of bystanders.

Among these were a couple of cyclists, a jobbing gardener I employed sometimes, a girl carrying a baby, Gregg the butcher and his little boy, and two or three loafers and golf caddies who were accustomed to hang about the railway station. There was very little talking. Few of the common people in England had anything but the vaguest astronomical ideas in those days. Most of them were staring quietly at the big tablelike end of the cylinder, which was still as Ogilvy and Henderson had left it. I fancy the popular expectation of a heap of charred corpses was disappointed at this inanimate bulk. Some went away while I was there, and other people came. I clambered into the pit and fancied I heard a faint movement under my feet. The top had certainly ceased to rotate.

It was only when I got thus close to it that the strangeness of this object was at all evident to me. At the first glance it was really no more exciting than an overturned carriage or a tree blown across the road. Not so much so, indeed. It looked like a rusty gas float. It required a certain amount of scientific education to perceive that the grey scale of the Thing was no common oxide, that the yellowish-white metal that gleamed in the crack between the lid and the cylinder had an unfamiliar hue. "Extra-terrestrial" had no meaning for most of the onlookers.

At that time it was quite clear in my own mind that the Thing had come from the planet Mars, but I judged it improbable that it contained any living creature. I thought the unscrewing might be automatic. In spite of Ogilvy, I still believed that there were men in Mars. My mind ran fancifully on the possibilities of its containing manuscript, on the difficulties in translation that might arise, whether we should find coins and models in it, and so forth. Yet it was a little too large for assurance on this idea. I felt an impatience to see it opened. About eleven, as nothing seemed happening, I walked back, full of such thought, to my home in Maybury. But I found it difficult to get to work upon my abstract investigations.

In the afternoon the appearance of the common had altered very much. The early editions of the evening papers had startled London with enormous headlines:

A MESSAGE RECEIVED FROM MARS
REMARKABLE STORY FROM WOKING

and so forth. In addition, Ogilvy's wire to the Astronomical Exchange had roused every observatory in the three kingdoms.

There were half a dozen flies or more from the Woking station standing in the road by the sand pits, a basketchaise from Chobham, and a rather lordly carriage. Besides that, there was quite a heap of bicycles. In addition, a large number of people must have walked, in spite of the heat of the day, from Woking and Chertsey, so that there was altogether quite a considerable crowd—one or two gaily dressed ladies among the others. It was glaringly hot, not a cloud in the sky nor a breath of wind, and the only shadow was that of the few scattered pine trees. The burning heather had been extinguished, but the level ground towards Ottershaw was blackened as far as one could see, and still giving off vertical streamers of smoke. An enterprising sweet-stuff dealer in the Chobham Road had sent up his son with a barrow-load of green apples and ginger beer.

Going to the edge of the pit, I found it occupied by a group of about half a dozen men—Henderson, Ogilvy, and a tall, fair-haired man that I afterwards learned was Stent, the Astronomer Royal, with several workmen wielding spades and pickaxes. Stent was giving directions in a clear, highpitched voice. He was standing on the cylinder, which was now evidently much cooler; his face was crimson and streaming with perspiration, and something seemed to have irritated him.

A large portion of the cylinder had been uncovered, though its lower end was still embedded. As soon as Ogilvy saw me among the staring crowd on the edge of the pit he called to me to come down, and asked me if I would mind going over to see Lord Hilton, the lord of the manor.

The growing crowd, he said, was becoming a serious impediment to their excavations, especially the boys. They wanted a light railing put up, and help to keep the people back. He told me that a faint stirring was occasionally still audible within the case, but that the workmen had failed to unscrew the top, as it afforded no grip to them. The case appeared to be enormously thick, and it was possible that the faint sounds we heard represented a noisy tumult in the interior.

I was very glad to do as he asked, and so become one of the privileged spectators within the contemplated enclosure. I failed to find Lord Hilton at his house, but I was told he was expected from London by the six o'clock train from Waterloo; and as it was then about a quarter past five, I went home, had some tea, and walked up to the station to waylay him.

Chapter Four
★ ★ ★
The Cylinder Opens

When I returned to the common the sun was setting. Scattered groups were hurrying from the direction of Woking, and one or two persons were returning. The crowd about the pit had increased, and stood out black against the lemon yellow of the sky—a couple of hundred people, perhaps. There were raised voices, and some sort of struggle appeared to be going on about the pit. Strange imaginings passed through my mind. As I drew nearer I heard Stent's voice:

"Keep back! Keep back!"

A boy came running towards me.

"It's a-movin'," he said to me as he passed; "a-screwin' and a-screwin' out. I don't like it. I'm a-goin' 'ome, I am."

I went on to the crowd. There were really, I should think, two or three hundred people elbowing and jostling one another, the one or two ladies there being by no means the least active.

"He's fallen in the pit!" cried some one.

"Keep back!" said several.

The crowd swayed a little, and I elbowed my way through. Every one seemed greatly excited. I heard a peculiar humming sound from the pit.

"I say!" said Ogilvy; "help keep these idiots back. We don't know what's in the confounded thing, you know!"

I saw a young man, a shop assistant in Woking I believe he was, standing on the cylinder and trying to scramble out of the hole again. The crowd had pushed him in.

The end of the cylinder was being screwed out from within. Nearly two feet of shining screw projected. Somebody blundered against me, and I narrowly missed being pitched onto the top of the screw. I turned, and as I did so the screw must have come out, for the lid of the cylinder fell upon the gravel with a ringing concussion. I stuck my elbow into the person behind me, and turned my head towards the Thing again. For a moment that circular cavity seemed perfectly black. I had the sunset in my eyes.

I think everyone expected to see a man emerge—possibly something a little unlike us terrestrial men, but in all essentials a man. I know I did. But, looking, I presently saw something stirring within the shadow: greyish billowy movements, one above another, and then two luminous disks—like eyes. Then something resembling a little grey snake, about the thickness of a walking stick, coiled up out of the writhing middle, and wriggled in the air towards me—and then another.

A sudden chill came over me. There was a loud shriek from a woman behind. I half turned, keeping my eyes fixed upon the cylinder still, from which other tentacles were now projecting, and began pushing my way back from the edge of the pit. I saw astonishment giving place to horror on the faces of the people about me. I heard inarticulate exclamations on all sides. There was a general movement backwards. I saw the shopman struggling still on the edge of the pit. I found myself alone, and saw the people on the other side of the pit running off, Stent among them. I looked again at the cylinder, and ungovernable terror gripped me. I stood petrified and staring.

A big greyish rounded bulk, the size, perhaps, of a bear, was rising slowly and painfully out of the cylinder. As it bulged up and caught the light, it glistened like wet leather.

Two large dark-coloured eyes were regarding me steadfastly. The mass that framed them, the head of the thing, was rounded, and had, one might say, a face. There was a mouth under the eyes, the lipless brim of which quivered and panted, and dropped saliva. The whole creature heaved and pulsated convulsively. A lank tentacular appendage gripped the edge of the cylinder, another swayed in the air.

Those who have never seen a living Martian can scarcely imagine the strange horror of its appearance. The peculiar V-shaped mouth with its pointed upper lip, the absence of brow ridges, the absence of a chin beneath the wedgelike lower lip, the incessant quivering of this mouth, the Gorgon groups of tentacles, the tumultuous breathing of the lungs in a strange atmosphere, the evident heaviness and painfulness of movement due to the greater gravitational energy of the

I ran slantingly and stumbling.

earth—above all, the extraordinary intensity of the immense eyes—were at once vital, intense, inhuman, crippled and monstrous. There was something fungoid in the oily brown skin, something in the clumsy deliberation of the tedious movements unspeakably nasty. Even at this first encounter, this first glimpse, I was overcome with disgust and dread.

Suddenly the monster vanished. It had toppled over the brim of the cylinder and fallen into the pit, with a thud like the fall of a great mass of leather. I heard it give a peculiar thick cry, and forthwith another of these creatures appeared darkly in the deep shadow of the aperture.

I turned and, running madly, made for the first group of trees, perhaps a hundred yards away; but I ran slantingly and stumbling, for I could not avert my face from these things.

There, among some young pine trees and furze bushes, I stopped, panting, and waited further developments. The common round the sand pits was dotted with people, standing like myself in a half-fascinated terror, staring at these creatures, or rather at the heaped gravel at the edge of the pit in which they lay. And then, with a renewed horror, I saw a round, black object bobbing up and down on the edge of the pit. It was the head of the shopman who had fallen in, but showing as a little black object against the hot western sun. Now he got his shoulder and knee up, and again he seemed to

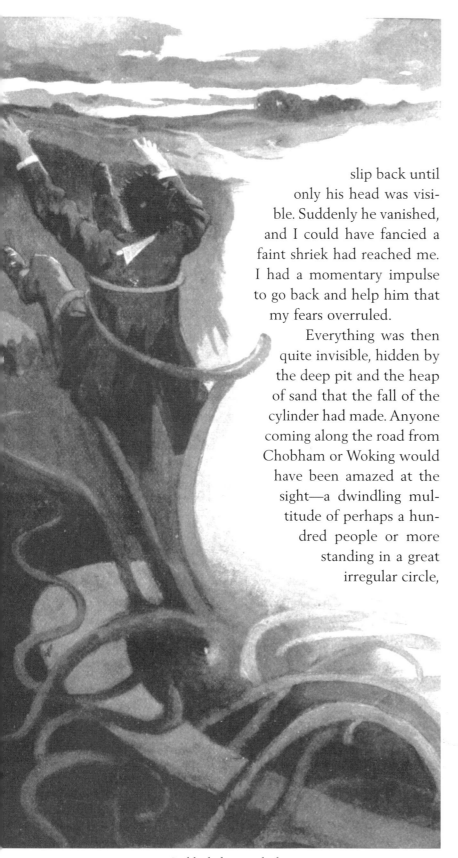

slip back until only his head was visible. Suddenly he vanished, and I could have fancied a faint shriek had reached me. I had a momentary impulse to go back and help him that my fears overruled.

Everything was then quite invisible, hidden by the deep pit and the heap of sand that the fall of the cylinder had made. Anyone coming along the road from Chobham or Woking would have been amazed at the sight—a dwindling multitude of perhaps a hundred people or more standing in a great irregular circle,

Suddenly he vanished.

in ditches, behind bushes, behind gates and hedges, saying little to one another and that in short, excited shouts, and staring, staring hard at a few heaps of sand. The barrow of ginger beer stood, a queer derelict, black against the burning sky, and in the sand pits was a row of deserted vehicles with their horses feeding out of nosebags or pawing the ground.

Chapter Five
★ ★ ★
The Heat-Ray

After the glimpse I had had of the Martians emerging from the cylinder in which they had come to the earth from their planet, a kind of fascination paralysed my actions. I remained standing knee-deep in the heather, staring at the mound that hid them. I was a battleground of fear and curiosity.

I did not dare to go back towards the pit, but I felt a passionate longing to peer into it. I began walking, therefore, in a big curve, seeking some point of vantage and continually looking at the sand heaps that hid these new-comers to our earth. Once a leash of thin black whips, like the arms of an octopus, flashed across the sunset and was immediately withdrawn, and afterwards a thin rod rose up, joint by joint, bearing at its apex a circular disk that spun with a wobbling motion. What could be going on there?

Most of the spectators had gathered in one or two groups—one a little crowd towards Woking, the other a knot of people in the direction of Chobham. Evidently they shared my mental conflict. There were few near me. One man I approached—he was, I perceived, a neighbour of mine, though I did not know his name—and accosted. But it was scarcely a time for articulate conversation.

"What ugly brutes!" he said. "Good God! What ugly brutes!" He repeated this over and over again.

"Did you see a man in the pit?" I said; but he made no answer to that. We became silent, and stood watching for a time side by side, deriving, I fancy, a certain comfort in one another's company. Then I shifted my position to a little knoll that gave me the advantage of a yard or more of elevation and when I looked for him presently he was walking towards Woking.

The sunset faded to twilight before anything further happened. The crowd far away on the left, towards Woking, seemed to grow, and I heard now a faint murmur from it. The little knot of people towards Chobham dispersed. There was scarcely an intimation of movement from the pit.

It was this, as much as anything, that gave people courage, and I suppose the new arrivals from Woking also helped to restore confidence. At any rate, as the dusk came on a slow, intermittent movement upon the sand pits began, a movement that seemed to gather force as the stillness of the evening about the cylinder remained unbroken. Vertical black figures in twos and threes would advance, stop, watch, and advance again, spreading out as they did so in a thin irregular crescent that promised to enclose the pit in its attenuated horns. I, too, on my side began to move towards the pit.

Then I saw some cabmen and others had walked boldly into the sand pits, and heard the clatter of hoofs and the gride of wheels. I saw a lad trundling off the barrow of apples. And then, within thirty yards of the pit, advancing from the direction of Horsell, I noted a little black knot of men, the foremost of whom was waving a white flag.

This was the Deputation. There had been a hasty consultation, and since the Martians were evidently, in spite of their repulsive forms, intelligent creatures, it had been resolved to show them, by approaching them with signals, that we too were intelligent.

Flutter, flutter, went the flag, first to the right, then to the left. It was too far for me to recognise anyone there, but afterwards I learned that Ogilvy, Stent, and Henderson were with others in this attempt at communication. This little group had in its advance dragged inward, so to speak, the circumference of the now almost complete circle of people, and a number of dim black figures followed it at discreet distances.

Suddenly there was a flash of light, and a quantity of luminous greenish smoke came out of the pit in three distinct puffs, which drove up, one after the other, straight into the still air.

This smoke (or flame, perhaps, would be the better word for it) was so bright that the deep blue sky overhead and the hazy stretches of brown common towards Chertsey, set with black pine trees, seemed to darken abruptly as these puffs arose, and to remain the darker after their dispersal. At the same time a faint hissing sound became audible.

Beyond the pit stood the little wedge of people with the white flag at its apex, arrested by these phenomena, a little knot of small vertical black shapes upon the black ground. As the green smoke arose, their faces flashed out pallid green, and faded again as it vanished. Then slowly the hissing passed into a humming, into a long, loud, droning noise. Slowly a humped shape rose out of the pit, and the ghost of a beam of light seemed to flicker out from it.

Forthwith flashes of actual flame, a bright glare leaping from one to another, sprang from the scattered group of men. It was as if some invisible jet impinged upon them and flashed into white flame. It was as if each man were suddenly and momentarily turned to fire.

Then, by the light of their own destruction, I saw them staggering and falling, and their supporters turning to run.

I stood staring, not as yet realising that this was death leaping from man to man in that little distant crowd. All I felt was that it was something very strange. An almost noiseless and blinding flash of light, and a man fell headlong and lay still; and as the unseen shaft of heat passed over them, pine trees burst into fire, and every dry furze bush became with one dull thud a mass of flames. And far away towards Knaphill I saw the flashes of trees and hedges and wooden buildings suddenly set alight.

It was sweeping round swiftly and steadily, this flaming death, this invisible, inevitable sword of heat. I perceived it coming towards me by the flashing bushes it touched, and was too astounded and stupefied to stir. I heard the crackle of fire in the sand pits and the sudden squeal of a horse that was as suddenly stilled. Then it was as if an invisible yet intensely heated finger were drawn through the heather between me and the Martians, and all along a curving line beyond the sand pits the dark ground smoked and crackled. Something fell with a crash far away to the left where the road from Woking station opens out on the common. Forthwith the hissing and humming ceased, and the black, domelike object sank slowly out of sight into the pit.

All this had happened with such swiftness that I had stood motionless, dumbfounded and dazzled by the flashes of light. Had that death swept through a full circle, it must inevitably have slain me in my surprise. But it passed and spared me, and left the night about me suddenly dark and unfamiliar.

The undulating common seemed now dark almost to blackness, except where its roadways lay grey and pale under the deep blue sky of the early night. It was dark, and suddenly void of men. Overhead the stars were mustering, and in the west the sky was still a pale, bright, almost greenish blue. The tops of the pine trees and the roofs of Horsell came out sharp and black against the western afterglow. The Martians and their appliances were altogether invisible, save for that thin mast upon which their restless mirror wobbled. Patches of bush and isolated trees here and there smoked and glowed still, and the houses towards Woking station were sending up spires of flame into the stillness of the evening air.

Nothing was changed save for that and a terrible astonishment. The little group of black specks with the flag of white had been swept out of existence, and the stillness of the evening, so it seemed to me, had scarcely been broken.

It came to me that I was upon this dark common, helpless, unprotected, and alone. Suddenly, like a thing falling upon me from without, came—fear.

With an effort I turned and began a stumbling run through the heather.

The fear I felt was no rational fear, but a panic terror not only of the Martians, but of the dusk and stillness all about me. Such an extraordinary effect in unmanning me it had that I ran weeping silently as a child might do. Once I had turned, I did not dare to look back.

I remember I felt an extraordinary persuasion that I was being played with, that presently, when I was upon

the very verge of safety, this mysterious death—as swift as the passage of light—would leap after me from the pit about the cylinder and strike me down.

Chapter Six
★ ★ ★
The Heat-Ray in the Chobham Road

It is still a matter of wonder how the Martians are able to slay men so swiftly and so silently. Many think that in some way they are able to generate an intense heat in a chamber of practically absolute non-conductivity. This intense heat they project in a parallel beam against any object they choose, by means of a polished parabolic mirror of unknown composition, much as the parabolic mirror of a lighthouse projects a beam

Slowly a humped shape rose out of the pit.

of light. But no one has absolutely proved these details. However it is done, it is certain that a beam of heat is the essence of the matter. Heat, and invisible, instead of visible, light. Whatever is combustible flashes into flame at its touch, lead runs like water, it softens iron, cracks and melts glass, and when it falls upon water, incontinently that explodes into steam.

That night nearly forty people lay under the starlight about the pit, charred and distorted beyond recognition, and all night long the common from Horsell to Maybury was deserted and brightly ablaze.

The news of the massacre probably reached Chobham, Woking, and Ottershaw about the same time. In Woking the shops had closed when the tragedy happened, and a number of people, shop people and so forth, attracted by the stories they had heard, were walking over the Horsell Bridge and along the road between the hedges that runs out at last upon the common. You may imagine the young people brushed up after the labours of the day, and making this novelty, as they would make any novelty, the excuse for walking together and enjoying a trivial flirtation. You may figure to yourself the hum of voices along the road in the gloaming....

As yet, of course, few people in Woking even knew that the cylinder had opened, though poor Henderson had sent a messenger on a bicycle to the post office with a special wire to an evening paper.

As these folks came out by twos and threes upon the open, they found little knots of people talking excitedly and peering at the spinning mirror over the sand pits, and the new-comers were, no doubt, soon infected by the excitement of the occasion.

By half past eight, when the Deputation was destroyed, there may have been a crowd of three hundred people or more at this place, besides those who had left the road to approach the Martians nearer. There were three policemen too, one of whom was mounted, doing their best, under instructions from Stent, to keep the people back and deter them from approaching the cylinder. There was some booing from those more thoughtless and excitable souls to whom a crowd is always an occasion for noise and horse-play.

The death seemed leaping from man to man.

Stent and Ogilvy, anticipating some possibilities of a collision, had telegraphed from Horsell to the barracks as soon as the Martians emerged, for the help of a company of soldiers to protect these strange creatures from violence. After that they returned to lead that ill-fated advance. The description of their death, as it was seen by the crowd, tallies very closely with my own impressions: the three puffs of green smoke, the deep humming note, and the flashes of flame.

But that crowd of people had a far narrower escape than mine. Only the fact that a hummock of heathery sand intercepted the lower part of the Heat-Ray saved them. Had the elevation of the parabolic mirror been a few yards higher, none could have lived to tell the tale. They saw the flashes and the men falling and an invisible hand, as it were, lit the bushes as it hurried towards them through the twilight. Then, with a whistling note

I perceived it coming towards me.

that rose above the droning of the pit, the beam swung close over their heads, lighting the tops of the beech trees that line the road, and splitting the bricks, smashing the windows, firing the window frames, and bringing down in crumbling ruin a portion of the gable of the house nearest the corner.

In the sudden thud, hiss, and glare of the igniting trees, the panic-stricken crowd seems to have swayed hesitatingly for some moments. Sparks and burning twigs began to fall into the road, and single leaves like puffs of flame. Hats and dresses caught fire. Then came a crying from the common. There were shrieks and shouts, and suddenly a mounted policeman came galloping through the confusion with his hands clasped over his head, screaming.

"They're coming!" a woman shrieked, and incontinently everyone was turning and pushing at those behind, in order to clear their way to Woking again. They must have bolted as blindly as a flock of sheep. Where the road grows narrow and black between the high banks the crowd jammed, and a desperate struggle occurred. All that crowd did not escape; three persons at least, two women and a little boy, were crushed and trampled there, and left to die amid the terror and the darkness.

Chapter Seven
★ ★ ★
How I Reached Home

For my own part, I remember nothing of my flight except the stress of blundering against trees and stumbling through the heather. All about me gathered the invisible terrors of the Martians; that pitiless sword of heat seemed whirling to and fro, flourishing overhead before it descended and smote me out of life. I came into the road between the crossroads and Horsell, and ran along this to the crossroads.

At last I could go no further; I was exhausted with the violence of my emotion and of my flight, and I staggered and fell by the wayside. That was near the bridge that crosses the canal by the gasworks. I fell and lay still.

I must have remained there some time.

I sat up, strangely perplexed. For a moment, perhaps, I could not clearly understand how I came there. My terror had fallen from me like a garment. My hat had gone, and my collar had burst away from its fastener. A few minutes before, there had only been three real things before me—the immensity of the night and space and nature, my own feebleness and anguish, and the near approach of death. Now it was as if something turned over, and the point of view altered abruptly. There was no sensible transition from one state of mind to the other. I was immediately the self of every day again—a decent, ordinary citizen. The silent common, the impulse of my flight, the starting flames, were as if they had been in a dream. I asked myself had these latter things indeed happened? I could not credit it.

I rose and walked unsteadily up the steep incline of the bridge. My mind was blank wonder. My muscles and nerves seemed drained of their strength. I dare say I staggered drunkenly. A head rose over the arch, and the figure of a workman carrying a basket appeared. Beside him ran a little boy. He passed me, wishing me good night. I was minded to speak to him, but did not. I answered his greeting with a meaningless mumble and went on over the bridge.

Over the Maybury arch a train, a billowing tumult of white, firelit smoke, and a long caterpillar of lighted

windows, went flying south—clatter, clatter, clap, rap, and it had gone. A dim group of people talked in the gate of one of the houses in the pretty little row of gables that was called Oriental Terrace. It was all so real and so familiar. And that behind me! It was frantic, fantastic! Such things, I told myself, could not be.

Perhaps I am a man of exceptional moods. I do not know how far my experience is common. At times I suffer from the strangest sense of detachment from myself and the world about me; I seem to watch it all from the outside, from somewhere inconceivably remote, out of time, out of space, out of the stress and tragedy of it all. This feeling was very strong upon me that night. Here was another side to my dream.

But the trouble was the blank incongruity of this serenity and the swift death flying yonder, not two miles away. There was a noise of business from the gasworks, and the electric lamps were all alight. I stopped at the group of people.

"What news from the common?" said I.

There were two men and a woman at the gate.

"Eh?" said one of the men, turning.

"What news from the common?" I said.

"'Ain't yer just *been* there?" asked the men.

"People seem fair silly about the common," said the woman over the gate. "What's it all abart?"

"Haven't you heard of the men from Mars?" said I; "the creatures from Mars?"

"Quite enough," said the woman over the gate. "Thenks"; and all three of them laughed.

I felt foolish and angry. I tried and found I could not tell them what I had seen. They laughed again at my broken sentences.

"You'll hear more yet," I said, and went on to my home.

I startled my wife at the doorway, so haggard was I. I went into the dining room, sat down, drank some wine, and so soon as I could collect myself sufficiently I told her the things I had seen. The dinner, which was a cold one, had already been served, and remained neglected on the table while I told my story.

"There is one thing," I said, to allay the fears I had aroused; "they are the most sluggish things I ever saw crawl. They may keep the pit and kill people who come near them, but they cannot get out of it.…But the horror of them!"

"Don't, dear!" said my wife, knitting her brows and putting her hand on mine.

"Poor Ogilvy!" I said. "To think he may be lying dead there!"

My wife at least did not find my experience incredible. When I saw how deadly white her face was, I ceased abruptly. "They may come here," she said again and again. I pressed her to take wine, and tried to reassure her. "They can scarcely move," I said.

I began to comfort her and myself by repeating all that Ogilvy had told me of the impossibility of the Martians establishing themselves on the earth. In particular I laid stress on the gravitational difficulty. On the surface of the earth the force of gravity is three times what it is on the surface of Mars. A Martian, therefore, would weigh three times more than on Mars, albeit his muscular strength would be the same. His own body would be a cope of lead to him. That, indeed, was the general opinion. Both *The Times* and the *Daily*

*I startled my wife at the doorway,
so haggard was I.*

Telegraph, for instance, insisted on it the next morning, and both overlooked, just as I did, two obvious modifying influences.

The atmosphere of the earth, we now know, contains far more oxygen or far less argon (whichever way one likes to put it) than does Mars. The invigorating influences of this excess of oxygen upon the Martians indisputably did much to counterbalance the increased weight of their bodies. And, in the second place, we all overlooked the fact that such mechanical intelligence as the Martian possessed was quite able to dispense with muscular exertion at a pinch.

But I did not consider these points at the time, and so my reasoning was dead against the chances of the invaders. With wine and food, the confidence of my own table, and the necessity of reassuring my wife, I grew by insensible degrees courageous and secure.

"They have done a foolish thing," said I, fingering my wineglass. "They are dangerous because, no doubt, they are mad with terror. Perhaps they expected to find no living things—certainly no intelligent living things.

"A shell in the pit" said I, "if the worst comes to the worst, will kill them all."

The intense excitement of the events had no doubt left my perceptive powers in a state of erethism. I remember that dinner table with extraordinary vividness even now. My dear wife's sweet anxious face peering at me from under the pink lamp shade, the white cloth with its silver and glass table furniture—for in those days even philosophical writers had many little luxuries—the crimson-purple wine in my glass, are photographically distinct. At the end of it I sat, tempering nuts with a cigarette, regretting Ogilvy's rashness, and denouncing the shortsighted timidity of the Martians.

So some respectable dodo in the Mauritius might have lorded it in his nest, and discussed the arrival of that shipful of pitiless sailors in want of animal food. "We will peck them to death tomorrow, my dear."

I did not know it, but that was the last civilised dinner I was to eat for very many strange and terrible days.

Chapter Eight
★ ★ ★
Friday Night

The most extraordinary thing to my mind, of all the strange and wonderful things that happened upon that Friday, was the dovetailing of the commonplace habits of our social order with the first beginnings of the series of events that was to topple that social order headlong. If on Friday night you had taken a pair of compasses and drawn a circle with a radius of five miles round the Woking sand pits, I doubt if you would have had one human being outside it, unless it were some relation of Stent or of the three or four cyclists or London people lying dead on the common, whose emotions or habits were at all affected by the new-comers. Many people had heard of the cylinder, of course, and talked about it in their leisure, but it certainly did not make the sensation that an ultimatum to Germany would have done.

In London that night poor Henderson's telegram describing the gradual unscrewing of the shot was judged to be a canard, and his evening paper, after wiring for authentication from him and receiving no reply—the man was killed—decided not to print a special edition.

Even within the five-mile circle the great majority of people were inert. I have already described the behaviour of the men and women to whom I spoke. All over the district people were dining and supping; working men were gardening after the labours of the day, children were being put to bed, young people were wandering through the lanes love-making, students sat over their books.

Maybe there was a murmur in the village streets, a novel and dominant topic in the public-houses, and here and there a messenger, or even an eye-witness of the later occurrences, caused a whirl of excitement, a shouting, and a running to and fro; but for the most part the daily routine of working, eating, drinking, sleeping, went on as it had done for countless years—as though no planet Mars existed in the sky. Even at Woking station and Horsell and Chobham that was the case.

One or two adventurous souls never returned.

In Woking junction, until a late hour, trains were stopping and going on, others were shunting on the sidings, passengers were alighting and waiting, and everything was proceeding in the most ordinary way. A boy from the town, trenching on Smith's monopoly, was selling papers with the afternoon's news. The ringing impact of trucks, the sharp whistle of the engines from the junction, mingled with their shouts of "Men from Mars!" Excited men came into the station about nine o'clock with incredible tidings, and caused no more disturbance than drunkards might have done. People rattling Londonwards peered into the darkness outside the carriage windows, and saw only a rare, flickering, vanishing spark dance up from the direction of Horsell, a red glow and a thin veil of smoke driving across the stars, and thought that nothing more serious than a heath fire was happening. It was only round the edge of the common that any disturbance was perceptible. There were half a dozen villas burning on the Woking border. There were lights in all the houses on the common side of the three villages, and the people there kept awake till dawn.

A curious crowd lingered restlessly, people coming and going but the crowd remaining, both on the Chobham and Horsell bridges. One or two adventurous souls, it was afterwards found, went into the darkness and crawled quite near the Martians; but they never returned, for now and again a light-ray, like the beam of a warship's searchlight swept the common, and the Heat-Ray was ready to follow. Save for such, that big area of common was silent and desolate, and the charred bodies lay about on it all night under the stars, and all the next day. A noise of hammering from the pit was heard by many people.

So you have the state of things on Friday night. In the centre, sticking into the skin of our old planet Earth like a poisoned dart, was this cylinder. But the poison was scarcely working yet. Around it was a patch of silent common, smouldering in places, and with a few dark, dimly seen objects lying in contorted attitudes here and there. Here and there was a burning bush or tree. Beyond was a fringe of excitement, and farther than

that fringe the inflammation had not crept as yet. In the rest of the world the stream of life still flowed as it had flowed for immemorial years. The fever of war that would presently clog vein and artery, deaden nerve and destroy brain, had still to develop.

All night long the Martians were hammering and stirring, sleepless, indefatigable, at work upon the machines they were making ready, and ever and again a puff of greenish-white smoke whirled up to the starlit sky.

About eleven a company of soldiers came through Horsell, and deployed along the edge of the common to form a cordon. Later a second company marched through Chobham to deploy on the north side of the common. Several officers from the Inkerman barracks had been on the common earlier in the day, and one, Major Eden, was reported to be missing. The colonel of the regiment came to the Chobham bridge and was busy questioning the crowd at midnight. The military authorities were certainly alive to the seriousness of the business. About eleven, the next morning's papers were able to say, a squadron of hussars, two Maxims, and about four hundred men of the Cardigan regiment started from Aldershot.

A few seconds after midnight the crowd in the Chertsey road, Woking, saw a star fall from heaven into the pine woods to the northwest. It had a greenish colour, and caused a silent brightness like summer lightning. This was the second cylinder.

Chapter Nine

★ ★ ★

The Fighting Begins

Saturday lives in my memory as a day of suspense. It was a day of lassitude too, hot and close, with, I am told, a rapidly fluctuating barometer. I had slept but little, though my wife had succeeded in sleeping, and I rose early. I went into my garden before breakfast and stood listening, but towards the common there was nothing stirring but a lark.

The milkman came as usual. I heard the rattle of his chariot and I went round to the side gate to ask the latest news. He told me that during the night the Martians

had been surrounded by troops, and that guns were expected. Then—a familiar, reassuring note—I heard a train running towards Woking.

"They aren't to be killed," said the milkman, "if that can possibly be avoided."

I saw my neighbour gardening, chatted with him for a time, and then strolled in to breakfast. It was a most unexceptional morning. My neighbour was of opinion that the troops would be able to capture or to destroy the Martians during the day.

"It's a pity they make themselves so unapproachable," he said. "It would be curious to know how they live on another planet; we might learn a thing or two."

He came up to the fence and extended a handful of strawberries, for his gardening was as generous as it was enthusiastic. At the same time he told me of the burning of the pine woods about the Byfleet Golf Links.

"They say," said he, "that there's another of those blessed things fallen there—number two. But one's enough, surely. This lot'll cost the insurance people a pretty penny before everything's settled." He laughed with an air of the greatest good humour as he said this. The woods, he said, were still burning, and pointed out a haze of smoke to me. "They will be hot under foot for days, on account of the thick soil of pine needles and turf," he said, and then grew serious over "poor Ogilvy."

After breakfast, instead of working, I decided to walk down towards the common. Under the railway bridge I found a group of soldiers—sappers, I think, men in small round caps, dirty red jackets unbuttoned, and showing their blue shirts, dark trousers, and boots coming to the calf. They told me no one was allowed over the canal, and, looking along the road towards the bridge, I saw one of the Cardigan men standing sentinel there. I talked with these soldiers for a time; I told them of my sight of the Martians on the previous evening. None of them had seen the Martians, and they had but the vaguest ideas of them, so that they plied me with questions. They said that they did not know who had authorised the movements of the troops; their idea was that a dispute had arisen at the Horse Guards. The ordinary sapper is a great deal better educated than the common soldier, and they discussed the peculiar conditions of the possible fight with some acuteness. I described the Heat-Ray to them, and they began to argue among themselves.

"Crawl up under cover and rush 'em, say I," said one.

"Get aht!," said another. "What's cover against this 'ere 'eat? Sticks to cook yer! What we got to do is to go as near as the ground'll let us, and then drive a trench."

"Blow yer trenches! You always want trenches; you ought to ha' been born a rabbit Snippy."

"'Ain't they got any necks, then?" said a third, abruptly—a little, contemplative, dark man, smoking a pipe.

I repeated my description.

"Octopuses," said he, "that's what I calls 'em. Talk about fishers of men—fighters of fish it is this time!"

"It ain't no murder killing beasts like that," said the first speaker.

"Why not shell the darned things strite off and finish 'em?" said the little dark man. "You carn tell what they might do."

"Where's your shells?" said the first speaker. "There ain't no time. Do it in a rush, that's my tip, and do it at once."

So they discussed it. After a while I left them, and went on to the railway station to get as many morning papers as I could.

But I will not weary the reader with a description of that long morning and of the longer afternoon. I did not succeed in getting a glimpse of the common, for even Horsell and Chobham church towers were in the hands of the military authorities. The soldiers I addressed didn't know anything; the officers were mysterious as well as busy. I found people in the town quite secure again in the presence of the military, and I heard for the first time from Marshall, the tobacconist, that his son was among the dead on the common. The soldiers had made the people on the outskirts of Horsell lock up and leave their houses.

I got back to lunch about two, very tired for, as I have said, the day was extremely hot and dull; and in order to refresh myself I took a cold bath in the afternoon. About half past four I went up to the railway station to get an evening paper, for the morning papers had contained only a very inaccurate description of the killing of Stent, Henderson, Ogilvy, and the others. But there was little I didn't know. The Martians did not show an inch of themselves. They seemed busy in their pit, and there was a sound of hammering and an almost continuous streamer of smoke. Apparently they were busy getting ready for a struggle. "Fresh attempts have been made to signal, but without success," was the stereotyped formula of the papers. A sapper told me it was done by a man in a ditch with a flag on a long pole. The Martians took as much notice of such advances as we should of the lowing of a cow.

I must confess the sight of all this armament, all this preparation, greatly excited me. My imagination became belligerent, and defeated the invaders in a dozen striking ways; something of my schoolboy dreams of battle and heroism came back. It hardly seemed a fair fight to me at that time. They seemed very helpless in that pit of theirs.

About three o'clock there began the thud of a gun at measured intervals from Chertsey or Addlestone. I learned that the smouldering pine wood into which the second cylinder had fallen was being shelled, in the hope of destroying that object before it opened. It was only about five, however, that a field gun reached Chobham for use against the first body of Martians.

About six in the evening, as I sat at tea with my wife in the summerhouse talking vigorously about the battle that was lowering upon us, I heard a muffled detonation from the common, and immediately after a gust of firing. Close on the heels of that came a violent rattling crash, quite close to us, that shook the ground; and, starting out upon the lawn, I saw the tops of the trees about the Oriental College burst into smoky red flame, and the tower of the little church beside it slide down into ruin. The pinnacle of the mosque had vanished, and the roof line of the college itself looked as if a hundred-ton gun had

been at work upon it. One of our chimneys cracked as if a shot had hit it, flew, and a piece of it came clattering down the tiles and made a heap of broken red fragments upon the flower bed by my study window.

I and my wife stood amazed. Then I realised that the crest of Maybury Hill must be within range of the Martians' Heat-Ray now that the college was cleared out of the way.

At that I gripped my wife's arm, and without ceremony ran her out into the road. Then I fetched out the servant, telling her I would go upstairs myself for the box she was clamouring for.

"We can't possibly stay here," I said; and as I spoke the firing reopened for a moment upon the common.

"But where are we to go?" said my wife in terror.

I thought perplexed. Then I remembered her cousins at Leatherhead.

"Leatherhead!" I shouted above the sudden noise.

She looked away from me downhill. The people were coming out of their houses, astonished.

"How are we to get to Leatherhead?" she said.

Down the hill I saw a bevy of hussars ride under the railway bridge; three galloped through the open gates of the Oriental College; two others dismounted, and began running from house to house. The sun, shining through the smoke that drove up from the tops of the trees, seemed blood red, and threw an unfamiliar lurid light upon everything.

"Stop here," said I; "you are safe here"; and I started off at once for the Spotted Dog, for I knew the landlord had a horse and dog cart. I ran, for I perceived that in a moment everyone upon this side of the hill would be moving. I found him in his bar, quite unaware of what was going on behind his house. A man stood with his back to me, talking to him.

"Fresh attempts have been made to signal."

"I must have a pound," said the landlord, "and I've no one to drive it."

"I'll give you two," said I, over the stranger's shoulder.

"What for?"

"And I'll bring it back by midnight," I said.

"Lord!" said the landlord; "what's the hurry? I'm selling my bit of a pig. Two pounds, and you bring it back? What's going on now?"

I explained hastily that I had to leave my home, and so secured the dog cart. At the time it did not seem to me nearly so urgent that the landlord should leave his. I took care to have the cart there and then, drove it off down the road, and, leaving it in charge of my wife and servant, rushed into my house and packed a few valuables, such plate as we had, and so forth. The beech trees below the house were burning while I did this, and the palings up the road glowed red. While I was occupied in this way, one of the dismounted hussars came running up. He was going from house to house, warning people to leave. He was going on as I came out of my front door, lugging my treasures, done up in a table-cloth. I shouted after him:

"What news?"

He turned, stared, bawled something about "crawling out in a thing like a dish cover," and ran on to the gate of the house at the crest. A sudden whirl of black smoke driving across the road hid him for a moment. I ran to my neighbour's door and rapped to satisfy myself of what I already knew, that his wife had gone to London with him and had locked up their house. I went in again, according to my promise, to get my servant's box, lugged it out, clapped it beside her on the tail of the dog cart, and then caught the reins and jumped up into the driver's seat beside my wife. In another moment we were clear of the smoke and noise, and spanking down the opposite slope of Maybury Hill towards Old Woking.

In front was a quiet sunny landscape, a wheat field ahead on either side of the road, and the Maybury Inn with its swinging sign. I saw the doctor's cart ahead of me. At the bottom of the hill I turned my head to look at the hillside I was leaving. Thick streamers of black smoke shot with threads of red fire were driving up into the still air, and throwing dark shadows upon the green treetops eastward. The smoke already extended far away to the east and west—to the Byfleet pine woods eastward, and to Woking on the west. The road was dotted with people running towards us. And very faint now, but very distinct through the hot, quiet air, one heard the whirr of a machine-gun that was presently stilled, and an intermittent cracking of rifles. Apparently the Martians were setting fire to everything within range of their Heat-Ray.

I am not an expert driver, and I had immediately to turn my attention to the horse. When I looked back again the second hill had hidden the black smoke. I slashed the horse with the whip, and gave him a loose rein until Woking and Send lay between us and that quivering tumult. I overtook and passed the doctor between Woking and Send.

Chapter Ten

★ ★ ★

In the Storm

Leatherhead is about twelve miles from Maybury Hill. The scent of hay was in the air through the lush meadows beyond Pyrford, and the hedges on either side were sweet and gay with multitudes of dog-roses. The heavy firing that had broken out while we were driving down Maybury Hill ceased as abruptly as it began, leaving the evening very peaceful and still. We got to Leatherhead without misadventure about nine o'clock, and the horse had an hour's rest while I took supper with my cousins and commended my wife to their care.

My wife was curiously silent throughout the drive, and seemed oppressed with forebodings of evil. I talked to her reassuringly, pointing out that the Martians were tied to the pit by sheer heaviness, and at the utmost could but crawl a little out of it; but she answered only in monosyllables. Had it not been for my promise to the innkeeper, she would, I think, have urged me to stay in Leatherhead that night. Would that I had! Her face, I remember, was very white as we parted.

For my own part, I had been feverishly excited all day. Something very like the war fever that occasionally runs through a civilised community had got into my blood, and in my heart I was not so very sorry that I had to return to Maybury that night. I was even afraid that that last fusillade I had heard might mean the extermination of our invaders from Mars. I can best express my state of mind by saying that I wanted to be in at the death.

It was nearly eleven when I started to return. The night was unexpectedly dark; to me, walking out of the lighted passage of my cousins' house, it seemed indeed black, and it was as hot and close as the day. Overhead the clouds were driving fast, albeit not a breath stirred the shrubs about us. My cousins' man lit both lamps. Happily, I knew the road intimately. My wife stood in the light of the doorway, and watched me until I jumped up into the dog cart. Then abruptly she turned and went in, leaving my cousins side by side wishing me good hap.

I was a little depressed at first with the contagion of my wife's fears, but very soon my thoughts reverted to the Martians. At that time I was absolutely in the dark as to the course of the evening's fighting. I did not know even the circumstances that had precipitated the conflict. As I came through Ockham (for that was the way I returned, and not through Send and Old Woking) I saw along the western horizon a blood-red glow, which as I drew nearer, crept slowly up the sky. The driving clouds of the gathering thunderstorm mingled there with masses of black and red smoke.

Ripley Street was deserted, and except for a lighted window or so the village showed not a sign of life; but I narrowly escaped an accident at the corner of the road to Pyrford, where a knot of people stood with their backs to me. They said nothing to me as I passed. I do not know what they knew of the things happening beyond the hill, nor do I know if the silent houses I passed on my way were sleeping securely, or deserted and empty, or harassed and watching against the terror of the night.

From Ripley until I came through Pyrford I was in the valley of the Wey, and the red glare was hidden from me. As I ascended the little hill beyond Pyrford Church the glare came into view again, and the trees about me shivered with the first intimation of the storm that was upon me. Then I heard midnight pealing out from Pyrford Church behind me, and then came the silhouette of Maybury Hill, with its treetops and roofs black and sharp against the red.

Even as I beheld this a lurid green glare lit the road about me and showed the distant woods towards Addlestone. I felt a tug at the reins. I saw that the driving clouds had been pierced as it were by a thread of green fire, suddenly lighting their confusion and falling into the field to my left. It was the third falling star!

Close on its apparition, and blindingly violet by contrast, danced out the first lightning of the gathering storm, and the thunder burst like a rocket overhead. The horse took the bit between his teeth and bolted.

A moderate incline runs towards the foot of Maybury Hill, and down this we clattered. Once the lightning had begun, it went on in as rapid a succession of flashes as I have ever seen. The thunderclaps, treading one on the heels of another and with a strange crackling accompaniment, sounded more like the working of a gigantic electric machine than the usual detonating reverberations. The flickering light was blinding and confusing, and a thin hail smote gustily at my face as I drove down the slope.

At first I regarded little but the road before me, and then abruptly my attention was arrested by something that was moving rapidly down the opposite slope of Maybury Hill. At first I took it for the wet roof of a house, but one flash following another showed it to be in swift rolling movement. It was an elusive vision—a moment of bewildering darkness, and then, in a flash like daylight, the red masses of the Orphanage near the crest of the hill, the green tops of the pine trees, and this problematical object came out clear and sharp and bright.

And this Thing I saw! How can I describe it? A monstrous tripod, higher than many houses, striding over the young pine trees, and smashing them aside in its career; a walking engine of glittering metal, striding now across the heather; articulate ropes of steel dangling from it, and the clattering tumult of its passage mingling with the riot of the thunder. A flash, and it came out vividly, heeling over one way with two feet in the air, to vanish and reappear almost instantly as it seemed, with the next flash, a hundred yards nearer. Can you imagine a milking stool tilted and bowled violently along the ground? That was the impression those instant flashes gave. But instead of a milking stool imagine it a great body of machinery on a tripod stand.

Then suddenly the trees in the pine wood ahead of me were parted, as brittle reeds are parted by a man thrusting through them; they were snapped off and driven headlong, and a second huge tripod appeared, rushing, as it seemed, headlong towards me. And I was galloping hard to meet it! At the sight of the second monster my nerve went altogether. Not stopping to look again, I wrenched the horse's head hard round to the right and in another moment the dog cart had heeled over upon the horse; the shafts smashed noisily, and I was flung sideways and fell heavily into a shallow pool of water.

I crawled out almost immediately, and crouched, my feet still in the water, under a clump of furze. The horse lay motionless (his neck was broken, poor brute!) and by the lightning flashes I saw the black bulk of the over-turned dog cart and the silhouette of the wheel still spinning slowly. In another moment the colossal mechanism went striding by me, and passed uphill towards Pyrford.

Seen nearer, the Thing was incredibly strange, for it was no mere insensate machine driving on its way. Machine it was, with a ringing metallic pace, and long, flexible, glittering tentacles (one of which gripped a young pine tree) swinging and rattling about its strange body. It picked its road as it went striding along, and the

Suddenly the trees in the pine wood were parted.

brazen hood that surmounted it moved to and fro with the inevitable suggestion of a head looking about. Behind the main body was a huge mass of white metal like a gigantic fisherman's basket, and puffs of green smoke squirted out from the joints of the limbs as the monster swept by me. And in an instant it was gone.

So much I saw then, all vaguely for the flickering of the lightning, in blinding highlights and dense black shadows.

As it passed it set up an exultant deafening howl that drowned the thunder —"Aloo! Aloo!"—and in another minute it was with its companion, half a mile away, stooping over something in the field. I have no doubt this Thing in the field was the third of the ten cylinders they had fired at us from Mars.

For some minutes I lay there in the rain and darkness watching, by the intermittent light, these monstrous beings of metal moving about in the distance over the hedge tops. A thin hail was now beginning, and as it came and went their figures grew misty and then flashed into clearness again. Now and then came a gap in the lightning, and the night swallowed them up.

I was soaked with hail above and puddle water below. It was some time before my blank astonishment would let me struggle up the bank to a drier position, or think at all of my imminent peril.

Not far from me was a little one-roomed squatter's hut of wood, surrounded by a patch of potato garden. I struggled to my feet at last, and, crouching and making use of every chance of cover, I made a run for this. I hammered at the door, but I could not make the people hear (if there were any people inside), and after a time I desisted, and, availing myself of a ditch for the greater part of the way, succeeded in crawling, unobserved by these monstrous machines, into the pine woods towards Maybury.

Under cover of this I pushed on, wet and shivering now, towards my own house. I walked among the trees trying to find the footpath. It was very dark indeed in the wood, for the lightning was now becoming infrequent, and the hail, which was pouring down in a torrent, fell in columns through the gaps in the heavy foliage.

If I had fully realised the meaning of all the things I had seen I should have immediately worked my way round through Byfleet to Street Cobham, and so gone back to rejoin my wife at Leatherhead. But that night the strangeness of things about me, and my physical wretchedness, prevented me, for I was bruised, weary, wet to the skin, deafened and blinded by the storm.

I had a vague idea of going on to my own house, and that was as much motive as I had. I staggered through the trees, fell into a ditch and bruised my knees against a plank, and finally splashed out into the lane that ran down from the College Arms. I say splashed, for the storm water was sweeping the sand down the hill in a muddy torrent. There in the darkness a man blundered into me and sent me reeling back.

He gave a cry of terror, sprang sideways, and rushed on before I could gather my wits sufficiently to speak to him. So heavy was the stress of the storm just at this place that I had the hardest task to win my way up the hill. I went close up to the fence on the left and worked my way along its palings.

Near the top I stumbled upon something soft, and, by a flash of lightning, saw between my feet a heap of black broadcloth and a pair of boots. Before I could distinguish clearly how the man lay, the flicker of light had passed. I stood over him waiting for the next flash. When it came, I saw that he was a sturdy man, cheaply but not shabbily dressed; his head was bent under his body, and he lay crumpled up close to the fence, as though he had been flung violently against it.

Overcoming the repugnance natural to one who had never before touched a dead body, I stooped and turned him over to feel for his heart. He was quite dead. Apparently his neck had been broken. The lightning flashed for a third time, and his face leaped upon me. I sprang to my feet. It was the landlord of the Spotted Dog, whose conveyance I had taken.

I stepped over him gingerly and pushed on up the hill. I made my way by the police station and the College Arms towards my own house. Nothing was burning on the hillside, though from the common there still came a red glare and a rolling tumult of ruddy smoke beating up against the drenching hail. So far as I could see by the flashes, the houses about me were mostly uninjured. By the College Arms a dark heap lay in the road.

Down the road towards Maybury Bridge there were voices and the sound of feet, but I had not the courage to shout or to go to them. I let myself in with my latchkey, closed, locked and bolted the door, staggered to the foot of the staircase, and sat down. My imagination was full of those striding metallic monsters, and of the dead body smashed against the fence.

I crouched at the foot of the staircase with my back to the wall, shivering violently.

Chapter Eleven
★ ★ ★
At the Window

I have already said that my storms of emotion have a trick of exhausting themselves. After a time I discovered that I was cold and wet, and with little pools of water about me on the stair carpet. I got up almost mechanically, went into the dining room and drank some whiskey, and then I was moved to change my clothes.

After I had done that I went upstairs to my study, but why I did so I do not know. The window of my study looks over the trees and the railway towards Horsell Common. In the hurry of our departure this window had been left open. The passage was dark, and, by contrast with the picture the window frame enclosed, the side of the room seemed impenetrably dark. I stopped short in the doorway.

The thunderstorm had passed. The towers of the Oriental College and the pine trees about it had gone, and very far away, lit by a vivid red glare, the common about the sand pits was visible. Across the light huge black shapes, grotesque and strange, moved busily to and fro.

It seemed indeed as if the whole country in that direction was on fire—a broad hillside set with minute tongues of flame, swaying and writhing with the gusts of the dying storm, and throwing a red reflection upon the cloud scud above. Every now and then a haze of smoke from some nearer conflagration drove across the window and hid the Martian shapes. I could not see what they were doing, nor the clear form of them, nor recognise the black objects they were busied upon. Neither could I see the nearer fire, though the reflections of it danced on the wall and ceiling of the study. A sharp, resinous tang of burning was in the air.

I closed the door noiselessly and crept towards the window. As I did so, the view opened out until, on the one hand, it reached to the houses about Woking station, and on the other to the charred and blackened pine woods of Byfleet. There was a light down below the hill, on the railway, near the arch, and several of the houses along the Maybury road and the streets near the station were glowing ruins. The light upon the railway puzzled me at first; there were a black heap and a vivid glare, and to the right of that a row of yellow oblongs. Then I perceived this was a wrecked train, the fore part smashed and on fire, the hinder carriages still upon the rails.

Between these three main centres of light—the houses, the train, and the burning county towards Chobham—stretched irregular patches of dark country, broken here and there by intervals of dimly glowing and smoking ground. It was the strangest spectacle, that black expanse set with fire. It reminded me, more than anything else, of the Potteries at night. At first I could distinguish no people at all, though I peered intently for them. Later I saw against the light of Woking station a number of black figures hurrying one after the other across the line.

And this was the little world in which I had been living securely for years, this fiery chaos! What had happened in the last seven hours I still did not know; nor

did I know, though I was beginning to guess, the relation between these mechanical colossi and the sluggish lumps I had seen disgorged from the cylinder. With a queer feeling of impersonal interest I turned my desk chair to the window, sat down, and stared at the blackened country, and particularly at the three gigantic black things that were going to and fro in the glare about the sand pits.

They seemed amazingly busy. I began to ask myself what they could be. Were they intelligent mechanisms? Such a thing I felt was impossible. Or did a Martian sit within each, ruling, directing, using, much as a man's brain sits and rules in his body? I began to compare the things to human machines, to ask myself for the first time in my life how an ironclad or a steam engine would seem to an intelligent lower animal.

The storm had left the sky clear, and over the smoke of the burning land the little fading pinpoint of Mars was dropping into the west, when a soldier came into my garden. I heard a slight scraping at the fence, and rousing myself from the lethargy that had fallen upon me, I looked down and saw him dimly, clambering over the palings. At the sight of another human being my torpor passed, and I leaned out of the window eagerly.

"Hist!" said I, in a whisper.

He stopped astride of the fence in doubt. Then he came over and across the lawn to the corner of the house. He bent down and stepped softly.

"Who's there?" he said, also whispering, standing under the window and peering up.

"Where are you going?" I asked.

"God knows."

"Are you trying to hide?"

"That's it."

"Come into the house," I said.

I went down, unfastened the door, and let him in, and locked the door again. I could not see his face. He was hatless, and his coat was unbuttoned.

"My God!" he said, as I drew him in.

"What has happened?" I asked.

"What hasn't?" In the obscurity I could see he made a gesture of despair. "They wiped us out—simply wiped us out," he repeated again and again.

He followed me, almost mechanically, into the dining room.

"Take some whiskey," I said, pouring out a stiff dose.

He drank it. Then abruptly he sat down before the table, put his head on his arms, and began to sob and weep like a little boy, in a perfect passion of emotion, while I, with a curious forgetfulness of my own recent despair, stood beside him, wondering.

It was a long time before he could steady his nerves to answer my questions, and then he answered perplexingly and brokenly. He was a driver in the artillery, and had only come into action about seven. At that time firing was going on across the common, and it was said the first party of Martians were crawling slowly towards their second cylinder under cover of a metal shield.

Later this shield staggered up on tripod legs and became the first of the fighting-machines I had seen. The gun he drove had been unlimbered near Horsell, in order to command the sand pits, and its arrival it was that had precipitated the action. As the limber gunners went to the

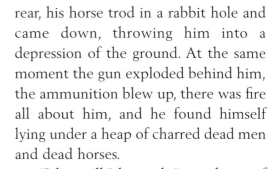

rear, his horse trod in a rabbit hole and came down, throwing him into a depression of the ground. At the same moment the gun exploded behind him, the ammunition blew up, there was fire all about him, and he found himself lying under a heap of charred dead men and dead horses.

"I lay still," he said, "scared out of my wits, with the fore quarter of a horse atop of me. We'd been wiped out. And the smell—good God! Like burnt meat! I was hurt across the back by the fall of the horse, and there I had to lie until I felt better. Just like parade it had been a minute before—then stumble, bang, swish!"

"Wiped out!" he said.

He had hid under the dead horse for a long time, peeping out furtively across the common. The Cardigan men had tried a rush, in skirmishing order, at the pit, simply to be swept out of existence. Then the monster had risen to its feet and had begun to walk leisurely to and fro across the common among the few fugitives, with its headlike hood turning about exactly like the head of a cowled human being. A kind of arm carried a complicated metallic case, about which green flashes scintillated, and out of the funnel of this there smoked the Heat-Ray.

In a few minutes there was, so far as the soldier could see, not a living thing left upon the common, and every bush and tree upon it that was not already a blackened skeleton was burning. The hussars had been on the road beyond the curvature of the ground, and he saw nothing of them. He heard the Martians rattle for a time and then become still. The giant saved Woking station and its cluster of houses until the last; then in a moment the Heat-Ray was brought to bear, and the town became a heap of fiery ruins. Then the Thing shut off the Heat-Ray, and turning its back upon the artilleryman, began to waddle away towards the smouldering pine woods that sheltered the second cylinder. As it did so a second glittering Titan built itself up out of the pit.

The second monster followed the first, and at that the artilleryman began to crawl very cautiously across the hot heather ash towards Horsell. He managed to get alive into the ditch by the side of the road, and so escaped to Woking. There his story became ejaculatory. The place was impassable. It seems there were a few people alive there, frantic for the most part and many burned and scalded. He was turned aside by the fire, and hid among some almost scorching heaps of broken wall as one of the Martian giants returned. He saw this one pursue a man, catch him up in one of its steely tentacles, and knock his head against the trunk of a pine tree. At last, after nightfall, the artilleryman made a rush for it and got over the railway embankment.

Since then he had been skulking along towards Maybury, in the hope of getting out of danger Londonward. People were hiding in trenches and cellars, and many of the survivors had made off towards Woking village and Send. He had been consumed with thirst until he found one of the water mains near the railway arch smashed, and the water bubbling out like a spring upon the road.

That was the story I got from him, bit by bit. He grew calmer telling me and trying to make me see the things he had seen. He had eaten no food since midday, he told me early in his narrative, and I found some mutton and bread in the pantry and brought it into the room. We lit no lamp for fear of attracting the Martians, and ever and again our hands would touch upon bread or meat. As he talked, things about us came darkly out of the darkness, and the trampled bushes and broken rose trees outside the window grew distinct. It would seem that a number of men or animals had rushed across the lawn. I began to see his face, blackened and haggard, as no doubt mine was also.

When we had finished eating we went softly upstairs to my study, and I looked again out of the open window. In one night the valley had become a valley of ashes. The fires had dwindled now. Where flames had been there were now streamers of smoke; but the countless ruins of shattered and gutted houses and blasted and blackened trees that the night had hidden stood out now gaunt and terrible in the pitiless light of dawn. Yet here and there some object had had the luck to escape—a white railway signal here, the end of a greenhouse there, white and fresh amid the wreckage. Never before in the history of warfare had destruction been so indiscriminate and so universal. And shining with the growing light of the east, three of the metallic giants stood about the pit, their cowls rotating as though they were surveying the desolation they had made.

It seemed to me that the pit had been enlarged, and ever and again puffs of vivid green vapour streamed up and out of it towards the brightening dawn—streamed up, whirled, broke, and vanished.

Beyond were the pillars of fire about Chobham. They became pillars of bloodshot smoke at the first touch of day.

Chapter Twelve

★ ★ ★

What I Saw of the Destruction of Weybridge and Shepperton

As the dawn grew brighter we withdrew from the window from which we had watched the Martians, and went very quietly downstairs.

The artilleryman agreed with me that the house was no place to stay in. He proposed, he said, to make his way Londonward, and thence rejoin his battery—No. 12, of the Horse Artillery. My plan was to return at once to Leatherhead; and so greatly had the strength of the Martians impressed me that I had determined to take my wife to Newhaven, and go with her out of the country forthwith. For I already perceived clearly that the country about London must inevitably be the scene of a disastrous struggle before such creatures as these could be destroyed.

Between us and Leatherhead, however, lay the third cylinder,

He saw this one pursue a man and catch him up in one of its steely tentacles.

with its guarding giants. Had I been alone, I think I should have taken my chance and struck across country. But the artilleryman dissuaded me: "It's no kindness to the right sort of wife," he said, "to make her a widow"; and in the end I agreed to go with him, under cover of the woods, northward as far as Street Cobham before I parted with him. Thence I would make a big detour by Epsom to reach Leatherhead.

I should have started at once, but my companion had been in active service and he knew better than that. He made me ransack the house for a flask, which he filled with whiskey; and we lined every available pocket with packets of biscuits and slices of meat. Then we crept out of the house, and ran as quickly as we could down the ill-made road by which I had come overnight. The houses seemed deserted. In the road lay a group of three charred bodies close together, struck dead by the Heat-Ray; and here and there were things that people had dropped—a clock, a slipper, a silver spoon, and the like poor valuables. At the corner turning up towards the post office a little cart, filled with boxes and furniture, and horseless, heeled over on a broken wheel. A cash box had been hastily smashed open and thrown under the débris.

Except the lodge at the Orphanage, which was still on fire, none of the houses had suffered very greatly here. The Heat-Ray had shaved the chimney tops and passed. Yet, save ourselves, there did not seem to be a living soul on Maybury Hill. The majority of the inhabitants had escaped, I suppose, by way of the Old Woking road—the road I had taken when I drove to Leatherhead—or they had hidden.

We went down the lane, by the body of the man in black, sodden now from the overnight hail, and broke into the woods at the foot of the hill. We pushed through these towards the railway without meeting a soul. The woods across the line were but the scarred and blackened ruins of woods; for the most part the trees had fallen, but a certain proportion still stood, dismal grey stems, with dark brown foliage instead of green.

On our side the fire had done no more than scorch the nearer trees; it had failed to secure its footing. In one place the woodmen had been at work on Saturday;

trees, felled and freshly trimmed, lay in a clearing, with heaps of sawdust by the sawing-machine and its engine. Hard by was a temporary hut, deserted. There was not a breath of wind this morning, and everything was strangely still. Even the birds were hushed, and as we hurried along I and the artilleryman talked in whispers and looked now and again over our shoulders. Once or twice we stopped to listen.

After a time we drew near the road, and as we did so we heard the clatter of hoofs and saw through the tree stems three cavalry soldiers riding slowly towards Woking. We hailed them, and they halted while we hurried towards them. It was a lieutenant and a couple of privates of the 8th Hussars, with a stand like a theodolite, which the artilleryman told me was a heliograph.

"You are the first men I've seen coming this way this morning," said the lieutenant. "What's brewing?"

His voice and face were eager. The men behind him stared curiously. The artilleryman jumped down the bank into the road and saluted.

"Gun destroyed last night, sir. Have been hiding. Trying to rejoin battery, sir. You'll come in sight of the Martians, I expect, about half a mile along this road."

"What the dickens are they like?" asked the lieutenant.

"Giants in armour, sir. Hundred feet high. Three legs and a body like 'luminium, with a mighty great head in a hood, sir."

"Get out!" said the lieutenant. "What confounded nonsense!"

"You'll see, sir. They carry a kind of box, sir, that shoots fire and strikes you dead."

"What d'ye mean—a gun?"

"No, sir," and the artilleryman began a vivid account of the Heat-Ray. Halfway through, the lieutenant interrupted him and looked up at me. I was still standing on the bank by the side of the road.

"It's perfectly true," I said.

"Well," said the lieutenant, "I suppose it's my business to see it too. Look here"—to the artilleryman—"we're detailed here clearing people out of their houses. You'd better go along and report yourself to Brigadier-General Marvin, and tell him all you know. He's at Weybridge. Know the way?"

"I do," I said; and he turned his horse southward again.

"Half a mile, you say?" said he.

"At most," I answered, and pointed over the treetops southward. He thanked me and rode on, and we saw them no more.

Farther along we came upon a group of three women and two children in the road, busy clearing out a labourer's cottage. They had got hold of a little hand truck, and were piling it up with unclean-looking bundles and shabby furniture. They were all too assiduously engaged to talk to us as we passed.

By Byfleet station we emerged from the pine trees, and found the country calm and peaceful under the morning sunlight. We were far beyond the range of the Heat-Ray there, and had it not been for the silent desertion of some of the houses, the stirring movement of packing in others, and the knot of soldiers standing on the bridge over the railway and staring down the line towards Woking, the day would have seemed very like any other Sunday.

Several farm waggons and carts were moving creakily along the road to Addlestone, and suddenly through the gate of a field we saw, across a stretch of flat meadow, six twelve-pounders standing neatly at equal distances pointing towards Woking. The gunners stood by the guns waiting, and the ammunition waggons were at a business-like distance. The men stood almost as if under inspection.

"That's good!" said I. "They will get one fair shot, at any rate."

The artilleryman hesitated at the gate.

"I shall go on," he said.

Farther on towards Weybridge, just over the bridge, there were a number of men in white fatigue jackets throwing up a long rampart, and more guns behind.

"It's bows and arrows against the lightning, anyhow," said the artilleryman. "They 'aven't seen that fire-beam yet."

The officers who were not actively engaged stood and stared over the treetops southwestward, and the men digging would stop every now and again to stare in the same direction.

Byfleet was in a tumult; people packing, and a score of hussars, some of them dismounted, some on horse-back, were hunting them about. Three or four black government waggons, with crosses in white circles, and an old omnibus, among other vehicles, were being loaded in the village street. There were scores of people, most of them sufficiently sabbatical to have assumed their best clothes. The soldiers were having the greatest difficulty in making them realise the gravity of their position. We saw one shrivelled old fellow with a huge box and a score or more of flower pots containing orchids, angrily expostulating with the corporal who would leave them behind. I stopped and gripped his arm.

"Do you know what's over there?" I said, pointing at the pine tops that hid the Martians.

"Eh?" said he, turning. "I was explainin' these is vallyble."

"Death!" I shouted. "Death is coming! Death!" and leaving him to digest that if he could, I hurried on after the artilleryman. At the corner I looked back. The soldier had left him, and he was still standing by his box, with the pots of orchids on the lid of it, and staring vaguely over the trees.

No one in Weybridge could tell us where the headquarters were established; the whole place was in such confusion as I had never seen in any town before. Carts, carriages everywhere, the most astonishing miscellany of conveyances and horseflesh. The respectable inhabitants of the place, men in golf and boating costumes, wives prettily dressed, were packing, river-side loafers energetically helping, children excited, and, for the most part, highly delighted at this astonishing variation of their Sunday experiences. In the midst of it all the worthy vicar was very pluckily holding an early celebration, and his bell was jangling out above the excitement.

I and the artilleryman, seated on the step of the drinking fountain, made a very passable meal upon what we had brought with us. Patrols of soldiers—here no longer hussars, but grenadiers in white—were warning people to move now or to take refuge in their cellars as soon as the firing began. We saw as we crossed the railway bridge that a growing crowd of people had assembled in and about the railway station, and the swarming platform was piled with boxes and packages. The ordinary traffic had been stopped, I believe, in order to allow of the passage of troops and guns to Chertsey, and I have heard since that a savage struggle occurred for places in the special trains that were put on at a later hour.

We remained at Weybridge until midday, and at that hour we found ourselves at the place near Shepperton Lock where the Wey and Thames join. Part of the time we spent helping two old women to pack a little cart. The Wey has a treble mouth, and at this point boats are to be hired, and there was a ferry across the river. On the Shepperton side was an inn with a lawn, and beyond that the tower of Shepperton Church—it has been replaced by a spire—rose above the trees.

Here we found an excited and noisy crowd of fugitives. As yet the flight had not grown to a panic, but there were already far more people than all the boats going to and fro could enable to cross. People came panting along under heavy burdens; one husband and wife were even carrying a small outhouse door between them, with some of their household goods piled thereon. One man told us he meant to try to get away from Shepperton station.

There was a lot of shouting, and one man was even jesting. The idea people seemed to have here was that the Martians were simply formidable human beings, who might attack and sack the town, to be certainly destroyed in the end. Every now and then people would glance nervously across the Wey, at the meadows towards Chertsey, but everything over there was still.

Across the Thames, except just where the boats landed, everything was quiet, in vivid contrast with the Surrey side. The people who landed there from the boats went tramping off down the lane. The big ferry-boat had just made a journey. Three or four soldiers stood on the lawn of the inn, staring and jesting at the fugitives, without offering to help. The inn was closed, as it was now within prohibited hours.

"What's that?" cried a boatman, and "Shut up, you fool!" said a man near me to a yelping dog. Then the sound came again, this time from the direction of

Chertsey, a muffled thud—the sound of a gun.

The fighting was beginning. Almost immediately unseen batteries across the river to our right, unseen because of the trees, took up the chorus, firing heavily one after the other. A woman screamed. Everyone stood arrested by the sudden stir of battle, near us and yet invisible to us. Nothing was to be seen save flat meadows, cows feeding unconcernedly for the most part, and silvery pollard willows motionless in the warm sunlight.

"The sojers'll stop 'em," said a woman beside me, doubtfully. A haziness rose over the treetops.

Then suddenly we saw a rush of smoke far away up the river, a puff of smoke that jerked up into the air and hung; and forthwith the ground heaved under foot and a heavy explosion shook the air, smashing two or three windows in the houses near, and leaving us astonished.

"Here they are!" shouted a man in a blue jersey. "Yonder! D'yer see them? Yonder!"

Quickly, one after the other, one, two, three, four of the armoured Martians appeared, far away over the little trees, across the flat meadows that stretched towards Chertsey, and striding hurriedly towards the river. Little cowled figures they seemed at first, going with a rolling motion and as fast as flying birds.

Then, advancing obliquely towards us, came a fifth. Their armoured bodies glittered in the sun as they swept swiftly forward upon the guns, growing rapidly larger as they drew nearer. One on the extreme left, the remotest that is, flourished a huge case high in the air, and the ghostly, terrible Heat-Ray I had already seen on Friday night smote towards Chertsey, and struck the town.

At sight of these strange, swift, and terrible creatures the crowd near the water's edge seemed to me to be for a moment horror-struck. There was no screaming or shouting, but a silence. Then a hoarse murmur and a movement of feet—a splashing from the water. A man, too frightened to drop the portmanteau he carried on his shoulder, swung round and sent me staggering with a blow from the corner of his burden. A woman thrust at me with her hand and rushed past me. I turned with the rush of the people, but I was not too terrified for thought. The terrible Heat-Ray was in my mind. To get under water! That was it!

"Get under water!" I shouted, unheeded.

I faced about again, and rushed towards the approaching Martian, rushed right down the gravelly beach and headlong into the water. Others did the same. A boatload of people put-

The Martians appeared.

ting back came leaping out as I rushed past. The stones under my feet were muddy and slippery, and the river was so low that I ran perhaps twenty feet scarcely waist-deep. Then, as the Martian towered overhead scarcely a couple of hundred yards away, I flung myself forward under the surface. The splashes of the people in the boats leaping into the river sounded like thunderclaps in my ears. People were landing hastily on both sides of the river. But the Martian machine took no more notice for the moment of the people running this way and that than a man would of the confusion of ants in a nest against which his foot has kicked. When, half suffocated, I raised my head above water, the Martian's hood pointed at the batteries that were still firing across the river, and as it advanced it swung loose what must have been the generator of the Heat-Ray.

In another moment it was on the bank, and in a stride wading halfway across. The knees of its foremost

The shell burst clean in the face of the Thing.

legs bent at the farther bank, and in another moment it had raised itself to its full height again, close to the village of Shepperton. Forthwith the six guns which, unknown to anyone on the right bank, had been hidden behind the outskirts of that village, fired simultaneously. The sudden near concussion, the last close upon the first, made my heart jump. The monster was already raising the case generating the Heat-Ray as the first shell burst six yards above the hood.

I gave a cry of astonishment. I saw and thought nothing of the other four Martian monsters; my attention was riveted upon the nearer incident. Simultaneously two other shells burst in the air near the body as the hood twisted round in time to receive, but not in time to dodge, the fourth shell.

The shell burst clean in the face of the Thing. The hood bulged, flashed, was whirled off in a dozen tattered fragments of red flesh and glittering metal.

"Hit!" shouted I, with something between a scream and a cheer.

I heard answering shouts from the people in the water about me. I could have leaped out of the water with that momentary exultation.

The decapitated colossus reeled like a drunken giant; but it did not fall over. It recovered its balance by a miracle, and, no longer heeding its steps and with the camera that fired the Heat-Ray now rigidly upheld, it reeled swiftly upon Shepperton. The living intelligence, the Martian within the hood, was slain and splashed to the four winds of heaven, and the Thing was now but a mere intricate device of metal whirling to destruction. It drove along in a straight line, incapable of guidance. It struck the tower of Shepperton Church, smashing it down as the impact of a battering ram might have done, swerved aside, blundered on and collapsed with tremendous force into the river out of my sight.

A violent explosion shook the air, and a spout of water, steam, mud, and shattered metal shot far up into the sky. As the camera of the Heat-Ray hit the water, the latter had immediately flashed into steam. In another moment a huge wave, like a muddy tidal bore but almost scaldingly hot, came sweeping round the bend upstream. I saw people struggling shorewards, and heard their screaming and shouting faintly above the seething and roar of the Martian's collapse.

For a moment I heeded nothing of the heat, forgot the patent need of self-preservation. I splashed through the tumultuous water, pushing aside a man in black to do so, until I could see round the bend. Half a dozen deserted boats pitched aimlessly upon the confusion of the waves. The fallen Martian came into sight downstream, lying across the river, and for the most part submerged.

Thick clouds of steam were pouring off the wreckage, and through the tumultuously whirling wisps I could see, intermittently and vaguely, the gigantic limbs churning the water and flinging a splash and spray of mud and froth into the air. The tentacles swayed and

struck like living arms, and, save for the helpless pur-
poselessness of these movements, it was as if some
wounded thing were struggling for its life amid the
waves. Enormous quantities of a ruddy-brown fluid
were spurting up in noisy jets out of the machine.

My attention was diverted from this death flurry by
a furious yelling, like that of the thing called a siren in
our manufacturing towns. A man, knee-deep near the
towing path, shouted inaudibly to me and pointed.
Looking back, I saw the other Martians advancing with
gigantic strides down the riverbank from the direction
of Chertsey. The Shepperton guns spoke this time
unavailingly.

At that I ducked at once under water, and, holding
my breath until movement was an agony, blundered
painfully ahead under the surface as long as I could.
The water was in a tumult about me, and rapidly growing hotter.

When for a moment I raised my head to take
breath and throw the hair and water from my eyes, the
steam was rising in a whirling white fog that at first
hid the Martians altogether. The noise was deafening.
Then I saw them dimly, colossal figures of grey, magnified by the mist. They had passed by me, and two
were stooping over the frothing, tumultuous ruins of
their comrade.

The third and fourth stood beside him in the water,
one perhaps two hundred yards from me, the other
towards Laleham. The generators of the Heat-Rays
waved high, and the hissing beams smote down this way
and that.

The air was full of sound, a deafening and confusing conflict of noises—the clangorous din of the
Martians, the crash of falling houses, the thud of trees,
fences, sheds flashing into flame, and the crackling and
roaring of fire. Dense black smoke was leaping up to
mingle with the steam from the river, and as the Heat-
Ray went to and fro over Weybridge its impact was
marked by flashes of incandescent white, that gave
place at once to a smoky dance of lurid flames. The
nearer houses still stood intact, awaiting their fate,
shadowy, faint and pallid in the steam, with the fire
behind them going to and fro.

As the camera and the Heat-Ray hit the water...

For a moment perhaps I stood there, breast-high in
the almost boiling water, dumbfounded at my position,
hopeless of escape. Through the reek I could see the
people who had been with me in the river scrambling
out of the water through the reeds, like little frogs hurrying through grass from the advance of a man, or running to and fro in utter dismay on the towing path.

Then suddenly the white flashes of the Heat-Ray
came leaping towards me. The houses caved in as they
dissolved at its touch, and darted out flames; the trees
changed to fire with a roar. The Ray flickered up and
down the towing path, licking off the people who ran
this way and that, and came down to the water's edge
not fifty yards from where I stood. It swept across the
river to Shepperton, and the water in its track rose in a
boiling weal crested with steam. I turned shoreward.

The tentacles swayed like living arms.

In another moment the huge wave, well-nigh at the boiling-point had rushed upon me. I screamed aloud, and scalded, half blinded, agonised, I staggered through the leaping, hissing water towards the shore. Had my foot stumbled, it would have been the end. I fell helplessly, in full sight of the Martians, upon the broad, bare gravelly spit that runs down to mark the angle of the Wey and Thames. I expected nothing but death.

I have a dim memory of the foot of a Martian coming down within a score of yards of my head, driving straight into the loose gravel, whirling it this way and that and lifting again; of a long suspense, and then of the four carrying the debris of their comrade between them, now clear and then presently faint through a veil of smoke, receding interminably, as it seemed to me, across a vast space of river and meadow. And then, very slowly, I realised that by a miracle I had escaped.

Chapter Thirteen

★ ★ ★

How I Fell in With the Curate

After getting this sudden lesson in the power of terrestrial weapons, the Martians retreated to their original position upon Horsell Common; and in their haste, and encumbered with the débris of their smashed companion, they no doubt overlooked many such a stray and negligible victim as myself. Had they left their comrade and pushed on forthwith, there was nothing at that time between them and London but batteries of twelve-pounder guns, and they would certainly have reached the capital in advance of the tidings of their approach; as sudden, dreadful, and destructive their advent would have been as the earthquake that destroyed Lisbon a century ago.

But they were in no hurry. Cylinder followed cylinder on its interplanetary flight; every twenty-four hours brought them reinforcement. And meanwhile the military and naval authorities, now fully alive to the tremendous power of their antagonists, worked with furious energy. Every minute a fresh gun came into position until, before twilight, every copse, every row of suburban villas on the hilly slopes about Kingston and Richmond, masked an expectant black muzzle. And through the charred and desolated area—perhaps twenty square miles altogether—that encircled the Martian encampment on Horsell Common, through charred and ruined villages among the green trees, through the blackened and smoking arcades that had been but a day ago pine spinneys, crawled the devoted scouts with the heliographs that were presently to warn the gunners of the Martian approach. But the Martians now understood our command of artillery and the danger of human proximity, and not a man ventured within a mile of either cylinder, save at the price of his life.

It would seem that these giants spent the earlier part of the afternoon in going to and fro, transferring everything from the second and third cylinders—the second in Addlestone Golf Links and the third at Pyrford—to their original pit on Horsell Common. Over that, above the blackened heather and ruined buildings that stretched far and wide, stood one as sentinel, while the rest abandoned their vast fighting-machines and descended into the pit. They were hard at work there far into the night, and the towering pillar of dense green smoke that rose therefrom could be seen from the hills about Merrow, and even, it is said, from Banstead and Epsom Downs.

And while the Martians behind me were thus preparing for their next sally, and in front of me Humanity gathered for the battle, I made my way with infinite pains and labour from the fire and smoke of burning Weybridge towards London.

I saw an abandoned boat, very small and remote, drifting down-stream; and throwing off the most of my sodden clothes, I went after it, gained it, and so escaped out of that destruction. There were no oars in the boat, but I contrived to paddle, as well as my parboiled hands would allow, down the river towards Halliford and Walton, going very tediously and continually looking behind me, as you may well understand. I followed the river, because I considered that the water gave me my best chance of escape should these giants return.

The hot water from the Martian's overthrow drifted downstream with me, so that for the best part of a mile I could see little of either bank. Once, however, I made out a string of black figures hurrying across the meadows from the direction of Weybridge. Halliford, it seemed, was deserted, and several of the houses facing the river were on fire. It was strange to see the place quite tranquil, quite desolate under the hot blue sky, with the smoke and little threads of flame going straight up into the heat of the afternoon. Never before had I seen houses burning without the accompaniment of an obstructive crowd. A little farther on the dry reeds up the bank were smoking and glowing, and a line of fire inland was marching steadily across a late field of hay.

For a long time I drifted, so painful and weary was I after the violence I had been through, and so intense the heat upon the water. Then my fears got the better of me again, and I resumed my paddling. The sun scorched my bare back. At last, as the bridge at Walton was coming into sight round the bend, my fever and faintness overcame my fears, and I landed on the Middlesex bank and

I contrived to paddle, as well as my parboiled hands would allow.

lay down, deadly sick, amid the long grass. I suppose the time was then about four or five o'clock. I got up presently, walked perhaps half a mile without meeting a soul, and then lay down again in the shadow of a hedge. I seem to remember talking, wanderingly, to myself during that last spurt. I was also very thirsty, and bitterly regretful I had drunk no more water. It is a curious thing that I felt angry with my wife; I cannot account for it, but my impotent desire to reach Leatherhead worried me excessively.

I do not clearly remember the arrival of the curate, so that probably I dozed. I became aware of him as a seated figure in soot-smudged shirt sleeves, and with his upturned, cleanshaven face staring at a faint flickering that danced over the sky. The sky was what is called a mackerel sky—rows and rows of faint down-plumes of cloud, just tinted with the midsummer sunset.

I sat up, and at the rustle of my motion he looked at me quickly.

"Have you any water?" I asked abruptly.

He shook his head.

"You have been asking for water for the last hour," he said.

For a moment we were silent, taking stock of each other. I dare say he found me a strange enough figure, naked, save for my water-soaked trousers and socks, scalded, and my face and shoulders blackened by the smoke. His face was a fair weakness, his chin retreated, and his hair lay in crisp, almost flaxen curls on his low forehead; his eyes were rather large, pale blue, and blankly staring. He spoke abruptly, looking vacantly away from me.

"What does it mean?" he said. "What do these things mean?"

I stared at him and made no answer.

He extended a thin white hand and spoke in almost a complaining tone.

"Why are these things permitted? What sins have we done? The morning service was over, I was walking through the roads to clear my brain for the afternoon, and then—fire, earthquake, death! As if it were Sodom and Gomorrah! All our work undone, all the work—— What are these Martians?"

"What are we?" I answered, clearing my throat.

He gripped his knees and turned to look at me again. For half a minute, perhaps, he stared silently.

"I was walking through the roads to clear my brain," he said. "And suddenly—fire, earthquake, death!"

He relapsed into silence, with his chin now sunken almost to his knees.

Presently he began waving his hand.

"All the work—all the Sunday schools—— What have we done—what has Weybridge done? Everything gone—everything destroyed. The church! We rebuilt it only three years ago. Gone! Swept out of existence! Why?"

Another pause, and he broke out again like one demented.

"The smoke of her burning goeth up for ever and ever!" he shouted.

His eyes flamed, and he pointed a lean finger in the direction of Weybridge.

By this time I was beginning to take his measure. The tremendous tragedy in which he had been involved—it was evident he was a fugitive from Weybridge—had driven him to the very verge of his reason.

"Are we far from Sunbury?" I said, in a matter-of-fact tone.

"What are we to do?" he asked. "Are these creatures everywhere? Has the earth been given over to them?"

"Are we far from Sunbury?"

"Only this morning I officiated at early celebration——"

"Things have changed," I said, quietly. "You must keep your head. There is still hope."

"Hope!"

"Yes. Plentiful hope—for all this destruction!"

I began to explain my view of our position. He listened at first, but as I went on the interest dawning in his eyes gave place to their former stare, and his regard wandered from me.

"This must be the beginning of the end," he said, interrupting me. "The end! The great and terrible day of the Lord! When men shall call upon the mountains and

"The smoke of her burning goeth up forever and ever!"

the rocks to fall upon them and hide them—hide them from the face of Him that sitteth upon the throne!"

I began to understand the position. I ceased my laboured reasoning, struggled to my feet, and, standing over him, laid my hand on his shoulder.

"Be a man!" said I. "You are scared out of your wits! What good is religion if it collapses under calamity? Think of what earthquakes and floods, wars and volcanoes, have done before to men! Did you think God had exempted Weybridge? He is not an insurance agent."

For a time he sat in blank silence.

"But how can we escape?" he asked, suddenly. "They are invulnerable, they are pitiless."

"Neither the one nor, perhaps, the other," I answered. "And the mightier they are the more sane and wary should we be. One of them was killed yonder not three hours ago."

"Killed!" he said, staring about him. "How can God's ministers be killed?"

"I saw it happen." I proceeded to tell him. "We have chanced to come in for the thick of it," said I, "and that is all."

"What is that flicker in the sky?" he asked abruptly.

I told him it was the heliograph signalling—that it was the sign of human help and effort in the sky.

"We are in the midst of it," I said, "quiet as it is. That flicker in the sky tells of the gathering storm. Yonder, I take it are the Martians, and Londonward, where those hills rise about Richmond and Kingston and the trees give cover, earthworks are being thrown up and guns are being placed. Presently the Martians will be coming this way again."

And even as I spoke he sprang to his feet and stopped me by a gesture.

"Listen!" he said.

From beyond the low hills across the water came the dull resonance of distant guns and a remote weird crying. Then everything was still. A cockchafer came droning over the hedge and past us. High in the west the crescent moon hung faint and pale above the smoke of Weybridge and Shepperton and the hot, still splendour of the sunset.

"We had better follow this path," I said, "northward."

Chapter Fourteen
★ ★ ★
In London

My younger brother was in London when the Martians fell at Woking. He was a medical student working for an imminent examination, and he heard nothing of the arrival until Saturday morning. The morning papers on Saturday contained, in addition to lengthy special articles on the planet Mars, on life in the planets, and so forth, a brief and vaguely worded telegram, all the more striking for its brevity.

The Martians, alarmed by the approach of a crowd, had killed a number of people with a quick-firing gun, so the story ran. The telegram concluded with the words: "Formidable as they seem to be, the Martians have not moved from the pit into which they have fallen, and, indeed, seem incapable of doing so. Probably this is due to the relative strength of the earth's gravitational energy." On that last text their leader-writer expanded very comfortingly.

*My brother was in London…
a medical student.*

Of course all the students in the crammer's biology class, to which my brother went that day, were intensely interested, but there were no signs of any unusual excitement in the streets. The afternoon papers puffed scraps of news under big headlines. They had nothing to tell beyond the movements of troops about the common, and the burning of the pine woods between Woking and Weybridge, until eight. Then the *St. James' Gazette*, in an extra-special edition, announced the bare fact of the interruption of telegraphic communication. This was thought to be due to the falling of burning pine trees across the line. Nothing more of the fighting was known that night, the night of my drive to Leatherhead and back.

My brother felt no anxiety about us, as he knew from the description in the papers that the cylinder was a good two miles from my house. He made up his mind to run down that night to me, in order, as he says, to see the Things before they were killed. He despatched a telegram, which never reached me, about four o'clock, and spent the evening at a music hall.

In London, also, on Saturday night there was a thunderstorm, and my brother reached Waterloo in a cab. On the platform from which the midnight train usually starts he learned, after some waiting, that an accident prevented trains from reaching Woking that night. The nature of the accident he could not ascertain; indeed, the railway authorities did not clearly know at that time. There was very little excitement in the station, as the officials, failing to realise that anything further than a breakdown between Byfleet and Woking junction had occurred, were running the theatre trains which usually passed through Woking round by Virginia Water or Guildford. They were busy making the necessary arrangements to alter the route of the

"The Martians appear to be moving slowly towards Chertsey or Windsor."

Southampton and Portsmouth Sunday League excursions. A nocturnal newspaper reporter, mistaking my brother for the traffic manager, to whom he bears a slight resemblance, waylaid and tried to interview him. Few people, excepting the railway officials, connected the breakdown with the Martians.

I have read, in another account of these events, that on Sunday morning "all London was electrified by the news from Woking." As a matter of fact, there was nothing to justify that very extravagant phrase. Plenty of Londoners did not hear of the Martians until the panic of Monday morning. Those who did took some time to realise all that the hastily worded telegrams in the Sunday papers conveyed. The majority of people in London do not read Sunday papers.

The habit of personal security, moreover, is so deeply fixed in the Londoner's mind, and startling intelligence so much a matter of course in the papers, that they could read without any personal tremors: "About seven o'clock last night the Martians came out of the cylinder, and, moving about under an armour of metallic shields, have completely wrecked Woking station with the adjacent houses, and massacred an entire battalion of the Cardigan Regiment. No details are known. Maxims have been absolutely useless against their armour; the field guns have been disabled by them. Flying hussars have been galloping into Chertsey. The Martians appear to be moving slowly towards Chertsey or Windsor. Great anxiety prevails in West Surrey, and earthworks are being thrown up to check the advance Londonward." That was how the Sunday *Sun* put it, and a clever and remarkably prompt "handbook" article in the *Referee* compared the affair to a menagerie suddenly let loose in a village.

No one in London knew positively of the nature of the armoured Martians, and there was still a fixed idea that these monsters must be sluggish: "crawling," "creeping painfully"—such expressions occurred in almost all the earlier reports. None of the telegrams could have been written by an eyewitness of their advance. The Sunday papers printed separate editions as further news came to hand, some even in default of it. But there was practically nothing more to tell people until late in the afternoon, when the authorities gave the press agencies the news in their possession. It was stated that the people of Walton and Weybridge, and all the district were pouring along the roads Londonward, and that was all.

My brother went to church at the Foundling Hospital in the morning, still in ignorance of what had happened on the previous night. There he heard allusions made to the invasion, and a special prayer for peace. Coming out, he bought a *Referee*. He became alarmed at the news in this, and went again to Waterloo station to find out if communication were restored. The omnibuses, carriages, cyclists, and innumerable people walking in their best clothes seemed scarcely affected by the strange intelligence that the news venders were disseminating. People were interested, or, if alarmed, alarmed only on account of the local residents. At the station he heard for the first time that the Windsor and Chertsey lines were now interrupted. The porters told him that several remarkable telegrams had been received in the morning from Byfleet and Chertsey stations, but that these had abruptly ceased. My brother could get very little precise detail out of them.

"There's fighting going on about Weybridge" was the extent of their information.

The train service was now very much disorganised. Quite a number of people who had been expecting friends from places on the South-Western network were standing about the station. One grey-headed old gentleman came and abused the South-Western Company bitterly to my brother. "It wants showing up," he said.

One or two trains came in from Richmond, Putney, and Kingston, containing people who had gone out for a day's boating and found the locks closed and a feeling of panic in the air. A man in a blue and white blazer addressed my brother, full of strange tidings.

"There's hosts of people driving into Kingston in traps and carts and things, with boxes of valuables and all that," he said. "They come from Molesey and Weybridge and Walton, and they say there's been guns heard at Chertsey, heavy firing, and that mounted soldiers have told them to get off at once because the Martians are coming. We heard guns firing at Hampton Court station, but we thought it was thunder. What the dickens does it all mean? The Martians can't get out of their pit, can they?"

My brother could not tell him.

Afterwards he found that the vague feeling of alarm had spread to the clients of the underground railway, and that the Sunday excursionists began to return from all over the South-Western "lung"—Barnes, Wimbledon, Richmond Park, Kew, and so forth—at unnaturally early hours; but not a soul had anything more than vague hearsay to tell of. Everyone connected with the terminus seemed ill-tempered.

About five o'clock the gathering crowd in the station was immensely excited by the opening of the line of communication, which is almost invariably closed, between the South-Eastern and the South-Western stations, and the passage of carriage trucks bearing huge guns and carriages crammed with soldiers. These were the guns that were brought up from Woolwich and Chatham to cover Kingston. There was an exchange of pleasantries: "You'll get eaten!" "We're the beast-tamers!" and so forth. A little while after that a squad of police came into the station and began to clear the public off the platforms, and my brother went out into the street again.

The church bells were ringing for evensong, and a squad of Salvation Army lassies came singing down Waterloo Road. On the bridge a number of loafers were watching a curious brown scum that came drifting down the stream in patches. The sun was just setting, and the Clock Tower and the Houses of Parliament rose against one of the most peaceful skies it is possible to imagine, a sky of gold, barred with long transverse stripes of reddish-purple cloud. There was talk of a

On the bridge were a number of idle loafers.

floating body. One of the men there, a reservist he said he was, told my brother he had seen the heliograph flickering in the west.

In Wellington Street my brother met a couple of sturdy roughs who had just been rushed out of Fleet Street with still-wet newspapers and staring placards. "Dreadful catastrophe!" they bawled one to the other down Wellington Street. "Fighting at Weybridge! Full description! Repulse of the Martians! London in Danger!" He had to give threepence for a copy of that paper.

Then it was, and then only, that he realised something of the full power and terror of these monsters. He learned that they were not merely a handful of small sluggish creatures, but that they were minds swaying vast mechanical bodies; and that they could move swiftly and smite with such power that even the mightiest guns could not stand against them.

They were described as "vast spiderlike machines, nearly a hundred feet high, capable of the speed of an express train, and able to shoot out a beam of intense heat." Masked batteries, chiefly of field guns, had been planted in the country about Horsell Common, and especially between the Woking district and London. Five of the machines had been seen moving towards the Thames, and one, by a happy chance, had been destroyed. In the other cases the shells had missed, and the batteries had been at once annihilated by the Heat-Rays. Heavy losses of soldiers were mentioned, but the tone of the despatch was optimistic.

The Martians had been repulsed; they were not invulnerable. They had retreated to their triangle of cylinders again, in the circle about Woking. Signallers with heliographs were pushing forward upon them from all sides. Guns were in rapid transit from Windsor, Portsmouth, Aldershot, Woolwich—even from the north; among others, long wire-guns of ninety-five tons from Woolwich. Altogether one hundred and sixteen were in position or being hastily placed, chiefly covering London. Never before in England had there been such a vast or rapid concentration of military material.

Any further cylinders that fell, it was hoped, could be destroyed at once by high explosives, which were being rapidly manufactured and distributed. No doubt, ran the report, the situation was of the strangest and gravest description, but the public was exhorted to avoid and discourage panic. No doubt the Martians were strange and terrible in the extreme, but at the outside there could not be more than twenty of them against our millions.

The authorities had reason to suppose, from the size of the cylinders, that at the outside there could not be more than five in each cylinder—fifteen altogether. And one at least was disposed of—perhaps more. The public would be fairly warned of the approach of danger, and elaborate measures were being taken for the protection of the people in the threatened southwestern suburbs. And so, with reiterated assurances of the safety of London and the ability of the authorities to cope with the difficulty, this quasi-proclamation closed.

This was printed in enormous type on paper so fresh that it was still wet, and there had been no time to add a word of comment. It was curious, my brother said, to see how ruthlessly the usual contents of the paper had been hacked and taken out to give this place.

All down Wellington Street people could be seen fluttering out the pink sheets and reading, and the Strand was suddenly noisy with the voices of an army of hawkers following these pioneers. Men came scrambling off buses to secure copies. Certainly this news excited people intensely, whatever their previous apathy. The

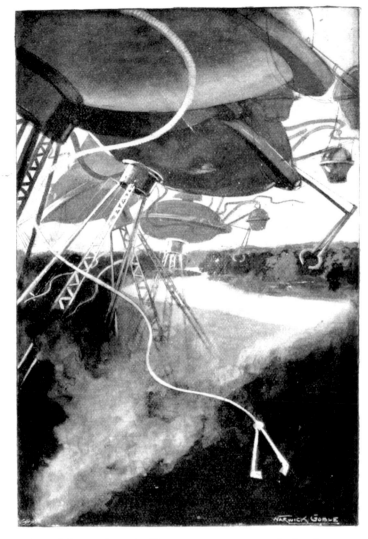

Five of the machines had been seen moving towards the Thames.

people on the omnibuses. People in fashionable clothing peeped at them out of cabs. They stopped at the Square as if undecided which way to take, and finally turned eastward along the Strand. Some way behind these came a man in workday clothes, riding one of those old-fashioned tricycles with a small front wheel. He was dirty and white in the face.

My brother turned down towards Victoria, and met a number of such people. He had a vague idea that he might see something of me. He noticed an unusual number of police regulating the traffic. Some of the refugees were exchanging news with the people on the omnibuses. One was professing to have seen the Martians. "Boilers on stilts, I tell you, striding along like men." Most of them were excited and animated by their strange experience.

Beyond Victoria the public-houses were doing a lively trade with these arrivals. At all the street corners groups of people were reading papers, talking excitedly, or staring at these unusual Sunday visitors. They seemed to increase as night drew on, until at last the roads, my brother said, were like Epsom High Street on a Derby Day. My brother addressed several of these fugitives and got unsatisfactory answers from most.

None of them could tell him any news of Woking except one man, who assured him that Woking had been entirely destroyed on the previous night.

"I come from Byfleet," he said; "man on a bicycle came through the place in the early morning, and ran from door to door warning us to come away. Then came soldiers. We went out to look, and there were clouds of smoke to the south—nothing but smoke, and not a soul coming that way. Then we heard the guns at Chertsey, and folks coming from Weybridge. So I've locked up my house and come on."

At the time there was a strong feeling in the streets that the authorities were to blame for their incapacity to dispose of the invaders without all this inconvenience.

About eight o'clock a noise of heavy firing was distinctly audible all over the south of London. My brother could not hear it for the traffic in the main thoroughfares, but by striking through the quiet back streets to the river he was able to distinguish it quite plainly.

shutters of a map shop in the Strand were being taken down, my brother said, and a man in his Sunday raiment, lemon-yellow gloves even, was visible inside the window hastily fastening maps of Surrey to the glass.

Going on along the Strand to Trafalgar Square, the paper in his hand, my brother saw some of the fugitives from West Surrey. There was a man with his wife and two boys and some articles of furniture in a cart such as greengrocers use. He was driving from the direction of Westminster Bridge; and close behind him came a hay waggon with five or six respectable-looking people in it, and some boxes and bundles. The faces of these people were haggard, and their entire appearance contrasted conspicuously with the Sabbath-best appearance of the

He walked from Westminster to his apartments near Regent's Park, about two. He was now very anxious on my account, and disturbed at the evident magnitude of the trouble. His mind was inclined to run, even as mine had run on Saturday, on military details. He thought of all those silent, expectant guns, of the suddenly nomadic countryside; he tried to imagine "boilers on stilts" a hundred feet high.

There were one or two cartloads of refugees passing along Oxford Street, and several in the Marylebone Road, but so slowly was the news spreading that Regent Street and Portland Place were full of their usual Sunday-night promenaders, albeit they talked in groups, and along the edge of Regent's Park there were as many silent couples "walking out" together under the scattered gas lamps as ever there had been. The night was warm and still, and a little oppressive; the sound of guns continued intermittently, and after midnight there seemed to be sheet lightning in the south.

He read and re-read the paper, fearing the worst had happened to me. He was restless, and after supper prowled out again aimlessly. He returned and tried in vain to divert his attention to his examination notes. He

Then he jumped out of bed
and ran to the window.

went to bed a little after midnight, and was awakened from lurid dreams in the small hours of Monday by the sound of door knockers, feet running in the street, distant drumming, and a clamour of bells. Red reflections danced on the ceiling. For a moment he lay astonished, wondering whether day had come or the world gone mad. Then he jumped out of bed and ran to the window.

His room was an attic and as he thrust his head out, up and down the street there were a dozen echoes to the noise of his window sash, and heads in every kind of night disarray appeared. Enquiries were being shouted. "They are coming!" bawled a policeman, hammering at the door; "the Martians are coming!" and hurried to the next door.

The sound of drumming and trumpeting came from the Albany Street Barracks, and every church within earshot was hard at work killing sleep with a vehement disorderly tocsin. There was a noise of doors opening, and window after window in the houses opposite flashed from darkness into yellow illumination.

Up the street came galloping a closed carriage, bursting abruptly into noise at the corner, rising to a clattering climax under the window, and dying away slowly in the distance. Close on the rear of this came a couple of cabs, the forerunners of a long procession of flying vehicles, going for the most part to Chalk Farm station, where the North-Western special trains were loading up, instead of coming down the gradient into Euston.

For a long time my brother stared out of the window in blank astonishment, watching the policemen hammering at door after door, and delivering their incomprehensible message. Then the door behind him opened, and the man who lodged across the landing came in, dressed only in shirt, trousers, and slippers, his braces loose about his waist, his hair disordered from his pillow.

"What the devil is it?" he asked. "A fire? What a devil of a row!"

They both craned their heads out of the window, straining to hear what the policemen were shouting. People were coming out of the side streets, and standing in groups at the corners talking.

"What the devil is it all about?" said my brother's fellow lodger.

My brother answered him vaguely and began to dress, running with each garment to the window in order to miss nothing of the growing excitement. And presently men selling unnaturally early newspapers came bawling into the street:

"London in danger of suffocation! The Kingston and Richmond defences forced! Fearful massacres in the Thames Valley!"

And all about him—in the rooms below, in the houses on each side and across the road, and behind in the Park Terraces and in the hundred other streets of that part of Marylebone, and the Westbourne Park district and St. Pancras, and westward and northward in Kilburn and St. John's Wood and Hampstead, and eastward in Shoreditch and Highbury and Haggerston and Hoxton, and, indeed, through all the vastness of London from Ealing to East Ham—people were rubbing their eyes, and opening windows to stare out and ask aimless questions, dressing hastily as the first breath of the coming storm of Fear blew through the streets. It was the dawn of the great panic. London, which had gone to bed on Sunday night oblivious and inert, was awakened, in the small hours of Monday morning, to a vivid sense of danger.

Unable from his window to learn what was happening, my brother went down and out into the street, just as the sky between the parapets of the houses grew pink with the early dawn. The flying people on foot and in vehicles grew more numerous every moment. "Black Smoke!" he heard people crying, and again "Black Smoke!" The contagion of such a unanimous fear was inevitable. As my brother hesitated on the door-step, he saw another news vender approaching, and got a paper forthwith. The man was running away with the rest, and selling his papers for a shilling each as he ran—a grotesque mingling of profit and panic.

And from this paper my brother read that catastrophic despatch of the Commander-in-Chief:

"The Martians are able to discharge enormous clouds of a black and poisonous vapour by means of rockets. They have smothered our batteries, destroyed Richmond, Kingston, and Wimbledon, and are advancing slowly towards London, destroying everything on

"The Martians are able to discharge enormous clouds of a black and poisonous vapour."

the way. It is impossible to stop them. There is no safety from the Black Smoke but in instant flight."

That was all, but it was enough. The whole population of the great six-million city was stirring, slipping, running; presently it would be pouring *en masse* northward.

"Black Smoke!" the voices cried. "Fire!"

The bells of the neighbouring church made a jangling tumult, a cart carelessly driven smashed, amid shrieks and curses, against the water trough up the street. Sickly yellow lights went to and fro in the houses, and some of the passing cabs flaunted unextinguished lamps. And overhead the dawn was growing brighter, clear and steady and calm.

He heard footsteps running to and fro in the rooms, and up and down stairs behind him. His landlady came to the door, loosely wrapped in dressing gown and shawl; her husband followed ejaculating.

As my brother began to realise the import of all these things, he turned hastily to his own room, put all his available money—some ten pounds altogether—into his pockets, and went out again into the streets.

Chapter Fifteen
★ ★ ★
What Had Happened in Surrey

It was while the curate had sat and talked so wildly to me under the hedge in the flat meadows near Halliford, and while my brother was watching the fugitives stream over Westminster Bridge, that the Martians had resumed the offensive. So far as one can ascertain from the conflicting accounts that have been put forth, the majority of them remained busied with preparations in the Horsell pit until nine that night, hurrying on some operation that disengaged huge volumes of green smoke.

But three certainly came out about eight o'clock and, advancing slowly and cautiously, made their way through Byfleet and Pyrford towards Ripley and Weybridge, and so came in sight of the expectant batteries against the setting sun. These Martians did not advance in a body, but in a line, each perhaps a mile and a half from his nearest fellow. They communicated with one another by means of sirenlike howls, running up and down the scale from one note to another.

It was this howling and firing of the guns at Ripley and St. George's Hill that we had heard at Upper Halliford. The Ripley gunners, unseasoned artillery volunteers who ought never to have been placed in such a position, fired one wild, premature, ineffectual volley, and bolted on horse and foot through the deserted village, while the Martian, without using his Heat-Ray, walked serenely over their guns, stepped gingerly among them, passed in front of them, and so came unexpectedly upon the guns in Painshill Park, which he destroyed.

The St. George's Hill men, however, were better led or of a better mettle. Hidden by a pine wood as they were, they seem to have been quite unsuspected by the Martian nearest to them. They laid their guns as deliberately as if they had been on parade, and fired at about a thousand yards' range.

The shells flashed all round him, and he was seen to advance a few paces, stagger, and go down. Everybody yelled together, and the guns were reloaded in frantic haste. The overthrown Martian set up a prolonged ululation, and immediately a second glittering giant, answering him, appeared over the trees to the south. It would seem that a leg of the tripod had been smashed by one of the shells. The whole of the second volley flew wide of the Martian on the ground, and, simultaneously, both his companions brought their Heat-Rays to bear on the battery. The ammunition blew up, the pine trees all about the guns flashed into fire, and only one or two of the men who were already running over the crest of the hill escaped.

After this it would seem that the three took counsel together and halted, and the scouts who were watching them report that they remained absolutely stationary for the next half hour. The Martian who had been overthrown crawled tediously out of his hood, a small brown figure, oddly suggestive from that distance of a speck of blight, and apparently engaged in the repair of his support. About nine he had finished, for his cowl was then seen above the trees again.

It was a few minutes past nine that night when these three sentinels were joined by four other Martians, each carrying a thick black tube. A similar tube was handed to each of the three, and the seven proceeded to distribute themselves at equal distances along a curved line between St. George's Hill, Weybridge, and the village of Send, southwest of Ripley.

A dozen rockets sprang out of the hills before them so soon as they began to move, and warned the waiting batteries about Ditton and Esher. At the same time four of their fighting machines, similarly armed with tubes, crossed the river, and two of them, black against the western sky, came into sight of myself and the curate as we hurried wearily and painfully along the road that runs northward out of Halliford. They moved, as it seemed to us, upon a cloud, for a milky mist covered the fields and rose to a third of their height.

At this sight the curate cried faintly in his throat, and began running; but I knew it was no good running from a Martian, and I turned aside and crawled through dewy nettles and brambles into the broad ditch by the side of the road. He looked back, saw what I was doing, and turned to join me.

The two halted, the nearer to us standing and facing Sunbury, the remoter being a grey indistinctness towards the evening star, away towards Staines.

The occasional howling of the Martians had ceased; they took up their positions in the huge crescent about their cylinders in absolute silence. It was a crescent with twelve miles between its horns. Never since the devising of gunpowder was the beginning of a battle so still. To us and to an observer about Ripley it would have had precisely the same effect—the Martians seemed in solitary possession of the darkling night, lit only as it was by the slender moon, the stars, the afterglow of the daylight, and the ruddy glare from St. George's Hill and the woods of Painshill.

But facing that crescent everywhere—at Staines, Hounslow, Ditton, Esher, Ockham, behind hills and woods south of the river, and across the flat grass meadows to the north of it, wherever a cluster of trees or village houses gave sufficient cover—the guns were waiting. The signal rockets burst and rained their sparks

through the night and vanished, and the spirit of all those watching batteries rose to a tense expectation. The Martians had but to advance into the line of fire, and instantly those motionless black forms of men, those guns glittering so darkly in the early night, would explode into a thunderous fury of battle.

No doubt the thought that was uppermost in a thousand of those vigilant minds, even as it was uppermost in mine, was the riddle—how much they understood of us. Did they grasp

A leg of the tripod had been smashed.

that we in our millions were organized, disciplined, working together? Or did they interpret our spurts of fire, the sudden stinging of our shells, our steady investment of their encampment, as we should the furious unanimity of onslaught in a disturbed hive of bees? Did they dream they might exterminate us? (At that time no one knew what food they needed.) A hundred such questions struggled together in my mind as I watched that vast sentinel shape. And in the back of my mind was the sense of all the huge unknown and hidden forces Londonward. Had they prepared pitfalls? Were the powder mills at Hounslow ready as a snare? Would the Londoners have the heart and courage to make a greater Moscow of their mighty province of houses?

Then, after an interminable time, as it seemed to us, crouching and peering through the hedge, came a sound like the distant concussion of a gun. Another nearer, and then another. And then the Martian beside us raised his tube on high and discharged it, gunwise, with a heavy report that made the ground heave. The one towards Staines answered him. There was no flash, no smoke, simply that loaded detonation.

I was so excited by these heavy minute-guns following one another that I so far forgot my personal safety and my scalded hands as to clamber up into the hedge and stare towards Sunbury. As I did so a second report followed, and a big projectile hurtled overhead towards Hounslow. I expected at least to see smoke or fire, or some such evidence of its work. But all I saw was the deep blue sky above, with one solitary star, and the white mist spreading wide and low beneath. And there had been no crash, no answering explosion. The silence was restored; the minute lengthened to three.

"What has happened?" said the curate, standing up beside me.

"Heaven knows!" said I.

A bat flickered by and vanished. A distant tumult of shouting began and ceased. I looked again at the Martian, and saw he was now moving eastward along the riverbank, with a swift, rolling motion.

Every moment I expected the fire of some hidden battery to spring upon him; but the evening calm was unbroken. The figure of the Martian grew smaller as he receded, and presently the mist and the gathering night had swallowed him up. By a common impulse we clambered higher. Towards Sunbury was a dark appearance, as though a conical hill had suddenly come into being there, hiding our view of the farther country; and then, remoter across the river, over Walton, we saw another such summit. These hill-like forms grew lower and broader even as we stared.

Moved by a sudden thought, I looked northward, and there I perceived a third of these cloudy black kopjes had risen.

Everything had suddenly become very still. Far away to the southeast, marking the quiet, we heard the Martians hooting to one another, and then the air quivered again with the distant thud of their guns. But the earthly artillery made no reply.

Now at the time we could not understand these things, but later I was to learn the meaning of these ominous kopjes that gathered in the twilight. Each of the Martians, standing in the great crescent I have described, had discharged, by means of the gunlike tube he carried, a huge canister over whatever hill, copse, cluster of houses, or other possible cover for guns, chanced to be in front of him. Some fired only one of these, some two—as in the case of the one we had seen; the one at Ripley is said to have discharged no fewer than five at that time. These canisters smashed on striking the ground—they did not explode—and incontinently disengaged an enormous volume of heavy, inky vapour, coiling and pouring upward in a huge and ebony cumulus cloud, a gaseous hill that sank and spread itself slowly over the surrounding country. And the touch of that vapour, the inhaling of its pungent wisps, was death to all that breathes.

It was heavy, this vapour, heavier than the densest smoke, so that, after the first tumultuous uprush and outflow of its impact, it sank down through the air and poured over the ground in a manner rather liquid than gaseous, abandoning the hills, and streaming into the valleys and ditches and watercourses even as I have heard the carbonic-acid gas that pours from volcanic clefts is wont to do. And where it came upon water some chemical action occurred, and the surface would be instantly covered with a powdery scum that sank slowly and made way for more. The scum was absolutely insoluble, and it is a strange thing, seeing the instant effect of the gas, that one could drink without hurt the water from which it had been strained. The vapour did not diffuse as a true gas would do. It hung together in banks, flowing sluggishly down the slope of the land and driving reluctantly before the wind, and very slowly it combined with the mist and moisture of the air, and sank to the earth in the form of dust. Save that an unknown element giving a group of four lines in the blue of the spectrum is concerned, we are still entirely ignorant of the nature of this substance.

Once the tumultuous upheaval of its dispersion was over, the black smoke clung so closely to the ground, even before its precipitation, that fifty feet up in the air, on the roofs and upper stories of high houses and on great trees, there was a chance of escaping its poison altogether, as was proved even that night at Street Cobham and Ditton.

The man who escaped at the former place tells a wonderful story of the strangeness of its coiling flow, and how he looked down from the church spire and saw the houses of the village rising like ghosts out of its inky nothingness. For a day and a half he remained there, weary, starving and sun-scorched, the earth under the blue sky and against the prospect of the distant hills a velvet-black expanse, with red roofs, green trees, and, later, black-veiled shrubs and gates, barns, outhouses, and walls, rising here and there into the sunlight.

But that was at Street Cobham, where the black vapour was allowed to remain until it sank of its own accord into the ground. As a rule the Martians, when it had served its purpose, cleared the air of it again by wading into it and directing a jet of steam upon it.

This they did with the vapour banks near us, as we saw in the starlight from the window of a deserted house at Upper Halliford, whither we had returned. From there we could see the searchlights on Richmond Hill and Kingston Hill going to and fro, and about eleven the windows rattled, and we heard the sound of the huge siege guns that had been put in position there. These continued intermittently for the space of a quarter of an hour, sending chance shots at the invisible Martians at Hampton and Ditton, and then the pale beams of the electric light vanished, and were replaced by a bright red glow.

Then the fourth cylinder fell—a brilliant green meteor—as I learned afterwards, in Bushey Park. Before the guns on the Richmond and Kingston line of hills

They moved, as it seemed to us, upon a cloud.

A strange and horrible antagonist of vapour striding upon its victims.

began, there was a fitful cannonade far away in the southwest, due, I believe, to guns being fired haphazard before the black vapour could overwhelm the gunners.

So, setting about it as methodically as men might smoke out a wasps' nest, the Martians spread this strange stifling vapour over the Londonward country. The horns of the crescent slowly moved apart, until at last they formed a line from Hanwell to Coombe and Malden. All night through their destructive tubes advanced. Never once, after the Martian at St. George's Hill was brought down, did they give the artillery the ghost of a chance against them. Wherever there was a possibility of guns being laid for them unseen, a fresh canister of the black vapour was discharged, and where the guns were openly displayed the Heat-Ray was brought to bear.

By midnight the blazing trees along the slopes of Richmond Park and the glare of Kingston Hill threw their light upon a network of black smoke, blotting out the whole valley of the Thames and extending as far as the eye could reach. And through this two Martians slowly waded, and turned their hissing steam jets this way and that.

They were sparing of the Heat-Ray that night, either because they had but a limited supply of material for its production or because they did not wish to destroy the country but only to crush and overawe the opposition they had aroused. In the latter aim they certainly succeeded. Sunday night was the end of the organised opposition to their movements. After that no body of men would stand against them, so hopeless was the enterprise. Even the crews of the torpedo-boats and destroyers that had brought their quickfirers up the Thames refused to stop, mutinied, and went down again. The only offensive operation men ventured upon after that night was the preparation of mines and pitfalls, and even in that their energies were frantic and spasmodic.

One has to imagine, as well as one may, the fate of those batteries towards Esher, waiting so tensely in the twilight. Survivors there were none. One may picture the orderly expectation, the officers alert and watchful, the gunners ready, the ammunition piled to hand, the limber gunners with their horses and waggons, the groups of civilian spectators standing as near as they were permitted, the evening stillness, the ambulances and hospital tents with the burned and wounded from Weybridge; then the dull resonance of the shots the Martians fired, and the clumsy projectile whirling over the trees and houses and smashing amid the neighbouring fields.

One may picture, too, the sudden shifting of the attention, the swiftly spreading coils and bellyings of that blackness advancing headlong, towering heavenward, turning the twilight to a palpable darkness, a strange and horrible antagonist of vapour striding upon its victims, men and horses near it seen dimly, running, shrieking, falling headlong, shouts of dismay, the guns suddenly abandoned, men choking and writhing on the ground, and the swift broadening-out of the opaque cone of smoke. And then night and extinction—nothing but a silent mass of impenetrable vapour hiding its dead.

Before dawn the black vapour was pouring through the streets of Richmond, and the disintegrating organism of government was, with a last expiring effort, rousing the population of London to the necessity of flight.

Chapter Sixteen

★ ★ ★

The Exodus from London

So you understand the roaring wave of fear that swept through the greatest city in the world just as Monday was dawning—the stream of flight rising swiftly to a torrent, lashing in a foaming tumult round the railway stations, banked up into a horrible struggle about the shipping in the Thames, and hurrying by every available channel northward and eastward. By ten o'clock the police organisation, and by midday even the railway organisations, were losing coherency, losing shape and efficiency, guttering, softening, running at last in that swift liquefaction of the social body.

All the railway lines north of the Thames and the SouthEastern people at Cannon Street had been warned by midnight on Sunday, and trains were being filled. People were fighting savagely for standing-room in the carriages even at two o'clock. By three, people were being trampled and crushed even in Bishopsgate Street, a couple of hundred yards or more from Liverpool Street station; revolvers were fired, people stabbed, and the policemen who had been sent to direct the traffic, exhausted and infuriated, were breaking the heads of the people they were called out to protect.

And as the day advanced and the engine drivers and stokers refused to return to London, the pressure of the flight drove the people in an ever-thickening multitude away from the stations and along the northward-running roads. By midday a Martian had been seen at Barnes, and a cloud of slowly sinking black vapour drove along the Thames and across the flats of Lambeth, cutting off all escape over the bridges in its sluggish advance. Another bank drove over Ealing, and surrounded a little island of survivors on Castle Hill, alive, but unable to escape.

After a fruitless struggle to get aboard a North-Western train at Chalk Farm—the engines of the trains that had loaded in the goods yard there *ploughed* through shrieking people, and a dozen stalwart men fought to keep the crowd from crushing the driver against his furnace—my brother emerged upon the Chalk Farm road, dodged across through a hurrying swarm of vehicles, and had the luck to be foremost in the sack of a cycle shop. The front tire of the machine he got was punctured in dragging it through the window, but he got up and off, notwithstanding, with no further injury than a cut wrist. The steep foot of Haverstock Hill was impassable owing to several overturned horses, and my brother struck into Belsize Road.

So he got out of the fury of the panic, and, skirting the Edgware Road, reached Edgware about seven, fasting and wearied, but well ahead of the crowd. Along the road people were standing in the roadway, curious, wondering. He was passed by a number of cyclists, some horsemen, and two motor cars. A mile from Edgware the rim of the wheel broke, and the machine became unridable. He left it by the roadside and trudged through the village. There were shops half opened in the main street of the place, and people crowded on the pavement and in the doorways and windows, staring astonished at this extraordinary procession of fugitives that was beginning. He succeeded in getting some food at an inn.

For a time he remained in Edgware not knowing what next to do. The flying people increased in number. Many of them, like my brother, seemed inclined to loiter in the place. There was no fresh news of the invaders from Mars.

At that time the road was crowded, but as yet far from congested. Most of the fugitives at that hour were mounted on cycles, but there were soon motor cars, hansom cabs, and carriages hurrying along, and the dust hung in heavy clouds along the road to St. Albans.

It was perhaps a vague idea of making his way to Chelmsford, where some friends of his lived, that at last induced my brother to strike into a quiet lane running eastward. Presently he came upon a stile, and, crossing it, followed a footpath northeastward. He passed near several farmhouses and some little places whose names he did not learn. He saw few fugitives until, in a grass lane towards High Barnet, he happened upon two ladies who became his fellow travellers. He came upon them just in time to save them.

He heard their screams, and, hurrying round the corner, saw a couple of men struggling to drag them out of the little pony-chaise in which they had been driving, while a third with difficulty held the frightened pony's head. One of the ladies, a short woman dressed in white, was simply screaming; the other, a dark, slender figure, slashed at the man who gripped her arm with a whip she held in her disengaged hand.

My brother immediately grasped the situation, shouted, and hurried towards the struggle. One of the men desisted and turned towards him, and my brother, realising from his antagonist's face that a fight was unavoidable, and being an expert boxer, went into him forthwith and sent him down against the wheel of the chaise.

It was no time for pugilistic chivalry and my brother laid him quiet with a kick, and gripped the collar of the man who pulled at the slender lady's arm. He heard the clatter of hoofs, the whip stung across his face, a third antagonist struck him between the eyes, and the man he held wrenched himself free and made off down the lane in the direction from which he had come.

Partly stunned, he found himself facing the man who had held the horse's head, and became aware of the chaise receding from him down the lane, swaying from side to side, and with the women in it looking back. The man before him, a burly rough, tried to close, and he stopped him with a blow in the face. Then, realising that he was deserted, he dodged round and made off down the lane after the chaise, with the sturdy man close behind him, and the fugitive, who had turned now, following remotely.

Suddenly he stumbled and fell; his immediate pursuer went headlong, and he rose to his feet to find himself with a couple of antagonists again. He would have had little chance against them had not the slender lady very pluckily pulled up and returned to his help. It seems she had had a revolver all this time, but it had been under the seat when she and her companion were attacked. She fired at six yards' distance, narrowly missing my brother. The less courageous of the robbers made off, and his companion followed him, cursing his cowardice. They both stopped in sight down the lane, where the third man lay insensible.

"Take this!" said the slender lady, and she gave my brother her revolver.

She fired at six yards' distance.

"Go back to the chaise," said my brother, wiping the blood from his split lip.

She turned without a word—they were both panting—and they went back to where the lady in white struggled to hold back the frightened pony.

The robbers had evidently had enough of it. When my brother looked again they were retreating.

"I'll sit here," said my brother, "if I may"; and he got upon the empty front seat. The lady looked over her shoulder.

"Give me the reins," she said, and laid the whip along the pony's side. In another moment a bend in the road hid the three men from my brother's eyes.

So, quite unexpectedly, my brother found himself, panting, with a cut mouth, a bruised jaw, and bloodstained knuckles, driving along an unknown lane with these two women.

He learned they were the wife and the younger sister of a surgeon living at Stanmore, who had come in the small hours from a dangerous case at Pinner, and heard at some railway station on his way of the Martian advance. He had hurried home, roused the women—their servant had left them two days before—packed some provisions, put his revolver under the seat—luckily for my brother—and told them to drive on to Edgware, with the idea of getting a train there. He stopped behind to tell the neighbours. He would overtake them, he said, at about half past four in the morning, and now it was nearly nine and they had seen nothing of him. They could not stop in Edgware because of the growing traffic through the place, and so they had come into this side lane.

That was the story they told my brother in fragments when presently they stopped again, nearer to New Barnet. He promised to stay with them, at least until they could determine what to do, or until the missing man arrived, and professed to be an expert shot with the revolver—a weapon strange to him—in order to give them confidence.

They made a sort of encampment by the wayside, and the pony became happy in the hedge. He told them of his own escape out of London, and all that he knew of these Martians and their ways. The sun crept higher in the sky, and after a time their talk died out and gave place to an uneasy state of anticipation. Several wayfarers came along the lane, and of these my brother gathered such news as he could. Every broken answer he had deepened his impression of the great disaster that had come on humanity, deepened his persuasion of the immediate necessity for prosecuting this flight. He urged the matter upon them.

"We have money," said the slender woman, and hesitated.

Her eyes met my brother's, and her hesitation ended.

"So have I," said my brother.

She explained that they had as much as thirty pounds in gold, besides a five-pound note, and suggested that with that they might get upon a train at St. Albans or New Barnet. My brother thought that was hopeless, seeing the fury of the Londoners to crowd upon the trains, and broached his own idea of striking across Essex towards Harwich and thence escaping from the country altogether.

Mrs. Elphinstone—that was the name of the woman in white—would listen to no reasoning, and kept calling upon "George"; but her sister-in-law was astonishingly quiet and deliberate, and at last agreed to my brother's suggestion. So, designing to cross the Great North Road, they went on towards Barnet, my brother leading the pony to save it as much as possible. As the sun crept up the sky the day became excessively hot, and under foot a thick, whitish sand grew burning and blinding, so that they travelled only very slowly. The hedges were grey with dust. And as they advanced towards Barnet a tumultuous murmuring grew stronger.

They began to meet more people. For the most part these were staring before them, murmuring indistinct questions, jaded, haggard, unclean. One man in evening dress passed them on foot, his eyes on the ground. They heard his voice, and, looking back at him, saw one hand clutched in his hair and the other beating invisible things. His paroxysm of rage over, he went on his way without once looking back.

As my brother's party went on towards the crossroads to the south of Barnet they saw a woman approaching the road across some fields on their left, carrying a child and with two other children; and then passed a man in dirty black, with a thick stick in one hand and a small portmanteau in the other. Then round the corner of the lane, from between the villas that guarded it at its confluence with the high road, came a little cart drawn by a sweating black pony and driven by a sallow youth in a bowler hat, grey with dust. There were three girls, East End factory girls, and a couple of little children crowded in the cart.

"This'll tike us rahnd Edgware?" asked the driver, wild-eyed, white-faced; and when my brother told him it would if he turned to the left, he whipped up at once without the formality of thanks.

My brother noticed a pale grey smoke or haze rising among the houses in front of them, and veiling the white facade of a terrace beyond the road that appeared between the backs of the villas. Mrs. Elphinstone suddenly cried out at a number of tongues of smoky red flame leaping up above the houses in front of them against the hot, blue sky. The tumultuous noise resolved itself now into the disorderly mingling of many voices, the gride of many wheels, the creaking of waggons, and the staccato of hoofs. The lane came round sharply not fifty yards from the crossroads.

"Good heavens!" cried Mrs. Elphinstone. "What is this you are driving us into?"

My brother stopped.

For the main road was a boiling stream of people, a torrent of human beings rushing northward, one pressing on another. A great bank of dust, white and luminous in the blaze of the sun, made everything within twenty feet of the ground grey and indistinct and was perpetually renewed by the hurrying feet of a dense crowd of horses and of men and women on foot, and by the wheels of vehicles of every description.

"Way!" my brother heard voices crying. "Make way!"

It was like riding into the smoke of a fire to approach the meeting point of the lane and road; the crowd roared like a fire, and the dust was hot and pungent. And, indeed, a little way up the road a villa was burning and sending rolling masses of black smoke across the road to add to the confusion.

Two men came past them. Then a dirty woman, carrying a heavy bundle and weeping. A lost retriever dog, with hanging tongue, circled dubiously round them, scared and wretched, and fled at my brother's threat.

So much as they could see of the road Londonward between the houses to the right was a tumultuous stream of dirty, hurrying people, pent in between the villas on either side; the black heads, the crowded forms, grew into distinctness as they rushed towards the corner, hurried past, and merged their individuality again in a receding multitude that was swallowed up at last in a cloud of dust.

"Go on! Go on!" cried the voices. "Way! Way!"

One man's hands pressed on the back of another. My brother stood at the pony's head. Irresistibly attracted, he advanced slowly, pace by pace, down the lane.

Edgware had been a scene of confusion, Chalk Farm a riotous tumult, but this was a whole population in movement. It is hard to imagine that host. It had no character of its own. The figures poured out past the corner, and receded with their backs to the group in the lane. Along the margin came those who were on foot threatened by the wheels, stumbling in the ditches, blundering into one another.

The carts and carriages crowded close upon one another, making little way for those swifter and more impatient vehicles that darted forward every now and then when an opportunity showed itself of doing so, sending the people scattering against the fences and gates of the villas.

"Push on!" was the cry. "Push on! They are coming!"

In one cart stood a blind man in the uniform of the Salvation Army, gesticulating with his crooked fingers and bawling, "Eternity! Eternity!" His voice was hoarse and very loud so that my brother could hear him long after he was lost to sight in the dust. Some of the people who crowded in the carts whipped stupidly at their horses and quarrelled with other drivers; some sat motionless, staring at nothing with miserable eyes; some gnawed their hands with thirst, or lay prostrate in the bottoms of their conveyances. The horses' bits were covered with foam, their eyes bloodshot.

There were cabs, carriages, shop cars, waggons, beyond counting; a mail cart, a road-cleaner's cart marked "Vestry of St. Pancras," a huge timber waggon crowded with roughs. A brewer's dray rumbled by with its two near wheels splashed with fresh blood.

"Clear the way!" cried the voices. "Clear the way!"

"Eter-nity! Eter-nity!" came echoing down the road.

There were sad, haggard women tramping by, well dressed, with children that cried and stumbled, their dainty clothes smothered in dust, their weary faces smeared with tears. With many of these came men, sometimes helpful, sometimes lowering and savage. Fighting side by side with them pushed some weary street outcast in faded black rags, wide-eyed, loud-voiced, and foul-mouthed. There were sturdy workmen thrusting their way along, wretched, unkempt men, clothed like clerks or shopmen, struggling spasmodically; a wounded soldier my brother noticed, men dressed in the clothes of railway porters, one wretched creature in a nightshirt with a coat thrown over it.

But varied as its composition was, certain things all that host had in common. There were fear and pain on their faces, and fear behind them. A tumult up the road, a quarrel for a place in a waggon, sent the whole host of them quickening their pace; even a man so scared and broken that his knees bent under him was galvanised for a moment into renewed activity. The heat and dust had already been at work upon this multitude. Their skins were dry, their lips black and cracked. They were all thirsty, weary, and footsore. And amid the various cries one heard disputes, reproaches, groans of weariness and fatigue; the voices of most of them were hoarse and weak. Through it all ran a refrain:

"Way! Way! The Martians are coming!"

Few stopped and came aside from that flood. The lane opened slantingly into the main road with a narrow opening, and had a delusive appearance of coming from the direction of London. Yet a kind of eddy of people drove into its mouth; weaklings elbowed out of the stream, who for the most part rested but a moment before plunging into it again. A little way down the lane, with two friends bending over him, lay a man with a bare leg, wrapped about with bloody rags. He was a lucky man to have friends.

A little old man, with a grey military moustache and a filthy black frock coat, limped out and sat down beside the trap, removed his boot—his sock was bloodstained—shook out a pebble, and hobbled on again; and then a little girl of eight or nine, all alone, threw herself under the hedge close by my brother, weeping.

"I can't go on! I can't go on!"

My brother woke from his torpor of astonishment and lifted her up, speaking gently to her, and carried her to Miss Elphinstone. So soon as my brother touched her she became quite still, as if frightened.

"Ellen!" shrieked a woman in the crowd, with tears in her voice—"Ellen!" And the child suddenly darted away from my brother, crying "Mother!"

His handbag split open and disgorged a mass of sovereigns.

"They are coming," said a man on horseback, riding past along the lane.

"Out of the way, there!" bawled a coachman, towering high; and my brother saw a closed carriage turning into the lane.

The people crushed back on one another to avoid the horse. My brother pushed the pony and chaise back into the hedge, and the man drove by and stopped at the turn of the way. It was a carriage, with a pole for a pair of horses, but only one was in the traces. My brother saw dimly through the dust that two men lifted out something on a white stretcher and put it gently on the grass beneath the privet hedge.

One of the men came running to my brother.

"Where is there any water?" he said. "He is dying fast, and very thirsty. It is Lord Garrick."

"Lord Garrick!" said my brother; "the Chief Justice?"

"The water?" he said.

"There may be a tap," said my brother, "in some of the houses. We have no water. I dare not leave my people."

The man pushed against the crowd towards the gate of the corner house.

"Go on!" said the people, thrusting at him. "They are coming! Go on!"

Then my brother's attention was distracted by a bearded, eagle-faced man lugging a small handbag, which split even as my brother's eyes rested on it and disgorged a mass of sovereigns that seemed to break up into separate coins as it struck the ground. They rolled hither and thither among the struggling feet of men and horses. The man stopped and looked stupidly at the heap, and the shaft of a cab struck his shoulder and sent him reeling. He gave a shriek and dodged back, and a cartwheel shaved him narrowly.

"Way!" cried the men all about him. "Make way!"

So soon as the cab had passed, he flung himself, with both hands open, upon the heap of coins, and began thrusting handfuls in his pocket. A horse rose close upon him, and in another moment, half rising, he had been borne down under the horse's hoofs.

"Stop!" screamed my brother, and pushing a woman out of his way, tried to clutch the bit of the horse.

Before he could get to it, he heard a scream under the wheels, and saw through the dust the rim passing over the poor wretch's back. The driver of the cart slashed his whip at my brother, who ran round behind the cart. The multitudinous shouting confused his ears. The man was writhing in the dust among his scattered money, unable to rise, for the wheel had broken his back, and his lower limbs lay limp and dead. My brother stood up and yelled at the next driver, and a man on a black horse came to his assistance.

"Get him out of the road," said he; and, clutching the man's collar with his free hand, my brother lugged him sideways. But he still clutched after his money, and regarded my brother fiercely, hammering at his arm with a handful of gold. "Go on! Go on!" shouted angry voices behind.

"Way! Way!"

There was a smash as the pole of a carriage crashed into the cart that the man on horseback stopped. My brother looked up, and the man with the gold twisted his head round and bit the wrist that held his collar. There was a concussion, and the black horse came staggering sideways, and the carthorse pushed beside it. A hoof missed my brother's foot by a hair's breadth. He released his grip on the fallen man and jumped back. He saw anger change to terror on the face of the poor wretch on the ground, and in a moment he was hidden and my brother was borne backward and carried past the entrance of the lane, and had to fight hard in the torrent to recover it.

He saw Miss Elphinstone covering her eyes, and a little child, with all a child's want of sympathetic imagination, staring with dilated eyes at a dusty something that lay black and still, ground and crushed under the rolling wheels. "Let us go back!" he shouted, and began turning the pony round. "We cannot cross this—hell," he said and they went back a hundred yards the way they had come, until the fighting crowd was hidden. As they passed the bend in the lane my brother saw the face of the dying man in the ditch under the privet, deadly white and drawn, and shining with perspiration. The two women sat silent, crouching in their seat and shivering.

Then beyond the bend my brother stopped again. Miss Elphinstone was white and pale, and her sister-in-law sat weeping, too wretched even to call upon "George." My brother was horrified and perplexed. So soon as they had retreated he realised how urgent and unavoidable it was to attempt this crossing. He turned to Miss Elphinstone, suddenly resolute.

"We must go that way," he said, and led the pony round again.

For the second time that day this girl proved her quality. To force their way into the torrent of people, my brother plunged into the traffic and held back a cab horse, while she drove the pony across its head. A waggon locked wheels for a moment and ripped a long splinter from the chaise. In another moment they were caught and swept forward by the stream. My brother, with the cabman's whip marks red across his face and hands, scrambled into the chaise and took the reins from her.

"Point the revolver at the man behind," he said, giving it to her, "if he presses us too hard. No!—point it at his horse."

Then he began to look out for a chance of edging to the right across the road. But once in the stream he seemed to lose volition, to become a part of that dusty rout. They swept through Chipping Barnet with the torrent; they were nearly a mile beyond the centre of the town before they had fought across to the opposite side of the way. It was din and confusion indescribable; but in and beyond the town the road forks repeatedly, and this to some extent relieved the stress.

They struck eastward through Hadley, and there on either side of the road, and at another place farther on they came upon a great multitude of people drinking at the stream, some fighting to come at the water. And farther on, from a lull near East Barnet, they saw two trains running slowly one after the other without signal or order—trains swarming with people, with men even among the coals behind the engines—going northward along the Great Northern Railway. My brother supposes they must have filled outside London, for at that time the furious terror of the people had rendered the central termini impossible.

Near this place they halted for the rest of the afternoon, for the violence of the day had already utterly exhausted all three of them. They began to suffer the beginnings of hunger; the night was cold, and none of them dared to sleep. And in the evening many people came hurrying along the road nearby their stopping place, fleeing from unknown dangers before them, and going in the direction from which my brother had come.

Chapter Seventeen
★ ★ ★
The "Thunder Child"

Had the Martians aimed only at destruction, they might on Monday have annihilated the entire population of London, as it spread itself slowly through the home counties. Not only along the road through Barnet, but also through Edgware and Waltham Abbey, and along the roads eastward to Southend and Shoeburyness, and south of the Thames to Deal and Broadstairs, poured the same frantic rout. If one could have hung that June morning in a balloon in the blazing blue above London every northward and eastward road running out of the tangled maze of streets would have seemed stippled black with the streaming fugitives, each dot a human agony of terror and physical distress. I have set forth at length in the last chapter my brother's account of the road through Chipping Barnet, in order that my readers may realise how that swarming of black dots appeared to one of those concerned. Never before in the history of the world had such a mass of human beings moved and suffered together. The legendary hosts of Goths and Huns, the hugest armies Asia has ever seen, would have been but a drop in that current. And this was no disciplined march; it was a stampede—a stampede gigantic and

terrible—without order and without a goal, six million people unarmed and unprovisioned, driving headlong. It was the beginning of the rout of civilisation, of the massacre of mankind.

Directly below him the balloonist would have seen the network of streets far and wide, houses, churches, squares, crescents, gardens—already derelict—spread out like a huge map, and in the southward *blotted*. Over Ealing, Richmond, Wimbledon, it would have seemed as if some monstrous pen had flung ink upon the chart. Steadily, incessantly, each black splash grew and spread, shooting out ramifications this way and that, now banking itself against rising ground, now pouring swiftly over a crest into a new-found valley, exactly as a gout of ink would spread itself upon blotting paper.

They wrecked the railways.

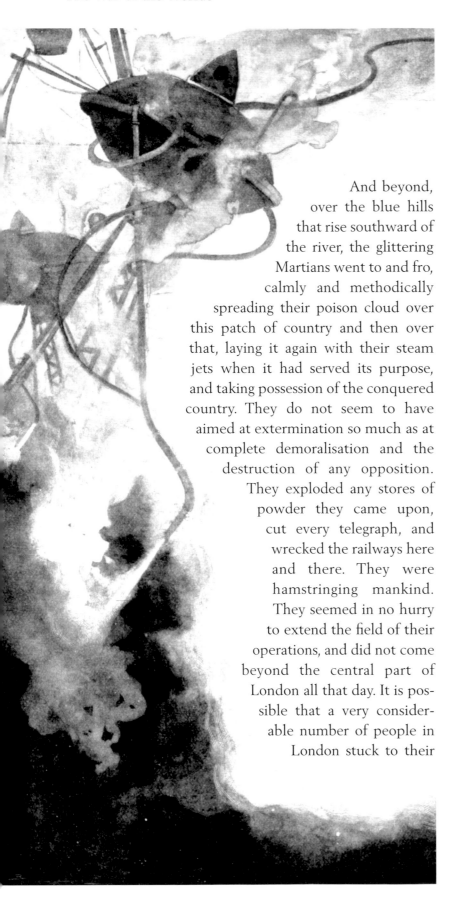

And beyond, over the blue hills that rise southward of the river, the glittering Martians went to and fro, calmly and methodically spreading their poison cloud over this patch of country and then over that, laying it again with their steam jets when it had served its purpose, and taking possession of the conquered country. They do not seem to have aimed at extermination so much as at complete demoralisation and the destruction of any opposition. They exploded any stores of powder they came upon, cut every telegraph, and wrecked the railways here and there. They were hamstringing mankind. They seemed in no hurry to extend the field of their operations, and did not come beyond the central part of London all that day. It is possible that a very considerable number of people in London stuck to their houses through Monday morning. Certain it is that many died at home suffocated by the Black Smoke.

Until about midday the Pool of London was an astonishing scene. Steamboats and shipping of all sorts lay there, tempted by the enormous sums of money offered by fugitives, and it is said that many who swam out to these vessels were thrust off with boathooks and drowned. About one o'clock in the afternoon the thinning remnant of a cloud of the black vapour appeared between the arches of Blackfriars Bridge. At that the Pool became a scene of mad confusion, fighting, and collision, and for some time a multitude of boats and barges jammed in the northern arch of the Tower Bridge, and the sailors and lightermen had to fight savagely against the people who swarmed upon them from the riverfront. People were actually clambering down the piers of the bridge from above.

When, an hour later, a Martian appeared beyond the Clock Tower and waded down the river, nothing but wreckage floated above Limehouse.

Of the falling of the fifth cylinder I have presently to tell. The sixth star fell at Wimbledon. My brother, keeping watch beside the women in the chaise in a meadow, saw the green flash of it far beyond the hills. On Tuesday the little party, still set upon getting across the sea, made its way through the swarming country towards Colchester. The news that the Martians were now in possession of the whole of London was confirmed. They had been seen at Highgate, and even, it was said, at Neasden. But they did not come into my brother's view until the morrow.

That day the scattered multitudes began to realise the urgent need of provisions. As they grew hungry the rights of property ceased to be regarded. Farmers were out to defend their cattle-sheds, granaries, and ripening root crops with arms in their hands. A number of people now, like my brother, had their faces eastward, and there were some desperate souls even going back towards London to get food. These were chiefly people from the northern suburbs, whose knowledge of the Black Smoke came by hearsay. He heard that about half the members of the government had gathered at Birmingham, and that enormous quantities of high explosives were being prepared to be used in automatic mines across the Midland counties.

He was also told that the Midland Railway Company had replaced the desertions of the first day's panic, had resumed traffic, and was running northward trains from St. Albans to relieve the congestion of the home counties. There was also a placard in Chipping Ongar announcing that large stores of flour were available in the northern towns and that within twenty-four hours bread would be distributed among the starving people in the neighbourhood. But this intelligence did not deter him from the plan of escape he had formed, and the three pressed eastward all day, and heard no more of the bread distribution than this promise. Nor, as a matter of fact, did anyone else hear more of it. That night fell the seventh star, falling upon Primrose Hill. It fell while Miss Elphinstone was watching, for she took that duty alternately with my brother. She saw it.

On Wednesday the three fugitives—they had passed the night in a field of unripe wheat—reached Chelmsford, and there a body of the inhabitants, calling itself the Committee of Public Supply, seized the pony as provisions, and would give nothing in exchange for it but the promise of a share in it the next day. Here there were rumours of Martians at Epping, and news of the destruction of Waltham Abbey Powder Mills in a vain attempt to blow up one of the invaders.

People were watching for Martians here from the church towers. My brother, very luckily for him as it chanced, preferred to push on at once to the coast rather than wait for food, although all three of them were very hungry. By midday they passed through Tillingham, which, strangely enough, seemed to be quite silent and deserted, save for a few furtive plunderers hunting for food. Near Tillingham they suddenly came in sight of the sea, and the most amazing crowd of shipping of all sorts that it is possible to imagine.

For after the sailors could no longer come up the Thames, they came on to the Essex coast, to Harwich and Walton and Clacton, and afterwards to Foulness and Shoebury, to bring off the people. They lay in a huge sickle-shaped curve that vanished into mist at last

towards the Naze. Close inshore was a multitude of fishing smacks—English, Scotch, French, Dutch, and Swedish; steam launches from the Thames, yachts, electric boats; and beyond were ships of large burden, a multitude of filthy colliers, trim merchantmen, cattle ships, passenger boats, petroleum tanks, ocean tramps, an old white transport even, neat white and grey liners from Southampton and Hamburg; and along the blue coast across the Blackwater my brother could make out dimly a dense swarm of boats chaffering with the people on the beach, a swarm which also extended up the Blackwater almost to Maldon.

About a couple of miles out lay an ironclad, very low in the water, almost, to my brother's perception, like a waterlogged ship. This was the ram *Thunder Child*. It was the only warship in sight, but far away to the right over the smooth surface of the sea—for that day there was a dead calm—lay a serpent of black smoke to mark the next ironclads of the Channel Fleet, which hovered in an extended line, steam up and ready for action, across the Thames estuary during the course of the Martian conquest, vigilant and yet powerless to prevent it.

At the sight of the sea, Mrs. Elphinstone, in spite of the assurances of her sister-in-law, gave way to panic. She had never been out of England before, she would rather die than trust herself friendless in a foreign country, and so forth. She seemed, poor woman, to imagine that the French and the Martians might prove very similar. She had been growing increasingly hysterical, fearful, and depressed during the two days' journeyings. Her great idea was to return to Stanmore. Things had been always well and safe at Stanmore. They would find George at Stanmore.

It was with the greatest difficulty they could get her down to the beach, where presently my brother succeeded in attracting the attention of some men on a paddle steamer from the Thames. They sent a boat and drove a bargain for thirty-six pounds for the three. The steamer was going, these men said, to Ostend.

It was about two o'clock when my brother, having paid their fares at the gangway, found himself safely aboard the steamboat with his charges. There was food aboard, albeit at exorbitant prices, and the three of them contrived to eat a meal on one of the seats forward.

There were already a couple of score of passengers aboard, some of whom had expended their last money in securing a passage, but the captain lay off the Blackwater until five in the afternoon, picking up passengers until the seated decks were even dangerously crowded. He would probably have remained longer had it not been for the sound of guns that began about that hour in the south. As if in answer, the ironclad seaward fired a small gun and hoisted a string of flags. A jet of smoke sprang out of her funnels.

Some of the passengers were of opinion that this firing came from Shoeburyness, until it was noticed that it was growing louder. At the same time, far away in the southeast the masts and upperworks of three ironclads rose one after the other out of the sea, beneath clouds of black smoke. But my brother's attention speedily reverted to the distant firing in the south. He fancied he saw a column of smoke rising out of the distant grey haze.

The little steamer was already flapping her way eastward of the big crescent of shipping, and the low Essex coast was growing blue and hazy, when a Martian appeared, small and faint in the remote distance, advancing along the muddy coast from the direction of Foulness. At that the captain on the bridge swore at the top of his voice with fear and anger at his own delay, and the paddles seemed infected with his terror. Every soul aboard stood at the bulwarks or on the seats of the steamer and stared at that distant shape, higher than the trees or church towers inland, and advancing with a leisurely parody of a human stride.

It was the first Martian my brother had seen, and he stood, more amazed than terrified, watching this Titan advancing deliberately towards the shipping, wading farther and farther into the water as the coast fell away. Then, far away beyond the Crouch, came another, striding over some stunted trees, and then yet another, still farther off, wading deeply through a shiny mudflat that seemed to hang halfway up between sea and sky. They were all stalking seaward, as if to intercept the escape of the multitudinous vessels that were crowded between Foulness and the Naze. In spite of the throbbing

exertions of the engines of the little paddleboat, and the pouring foam that her wheels flung behind her, she receded with terrifying slowness from this ominous advance.

Glancing northwestward, my brother saw the large crescent of shipping already writhing with the approaching terror; one ship passing behind another, another coming round from broadside to end on, steamships whistling and giving off volumes of steam, sails being let out, launches rushing hither and thither. He was so fascinated by this and by the creeping danger away to the left that he had no eyes for anything seaward. And then a swift movement of the steamboat (she had suddenly come round to avoid being run down)

They were all stalking seaward.

flung him headlong from the seat upon which he was standing. There was a shouting all about him, a trampling of feet, and a cheer that seemed to be answered faintly. The steamboat lurched and rolled him over upon his hands.

He sprang to his feet and saw to starboard, and not a hundred yards from their heeling, pitching boat, a vast iron bulk like the blade of a plough tearing through the water, tossing it on either side in huge waves of foam that leaped towards the steamer, flinging her paddles helplessly in the air, and then sucking her deck down almost to the waterline.

A douche of spray blinded my brother for a moment. When his eyes were clear again he saw the monster had passed and was rushing landward. Big iron upperworks rose out of this headlong structure, and from that twin funnels projected and spat a smoking blast shot with fire. It was the torpedo ram, *Thunder Child*, steaming headlong, coming to the rescue of the threatened shipping.

Keeping his footing on the heaving deck by clutching the bulwarks, my brother looked past this charging leviathan at the Martians again, and he saw the three of them now close together, and standing so far out to sea that their tripod supports were almost entirely submerged. Thus sunken, and seen in remote perspective, they appeared far less formidable than the huge iron bulk in whose wake the steamer was pitching so helplessly. It would seem they were regarding this new antagonist with astonishment. To their intelligence, it may be, the giant was even such another as themselves. The *Thunder Child* fired no gun, but simply drove full speed towards them. It was probably her not firing that enabled her to get so near the enemy as she did. They did not know what to make of her. One shell, and they would have sent her to the bottom forthwith with the Heat-Ray.

She was steaming at such a pace that in a minute she seemed halfway between the steamboat and the Martians—a diminishing black bulk against the receding horizontal expanse of the Essex coast.

Suddenly the foremost Martian lowered his tube and discharged a canister of the black gas at the ironclad. It hit her larboard side and glanced off in an inky jet that rolled away to seaward, an unfolding torrent of Black Smoke, from which the ironclad drove clear. To the watchers from the steamer, low in the water and with the sun in their eyes, it seemed as though she were already among the Martians.

They saw the gaunt figures separating and rising out of the water as they retreated shoreward, and one of them raised the camera-like generator of the Heat-Ray. He held it pointing obliquely downward, and a bank of steam sprang from the water at its touch. It must have driven through the iron of the ship's side like a white-hot iron rod through paper.

A flicker of flame went up through the rising steam, and then the Martian reeled and staggered. In another moment he was cut down, and a great body of water and steam shot high in the air. The guns of the *Thunder Child* sounded through the reek, going off one after the other, and one shot splashed the water high close by the steamer, ricocheted towards the other flying ships to the north, and smashed a smack to matchwood.

But no one heeded that very much. At the sight of the Martian's collapse the captain on the bridge yelled inarticulately, and all the crowding passengers on the steamer's stern shouted together. And then they yelled again. For, surging out beyond the white tumult, drove something long and black, the flames streaming from its middle parts, its ventilators and funnels spouting fire.

She was alive still; the steering gear, it seems, was intact and her engines working. She headed straight for a second Martian, and was within a hundred yards of him when the Heat-Ray came to bear. Then with a violent thud, a blinding flash, her decks, her funnels, leaped upward. The Martian staggered with the violence of her explosion, and in another moment the flaming wreckage, still driving forward with the impetus of its pace, had struck him and crumpled him up like a thing of cardboard. My brother shouted involuntarily. A boiling tumult of steam hid everything again.

"Two!" yelled the captain.

Everyone was shouting. The whole steamer from end to end rang with frantic cheering that was taken up first by one and then by all in the crowding multitude of ships and boats that was driving out to sea.

The steam hung upon the water for many minutes, hiding the third Martian and the coast altogether. And all this time the boat was paddling steadily out to sea and away from the fight; and when at last the confusion cleared, the drifting bank of black vapour intervened, and nothing of the *Thunder Child* could be made out, nor could the third Martian be seen. But the ironclads to seaward were now quite close and standing in towards shore past the steamboat.

The little vessel continued to beat its way seaward, and the ironclads receded slowly towards the coast, which was hidden still by a marbled bank of vapour, part steam, part black gas, eddying and combining in the strangest way. The fleet of refugees was scattering to the northeast; several smacks were sailing between

In another moment he was cut down.

the ironclads and the steamboat. After a time, and before they reached the sinking cloud bank, the warships turned northward, and then abruptly went about and passed into the thickening haze of evening southward. The coast grew faint, and at last indistinguishable amid the low banks of clouds that were gathering about the sinking sun.

Then suddenly out of the golden haze of the sunset came the vibration of guns, and a form of black shadows moving. Everyone struggled to the rail of the steamer and peered into the blinding furnace of the west, but nothing was to be distinguished clearly. A mass of smoke rose slanting and barred the face of the sun. The steamboat throbbed on its way through an interminable suspense.

The sun sank into grey clouds, the sky flushed and darkened, the evening star trembled into sight. It was deep twilight when the captain cried out and pointed. My brother strained his eyes. Something rushed up into the sky out of the greyness—rushed slantingly upward and very swiftly into the luminous clearness above the clouds in the western sky; something flat and broad, and very large, that swept round in a vast curve, grew smaller, sank slowly, and vanished again into the grey mystery of the night. And as it flew it rained down darkness upon the land.

BOOK II
THE EARTH UNDER THE MARTIANS

Chapter One
★ ★ ★
Under Foot

In the first book I have wandered so much from my own adventures to tell of the experiences of my brother that all through the last two chapters I and the curate have been lurking in the empty house at Halliford whither we fled to escape the Black Smoke. There I will resume. We stopped there all Sunday night and all the next day—the day of the panic—in a little island of daylight, cut off by the Black Smoke from the rest of the world. We could do nothing but wait in aching inactivity during those two weary days.

My mind was occupied by anxiety for my wife. I figured her at Leatherhead, terrified, in danger, mourning me already as a dead man. I paced the rooms and cried aloud when I thought of how I was cut off from her, of all that might happen to her in my absence. My cousin I knew was brave enough for any emergency, but he was not the sort of man to realise danger quickly, to rise promptly. What was needed now was not bravery, but circumspection. My only consolation was to believe that the Martians were moving Londonward and away from her. Such vague anxieties keep the mind sensitive and painful. I grew very weary and irritable with the curate's perpetual ejaculations; I tired of the sight of his selfish despair. After some ineffectual remonstrance I kept away from him, staying in a room—evidently a children's schoolroom—containing globes, forms, and copybooks. When he followed me thither, I went to a box room at the top of the house and, in order to be alone with my aching miseries, locked myself in.

We were hopelessly hemmed in by the Black Smoke all that day and the morning of the next. There were signs of people in the next house on Sunday evening—a face at a window and moving lights, and later the slamming of a door. But I do not know who these people were, nor what became of them. We saw nothing of them next day. The Black Smoke drifted slowly riverward all through Monday morning, creeping nearer and nearer to us, driving at last along the roadway outside the house that hid us.

A Martian came across the fields about midday, laying the stuff with a jet of superheated steam that hissed against the walls, smashed all the windows it touched, and scalded the curate's hand as he fled out of the front room. When at last we crept across the sodden rooms and looked out again, the country northward was as though a black snowstorm had passed over it. Looking towards the river, we were astonished to see an unaccountable redness mingling with the black of the scorched meadows.

For a time we did not see how this change affected our position, save that we were relieved of our fear of the Black Smoke. But later I perceived that we were no longer hemmed in, that now we might get away. So soon as I realised that the way of escape was open, my dream of action returned. But the curate was lethargic, unreasonable.

"We are safe here," he repeated; "safe here."

I resolved to leave him—would that I had! Wiser now for the artilleryman's teaching, I sought out food and drink. I had found oil and rags for my burns, and I also took a hat and a flannel shirt that I found in one of the bedrooms. When it was clear to him that I meant to go alone—had reconciled myself to going alone—he suddenly roused himself to come. And all being quiet throughout the afternoon, we started about five o'clock, as I should judge, along the blackened road to Sunbury.

In Sunbury, and at intervals along the road, were dead bodies lying in contorted attitudes, horses as well as men, overturned carts and luggage, all covered thickly with black dust. That pall of cindery powder made me think of what I had read of the destruction of Pompeii. We got to Hampton Court without misadventure, our minds full of strange and unfamiliar appearances, and at Hampton Court our eyes were relieved to find a patch of green that had escaped the suffocating drift. We went through Bushey Park, with its deer going to and fro under the chestnuts, and some men and women hurrying in the distance towards Hampton, and so we came to Twickenham. These were the first people we saw.

Away across the road the woods beyond Ham and Petersham were still afire. Twickenham was uninjured by either Heat-Ray or Black Smoke, and there were more people about here, though none could give us news. For the most part they were like ourselves, taking advantage of a lull to shift their quarters. I have an impression that many of the houses here were still occupied by scared inhabitants, too frightened even for flight. Here too the evidence of a hasty rout was abundant along the road. I remember most vividly three smashed bicycles in a heap, pounded into the road by the wheels of subsequent carts. We crossed Richmond Bridge about half past eight. We hurried across the exposed bridge, of course, but I noticed floating down the stream a number of red masses, some many feet across. I did not know

We hurried across the exposed bridge.

what these were—there was no time for scrutiny—and I put a more horrible interpretation on them than they deserved. Here again on the Surrey side were black dust that had once been smoke, and dead bodies—a heap near the approach to the station; but we had no glimpse of the Martians until we were some way towards Barnes.

We saw in the blackened distance a group of three people running down a side street towards the river, but otherwise it seemed deserted. Up the hill Richmond town was burning briskly; outside the town of Richmond there was no trace of the Black Smoke.

Then suddenly, as we approached Kew, came a number of people running, and the upperworks of a Martian fighting-machine loomed in sight over the housetops, not a hundred yards away from us. We stood aghast at our danger, and had the Martian looked down we must immediately have perished. We were so terrified that we dared not go on, but turned aside and hid in a shed in a garden. There the curate crouched, weeping silently, and refusing to stir again.

But my fixed idea of reaching Leatherhead would not let me rest, and in the twilight I ventured out again. I went through a shrubbery, and along a passage beside a big house standing in its own grounds, and so emerged upon the road towards Kew. The curate I left in the shed, but he came hurrying after me.

That second start was the most foolhardy thing I ever did. For it was manifest the Martians were about us. No sooner had the curate overtaken me than we saw either the fighting-machine we had seen before or another, far away across the meadows in the direction of Kew Lodge. Four or five little black figures hurried before it across the green-grey of the field, and in a moment it was evident this Martian pursued them. In three strides he was among them, and they ran radiating from his feet in all directions. He used no Heat-Ray to destroy them, but picked them up one by one. Apparently he tossed them into the great metallic carrier which projected behind him, much as a workman's basket hangs over his shoulder.

It was the first time I realised that the Martians might have any other purpose than destruction with defeated humanity. We stood for a moment petrified, then turned and fled through a gate behind us into a walled garden, fell into, rather than found, a fortunate ditch, and lay there, scarce daring to whisper to each other until the stars were out.

I suppose it was nearly eleven o'clock before we gathered courage to start again, no longer venturing into the road, but sneaking along hedgerows and through plantations, and watching keenly through the darkness, he on the right and I on the left, for the Martians, who seemed to be all about us. In one place we blundered upon a scorched and blackened area, now cooling and ashen, and a number of scattered dead bodies of men, burned horribly about the heads and trunks but with their legs and boots mostly intact; and of dead horses, fifty feet, perhaps, behind a line of four ripped guns and smashed gun carriages.

Sheen, it seemed, had escaped destruction, but the place was silent and deserted. Here we happened on no dead, though the night was too dark for us to see into the side roads of the place. In Sheen my companion suddenly complained of faintness and thirst, and we decided to try one of the houses.

The first house we entered, after a little difficulty with the window, was a small semi-detached villa, and I found nothing eatable left in the place but some mouldy cheese. There was, however, water to drink; and I took a hatchet, which promised to be useful in our next housebreaking.

We then crossed to a place where the road turns towards Mortlake. Here there stood a white house within a walled garden, and in the pantry of this domicile we found a store of food—two loaves of bread in a pan, an uncooked steak, and the half of a ham. I give this catalogue so precisely because, as it happened, we were destined to subsist upon this store for the next

In three strides he was among them.

fortnight. Bottled beer stood under a shelf, and there were two bags of haricot beans and some limp lettuces. This pantry opened into a kind of wash-up kitchen, and in this was firewood; there was also a cupboard, in which we found nearly a dozen of burgundy, tinned soups and salmon, and two tins of biscuits.

We sat in the adjacent kitchen in the dark—for we dared not strike a light—and ate bread and ham, and drank beer out of the same bottle. The curate, who was still timorous and restless, was now, oddly enough, for pushing on, and I was urging him to keep up his strength by eating when the thing happened that was to imprison us.

"It can't be midnight yet," I said, and then came a blinding glare of vivid green light. Everything in the kitchen leaped out, clearly visible in green and black, and vanished again. And then followed such a concussion as I have never heard before or since. So close on the heels of this as to seem instantaneous came a thud behind me, a clash of glass, a crash and rattle of falling masonry all about us, and the plaster of the ceiling came down upon us, smashing into a multitude of fragments upon our heads. I was knocked headlong across the floor against the oven handle and stunned. I was insensible for a long time, the curate told me, and when I came to we were in darkness again, and he, with a face wet, as I found afterwards, with blood from a cut forehead, was dabbing water over me.

For some time I could not recollect what had happened. Then things came to me slowly. A bruise on my temple asserted itself.

"Are you better?" asked the curate in a whisper.

At last I answered him. I sat up.

"Don't move," he said. "The floor is covered with smashed crockery from the dresser. You can't possibly move without making a noise, and I fancy *they* are outside."

We both sat quite silent, so that we could scarcely hear each other breathing. Everything seemed deadly still, but once something near us, some plaster or broken brickwork, slid down with a rumbling sound. Outside and very near was an intermittent, metallic rattle.

"That!" said the curate, when presently it happened again.

"Yes," I said. "But what is it?"

"A Martian!" said the curate.

I listened again.

"It was not like the Heat-Ray," I said, and for a time I was inclined to think one of the great fighting-machines had stumbled against the house, as I had seen one stumble against the tower of Shepperton Church.

Our situation was so strange and incomprehensible that for three or four hours, until the dawn came, we scarcely moved. And then the light filtered in, not through the window, which remained black, but through a triangular aperture between a beam and a heap of broken bricks in the wall behind us. The interior of the kitchen we now saw greyly for the first time.

The window had been burst in by a mass of garden mould, which flowed over the table upon which we had been sitting and lay about our feet. Outside, the soil was banked high against the house. At the top of the window frame we could see an uprooted drainpipe. The floor was littered with smashed hardware; the end of the kitchen towards the house was broken into, and since the daylight shone in there, it was evident the greater part of the house had collapsed. Contrasting vividly with this ruin was the neat dresser, stained in the fashion, pale green, and with a number of copper and tin vessels below it, the wallpaper imitating blue and white tiles, and a couple of coloured supplements fluttering from the walls above the kitchen range.

As the dawn grew clearer, we saw through the gap in the wall the body of a Martian, standing sentinel, I suppose, over the still glowing cylinder. At the sight of that we crawled as circumspectly as possible out of the twilight of the kitchen into the darkness of the scullery.

Abruptly the right interpretation dawned upon my mind.

"The fifth cylinder," I whispered, "the fifth shot from Mars, has struck this house and buried us under the ruins!"

For a time the curate was silent, and then he whispered:

"God have mercy upon us!"

I heard him presently whimpering to himself.

Save for that sound we lay quite still in the scullery; I for my part scarce dared breathe, and sat with my eyes fixed on the faint light of the kitchen door. I could just see the curate's face, a dim, oval shape, and his collar and cuffs. Outside there began a metallic hammering, then a violent hooting, and then again, after a quiet interval, a hissing like the hissing of an engine. These noises, for the most part problematical, continued intermittently, and seemed if anything to increase in number as time wore on. Presently a measured thudding and a vibration that made everything about us quiver and the vessels in the pantry ring and shift, began and continued. Once the light was eclipsed, and the ghostly kitchen doorway became absolutely dark. For many hours we must have crouched there, silent and shivering, until our tired attention failed. . . .

At last I found myself awake and very hungry. I am inclined to believe we must have spent the greater portion of a day before that awakening. My hunger was at a stride so insistent that it moved me to action. I told the curate I was going to seek food, and felt my way towards the pantry. He made me no answer, but so soon as I began eating the faint noise I made stirred him up and I heard him crawling after me.

Chapter Two
★ ★ ★
What We Saw from the Ruined House

After eating we crept back to the scullery, and there I must have dozed again, for when presently I looked round I was alone. The thudding vibration continued with wearisome persistence. I whispered for the curate several times, and at last felt my way to the door of the kitchen. It was still daylight, and I perceived him across the room, lying against the triangular hole that looked out upon the Martians. His shoulders were hunched, so that his head was hidden from me.

I could hear a number of noises almost like those in an engine shed; and the place rocked with that beating thud. Through the aperture in the wall I could see the top of a tree touched with gold and the warm blue of a tranquil evening sky. For a minute or so I remained watching the curate, and then I advanced, crouching and stepping with extreme care amid the broken crockery that littered the floor.

I touched the curate's leg, and he started so violently that a mass of plaster went sliding down outside and fell with a loud impact. I gripped his arm, fearing he might cry out, and for a long time we crouched motionless. Then I turned to see how much of our rampart remained. The detachment of the plaster had left a vertical slit open in the débris, and by raising myself cautiously across a beam I was able to see out of this gap into what had been overnight a quiet suburban roadway. Vast, indeed, was the change that we beheld.

The fifth cylinder must have fallen right into the midst of the house we had first visited. The building had vanished, completely smashed, pulverised, and dispersed by the blow. The cylinder lay now far beneath the original foundations— deep in a hole, already vastly larger than the pit I had looked into at Woking. The earth all round it had splashed under that tremendous impact—"splashed" is the only word—and lay in heaped piles that hid the masses of the adjacent houses. It had behaved exactly like mud under the violent blow of a hammer. Our house had collapsed backward; the front portion, even on the ground floor, had been destroyed completely; by a chance the kitchen and scullery had escaped, and stood buried now under soil and ruins, closed in by tons of earth on every side save towards the cylinder. Over that aspect we hung now on the very edge of the great circular pit the Martians were engaged in making. The heavy beating sound was evidently just behind us, and ever and again a bright green vapour drove up like a veil across our peephole.

The cylinder was already opened in the centre of the pit, and on the farther edge of the pit, amid the smashed and gravel-heaped shrubbery, one of the great fighting-machines, deserted by its occupant, stood stiff and tall against the evening sky. At first I scarcely noticed the pit and the cylinder, although it has been convenient to describe them first, on account of the extraordinary glittering mechanism I saw busy in the excavation, and on account of the strange creatures that were crawling slowly and painfully across the heaped mould near it.

The mechanism it certainly was that held my attention first. It was one of those complicated fabrics that have since been called handling-machines, and the study of which has already given such an enormous impetus to terrestrial invention. As it dawned upon me first, it presented a sort of metallic spider with five jointed, agile legs, and with an extraordinary number of jointed levers, bars, and reaching and clutching tentacles about its body. Most of its arms were retracted, but with three long tentacles it was fishing out a number of rods, plates, and bars which lined the covering and apparently strengthened the walls of the cylinder. These, as it extracted them, were lifted out and deposited upon a level surface of earth behind it.

Its motion was so swift, complex, and perfect that at first I did not see it as a machine, in spite of its metallic

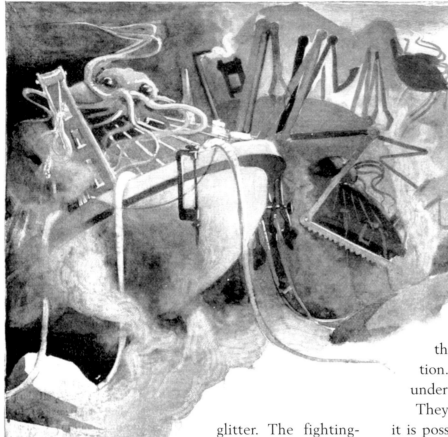

At first, I say, the handling-machine did not impress me as a machine, but as a crablike creature with a glittering integument, the controlling Martian whose delicate tentacles actuated its movements seeming to be simply the equivalent of the crab's cerebral portion. But then I perceived the resemblance of its grey-brown, shiny, leathery integument to that of the other sprawling bodies beyond, and the true nature of this dexterous workman dawned upon me. With that realisation my interest shifted to those other creatures, the real Martians. Already I had had a transient impression of these, and the first nausea no longer obscured my observation. Moreover, I was concealed and motionless, and under no urgency of action.

They were, I now saw, the most unearthly creatures it is possible to conceive. They were huge round bodies—or, rather, heads—about four feet in diameter, each body having in front of it a face. This face had no nostrils—indeed, the Martians do not seem to have had any sense of smell, but it had a pair of very large dark-coloured eyes, and just beneath this a kind of fleshy beak. In the back of this head or body—I scarcely know how to speak of it—was the single tight tympanic surface, since known to be anatomically an ear, though it must have been almost useless in our dense air. In a group round the mouth were sixteen slender, almost whiplike tentacles, arranged in two bunches of eight each. These bunches have since been named rather aptly, by that distinguished anatomist, Professor Howes, the *hands*. Even as I saw these Martians for the first time they seemed to be endeavouring to raise themselves on these hands, but of course, with the increased weight of terrestrial conditions, this was impossible. There is reason to suppose that on Mars they may have progressed upon them with some facility.

The internal anatomy, I may remark here, as dissection has since shown, was almost equally simple. The

glitter. The fighting-machines were co-ordinated and animated to an extraordinary pitch, but nothing to compare with this. People who have never seen these structures, and have only the ill-imagined efforts of artists or the imperfect descriptions of such eye-witnesses as myself to go upon, scarcely realise that living quality.

I recall particularly the illustration of one of the first pamphlets to give a consecutive account of the war. The artist had evidently made a hasty study of one of the fighting-machines, and there his knowledge ended. He presented them as tilted, stiff tripods, without either flexibility or subtlety, and with an altogether misleading monotony of effect. The pamphlet containing these renderings had a considerable vogue, and I mention them here simply to warn the reader against the impression they may have created. They were no more like the Martians I saw in action than a Dutch doll is like a human being. To my mind, the pamphlet would have been much better without them.

greater part of the structure was the brain, sending enormous nerves to the eyes, ear, and tactile tentacles. Besides this were the bulky lungs, into which the mouth opened, and the heart and its vessels. The pulmonary distress caused by the denser atmosphere and greater gravitational attraction was only too evident in the convulsive movements of the outer skin.

And this was the sum of the Martian organs. Strange as it may seem to a human being, all the complex apparatus of digestion, which makes up the bulk of our bodies, did not exist in the Martians. They were heads—merely heads. Entrails they had none. They did not eat, much less digest. Instead, they took the fresh, living blood of other creatures, and *injected* it into their own veins. I have myself seen this being done, as I shall mention in its place. But, squeamish as I may seem, I cannot bring myself to describe what I could not endure even to continue watching. Let it suffice to say, blood obtained from a still living animal, in most cases from a human being, was run directly by means of a little pipette into the recipient canal....

The bare idea of this is no doubt horribly repulsive to us, but at the same time I think that we should remember how repulsive our carnivorous habits would seem to an intelligent rabbit.

The physiological advantages of the practice of injection are undeniable, if one thinks of the tremendous waste of human time and energy occasioned by eating and the digestive process. Our bodies are half made up of glands and tubes and organs, occupied in turning heterogeneous food into blood. The digestive processes and their reaction upon the nervous system sap our strength and colour our minds. Men go happy or miserable as they have healthy or unhealthy livers, or sound gastric glands. But the Martians were lifted above all these organic fluctuations of mood and emotion.

Their undeniable preference for men as their source of nourishment is partly explained by the nature of the remains of the victims they had brought with them as provisions from Mars. These creatures, to judge from the shrivelled remains that have fallen into human hands, were bipeds with flimsy, silicious skeletons (almost like those of the silicious sponges) and feeble musculature, standing about six feet high and having round, erect heads, and large eyes in flinty sockets. Two or three of these seem to have been brought in each cylinder, and all were killed before earth was reached. It was just as well for them, for the mere attempt to stand upright upon our planet would have broken every bone in their bodies.

And while I am engaged in this description, I may add in this place certain further details which, although they were not all evident to us at the time, will enable the reader who is unacquainted with them to form a clearer picture of these offensive creatures.

In three other points their physiology differed strangely from ours. Their organisms did not sleep, any more than the heart of man sleeps. Since they had no extensive muscular mechanism to recuperate, that periodical extinction was unknown to them. They had little or no sense of fatigue, it would seem. On earth they could never have moved without effort, yet even to the last they kept in action. In twenty-four hours they did twenty-four hours of work, as even on earth is perhaps the case with the ants.

In the next place, wonderful as it seems in a sexual world, the Martians were absolutely without sex, and therefore without any of the tumultuous emotions that arise from that difference among men. A young Martian, there can now be no dispute, was really born upon earth during the war, and it was found attached to its parent, partially *budded* off, just as young lily-bulbs bud off, or like the young animals in the fresh-water polyp.

In man, in all the higher terrestrial animals, such a method of increase has disappeared; but even on this earth it was certainly the primitive method. Among the lower animals, up even to those first cousins of the vertebrated animals, the Tunicates, the two processes occur side by side, but finally the sexual method superseded its competitor altogether. On Mars, however, just the reverse has apparently been the case.

It is worthy of remark that a certain speculative writer of quasi-scientific repute, writing long before the Martian invasion, did forecast for man a final structure not unlike the actual Martian condition. His prophecy,

I remember, appeared in November or December, 1893, in a long-defunct publication, the *Pall Mall Budget*, and I recall a caricature of it in a pre-Martian periodical called *Punch*. He pointed out—writing in a foolish, facetious tone—that the perfection of mechanical appliances must ultimately supersede limbs; the perfection of chemical devices, digestion; that such organs as hair, external nose, teeth, ears, and chin were no longer essential parts of the human being, and that the tendency of natural selection would lie in the direction of their steady diminution through the coming ages. The brain alone remained a cardinal necessity. Only one other part of the body had a strong case for survival, and that was the hand, "teacher and agent of the brain." While the rest of the body dwindled, the hands would grow larger.

There is many a true word written in jest, and here in the Martians we have beyond dispute the actual accomplishment of such a suppression of the animal side of the organism by the intelligence. To me it is quite credible that the Martians may be descended from beings not unlike ourselves, by a gradual development of brain and hands (the latter giving rise to the two bunches of delicate tentacles at last) at the expense of the rest of the body. Without the body the brain would, of course, become a mere selfish intelligence, without any of the emotional substratum of the human being.

The last salient point in which the systems of these creatures differed from ours was in what one might have thought a very trivial particular. Micro-organisms, which cause so much disease and pain on earth, have either never appeared upon Mars or Martian sanitary science eliminated them ages ago. A hundred diseases, all the fevers and contagions of human life, consumption, cancers, tumours and such morbidities, never enter the scheme of their life. And speaking of the differences between the life on Mars and terrestrial life, I may allude here to the curious suggestions of the red weed.

Apparently the vegetable kingdom in Mars, instead of having green for a dominant colour, is of a vivid blood-red tint. At any rate, the seeds which the Martians (intentionally or accidentally) brought with them gave rise in all cases to red-coloured growths.

The actual Martians were the most extraordinary creatures it is possible to conceive.

Only that known popularly as the red weed, however, gained any footing in competition with terrestrial forms. The red creeper was quite a transitory growth, and few people have seen it growing. For a time, however, the red weed grew with astonishing vigour and luxuriance. It spread up the sides of the pit by the third or fourth day of our imprisonment, and its cactus-like branches formed a carmine fringe to the edges of our triangular window. And afterwards I found it broadcast throughout the country, and especially wherever there was a stream of water.

The Martians had what appears to have been an auditory organ, a single round drum at the back of the head-body, and eyes with a visual range not very different from ours except that, according to Philips, blue and violet were as black to them. It is commonly supposed that they communicated by sounds and tentacular gesticulations; this is asserted, for instance, in the able but hastily compiled pamphlet (written evidently by someone not an eye-witness of Martian actions) to which I have already alluded, and which, so far, has been the chief source of information concerning them. Now no surviving human being saw so much of the Martians in action as I did. I take no credit to myself for an accident, but the fact is so. And I assert that I watched them closely time after time, and that I have seen four, five, and (once) six of them sluggishly performing the most elaborately complicated operations together without either sound or gesture. Their peculiar hooting invariably preceded feeding; it had no modulation, and was, I believe, in no sense a signal, but merely the expiration of air preparatory to the suctional operation. I have a certain claim to at least an elementary knowledge of psychology, and in this matter I am convinced—as firmly as I am convinced of anything—that the Martians interchanged thoughts without any physical intermediation. And I have been convinced of this in spite of strong preconceptions. Before the Martian invasion, as an occasional reader here or there may remember, I had written with some little vehemence against the telepathic theory.

The Martians wore no clothing. Their conceptions of ornament and decorum were necessarily different from ours; and not only were they evidently much less sensible of changes of temperature than we are, but changes of pressure do not seem to have affected their health at all seriously. Yet though they wore no clothing, it was in the other artificial additions to their bodily resources that their great superiority over man lay. We men, with our bicycles and road-skates, our Lilienthal soaring-machines, our guns and sticks and so forth, are just in the beginning of the evolution that the Martians have worked out. They have become practically mere brains, wearing different bodies according to their needs just as men wear suits of clothes and take a bicycle in a hurry or an umbrella in the wet. And of their appliances, perhaps nothing is more wonderful to a man than the curious fact that what is the dominant feature of almost all human devices in mechanism is absent—the

wheel is absent; among all the things they brought to earth there is no trace or suggestion of their use of wheels. One would have at least expected it in locomotion. And in this connection it is curious to remark that even on this earth Nature has never hit upon the wheel, or has preferred other expedients to its development. And not only did the Martians either not know of (which is incredible), or abstain from, the wheel, but in their apparatus singularly little use is made of the fixed pivot or relatively fixed pivot, with circular motions thereabout confined to one plane. Almost all the joints of the machinery present a complicated system of sliding parts moving over small but beautifully curved friction bearings. And while upon this matter of detail, it is remarkable that the long leverages of their machines are in most cases actuated by a sort of sham musculature of the disks in an elastic sheath; these disks become polarised and drawn closely and powerfully together when traversed by a current of electricity. In this way the curious parallelism to animal motions, which was so striking and disturbing to the human beholder, was attained. Such quasi-muscles abounded in the crablike handling-machine which, on my first peeping out of the slit, I watched unpacking the cylinder. It seemed infinitely more alive than the actual Martians lying beyond it in the sunset light, panting, stirring ineffectual tentacles, and moving feebly after their vast journey across space.

While I was still watching their sluggish motions in the sunlight, and noting each strange detail of their form, the curate reminded me of his presence by pulling violently at my arm. I turned to a scowling face, and silent, eloquent lips. He wanted the slit, which permitted only one of us to peep through; and so I had to forego watching them for a time while he enjoyed that privilege.

When I looked again, the busy handling-machine had already put together several of the pieces of apparatus it had taken out of the cylinder into a shape having an unmistakable likeness to its own; and down on the left a busy little digging mechanism had come into view, emitting jets of green vapour and working its way round the pit, excavating and embanking in a methodical and discriminating manner. This it was which had caused the regular beating noise, and the rhythmic shocks that had kept our ruinous refuge quivering. It piped and whistled as it worked. So far as I could see, the thing was without a directing Martian at all.

Chapter Three

★ ★ ★

The Days of Imprisonment

The arrival of a second fighting-machine drove us from our peephole into the scullery, for we feared that from his elevation the Martian might see down upon us behind our barrier. At a later date we began to feel less in danger of their eyes, for to an eye in the dazzle of the sunlight outside our refuge must have been blank blackness, but at first the slightest suggestion of approach drove us into the scullery in heart-throbbing retreat. Yet terrible as was the danger we incurred, the attraction of peeping was for both of us irresistible. And I recall now with a sort of wonder that, in spite of the infinite danger in which we were between starvation and a still more terrible death, we could yet struggle bitterly for that horrible privilege of sight. We would race across the kitchen in a grotesque way between eagerness and the dread of making a noise, and strike each other, and thrust and kick, within a few inches of exposure.

The fact is that we had absolutely incompatible dispositions and habits of thought and action, and our danger and isolation only accentuated the incompatibility. At Halliford I had already come to hate the curate's trick of helpless exclamation, his stupid rigidity of mind. His endless muttering monologue vitiated every effort I made to think out a line of action, and drove me at times, thus pent up and intensified, almost to the verge of craziness. He was as lacking in restraint as a silly woman. He would weep for hours together, and I verily believe that to the very end this spoiled child of life thought his weak tears in some way efficacious. And I would sit in the darkness unable to keep my mind off him by reason of his importunities. He ate more than I did, and it was in vain I pointed out that our only

chance of life was to stop in the house until the Martians had done with their pit, that in that long patience a time might presently come when we should need food. He ate and drank impulsively in heavy meals at long intervals. He slept little.

As the days wore on, his utter carelessness of any consideration so intensified our distress and danger that I had, much as I loathed doing it, to resort to threats, and at last to blows. That brought him to reason for a time. But he was one of those weak creatures, void of pride, timorous, anaemic, hateful souls, full of shifty cunning, who face neither God nor man, who face not even themselves.

It is disagreeable for me to recall and write these things, but I set them down that my story may lack nothing. Those who have escaped the dark and terrible aspects of life will find my brutality, my flash of rage in our final tragedy, easy enough to blame; for they know what is wrong as well as any, but not what is possible to tortured men. But those who have been under the shadow, who have gone down at last to elemental things, will have a wider charity.

And while within we fought out our dark, dim contest of whispers, snatched food and drink, and gripping hands and blows, without, in the pitiless sunlight of that terrible June, was the strange wonder, the unfamiliar routine of the Martians in the pit. Let me return to those first new experiences of mine. After a long time I ventured back to the peephole, to find that the newcomers had been reinforced by the occupants of no fewer than three of the fighting-machines. These last had brought with them certain fresh appliances that stood in an orderly manner about the cylinder. The second handling-machine was now completed, and was busied in serving one of the novel contrivances the big machine had brought. This was a body resembling a milk can in its general form, above which oscillated a pear-shaped receptacle, and from which a stream of white powder flowed into a circular basin below.

The oscillatory motion was imparted to this by one tentacle of the handling-machine. With two spatulate hands the handling-machine was digging out and flinging masses of clay into the pear-shaped receptacle above, while with another arm it periodically opened a door and removed rusty and blackened clinkers from the middle part of the machine. Another steely tentacle directed the powder from the basin along a ribbed channel towards some receiver that was hidden from me by the mound of bluish dust. From this unseen receiver a little thread of green smoke rose vertically into the quiet air. As I looked, the handling-machine, with a faint and musical clinking, extended, telescopic fashion, a tentacle that had been a moment before a mere blunt projection, until its end was hidden behind the mound of clay. In another second it had lifted a bar of white aluminium into sight, untarnished as yet, and shining dazzlingly, and deposited it in a growing stack of bars that stood at the side of the pit. Between sunset and starlight this dexterous machine must have made more than a hundred such bars out of the crude clay, and the mound of bluish dust rose steadily until it topped the side of the pit.

The contrast between the swift and complex movements of these contrivances and the inert panting clumsiness of their masters was acute, and for days I had to tell myself repeatedly that these latter were indeed the living of the two things.

The curate had possession of the slit when the first men were brought to the pit. I was sitting below, huddled up, listening with all my ears. He made a sudden movement backward, and I, fearful that we were observed, crouched in a spasm of terror. He came sliding down the rubbish and crept beside me in the darkness, inarticulate, gesticulating, and for a moment I shared his panic. His gesture suggested a resignation of the slit, and after a little while my curiosity gave me courage, and I rose up, stepped across him, and clambered up to it. At first I could see no reason for his frantic behaviour. The twilight had now come, the stars were little and faint, but the pit was illuminated by the flickering green fire that came from the aluminium-making. The whole picture was a flickering scheme of green gleams and shifting rusty black shadows, strangely trying to the eyes. Over and through it all went the bats, heeding it not at all. The sprawling Martians were no longer to be seen, the mound of blue-green powder had

risen to cover them from sight, and a fighting-machine, with its legs contracted, crumpled, and abbreviated, stood across the corner of the pit. And then, amid the clangour of the machinery, came a drifting suspicion of human voices, that I entertained at first only to dismiss.

I crouched, watching this fighting-machine closely, satisfying myself now for the first time that the hood did indeed contain a Martian. As the green flames lifted I could see the oily gleam of his integument and the brightness of his eyes. And suddenly I heard a yell, and saw a long tentacle reaching over the shoulder of the machine to the little cage that hunched upon its back. Then something—something struggling violently—was lifted high against the sky, a black, vague enigma against the starlight; and as this black object came down again, I saw by the green brightness that it was a man. For an instant he was clearly visible. He was a stout, ruddy, middle-aged man, well dressed; three days before, he must have been walking the world, a man of considerable consequence. I could see his staring eyes and gleams of light on his studs and watch chain. He vanished behind the mound, and for a moment there was silence. And then began a shrieking and a sustained and cheerful hooting from the Martians.

I slid down the rubbish, struggled to my feet, clapped my hands over my ears, and bolted into the scullery. The curate, who had been crouching silently with his arms over his head, looked up as I passed, cried out quite loudly at my desertion of him, and came running after me.

That night, as we lurked in the scullery, balanced between our horror and the terrible fascination this peeping had, although I felt an urgent need of action I tried in vain to conceive some plan of escape; but afterwards, during the second day, I was able to consider our position with great clearness. The curate, I found, was quite incapable of discussion; this new and culminating atrocity had robbed him of all vestiges of reason or forethought. Practically he had already sunk to the level of an animal. But as the saying goes, I gripped myself with both hands. It grew upon my mind, once I could face the facts, that terrible as our position was, there was as yet no justification for absolute despair. Our chief chance lay in the possibility of the Martians making the pit nothing more than a temporary encampment. Or even if they kept it permanently, they might not consider it necessary to guard it, and a chance of escape might be afforded us. I also weighed very carefully the possibility of our digging a way out in a direction away from the pit, but the chances of our emerging within sight of some sentinel fighting-machine seemed at first too great. And I should have had to do all the digging myself. The curate would certainly have failed me.

It was on the third day, if my memory serves me right, that I saw the lad killed. It was the only occasion on which I actually saw the Martians feed. After that experience I avoided the hole in the wall for the better part of a day. I went into the scullery, removed the door, and spent some hours digging with my hatchet as silently as possible; but when I had made a hole about a couple of feet deep the loose earth collapsed noisily, and I did not dare continue. I lost heart, and lay down on the scullery floor for a long time, having no spirit even to move. And after that I abandoned altogether the idea of escaping by excavation.

It says much for the impression the Martians had made upon me that at first I entertained little or no hope of our escape being brought about by their overthrow through any human effort. But on the fourth or fifth night I heard a sound like heavy guns.

It was very late in the night, and the moon was shining brightly. The Martians had taken away the excavating-machine, and, save for a fighting-machine that stood in the remoter bank of the pit and a handling-machine that was buried out of my sight in a corner of the pit immediately beneath my peephole, the place was deserted by them. Except for the pale glow from the handling-machine and the bars and patches of white moonlight the pit was in darkness, and, except for the clinking of the handling-machine, quite still. That night was a beautiful serenity; save for one planet, the moon seemed to have the sky to herself. I heard a dog howling, and that familiar sound it was that made me listen. Then I heard quite distinctly a booming exactly like the sound of great guns. Six distinct reports I counted, and after a long interval six again. And that was all.

Chapter Four
★ ★ ★
The Death of the Curate

It was on the sixth day of our imprisonment that I peeped for the last time, and presently found myself alone. Instead of keeping close to me and trying to oust me from the slit, the curate had gone back into the scullery. I was struck by a sudden thought. I went back quickly and quietly into the scullery. In the darkness I heard the curate drinking. I snatched in the darkness, and my fingers caught a bottle of burgundy.

For a few minutes there was a tussle. The bottle struck the floor and broke, and I desisted and rose. We stood panting and threatening each other. In the end I planted myself between him and the food, and told him of my determination to begin a discipline. I divided the food in the pantry, into rations to last us ten days. I would not let him eat any more that day. In the afternoon he made a feeble effort to get at the food. I had been dozing, but in an instant I was awake. All day and all night we sat face to face, I weary but resolute, and he weeping and complaining of his immediate hunger. It was, I know, a night and a day, but to me it seemed—it seems now—an interminable length of time.

And so our widened incompatibility ended at last in open conflict. For two vast days we struggled in undertones and wrestling contests. There were times when I beat and kicked him madly, times when I cajoled and persuaded him, and once I tried to bribe him with the last bottle of burgundy, for there was a rain-water pump from which I could get water. But neither force nor kindness availed; he was indeed beyond reason. He would neither desist from his attacks on the food nor from his noisy babbling to himself. The rudimentary precautions to keep our imprisonment endurable he would not observe. Slowly I began to realise the complete overthrow of his intelligence, to perceive that my sole companion in this close and sickly darkness was a man insane.

From certain vague memories I am inclined to think my own mind wandered at times. I had strange and hideous dreams whenever I slept. It sounds paradoxical, but I am inclined to think that the weakness and insanity of the curate warned me, braced me, and kept me a sane man.

On the eighth day he began to talk aloud instead of whispering, and nothing I could do would moderate his speech.

"It is just, O God!" he would say, over and over again. "It is just. On me and mine be the punishment laid. We have sinned, we have fallen short. There was poverty, sorrow; the poor were trodden in the dust, and I held my peace. I preached acceptable folly—my God, what folly!—when I should have stood up, though I died for it, and called upon them to repent-repent!…Oppressors of the poor and needy…! The wine press of God!"

Then he would suddenly revert to the matter of the food I withheld from him, praying, begging, weeping, at last threatening. He began to raise his voice—I prayed him not to. He perceived a hold on me—he threatened he would shout and bring the Martians upon us. For a time that scared me; but any concession would have shortened our chance of escape beyond estimating. I defied him, although I felt no assurance that he might not do this thing. But that day, at any rate, he did not. He talked with his voice rising slowly, through the greater part of the eighth and ninth days— threats, entreaties, mingled with a torrent of half-sane and always frothy repentance for his vacant sham of God's service, such as made me pity him. Then he slept awhile, and began again with renewed strength, so loudly that I must needs make him desist.

"Be still!" I implored.

He rose to his knees, for he had been sitting in the darkness near the copper.

"I have been still too long," he said, in a tone that must have reached the pit, "and now I must bear my witness. Woe unto this unfaithful city! Woe! Woe! Woe! Woe! Woe! To the inhabitants of the earth by reason of the other voices of the trumpet——"

"Shut up!" I said, rising to my feet, and in a terror lest the Martians should hear us. "For God's sake——"

"Nay," shouted the curate, at the top of his voice, standing likewise and extending his arms. "Speak! The word of the Lord is upon me!"

In three strides he was at the door leading into the kitchen.

"I must bear my witness! I go! It has already been too long delayed."

I put out my hand and felt the meat chopper hanging to the wall. In a flash I was after him. I was fierce with fear. Before he was halfway across the kitchen I had overtaken him. With one last touch of humanity I turned the blade back and struck him with the butt. He went headlong forward and lay stretched on the ground. I stumbled over him and stood panting. He lay still.

Suddenly I heard a noise without, the run and smash of slipping plaster, and the triangular aperture in the wall was darkened. I looked up and saw the lower surface of a handling-machine coming slowly across the hole. One of its gripping limbs curled amid the débris; another limb appeared, feeling its way over the fallen beams. I stood petrified, staring. Then I saw through a sort of glass plate near the edge of the body the face, as we may call it, and the large dark eyes of a Martian, peering, and then a long metallic snake of tentacle came feeling slowly through the hole.

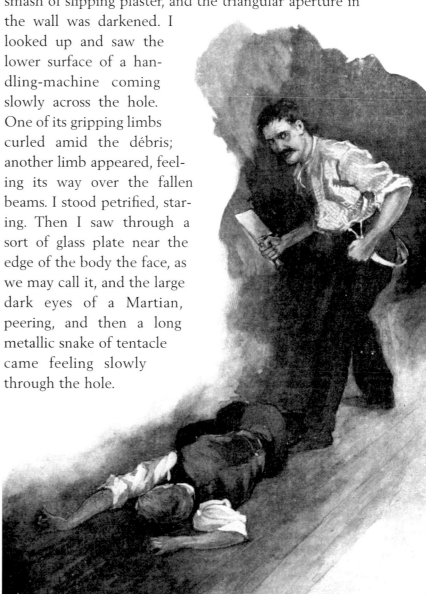

I turned by an effort, stumbled over the curate, and stopped at the scullery door. The tentacle was now some way, two yards or more, in the room, and twisting and turning, with queer sudden movements, this way and that. For a while I stood fascinated by that slow, fitful advance. Then, with a faint, hoarse cry, I forced myself across the scullery. I trembled violently; I could scarcely stand upright. I opened the door of the coal cellar, and stood there in the darkness staring at the faintly lit doorway into the kitchen, and listening. Had the Martian seen me? What was it doing now?

Something was moving to and fro there, very quietly; every now and then it tapped against the wall, or started on its movements with a faint metallic ringing, like the movements of keys on a split-ring. Then a heavy body—I knew too well what—was dragged across the floor of the kitchen towards the opening. Irresistibly attracted, I crept to the door and peeped into the kitchen. In the triangle of bright outer sunlight I saw the Martian, in its Briareus of a handling-machine, scrutinizing the curate's head. I thought at once that it would infer my presence from the mark of the blow I had given him.

I crept back to the coal cellar, shut the door, and began to cover myself up as much as I could, and as noiselessly as possible in the darkness, among the firewood and coal therein. Every now and then I paused, rigid, to hear if the Martian had thrust its tentacles through the opening again.

Then the faint metallic jingle returned. I traced it slowly feeling over the kitchen. Presently I heard it nearer—in the scullery, as I judged. I thought that its length might be insufficient to reach me. I prayed copiously. It passed, scraping faintly across the cellar door. An age of almost intolerable suspense intervened; then I heard it fumbling at the latch! It had found the door! The Martians understood doors!

It worried at the catch for a minute, perhaps, and then the door opened.

In the darkness I could just see the thing—like an elephant's trunk more than anything else—waving towards me and touching and examining the wall, coals, wood and ceiling. It was like a black worm swaying its blind head to and fro.

Once, even, it touched the heel of my boot. I was on the verge of screaming; I bit my hand. For a time the tentacle was silent. I could have fancied it had been withdrawn. Presently, with an abrupt click, it gripped something—I thought it had me!—and seemed to go out of the cellar again. For a minute I was not sure. Apparently it had taken a lump of coal to examine.

I seized the opportunity of slightly shifting my position, which had become cramped, and then listened. I whispered passionate prayers for safety.

Then I heard the slow, deliberate sound creeping towards me again. Slowly, slowly it drew near, scratching against the walls and tapping the furniture.

While I was still doubtful, it rapped smartly against the cellar door and closed it. I heard it go into the pantry, and the biscuit-tins rattled and a bottle smashed, and then came a heavy bump against the cellar door. Then silence that passed into an infinity of suspense.

Had it gone?

At last I decided that it had.

It came into the scullery no more; but I lay all the tenth day in the close darkness, buried among coals and firewood, not daring even to crawl out for the drink for which I craved. It was the eleventh day before I ventured so far from my security.

Chapter Five

★ ★ ★

The Stillness

My first act before I went into the pantry was to fasten the door between the kitchen and the scullery. But the pantry was empty; every scrap of food had gone. Apparently, the Martian had taken it all on the previous day. At that discovery I despaired for the first time. I took no food, or no drink either, on the eleventh or the twelfth day.

At first my mouth and throat were parched, and my strength ebbed sensibly. I sat about in the darkness of the scullery, in a state of despondent wretchedness. My mind ran on eating. I thought I had become deaf, for the noises of movement I had been accustomed to hear from the pit had ceased absolutely. I did not feel strong enough to crawl noiselessly to the peephole, or I would have gone there.

On the twelfth day my throat was so painful that, taking the chance of alarming the Martians, I attacked the creaking rain-water pump that stood by the sink, and got a couple of glassfuls of blackened and tainted rain water. I was greatly refreshed by this, and emboldened by the fact that no enquiring tentacle followed the noise of my pumping.

During these days, in a rambling, inconclusive way, I thought much of the curate and of the manner of his death.

On the thirteenth day I drank some more water, and dozed and thought disjointedly of eating and of vague impossible plans of escape. Whenever I dozed I dreamt of horrible phantasms, of the death of the curate, or of sumptuous dinners; but, asleep or awake, I felt a keen pain that urged me to drink again and again. The light that came into the scullery was no longer grey, but red. To my disordered imagination it seemed the colour of blood.

On the fourteenth day I went into the kitchen, and I was surprised to find that the fronds of the red weed had grown right across the hole in the wall, turning the half-light of the place into a crimson-coloured obscurity.

It was early on the fifteenth day that I heard a curious, familiar sequence of sounds in the kitchen, and, listening, identified it as the snuffing and scratching of a dog. Going into the kitchen, I saw a dog's nose peering in through a break among the ruddy fronds. This greatly surprised me. At the scent of me he barked shortly.

I thought if I could induce him to come into the place quietly I should be able, perhaps, to kill and eat him; and in any case, it would be advisable to kill him, lest his actions attracted the attention of the Martians.

I crept forward, saying "Good dog!" very softly; but he suddenly withdrew his head and disappeared.

I listened—I was not deaf—but certainly the pit was still. I heard a sound like the flutter of a bird's wings, and a hoarse croaking, but that was all.

For a long while I lay close to the peephole, but not daring to move aside the red plants that obscured it. Once or twice I heard a faint pitter-patter like the feet of the dog going hither and thither on the sand far below me, and there were more birdlike sounds, but that was all. At length, encouraged by the silence, I looked out.

Except in the corner, where a multitude of crows hopped and fought over the skeletons of the dead the Martians had consumed, there was not a living thing in the pit.

I stared about me, scarcely believing my eyes. All the machinery had gone. Save for the big mound of greyish-blue powder in one corner, certain bars of aluminium in another, the black birds, and the skeletons of the killed, the place was merely an empty circular pit in the sand.

Slowly I thrust myself out through the red weed, and stood upon the mound of rubble. I could see in any direction save behind me, to the north, and neither Martians nor sign of Martians were to be seen. The pit dropped sheerly from my feet, but a little way

A multitude of crows hopped and fought over the skeletons of the dead.

along the rubbish afforded a practicable slope to the summit of the ruins. My chance of escape had come. I began to tremble.

I hesitated for some time, and then, in a gust of desperate resolution, and with a heart that throbbed violently, I scrambled to the top of the mound in which I had been buried so long.

I looked about again. To the northward, too, no Martian was visible.

When I had last seen this part of Sheen in the daylight it had been a straggling street of comfortable white and red houses, interspersed with abundant shady trees. Now I stood on a mound of smashed brickwork, clay, and gravel, over which spread a multitude of red cactus-shaped plants, knee-high, without a solitary terrestrial growth to dispute their footing. The trees near me were dead and brown, but further a network of red thread scaled the still living stems.

The neighbouring houses had all been wrecked, but none had been burned; their walls stood, sometimes to the second story, with smashed windows and shattered doors. The red weed grew tumultuously in their roofless rooms. Below me was the great pit, with the crows struggling for its refuse. A number of other birds hopped about among the ruins. Far away I saw a gaunt cat slink crouchingly along a wall, but traces of men there were none.

The day seemed, by contrast with my recent confinement, dazzlingly bright, the sky a glowing blue. A gentle breeze kept the red weed that covered every scrap of unoccupied ground gently swaying. And oh! the sweetness of the air!

Chapter Six

★ ★ ★

The Work of Fifteen Days

For some time I stood tottering on the mound regardless of my safety. Within that noisome den from which I had emerged I had thought with a narrow intensity only of our immediate security. I had not realised what had been happening to the world, had not anticipated this startling vision of unfamiliar things. I had expected to see Sheen in ruins—I found about me the landscape, weird and lurid, of another planet.

For that moment I touched an emotion beyond the common range of men, yet one that the poor brutes we dominate know only too well. I felt as a rabbit might feel returning to his burrow and suddenly confronted by the work of a dozen busy navvies digging the foundations of a house. I felt the first inkling of a thing that presently grew quite clear in my mind, that oppressed me for many days, a sense of dethronement, a persuasion that I was no longer a master, but an animal among the animals, under the Martian heel. With us it would be as with them, to lurk and watch, to run and hide; the fear and empire of man had passed away.

But so soon as this strangeness had been realised it passed, and my dominant motive became the hunger of my long and dismal fast. In the direction away from the pit I saw, beyond a red-covered wall, a patch of garden ground unburied. This gave me a hint, and I went knee-deep, and sometimes neck-deep, in the red weed. The density of the weed gave me a reassuring sense of hiding. The wall was some six feet high, and when I attempted to clamber it I found I could not lift my feet to the crest. So I went along by the side of it, and came to a corner and a rockwork that enabled me to get to the top, and tumble into the garden I coveted. Here I found some young onions, a couple of gladiolus bulbs, and a quantity of immature carrots, all of which I secured, and, scrambling over a ruined wall, went on my way through scarlet and crimson trees towards Kew—it was like walking through an avenue of gigantic blood drops—possessed with two ideas: to get more food, and to limp, as soon and as far as my strength permitted, out of this accursed unearthly region of the pit.

Some way farther, in a grassy place, was a group of mushrooms which also I devoured, and then I came upon a brown sheet of flowing shallow water, where meadows used to be. These fragments of nourishment served only to whet my hunger. At first I was surprised at this flood in a hot, dry summer, but afterwards I discovered that it was caused by the tropical exuberance of the red weed. Directly this extraordinary growth encountered water it straightway became gigantic and of unparalleled fecundity. Its seeds were simply poured down into the water of the Wey and Thames, and its swiftly growing and Titanic water fronds speedily choked both those rivers.

At Putney, as I afterwards saw, the bridge was almost lost in a tangle of this weed, and at Richmond, too, the Thames water poured in a broad and shallow stream across the meadows of Hampton and Twickenham. As the water spread the weed followed them, until the ruined villas of the Thames valley were for a time lost in this red swamp, whose margin I explored, and much of the desolation the Martians had caused was concealed.

In the end the red weed succumbed almost as quickly as it had spread. A cankering disease, due, it is believed, to the action of certain bacteria, presently seized upon it. Now by the action of natural selection, all terrestrial plants have acquired a resisting power against bacterial diseases—they never succumb without a severe struggle, but the red weed rotted like a thing already dead. The fronds became bleached, and then shrivelled and brittle. They broke off at the least touch, and the waters that had stimulated their early growth carried their last vestiges out to sea.

My first act on coming to this water was, of course, to slake my thirst. I drank a great deal of it and, moved by an impulse, gnawed some fronds of red weed; but they were watery, and had a sickly, metallic taste. I found the water was sufficiently shallow for me to wade securely, although the red weed impeded my feet a little; but the flood evidently got deeper towards the river, and I turned back to Mortlake. I managed to make out the road by means of occasional ruins of its villas and fences and lamps, and so presently I got out of this spate and made my way to the hill going up towards Roehampton and came out on Putney Common.

Here the scenery changed from the strange and unfamiliar to the wreckage of the familiar: patches of ground exhibited the devastation of a cyclone, and in a few score yards I would come upon perfectly undisturbed spaces, houses with their blinds trimly drawn and doors closed, as if they had been left for a day by

At Putney, the bridge was almost lost in a tangle of this weed.

the owners, or as if their inhabitants slept within. The red weed was less abundant; the tall trees along the lane were free from the red creeper. I hunted for food among the trees, finding nothing, and I also raided a couple of silent houses, but they had already been broken into and ransacked. I rested for the remainder of the daylight in a shrubbery, being, in my enfeebled condition, too fatigued to push on.

All this time I saw no human beings, and no signs of the Martians. I encountered a couple of hungry-looking dogs, but both hurried circuitously away from the advances I made them. Near Roehampton I had seen two human skeletons—not bodies, but skeletons, picked clean—and in the wood by me I found the crushed and scattered bones of several cats and rabbits and the skull of a sheep. But though I gnawed parts of these in my mouth, there was nothing to be got from them.

After sunset I struggled on along the road towards Putney, where I think the Heat-Ray must have been used for some reason. And in the garden beyond Roehampton I got a quantity of immature potatoes, sufficient to stay my hunger. From this garden one looked down upon Putney and the river. The aspect of the place in the dusk was singularly desolate: blackened trees, blackened, desolate ruins, and down the hill the sheets of the flooded river, red-tinged with the weed. And over all—silence. It filled me with indescribable terror to think how swiftly that desolating change had come.

For a time I believed that mankind had been swept out of existence, and that I stood there alone, the last man left alive. Hard by the top of Putney Hill I came upon another skeleton, with the arms dislocated and removed several yards from the rest of the body. As I proceeded I became more and more convinced that the extermination of mankind was, save for such stragglers as myself, already accomplished in this part of the world. The Martians, I thought, had gone on and left the country desolated, seeking food elsewhere. Perhaps even now they were destroying Berlin or Paris, or it might be they had gone northward.

Chapter Seven
★ ★ ★
The Man on Putney Hill

I spent that night in the inn that stands at the top of Putney Hill, sleeping in a made bed for the first time since my flight to Leatherhead. I will not tell the needless trouble I had breaking into that house—afterwards I found the front door was on the latch—nor how I ransacked every room for food, until just on the verge of despair, in what seemed to me to be a servant's bedroom, I found a ratgnawed crust and two tins of pineapple. The place had been already searched and emptied. In the bar I afterwards found some biscuits and sandwiches that had been overlooked. The latter I could not eat, they were too rotten, but the former not only stayed my hunger, but filled my pockets. I lit no lamps, fearing some Martian might come beating that part of London for food in the night. Before I went to bed I had an interval of restlessness, and prowled from window to window, peering out for some sign of these monsters. I slept little. As I lay in bed I found myself thinking consecutively—a thing I do not remember to have done since my last argument with the curate. During all the intervening time my mental condition had been a hurrying succession of vague emotional states or a sort of stupid receptivity. But in the night my brain, reinforced, I suppose, by the food I had eaten, grew clear again, and I thought.

Three things struggled for possession of my mind: the killing of the curate, the whereabouts of the Martians, and the possible fate of my wife. The former gave me no sensation of horror or remorse to recall; I saw it simply as a thing done, a memory infinitely disagreeable but quite without the quality of remorse. I saw myself then as I see myself now, driven step by step towards that hasty blow, the creature of a sequence of accidents leading inevitably to that. I felt no condemnation; yet the memory, static, unprogressive, haunted me. In the silence of the night, with that sense of the nearness of God that sometimes comes into the stillness and the darkness, I stood my trial, my only trial, for that moment of wrath and fear. I retraced every step of our conversation from the moment when I had found him crouching beside me, heedless of my thirst, and pointing to the fire and smoke that streamed up from the ruins of Weybridge. We had been incapable of co-operation—grim chance had taken no heed of that. Had I foreseen, I should have left him at Halliford. But I did not foresee; and crime is to foresee and do. And I set this down as I have set all this story down, as it was. There were no witnesses—all these things I might have concealed. But I set it down, and the reader must form his judgment as he will.

And when, by an effort, I had set aside that picture of a prostrate body, I faced the problem of the Martians and the fate of my wife. For the former I had no data; I could imagine a hundred things, and so, unhappily, I could for the latter. And suddenly that night became terrible. I found myself sitting up in bed, staring at the dark. I found myself praying that the Heat-Ray might have suddenly and painlessly struck her out of being. Since the night of my return from Leatherhead I had not prayed. I had uttered prayers, fetish prayers, had prayed as heathens mutter charms when I was in extremity; but now I prayed indeed, pleading steadfastly and sanely, face to face with the darkness of God. Strange night! Strangest in this, that so soon as dawn had come, I, who had talked with God, crept out of the house like a rat leaving its hiding place—a creature scarcely larger, an inferior animal, a thing that for any passing whim of our masters might be hunted and killed. Perhaps they also prayed confidently to God. Surely, if we have learned nothing else, this war has taught us pity—pity for those witless souls that suffer our dominion.

The morning was bright and fine, and the eastern sky glowed pink, and was fretted with little golden clouds. In the road that runs from the top of Putney Hill to Wimbledon was a number of poor vestiges of the panic torrent that must have poured Londonward on the Sunday night after the fighting began. There was a little two-wheeled cart inscribed with the name of Thomas Lobb, Greengrocer, New Malden, with a smashed wheel and an abandoned tin trunk; there was a straw hat trampled into the now hardened mud, and at the top of West Hill a lot of blood-stained glass about the overturned water trough. My movements were languid, my plans of the vaguest. I had an idea of going to Leatherhead, though I knew that there I had the poorest chance of finding my wife. Certainly, unless death had overtaken them suddenly, my cousins and she would have fled thence; but it seemed to me I might find or learn there whither the Surrey people had fled. I knew I wanted to find my wife, that my heart ached for her and the world of men, but I had no clear idea how the finding might be done. I was also sharply aware now of my intense loneliness. From the corner I went, under cover of a thicket of trees and bushes, to the edge of Wimbledon Common, stretching wide and far.

That dark expanse was lit in patches by yellow gorse and broom; there was no red weed to be seen, and as I prowled, hesitating, on the verge of the open, the sun rose, flooding it all with light and vitality. I came upon a busy swarm of little frogs in a swampy place among the trees. I stopped to look at them, drawing a lesson from their stout resolve to live. And presently, turning suddenly, with an odd feeling of being watched, I beheld something crouching amid a clump of bushes. I stood regarding this. I made a step towards it, and it rose up and became a man armed with a cutlass. I approached him slowly. He stood silent and motionless, regarding me.

As I drew nearer I perceived he was dressed in clothes as dusty and filthy as my own; he looked, indeed, as though he had been dragged through a culvert. Nearer, I distinguished the green slime of ditches mixing with the pale drab of dried clay and shiny, coaly patches. His black hair fell over his eyes, and his face was dark and dirty and sunken, so that at first I did not recognise him. There was a red cut across the lower part of his face.

"Stop!" he cried, when I was within ten yards of him, and I stopped. His voice was hoarse. "Where do you come from?" he said.

I thought, surveying him.

"I come from Mortlake," I said. "I was buried near the pit the Martians made about their cylinder. I have worked my way out and escaped."

"There is no food about here," he said. "This is my country. All this hill down to the river, and back to Clapham, and up to the edge of the common. There is only food for one. Which way are you going?"

I answered slowly.

"I don't know," I said. "I have been buried in the ruins of a house thirteen or fourteen days. I don't know what has happened."

He looked at me doubtfully, then started, and looked with a changed expression.

"I've no wish to stop about here," said I. "I think I shall go to Leatherhead, for my wife was there."

He shot out a pointing finger.

"It is you," said he; "the man from Woking. And you weren't killed at Weybridge?"

I recognised him at the same moment.

"You are the artilleryman who came into my garden."

"Good luck!" he said. "We are lucky ones! Fancy *you*!" He put out a hand, and I took it. "I crawled up a drain," he said. "But they didn't kill everyone. And after they went away I got off towards Walton across the fields. But—— It's not sixteen days altogether—and your hair is grey." He looked over his shoulder suddenly. "Only a rook," he said. "One gets to know that birds have shadows these days. This is a bit open. Let us crawl under those bushes and talk."

"Have you seen any Martians?" I said. "Since I crawled out——"

"They've gone away across London," he said. "I guess they've got a bigger camp there. Of a night, all over there, Hampstead way, the sky is alive with their lights. It's like a great city, and in the glare you can just see them moving. By daylight you can't. But nearer—I haven't seen them—" (he counted on his fingers) "five days. Then I saw a couple across Hammersmith way carrying something big. And the night before last"—he stopped and spoke impressively—"it was just a matter of lights, but it was something up in the air. I believe they've built a flying-machine, and are learning to fly."

I stopped, on hands and knees, for we had come to the bushes.

"Fly!"

"Yes," he said, "fly."

I went on into a little bower, and sat down.

"It is all over with humanity," I said. "If they can do that they will simply go round the world."

He nodded.

"They will. But—— It will relieve things over here a bit. And besides——" He looked at me. "Aren't you satisfied it *is* up with humanity? I am. We're down; we're beat."

I stared. Strange as it may seem, I had not arrived at this fact—a fact perfectly obvious so soon as he spoke. I had still held a vague hope; rather, I had kept a lifelong habit of mind. He repeated his words, "We're beat." They carried absolute conviction.

"It's all over," he said. "They've lost *one*—just *one*. And they've made their footing good and crippled the greatest power in the world. They've walked over us. The death of that one at Weybridge was an accident. And these are only pioneers. They kept on coming. These green stars—I've seen none these five or six days, but I've no doubt they're falling somewhere every night. Nothing's to be done. We're under! We're beat!"

I made him no answer. I sat staring before me, trying in vain to devise some countervailing thought.

"This isn't a war," said the artilleryman. "It never was a war, any more than there's war between man and ants."

Suddenly I recalled the night in the observatory.

"After the tenth shot they fired no more—at least, until the first cylinder came."

"How do you know?" said the artilleryman. I explained. He thought. "Something wrong with the gun," he said. "But what if there is? They'll get it right again. And even if there's a delay, how can it alter the end? It's just men and ants. There's the ants builds their cities, live their lives, have wars, revolutions, until the men want them out of the way, and then they go out of the way. That's what we are now—just ants. Only——"

"Yes," I said.

"We're eatable ants."

We sat looking at each other.

"And what will they do with us?" I said.

"That's what I've been thinking," he said; "that's what I've been thinking. After Weybridge I went south—thinking. I saw what was up. Most of the people were hard at it squealing and exciting themselves. But I'm not so fond of squealing. I've been in sight of death once or twice; I'm not an ornamental soldier, and at the best and worst, death—it's just death. And it's the man that keeps on thinking comes through. I saw everyone tracking away south. Says I, "Food won't last this way," and I turned right back. I went for the Martians like a sparrow goes for man. All round"—he waved a hand to the horizon—"they're starving in heaps, bolting, treading on each other...."

He saw my face, and halted awkwardly.

"No doubt lots who had money have gone away to France," he said. He seemed to hesitate whether to apologise, met my eyes, and went on: "There's food all about here. Canned things in shops; wines, spirits, mineral waters; and the water mains and drains are empty. Well, I was telling you what I was thinking. 'Here's intelligent things,' I said, 'and it seems they want us for food. First, they'll smash us up—ships, machines, guns, cities, all the order and organisation. All that will go. If we were the size of ants we might pull through. But we're not. It's all too bulky to stop. That's the first certainty.' Eh?"

I assented.

"It is; I've thought it out. Very well, then—next; at present we're caught as we're wanted. A Martian has only to go a few miles to get a crowd on the run. And I saw one, one day, out by Wandsworth, picking houses to pieces and routing among the wreckage. But they won't keep on doing that. So soon as they've settled all our guns and ships, and smashed our railways, and done all the things they are doing over there, they will begin catching us systematic, picking the best and storing us in cages and things. That's what they will start doing in a bit. Lord! They haven't begun on us yet. Don't you see that?"

"Not begun!" I exclaimed.

"Not begun. All that's happened so far is through our not having the sense to keep quiet—worrying them with guns and such foolery. And losing our heads, and rushing off in crowds to where there wasn't any more safety than where we were. They don't want to bother us yet. They're making their things—making all the things they couldn't bring with them, getting things ready for the rest of their people. Very likely that's why the cylinders have stopped for a bit, for fear of hitting those who are here. And instead of our rushing about blind, on the howl, or getting dynamite on the chance of busting them up, we've got to fix ourselves up according to the new state of affairs. That's how I figure it out. It isn't quite according to what a man wants for his species, but it's about what the facts point to. And that's the principle I acted upon. Cities, nations, civilisation, progress—it's all over. That game's up. We're beat."

"But if that is so, what is there to live for?"

The artilleryman looked at me for a moment.

"There won't be any more blessed concerts for a million years or so; there won't be any Royal Academy of Arts, and no nice little feeds at restaurants. If it's amusement you're after, I reckon the game is up. If you've got any drawing-room manners or a dislike to eating peas with a knife or dropping aitches, you'd better chuck 'em away. They ain't no further use."

"You mean——"

"I mean that men like me are going on living—for the sake of the breed. I tell you, I'm grim set on living. And if I'm not mistaken, you'll show what insides *you've* got, too, before long. We aren't going to be exterminated. And I don't mean to be caught either, and tamed and fattened and bred like a thundering ox. Ugh! Fancy those brown creepers!"

"You don't mean to say——"

"I do. I'm going on, under their feet. I've got it planned; I've thought it out. We men are beat. We don't know enough. We've got to learn before we've got a chance. And we've got to live and keep independent while we learn. See! That's what has to be done."

I stared, astonished, and stirred profoundly by the man's resolution.

"Great God!," cried I. "But you are a man indeed!" And suddenly I gripped his hand.

"Eh!" he said, with his eyes shining. "I've thought it out, eh?"

"Go on," I said.

"Well, those who mean to escape their catching must get ready. I'm getting ready. Mind you, it isn't all of us that are made for wild beasts; and that's what it's got to be. That's why I watched you. I had my doubts. You're slender. I didn't know that it was you, you see, or just how you'd been buried. All these—the sort of people that lived in these houses, and all those damn little clerks that used to live down that way—they'd be no good. They haven't any spirit in them—no proud dreams and no proud lusts; and a man who hasn't one or the other—Lord! What is he but funk and precautions? They just used to skedaddle off to work—I've seen hundreds of 'em, bit of breakfast in hand, running wild and shining to catch their little season-ticket train, for fear they'd get dismissed if they didn't; working at businesses they were afraid to take the trouble to understand; skedaddling back for fear they wouldn't be in time for dinner; keeping indoors after dinner for fear of the back streets, and sleeping with the wives they married, not because they wanted them, but because they had a bit of money that would make for safety in their one little miserable skedaddle through the world. Lives insured and a bit invested for fear of accidents. And on Sundays—fear of the hereafter. As if hell was built for rabbits! Well, the Martians will just be a godsend to these. Nice roomy cages, fattening food, careful breeding, no worry. After a week or so chasing about the fields and lands on empty stomachs, they'll come and be caught cheerful. They'll be quite glad after a bit. They'll wonder what people did before there were Martians to take care of them. And the bar loafers, and mashers, and singers—I can imagine them. I can imagine them," he said, with a sort of sombre gratification. "There'll be any amount of sentiment and religion loose among them. There's hundreds of things I saw with my eyes that I've only begun to see clearly these last few days. There's lots will take things as they are—fat and stupid; and lots will be worried by a sort of feeling that it's all wrong, and that they ought to be doing something. Now whenever things are so that a lot of people feel they ought to be doing something, the weak, and those who go weak with a lot of complicated thinking, always make for a sort of do-nothing religion, very pious and superior, and submit to persecution and the will of the Lord. Very likely you've seen the same thing. It's energy in a gale of funk, and turned clean inside out. These cages will be full of psalms and hymns and piety. And those of a less simple sort will work in a bit of—what is it?—eroticism."

He paused.

"Very likely these Martians will make pets of some of them; train them to do tricks—who knows?—get sentimental over the pet boy who grew up and had to be killed. And some, maybe, they will train to hunt us."

"No," I cried, "that's impossible! No human being——"

"What's the good of going on with such lies?" said the artilleryman. "There's men who'd do it cheerful. What nonsense to pretend there isn't!"

And I succumbed to his conviction.

"If they come after me," he said; "Lord, if they come after me!" and subsided into a grim meditation.

I sat contemplating these things. I could find nothing to bring against this man's reasoning. In the days before the invasion no one would have questioned my intellectual superiority to his—I, a professed and recognised writer on philosophical themes, and he, a common soldier; and yet he had already formulated a situation that I had scarcely realised.

"What are you doing?" I said presently. "What plans have you made?"

He hesitated.

"Well, it's like this," he said. "What have we to do? We have to invent a sort of life where men can live and breed, and be sufficiently secure to bring the children up. Yes—wait a bit, and I'll make it clearer what I think ought to be done. The tame ones will go like all tame beasts; in a few generations they'll be big, beautiful, rich-blooded, stupid—rubbish! The risk is that we who keep wild will go savage—degenerate into a sort of big, savage rat....You see, how I mean to live is underground. I've been thinking about the drains. Of course those who don't know drains think horrible things; but under this London are miles and miles—hundreds of miles—and a few days' rain and London empty will leave them sweet and clean. The main drains are big enough and airy enough for anyone. Then there's cellars, vaults, stores, from which bolting passages may be made to the drains. And the railway tunnels and subways. Eh? You begin to see? And we form a band—able-bodied, clean-minded men. We're not going to pick up any rubbish that drifts in. Weaklings go out again."

"As you meant me to go?"

"Well—I parleyed, didn't I?"

"We won't quarrel about that. Go on."

"Those who stop obey orders. Able-bodied, clean-minded women we want also—mothers and teachers. No lackadaisical ladies—no blasted rolling eyes. We can't have any weak or silly. Life is real again, and the useless and cumbersome and mischievous have to die. They ought to die. They ought to be willing to die. It's a sort of disloyalty, after all, to live and taint the race. And they can't be happy. Moreover, dying's none so dreadful; it's the funking makes it bad. And in all those places we shall gather. Our district will be London. And we may even be

I hurried through the red weed.

able to keep a watch, and run about in the open when the Martians keep away. Play cricket, perhaps. That's how we shall save the race. Eh? It's a possible thing? But saving the race is nothing in itself. As I say, that's only being rats. It's saving our knowledge and adding to it is the thing. There men like you come in. There's books, there's models. We must make great safe places down deep, and get all the books we can; not novels and poetry swipes, but ideas, science books. That's where men like you come in. We must go to the British Museum and pick all those books through. Especially we must keep up our science—learn more. We must watch these Martians. Some of us must go as spies. When it's all working, perhaps I will. Get caught, I mean. And the great thing is, we must leave the Martians alone. We mustn't even steal. If we get in their way, we clear out. We must show them we mean no harm. Yes, I know. But they're intelligent things, and they won't hunt us down if they have all they want, and think we're just harmless vermin."

The artilleryman paused and laid a brown hand upon my arm.

"After all, it may not be so much we may have to learn before—Just imagine this: four or five of their fighting machines suddenly starting off—Heat-Rays right and left, and not a Martian in 'em. Not a Martian in 'em, but men—men who have learned the way how. It may be in my time, even—those men. Fancy having one of them lovely things, with its Heat-Ray wide and free! Fancy having it in control! What would it matter if you smashed to smithereens at the end of the run, after a bust like that? I reckon the Martians'll open their beautiful eyes! Can't you see them, man? Can't you see them hurrying, hurrying—puffing and blowing and hooting to their other mechanical affairs? Something out of gear in every case. And swish, bang, rattle, swish! Just as they are fumbling over it, *swish* comes the Heat-Ray, and, behold! man has come back to his own."

For a while the imaginative daring of the artilleryman, and the tone of assurance and courage he assumed, completely dominated my mind. I believed unhesitatingly both in his forecast of human destiny and in the practicability of his astonishing scheme, and the reader who thinks me susceptible and foolish must contrast his position, reading steadily with all his thoughts about his subject, and mine, crouching fearfully in the bushes and listening, distracted by apprehension. We talked in this manner through the early morning time, and later crept out of the bushes, and, after scanning the sky for Martians, hurried precipitately to the house on Putney Hill where he had made his lair. It was the coal cellar of the place, and when I saw the work he had spent a week upon—it was a burrow scarcely ten yards long, which he designed to reach to the main drain on Putney Hill—I had my first inkling of the gulf between his dreams and his powers. Such a hole I could have dug in a day. But I believed in him sufficiently to work with him all that morning until past midday at his digging. We had a garden barrow and shot the earth we removed against the kitchen range. We refreshed ourselves with a tin of mock-turtle soup and wine from the neighbouring pantry. I found a curious relief from the aching strangeness of the world in this steady labour. As we worked, I turned his project over in my mind, and presently objections and doubts began to arise; but I worked there all the morning, so glad was I to find myself with a purpose again. After working an hour I began to speculate on the distance one had to go before the cloaca was reached, the chances we had of missing it altogether. My immediate trouble was why we should dig this long tunnel, when it was possible to get into the drain at once down one of the manholes, and work back to the house. It seemed to me, too, that the house was inconveniently chosen, and required a needless length of tunnel. And just as I was beginning to face these things, the artilleryman stopped digging, and looked at me.

"We're working well," he said. He put down his spade. "Let us knock off a bit" he said. "I think it's time we reconnoitred from the roof of the house."

I was for going on, and after a little hesitation he resumed his spade; and then suddenly I was struck by a thought. I stopped, and so did he at once.

"Why were you walking about the common," I said, "instead of being here?"

"Taking the air," he said. "I was coming back. It's safer by night."

"But the work?"

"Oh, one can't always work," he said, and in a flash I saw the man plain. He hesitated, holding his spade. "We ought to reconnoitre now," he said, "because if any come near they may hear the spades and drop upon us unawares."

I was no longer disposed to object. We went together to the roof and stood on a ladder peeping out of the roof door. No Martians were to be seen, and we ventured out on the tiles, and slipped down under shelter of the parapet.

From this position a shrubbery hid the greater portion of Putney, but we could see the river below, a bubbly mass of red weed, and the low parts of Lambeth flooded and red. The red creeper swarmed up the trees about the old palace, and their branches stretched gaunt and dead, and set with shrivelled leaves, from amid its clusters. It was strange how entirely dependent both these things were upon flowing water for their propagation. About us neither had gained a footing; laburnums, pink mays, snowballs, and trees of arborvitae, rose out of laurels and hydrangeas, green and brilliant into the sunlight. Beyond Kensington dense smoke was rising, and that and a blue haze hid the northward hills.

The artilleryman began to tell me of the sort of people who still remained in London.

"One night last week," he said, "some fools got the electric light in order, and there was all Regent Street and the Circus ablaze, crowded with painted and ragged drunkards, men and women, dancing and shouting till dawn. A man who was there told me. And as the day came they became aware of a fighting-machine standing near by the Langham and looking down at them. Heaven knows how long he had been there. It must have given some of them a nasty turn. He came down the road towards them, and picked up nearly a hundred too drunk or frightened to run away."

Grotesque gleam of a time no history will ever fully describe!

From that, in answer to my questions, he came round to his grandiose plans again. He grew enthusiastic. He talked so eloquently of the possibility of capturing a fighting-machine that I more than half believed in him again. But now that I was beginning to understand something of his quality, I could divine the stress he laid on doing nothing precipitately. And I noted that now there was no question that he personally was to capture and fight the great machine.

After a time we went down to the cellar. Neither of us seemed disposed to resume digging, and when he suggested a meal, I was nothing loath. He became suddenly very generous, and when we had eaten he went away and returned with some excellent cigars. We lit these, and his optimism glowed. He was inclined to regard my coming as a great occasion.

"There's some champagne in the cellar," he said.

"We can dig better on this Thames-side burgundy," said I.

"No," said he; "I am host today. Champagne! Great God! We've a heavy enough task before us! Let us take a rest and gather strength while we may. Look at these blistered hands!"

And pursuant to this idea of a holiday, he insisted upon playing cards after we had eaten. He taught me euchre, and after dividing London between us, I taking the northern side and he the southern, we played for parish points. Grotesque and foolish as this will seem to the sober reader, it is absolutely true, and what is more remarkable, I found the card game and several others we played extremely interesting.

Strange mind of man! that, with our species upon the edge of extermination or appalling degradation, with no clear prospect before us but the chance of a horrible death, we could sit following the chance of this painted pasteboard, and playing the "joker" with vivid delight. Afterwards he taught me poker, and I beat him at three tough chess games. When dark came we decided to take the risk, and lit a lamp.

After an interminable string of games, we supped, and the artilleryman finished the champagne. We went on smoking the cigars. He was no longer the energetic regenerator of his species I had encountered in the morning. He was still optimistic, but it was a less kinetic, a more thoughtful optimism. I remember he wound up with my health, proposed in a speech of small variety and considerable intermittence. I took a cigar, and went upstairs to look at the lights of which he had spoken that blazed so greenly along the Highgate hills.

At first I stared unintelligently across the London valley. The northern hills were shrouded in darkness; the fires near Kensington glowed redly, and now and then an orange-red tongue of flame flashed up and vanished in the deep blue night. All the rest of London was black. Then, nearer, I perceived a strange light, a pale, violet-purple fluorescent glow, quivering under the night breeze. For a space I could not understand it, and then I knew that it must be the red weed from which this faint irradiation proceeded. With that realisation my dormant sense of wonder, my sense of the proportion of things, awoke again. I glanced from that to Mars, red and clear, glowing high in the west, and then gazed long and earnestly at the darkness of Hampstead and Highgate.

I remained a very long time upon the roof, wondering at the grotesque changes of the day. I recalled my mental states from the midnight prayer to the foolish card-playing. I had a violent revulsion of feeling. I remember I flung away the cigar with a certain wasteful symbolism. My folly came to me with glaring exaggeration. I seemed a traitor to my wife and to my kind; I was filled with remorse. I resolved to leave this strange undisciplined dreamer of great things to his drink and gluttony, and to go on into London. There, it seemed to me, I had the best chance of learning what the Martians and my fellow-men were doing. I was still upon the roof when the late moon rose.

Chapter Eight

★ ★ ★

Dead London

After I had parted from the artilleryman, I went down the hill, and by the High Street across the bridge to Fulham. The red weed was tumultuous at that time, and nearly choked the bridge roadway; but its fronds were already whitened in patches by the spreading disease that presently removed it so swiftly.

At the corner of the lane that runs to Putney Bridge station I found a man lying. He was as black as a sweep with the black dust, alive, but helplessly and speechlessly drunk. I could get nothing from him but curses and furious lunges at my head. I think I should have stayed by him but for the brutal expression of his face.

There was black dust along the roadway from the bridge onwards, and it grew thicker in Fulham. The streets were horribly quiet. I got food—sour, hard, and mouldy, but quite eatable—in a baker's shop here. Some way towards Walham Green the streets became clear of powder, and I passed a white terrace of houses on fire; the noise of the burning was an absolute relief. Going on towards Brompton, the streets were quiet again.

Here I came once more upon the black powder in the streets and upon dead bodies. I saw altogether about a dozen in the length of the Fulham Road. They had been dead many days, so that I hurried quickly past them. The black powder covered them over, and softened their outlines. One or two had been disturbed by dogs.

Where there was no black powder, it was curiously like a Sunday in the City, with the closed shops, the houses locked up and the blinds drawn, the desertion, and the stillness. In some places plunderers had been at work, but rarely at other than the provision and wine shops. A jeweller's window had been broken open in one place, but apparently the thief had been disturbed, and a number of gold chains and a watch lay scattered on the pavement. I did not trouble to touch them. Farther on was a tattered woman in a heap on a doorstep; the hand that hung over her knee was gashed and bled down her rusty brown dress, and a smashed magnum of champagne formed a pool across the pavement. She seemed asleep, but she was dead.

The farther I penetrated into London, the profounder grew the stillness. But it was not so much the stillness of death—it was the stillness of suspense, of expectation. At any time the destruction that had already singed the northwestern borders of the metropolis, and had annihilated Ealing and Kilburn, might strike among these houses and leave them smoking ruins. It was a city condemned and derelict....

In South Kensington the streets were clear of dead and of black powder. It was near South Kensington that I first heard the howling. It crept almost imperceptibly upon my senses. It was a sobbing alternation of two notes, "Ulla, ulla, ulla, ulla," keeping on perpetually. When I passed streets that ran northward it grew in volume, and houses and buildings seemed to deaden and cut it off again. It came in a full tide down Exhibition Road. I stopped, staring towards Kensington Gardens, wondering at this strange, remote wailing. It was as if that mighty desert of houses had found a voice for its fear and solitude.

"Ulla, ulla, ulla, ulla," wailed that superhuman note—great waves of sound sweeping down the broad, sunlit roadway, between the tall buildings on each side. I turned northwards, marvelling, towards the iron gates of Hyde Park. I had half a mind to break into the Natural History Museum and find my way up to the summits of the towers, in order to see across the park. But I decided to keep to the ground, where quick hiding was possible, and so went on up the Exhibition Road. All the large mansions on each side of the road were empty and still, and my footsteps echoed against the sides of the houses. At the top, near the park gate, I came upon a strange sight—a bus overturned, and the skeleton of a horse picked clean. I puzzled over this for a time, and then went on to the bridge over the Serpentine. The voice grew stronger and stronger, though I could see nothing above the housetops on the north side of the park, save a haze of smoke to the northwest.

"Ulla, ulla, ulla, ulla," cried the voice, coming, as it

seemed to me, from the district about Regent's Park. The desolating cry worked upon my mind. The mood that had sustained me passed. The wailing took possession of me. I found I was intensely weary, footsore, and now again hungry and thirsty.

It was already past noon. Why was I wandering alone in this city of the dead? Why was I alone when all London was lying in state, and in its black shroud? I felt intolerably lonely. My mind ran on old friends that I had forgotten for years. I thought of the poisons in the chemists' shops, of the liquors the wine merchants stored; I recalled the two sodden creatures of despair, who so far as I knew, shared the city with myself....

I came into Oxford Street by the Marble Arch, and here again were black powder and several bodies, and an evil, ominous smell from the gratings of the cellars of some of the houses. I grew very thirsty after the heat of my long walk. With infinite trouble I managed to break into a public-house and get food and drink. I was weary after eating, and went into the parlour behind the bar, and slept on a black horsehair sofa I found there.

I awoke to find that dismal howling still in my ears, "Ulla, ulla, ulla, ulla." It was now dusk, and after I had routed out some biscuits and a cheese in the bar—there was a meat safe, but it contained nothing but maggots—I wandered on through the silent residential squares to Baker Street—Portman Square is the only one I can name—and so came out at last upon Regent's Park. And as I emerged from the top of Baker Street, I saw far away over the trees in the clearness of the sunset the hood of the Martian giant from which this howling proceeded. I was not terrified. I came upon him as if it were a matter of course. I watched him for some time, but he

A dozen of them stark and silent and laid in a row...

did not move. He appeared to be standing and yelling, for no reason that I could discover.

I tried to formulate a plan of action. That perpetual sound of "Ulla, ulla, ulla, ulla," confused my mind. Perhaps I was too tired to be very fearful. Certainly I was more curious to know the reason of this monotonous crying than afraid. I turned back away from the park and struck into Park Road, intending to skirt the park, went along under the shelter of the terraces, and got a view of this stationary, howling Martian from the direction of St. John's Wood. A couple of hundred yards out of Baker Street I heard a yelping chorus, and saw, first a dog with a piece of putrescent red meat in his jaws coming headlong towards me, and then a pack of starving mongrels in pursuit of him. He made a wide curve to avoid me, as though he feared I might prove a fresh competitor. As the yelping died away down the silent road, the wailing sound of "Ulla, ulla, ulla, ulla," reasserted itself.

I came upon the wrecked handling-machine halfway to St. John's Wood station. At first I thought a house had fallen across the road. It was only as I clambered among the ruins that I saw, with a start, this mechanical Samson lying, with its tentacles bent and smashed and twisted, among the ruins it had made. The forepart was shattered. It seemed as if it had driven blindly straight at the house, and had been overwhelmed in its overthrow. It seemed to me then that this might have happened by a handling-machine escaping from the guidance of its Martian. I could not clamber among the ruins to see it, and the twilight was now so far advanced that the blood with which its seat was smeared, and the gnawed gristle of the Martian that the dogs had left, were invisible to me.

Wondering still more at all that I had seen, I pushed on towards Primrose Hill. Far away, through a gap in the trees, I saw a second Martian, as motionless as the first, standing in the park towards the Zoological Gardens, and silent. A little beyond the ruins about the smashed handling-machine I came upon the red weed again, and found the Regent's Canal, a spongy mass of dark-red vegetation.

As I crossed the bridge, the sound of "Ulla, ulla, ulla, ulla," ceased. It was, as it were, cut off. The silence came like a thunderclap.

The dusky houses about me stood faint and tall and dim; the trees towards the park were growing black. All about me the red weed clambered among the ruins, writhing to get above me in the dimness. Night, the mother of fear and mystery, was coming upon me. But while that voice sounded the solitude, the desolation, had been endurable; by virtue of it London had still seemed alive, and the sense of life about me had upheld me. Then suddenly a change, the passing of something—I knew not what—and then a stillness that could be felt. Nothing but this gaunt quiet.

London about me gazed at me spectrally. The windows in the white houses were like the eye sockets of skulls. About me my imagination found a thousand noiseless enemies moving. Terror seized me, a horror of my temerity. In front of me the road became pitchy black as though it was tarred, and I saw a contorted shape lying across the pathway. I could not bring myself to go on. I turned down St. John's Wood Road, and ran headlong from this unendurable stillness towards Kilburn. I hid from the night and the silence, until long after midnight, in a cabmen's shelter in Harrow Road. But before the dawn my courage returned, and while the stars were still in the sky I turned once more towards Regent's Park. I missed my way among the streets, and presently saw down a long avenue, in the half-light of the early dawn, the curve of Primrose Hill. On the summit, towering up to the fading stars, was a third Martian, erect and motionless like the others.

An insane resolve possessed me. I would die and end it. And I would save myself even the trouble of killing myself. I marched on recklessly towards this Titan, and then, as I drew nearer and the light grew, I saw that a multitude of black birds was circling and clustering about the hood. At that my heart gave a bound, and I began running along the road.

I hurried through the red weed that choked St. Edmund's Terrace (I waded breast-high across a torrent of water that was rushing down from the waterworks towards the Albert Road), and emerged upon the grass before the rising of the sun. Great mounds had been heaped about the crest of the hill, making a huge redoubt of it—it was the final and largest place the Martians had made—and from behind these heaps there rose a thin smoke against the sky. Against the sky line an eager dog ran and disappeared. The thought that had flashed into my mind grew real, grew credible. I felt no fear, only a wild, trembling exultation, as I ran up the hill towards the motionless monster. Out of the hood hung lank shreds of brown, at which the hungry birds pecked and tore.

In another moment I had scrambled up the earthen rampart and stood upon its crest, and the interior of the redoubt was below me. A mighty space it was, with gigantic machines here and there within it, huge mounds of material and strange shelter places. And scattered about it, some in their overturned war-machines, some in the now rigid handling-machines, and a dozen of them stark and silent and laid in a row, were the Martians—*dead!*—slain by the putrefactive and disease bacteria against which their systems were unprepared; slain as the red weed was being slain; slain, after all man's devices had failed, by the humblest things that God, in his wisdom, has put upon this earth.

For so it had come about, as indeed I and many men might have foreseen had not terror and disaster blinded our minds. These germs of disease have taken toll of humanity since the beginning of things—taken toll of our prehuman ancestors since life began here. But by virtue of this natural selection of our kind we have developed resisting power; to no germs do we succumb without a struggle, and to many—those that cause putrefaction in dead matter, for instance—our living frames are altogether immune. But there are no bacteria in Mars, and directly these invaders arrived, directly they drank and fed, our microscopic allies began to work their overthrow. Already when I watched them they were irrevocably doomed, dying and rotting even as they went to and fro. It was inevitable. By the toll of a billion deaths man has bought his birthright of the earth, and it is his against all comers; it would still be his were the Martians ten times as mighty as they are. For neither do men live nor die in vain.

Here and there they were scattered, nearly fifty altogether, in that great gulf they had made, overtaken by a death that must have seemed to them as incomprehensible as any death could be. To me also at that time this death was incomprehensible. All I knew was that these things that had been alive and so terrible to men were dead. For a moment I believed that the destruction of Sennacherib had been repeated, that God had repented, that the Angel of Death had slain them in the night.

I stood staring into the pit, and my heart lightened gloriously, even as the rising sun struck the world to fire about me with his rays. The pit was still in darkness; the mighty engines, so great and wonderful in their power and complexity, so unearthly in their tortuous forms, rose weird and vague and strange out of the shadows towards the light. A multitude of dogs, I could hear, fought over the bodies that lay darkly in the depth of the pit, far below me. Across the pit on its farther lip, flat and vast and strange, lay the great flying-machine with which they had been experimenting upon our denser atmosphere when decay and death arrested them. Death had come not a day too soon. At the sound of a cawing overhead I looked up at the huge fighting-machine that would fight no more for ever, at the tattered red shreds of flesh that dripped down upon the overturned seats on the summit of Primrose Hill.

I turned and looked down the slope of the hill to where, enhaloed now in birds, stood those other two Martians that I had seen overnight, just as death had overtaken them. The one had died, even as it had been crying to its companions; perhaps it was the last to die, and its voice had gone on perpetually until the force of its machinery was exhausted. They glittered now, harm-

less tripod towers of shining metal, in the brightness of the rising sun.

All about the pit, and saved as by a miracle from everlasting destruction, stretched the great Mother of Cities. Those who have only seen London veiled in her sombre robes of smoke can scarcely imagine the naked clearness and beauty of the silent wilderness of houses.

Eastward, over the blackened ruins of the Albert Terrace and the splintered spire of the church, the sun blazed dazzling in a clear sky, and here and there some facet in the great wilderness of roofs caught the light and glared with a white intensity.

Northward were Kilburn and Hampsted, blue and crowded with houses; westward the great city was dimmed; and southward, beyond the Martians, the green waves of Regent's Park, the Langham Hotel, the dome of the Albert Hall, the Imperial Institute, and the giant mansions of the Brompton Road came out clear and little in the sunrise, the jagged ruins of Westminster rising hazily beyond. Far away and blue were the Surrey hills, and the towers of the Crystal Palace glittered like two silver rods. The dome of St. Paul's was dark against the sunrise, and injured, I saw for the first time, by a huge gaping cavity on its western side.

And as I looked at this wide expanse of houses and factories and churches, silent and abandoned; as I thought of the multitudinous hopes and efforts, the innumerable hosts of lives that had gone to build this human reef, and of the swift and ruthless destruction that had hung over it all; when I realised that the shadow had been rolled back, and that men might still live in the streets, and this dear vast dead city of mine be once more alive and powerful, I felt a wave of emotion that was near akin to tears.

The torment was over. Even that day the healing would begin. The survivors of the people scattered over the country—leaderless, lawless, foodless, like sheep without a shepherd—the thousands who had fled by sea, would begin to return; the pulse of life, growing stronger and stronger, would beat again in the empty streets and pour across the vacant squares. Whatever destruction was done, the hand of the destroyer was stayed. All the gaunt wrecks, the blackened skeletons of houses that stared so dismally at the sunlit grass of the hill, would presently be echoing with the hammers of the restorers and ringing with the tapping of their trowels. At the thought I extended my hands towards the sky and began thanking God. In a year, thought I—in a year. . .

With overwhelming force came the thought of myself, of my wife, and the old life of hope and tender helpfulness that had ceased for ever.

Chapter Nine

★ ★ ★

Wreckage

And now comes the strangest thing in my story. Yet, perhaps, it is not altogether strange. I remember, clearly and coldly and vividly, all that I did that day until the time that I stood weeping and praising God upon the summit of Primrose Hill. And then I forget.

Of the next three days I know nothing. I have learned since that, so far from my being the first discoverer of the Martian overthrow, several such wanderers as myself had already discovered this on the previous night. One man—the first—had gone to St. Martin's-le-Grand, and, while I sheltered in the cabmen's hut, had contrived to telegraph to Paris. Thence the joyful news had flashed all over the world; a thousand cities, chilled by ghastly apprehensions, suddenly flashed into frantic illuminations; they knew of it in Dublin, Edinburgh, Manchester, Birmingham, at the time when I stood upon the verge of the pit. Already men, weeping with joy, as I have heard, shouting and staying their work to shake hands and shout, were making up trains, even as near as Crewe, to descend upon London. The church bells that had ceased a fortnight since suddenly caught the news, until all England was bell-ringing. Men on cycles, lean-faced, unkempt, scorched along every country lane shouting of unhoped deliverance, shouting to gaunt, staring figures of despair. And for the food! Across the Channel, across the Irish Sea, across the Atlantic, corn, bread, and meat were tearing to our relief. All the shipping in the world seemed going Londonward in those days. But of all this

I have no memory. I drifted—a demented man. I found myself in a house of kindly people, who had found me on the third day wandering, weeping, and raving through the streets of St. John's Wood. They have told me since that I was singing some insane doggerel about "The Last Man Left Alive! Hurrah! The Last Man Left Alive!" Troubled as they were with their own affairs, these people, whose name, much as I would like to express my gratitude to them, I may not even give here, nevertheless cumbered themselves with me, sheltered me, and protected me from myself. Apparently they had learned something of my story from me during the days of my lapse.

Very gently, when my mind was assured again, did they break to me what they had learned of the fate of Leatherhead. Two days after I was imprisoned it had been destroyed, with every soul in it, by a Martian. He had swept it out of existence, as it seemed, without any provocation, as a boy might crush an ant hill, in the mere wantonness of power.

I was a lonely man, and they were very kind to me. I was a lonely man and a sad one, and they bore with me. I remained with them four days after my recovery. All that time I felt a vague, a growing craving to look once more on whatever remained of the little life that seemed so happy and bright in my past. It was a mere hopeless desire to feast upon my misery. They dissuaded me. They did all they could to divert me from this morbidity. But at last I could resist the impulse no longer, and, promising faithfully to return to them, and parting, as I will confess, from these four-day friends with tears, I went out again into the streets that had lately been so dark and strange and empty.

Already they were busy with returning people; in places even there were shops open, and I saw a drinking fountain running water.

I remember how mockingly bright the day seemed as I went back on my melancholy pilgrimage to the little house at Woking, how busy the streets and vivid the moving life about me. So many people were abroad everywhere, busied in a thousand activities, that it seemed incredible that any great proportion of the population could have been slain. But then I noticed

I stood weeping and praising God upon the summit of Promise Hill.

distributing bread sent us by the French government. The ribs of the few horses showed dismally. Haggard special constables with white badges stood at the corners of every street. I saw little of the mischief wrought by the Martians until I reached Wellington Street, and there I saw the red weed clambering over the buttresses of Waterloo Bridge.

At the corner of the bridge, too, I saw one of the common contrasts of that grotesque time—a sheet of paper flaunting against a thicket of the red weed, transfixed by a stick that kept it in place. It was the placard of the first newspaper to resume publication—the *Daily Mail*. I bought a copy for a blackened shilling I found in my pocket. Most of it was in blank, but the solitary compositor who did the thing had amused himself by making a grotesque scheme of advertisement stereo on the back page. The matter he printed was emotional; the news organisation had not as yet found its way back. I learned nothing fresh except that already in one week the examination of the Martian mechanisms had yielded astonishing results. Among other things, the article assured me what I did not believe at the time, that the "Secret of Flying" was discovered. At Waterloo I found the free trains that were taking people to their homes. The first rush was already over. There were few people in the train, and I was in no mood for casual conversation. I got a compartment to myself, and sat with folded arms, looking greyly at the sunlit devastation that flowed past the windows. And just outside the terminus the train jolted over temporary rails, and on either side of the railway the houses were blackened ruins. To Clapham Junction the face of London was grimy with powder of the Black Smoke, in spite of two days of thunderstorms and rain, and at Clapham Junction the line had been wrecked again; there were hundreds of out-of-work clerks and shopmen working side by side with the customary navvies, and we were jolted over a hasty relaying.

All down the line from there the aspect of the country was gaunt and unfamiliar; Wimbledon particularly had suffered. Walton, by virtue of its unburned pine woods, seemed the least hurt of any place along the line. The Wandle, the Mole, every little stream, was a heaped

how yellow were the skins of the people I met, how shaggy the hair of the men, how large and bright their eyes, and that every other man still wore his dirty rags. Their faces seemed all with one of two expressions—a leaping exultation and energy or a grim resolution. Save for the expression of the faces, London seemed a city of tramps. The vestries were indiscriminately mass of red weed, in appearance between butcher's meat and pickled cabbage. The Surrey pine woods were too dry, however, for the festoons of the red climber. Beyond Wimbledon, within sight of the line, in certain nursery grounds, were the heaped masses of earth about the sixth cylinder. A number of people were standing about it, and some sappers were busy in the midst of it. Over it flaunted a Union Jack, flapping cheerfully in the morning breeze. The nursery grounds were everywhere crimson with the weed, a wide expanse of livid colour cut with purple shadows, and very painful to the eye. One's gaze went with infinite relief from the scorched greys and sullen reds of the foreground to the blue-green softness of the eastward hills.

The line on the London side of Woking station was still undergoing repair, so I descended at Byfleet station and took the road to Maybury, past the place where I and the artilleryman had talked to the hussars, and on by the spot where the Martian had appeared to me in the thunderstorm. Here, moved by curiosity, I turned aside to find, among a tangle of red fronds, the warped and broken dog cart with the whitened bones of the horse scattered and gnawed. For a time I stood regarding these vestiges....

Then I returned through the pine wood, neck-high with red weed here and there, to find the landlord of the Spotted Dog had already found burial, and so came home past the College Arms. A man standing at an open cottage door greeted me by name as I passed.

I looked at my house with a quick flash of hope that faded immediately. The door had been forced; it was unfast and was opening slowly as I approached.

It slammed again. The curtains of my study fluttered out of the open window from which I and the artillery-man had watched the dawn. No one had closed it since. The smashed bushes were just as I had left them nearly four weeks ago. I stumbled into the hall, and the house felt empty. The stair carpet was ruffled and discoloured where I had crouched, soaked to the skin from the thunderstorm the night of the catastrophe. Our muddy footsteps I saw still went up the stairs.

I followed them to my study, and found lying on my writing-table still, with the selenite paper weight upon

I turned aside to find the warped and broken dog cart with the whitened bones of the horse.

it, the sheet of work I had left on the afternoon of the opening of the cylinder. For a space I stood reading over my abandoned arguments. It was a paper on the probable development of Moral Ideas with the development of the civilising process; and the last sentence was the opening of a prophecy: "In about two hundred years," I had written, "we may expect——" The sentence ended abruptly. I remembered my inability to fix my mind that morning, scarcely a month gone by, and how I had broken off to get my *Daily Chronicle* from the newsboy. I remembered how I went down to the garden gate as he came along, and how I had listened to his odd story of "Men from Mars."

I came down and went into the dining room. There were the mutton and the bread, both far gone now in decay, and a beer bottle overturned, just as I and the artilleryman had left them. My home was desolate. I perceived the folly of the faint hope I had cherished so long. And then a strange thing occurred. "It is no use," said a voice. "The house is deserted. No one has been here these ten days. Do not stay here to torment yourself. No one escaped but you."

I was startled. Had I spoken my thought aloud? I turned, and the French window was open behind me. I made a step to it, and stood looking out.

And there, amazed and afraid, even as I stood amazed and afraid, were my cousin and my wife—my wife white and tearless. She gave a faint cry.

"I came," she said. "I knew—knew——"

She put her hand to her throat—swayed. I made a step forward, and caught her in my arms.

And there, amazed and afraid, were my cousin and my wife.

Chapter Ten
★ ★ ★
The Epilogue

I cannot but regret, now that I am concluding my story, how little I am able to contribute to the discussion of the many debatable questions which are still unsettled. In one respect I shall certainly provoke criticism. My particular province is speculative philosophy. My knowledge of comparative physiology is confined to a book or two, but it seems to me that Carver's suggestions as to the reason of the rapid death of the Martians is so probable as to be regarded almost as a proven conclusion. I have assumed that in the body of my narrative.

At any rate, in all the bodies of the Martians that were examined after the war, no bacteria except those already known as terrestrial species were found. That they did not bury any of their dead, and the reckless slaughter they perpetrated, point also to an entire ignorance of the putrefactive process. But probable as this seems, it is by no means a proven conclusion.

Neither is the composition of the Black Smoke known, which the Martians used with such deadly effect, and the generator of the Heat-Rays remains a puzzle. The terrible disasters at the Ealing and South Kensington laboratories have disinclined analysts for further investigations upon the latter. Spectrum analysis of the black powder points unmistakably to the presence of an unknown element with a brilliant group of three lines in the green, and it is possible that it combines with argon to form a compound which acts at once with deadly effect upon some constituent in the blood. But such unproven speculations will scarcely be of interest to the general reader, to whom this story is addressed. None of the brown scum that drifted down the Thames after the destruction of Shepperton was examined at the time, and now none is forthcoming.

The results of an anatomical examination of the Martians, so far as the prowling dogs had left such an examination possible, I have already given. But everyone is familiar with the magnificent and almost complete specimen in spirits at the Natural History Museum, and the countless drawings that have been made from it; and beyond that the interest of their physiology and structure is purely scientific.

A question of graver and universal interest is the possibility of another attack from the Martians. I do not think that nearly enough attention is being given to this aspect of the matter. At present the planet Mars is in conjunction, but with every return to opposition I, for one, anticipate a renewal of their adventure. In any case, we should be prepared. It seems to me that it should be possible to define the position of the gun from which the shots are discharged, to keep a sustained watch upon this part of the planet, and to anticipate the arrival of the next attack.

In that case the cylinder might be destroyed with dynamite or artillery before it was sufficiently cool for the Martians to emerge, or they might be butchered by means of guns so soon as the screw opened. It seems to me that they have lost a vast advantage in the failure of their first surprise. Possibly they see it in the same light.

Lessing has advanced excellent reasons for supposing that the Martians have actually succeeded in effecting a landing on the planet Venus. Seven months ago now, Venus and Mars were in alignment with the sun; that is to say, Mars was in opposition from the point of view of an observer on Venus. Subsequently a peculiar luminous and sinuous marking appeared on the unillumined half of the inner planet, and almost simultaneously a faint dark mark of a similar sinuous character was detected upon a photograph of the Martian disk. One needs to see the drawings of these appearances in order to appreciate fully their remarkable resemblance in character.

At any rate, whether we expect another invasion or not, our views of the human future must be greatly modified by these events. We have learned now that we cannot regard this planet as being fenced in and a secure abiding place for Man; we can never anticipate the unseen good or evil that may come upon us suddenly out of space. It may be that in the larger design of the universe this invasion from Mars is not without its ultimate benefit for men; it has robbed us of that serene confidence in the future which is the most fruitful source of decadence, the gifts to human science it has brought are enormous, and it has done much to promote the conception of the commonweal of mankind. It may be that across the immensity of space the Martians have watched the fate of these pioneers of theirs and learned their lesson, and that on the planet Venus they have found a securer settlement. Be that as it may, for many years yet there will certainly be no relaxation of the eager scrutiny of the Martian disk, and those fiery darts of the sky, the shooting stars, will bring with them as they fall an unavoidable apprehension to all the sons of men.

The broadening of men's views that has resulted can scarcely be exaggerated. Before the cylinder fell there was a general persuasion that through all the deep of space no life existed beyond the petty surface of our minute sphere. Now we see further. If the Martians can reach Venus, there is no reason to suppose that the thing is impossible for men, and when the slow cooling of the sun makes this earth uninhabitable, as at last it must do, it may be that the thread of life that has begun here will have streamed out and caught our sister planet within its toils.

Dim and wonderful is the vision I have conjured up in my mind of life spreading slowly from this little seed bed of the solar system throughout the inanimate vastness of sidereal space. But that is a remote dream. It may be, on the other hand, that the destruction of the Martians is only a reprieve. To them, and not to us, perhaps, is the future ordained.

I must confess the stress and danger of the time have left an abiding sense of doubt and insecurity in my mind. I sit in my study writing by lamplight, and suddenly I see again the healing valley below set with writhing flames, and feel the house behind and about me empty and desolate. I go out into the Byfleet Road, and vehicles pass me, a butcher boy in a cart, a cabful of visitors, a workman on a bicycle, children going to school, and suddenly they become vague and unreal, and I hurry again with the artilleryman through the hot, brooding silence. Of a night I see the black powder darkening the silent streets, and the contorted bodies shrouded in that layer; they rise upon me tattered and dog-bitten. They gibber and grow fiercer, paler, uglier, mad distortions of humanity at last, and I wake, cold and wretched, in the darkness of the night.

I go to London and see the busy multitudes in Fleet Street and the Strand, and it comes across my mind that they are but the ghosts of the past, haunting the streets that I have seen silent and wretched, going to and fro, phantasms in a dead city, the mockery of life in a galvanised body. And strange, too, it is to stand on Primrose Hill, as I did but a day before writing this last chapter, to see the great province of houses, dim and blue through the haze of the smoke and mist, vanishing at last into the vague lower sky, to see the people walking to and fro among the flower beds on the hill, to see the sight-seers about the Martian machine that stands there still, to hear the tumult of playing children, and to recall the time when I saw it all bright and clear-cut, hard and silent, under the dawn of that last great day....

And strangest of all is it to hold my wife's hand again, and to think that I have counted her, and that she has counted me, among the dead.

They gibber and grow fiercer...

Afterword by Ben Bova

The Once and Future Mars

What is there that fascinates us so about the planet Mars? What is there about this planet, above all others, that inspired H.G. Wells to write *The War of the Worlds* and Orson Welles to dramatize the story so chillingly on radio? The answer lies in a single word: life. For generations, people have thought that if any world beyond our own Earth could harbor life, even intelligent life, Mars would be the place.

Mars is the only planet whose surface can be seen from earthbound telescopes. Venus and the distant gas giant worlds of Jupiter and beyond are perpetually covered with clouds. Mercury is barely discernable from Earth; far-off Pluto a mere speck of light. Our own moon, airless and waterless, is a barren ball of rock.

Mars is a nearby neighbor, as planets go. About every twenty-six months, the red planet comes to within 35 million miles of Earth. Only Venus gets closer, about 25 million miles. Spacecraft make the journey to Mars in nine months or less; with only a modest extension of existing technology, humans could explore Mars in person.

Mars is the most Earthlike planet in the solar system. Its axial tilt is similar to Earth's. It spins about its axis in just a little over twenty-four hours. It has obvious polar caps, which melt in the summer and form again in the winter. Mars has seasons.

But does life exist there?

In 1877, Italian astronomer Giovanni Schiaparelli reported seeing straight-line markings on the ruddy face of Mars. He called them *canali*, meaning "channels." American astronomer Percival Lowell, among others, misinterpreted Schiapparelli's conservative description. When Lowell peered at the red planet he saw canals. Lots of them.

Scion of a wealthy Boston family, Lowell had the money and time to build an observatory in Flagstaff. There, in Arizona's clear air, he spent the rest of his life studying those "canals." He postulated that Mars was a dying world, its supply of water (and air) slowly leaking away into space. Intelligent Martian engineers had built the canal system, Lowell believed, to carry water from the polar caps to the cities in the encroaching global desert.

Most astronomers pointed out that Mars was too cold and dry for liquid water to exist on its surface. They even claimed that the polar caps were not water ice at all, but frozen carbon dioxide: dry ice.

Still Lowell doggedly produced extensive maps of Martian canal systems for several decades. When skeptics pointed out that canals would be much too thin to be discerned over the distance between the two planets, Lowell and his followers ingeniously countered that what the telescopes detected was not the canals themselves, but the bands of vegetation—farmlands—on either side of the canals.

Faced with the contention that water would quickly evaporate in the dry, thin Martian atmosphere, the "canalists" proposed that the Martians were clever enough to cover the water's surface with a slick of oil or perhaps even a roof over their canals.

It was Lowell's vision of Mars that inspired H.G. Wells' *War of the Worlds* in 1898. Forty years later, when Orson Welles broadcast his Halloween version of "The War of the Worlds," many in his radio audience were perfectly willing to believe that Martians might exist and could invade the Earth.

In a sense, the Martian canals were indeed created by intelligent minds: the minds of Lowell and other human observers who believed they saw them. With the telescopes available in their day, those astronomers were peering out at the far edge of observability. They saw a faint, ruddy disc, shimmering in and out of focus because of the turbulence in Earth's atmosphere. Their minds connected faint blobs of markings into straight lines—partially an optical illusion, partially a classic case of seeing what you dearly want to see.

When spacecraft began observing Mars from close-up, in the 1960s, the canals disappeared. They were never there. The pitiless cameras aboard a succession of NASA Mariner spacecraft showed no canals, no cities, no Martians: only an utterly barren sandy waste of desert—and lots of craters. To the earliest space probes, such as Mariner 4, Mars looked more like the battered lifeless face of the Moon than a planet that could spawn invading aliens.

Spacecraft observations have shown that Mars is indeed very cold and very dry. As I said in my 1992 novel, *Mars*:

> Picture Death Valley at its worst. Barren desert. Nothing but rock and sand. Remove every trace of life: get rid of each and every cactus, every bit of scrub, all the lizards and insects and sun-bleached bones and anything that even looks as if it might once have been alive.
>
> Now freeze-dry the whole landscape. Plunge it down to a temperature of a hundred below zero. And suck away the air until there's not even as much as you would find on Earth a hundred thousand feet above the ground.
>
> That is roughly what Mars is like.

If you were standing on the equator of Mars in mid-summer, the ground temperature might climb as high as 70° Fahrenheit. But the temperature at the level of your nose would be close to zero, because the Martian atmosphere is so thin that it retains very little heat. If there are any Martians, one thing they don't have to worry about is a greenhouse effect!

The overnight temperature would plummet to lower than a hundred degrees below zero. That's in midsummer. On the equator.

If you uncapped a bottle of water anywhere on Mars, any time of the night or day, the water would quickly boil away, despite the frigid temperature. The atmospheric pressure is far too low to permit water to remain liquid.

Most of Mars is a bone-dry desert of sandy iron oxides: rusty iron dust. Because its atmosphere is so thin, and its planetary magnetic field so weak, hard radiation from the Sun and cosmic rays from deep space bathe Mars' surface with lethal radiation doses.

There is water on the surface of Mars, although it is not liquid. The bright polar caps are composed partially of frozen water, covered over most of the year by dry ice. Spacecraft studies have indicated that liquid water may well exist underground; certainly the ground is underlain with permafrost, much like northern Canada, Alaska, and Siberia.

In 1976, two Viking spacecraft soft-landed on Mars. Each carried three experiments designed to detect possible Martian life: 1) Radioactive carbon-14 was introduced to samples of soil scooped up by Viking's remotely controlled arm, together with a nutrient mixture designed to feed any microorganisms that might be in the soil. If there were organisms present, the gases given off by the soil sample would show a high percentage of carbon-14. 2) A soil sample was mixed with gases that simulated the Martian atmosphere (mostly carbon dioxide), dosed with a slight amount of radioactive carbon-14 as a "tracer," and then exposed to a fluorescent light that simulated sunshine. If there were any Martian organisms present that depended on photosynthesis, they should have multiplied vigorously in such an environment. After five days, the gases were flushed

out of the chamber and the soil was baked at a temperature of 1,157° Fahrenheit. If the baked soil released a significant amount of carbon-14, it would be coming from organisms in the soil that took in the carbon dioxide. 3) Soil samples were "incubated" in a water-rich nutrient bath (which the Viking scientists called "chicken soup") and an atmosphere of carbon dioxide, krypton, and hydrogen. Living Martian organisms, if anything like those on Earth, would convert some of the carbon dioxide to free oxygen.

Each of the three biology experiments showed results that seemed to indicate life—at first.

The gas exchange experiment showed a sharp increase in the amount of oxygen given off by the soil samples, although this soon levelled off. Both the pyrolitic release and the label release experiments also gave strong positive returns at first, followed by lower returns afterward.

In short, all three Viking experiments showed results that were neither straight inorganic chemistry nor obvious Earth-type biology. Moreover, Viking's gas chromatograph-mass spectrometers failed to detect any evidence of organic, long-chain carbon molecules in the Martian soil, down to a level of one part per billion.

Most investigators eventually concluded that the Martian soil is lifeless. The surprising positive results from the biology experiments were attributed to superoxides in the soil, an excess of volatile oxygen molecules. The Martian soil, apparently, is something like powdered bleach.

Even though a few scientists still insist that their colleagues have interpreted Viking's results much too conservatively, the consensus is that life does not—and cannot—exist on the surface of Mars.

On the other hand, researchers in Antarctica used a technique similar to Viking's label release experiment to search for life in the near-freezing water of Lake Vostok, which is perpetually covered by two-and-a-half miles of ice. They not only got positive results, much as Viking did, but they also pulled living microorganisms out of the ice.

Has the scientific community written off the Viking results too soon? The answer may have to wait until scientists get to Mars.

Or perhaps not. Martians may have already "invaded" Earth.

Researchers have identified thirteen meteorites that originated on Mars and landed in Antarctica, Africa, Europe, and the Americas. The largest such meteorite is named Zagami; it was discovered in Nigeria in 1962. It weighs almost forty pounds.

The "Martian Thirteen" are known to be from Mars because the gases trapped within these rocks have the same ratios of noble gases (argon, neon, etc.) as the atmosphere of Mars. They were blasted off the surface of Mars by the impact of much larger meteoroids, cruised through space for millennia and eventually were caught by Earth's gravity field and crashed into our planet after a fiery plunge through our atmosphere.

In 1996, a team of NASA investigators announced finding possible fossils of ancient bacteria in one of the Martian meteorites, ALH84001, a four-pound rock discovered in 1984 in the Allan Hills ice fields in eastern Antarctica.

Scientists have hotly debated the idea that the nanometer-scale structures found deep inside ALH84001 are the fossils of once-living Martian bacteria. Similar structures have been found in a few of the other Martian meteorites.

Lending credence to the idea of microscopic underground life, however, is the fact that geologists have discovered colonies of thermophilic (heat-loving) bacteria living in the intense heat and pressures deep below-ground on Earth. These bacteria never see sunlight. They metabolize solid rock with water to produce the energy of life.

Until these discoveries (the first of which came in 1995) it was tacitly assumed that life needed sunlight to exist. After all, all life on Earth is dependent on photosynthetic organisms that convert solar energy into foodstuffs.

Well, not quite all life. Years earlier, oceanographers had been stunned by the discovery of whole colonies of deep-sea creatures that live around hydrothermal vents at the bottom of the ocean. Their food chain begins with bacteria that can metabolize the sulfur welling up from the hot springs.

Meanwhile, maverick astrophysicist Thomas Gold hypothesized that vast ecologies of subterranean bacteria exist far below the surface of the Earth—and other worlds, as well.

The discovery of thermophilic bacteria far below Earth's surface vindicated Gold's idea of a "deep, hot biosphere." It also meant that similar organisms might exist on Mars. And maybe elsewhere. Gold believes that "deep, hot biospheres" can exist on virtually any solid body in the solar system that has a heat source at its core.

While the surface of Mars seems strongly inhospitable to life, deep underground there could be whole biospheres of thermophilic bacteria, just as there are on Earth.

The possibility that Martian organisms could have survived a ride to Earth brings up the question of whether Earth life might have originated on Mars. Was our world "seeded" by inadvertent Martian space travellers?

Planetary scientists believe that Mars was once much warmer and wetter than it is today. Spacecraft photos show sinuous trails that look like dried-out river beds, and other signs of water erosion. The 1998 Pathfinder lander photographed surface features that were most likely formed by rushing flood waters. Many scientists believe much of the Martian landscape is underlain by permafrost: frozen water reposing underground.

When Mars first coalesced out of the ring of dust and rubble around the newly-formed Sun, more than four billion years ago, its interior was hot from the energy of uncountable impacts by objects ranging in size from dust grains to mini-planets, as well as heat generated by radioactive elements. As the surface of the planet cooled and solidified, Mars was sheathed in a much thicker atmosphere than it has today, and the surface was warm enough to contain liquid water.

Huge volcanoes belched titanic outflows of magma and steam. One of them, the aptly-named Olympus Mons, is the tallest mountain in the solar system, three times higher than Mt. Everest. Its base is roughly the size of Iowa.

Mars was much more Earthlike at the outset. But, because it is such a small planet—barely half Earth's size and with a surface gravity only one-third of Earth's—its atmosphere leaked away, together with its interior heat, until it became the cold, dry, barren world we see today.

Is it really barren, though?

In the coming decade, a dozen or more probes will be launched at Mars by NASA, Russian, European, and Japanese rockets. Some of the spacecraft will orbit Mars; others will land at various spots on Mars' surface; several will send samples of Martian soil, rock, and atmosphere back to eager scientists on Earth.

While there are plans afoot to send probes that can dig into the Martian sands, none of the missions proposed so far will be capable of drilling deep enough—a few miles, at least—to hit colonies of thermophilic bacteria. The probes might, however, detect permafrost ice beneath the surface of the ground; that would be a major encouragement to press on with the search for life.

Sooner or later, human explorers will go to Mars. This, too, depends largely on political decisions, although it is not beyond the realm of possibility to mount a human expedition through private funding, as I examined in my novel, *Return to Mars*.

A key factor is the cost of such an expedition, which NASA pegged at some half-trillion dollars nearly ten years ago. However, innovative ideas such as Robert Zubrin's "Mars Direct" scheme could bring the cost down to the point where a few private philanthropists of the Gates and Spielberg caliber might be able to fund an expedition.

Zubrin's "Mars Direct" idea is simply this: live off the land. Instead of bringing every molecule of fuel, air, and food that an expedition would need, send automated machinery that can produce fuel and breathable air and food crops out of the local Martian resources. Once these precursors have landed on Mars and produced the materials that human explorers need, then send the human team. It could be done, with only a modest advance on existing technology, and for a fraction of NASA's pricetag. Mars is a unique world and should be explored. But it should also be kept as unspoiled as pos-

sible. Talk of terraforming and colonization is not only premature, it's silly. The costs, the risks, the sheer time it would take to transform a planet into a shirtsleeve, Earthlike world simply beggars the imagination.

Who should go to Mars? Scientists, of course. And you and I. But when you and I go, it should be through virtual reality visits. We can walk on the red sands of Mars, climb the solar system's tallest mountain, gasp with awe at the titanic Valles Marineris—a chasm that makes our Grand Canyon look picayune. And we can do it all without leaving our living rooms, through virtual reality systems. Take nothing but pictures; leave nothing but footprints. With VR we can enjoy Mars, revel in its strange, harsh beauty—and not even leave footprints to mar its rust-red sands.

The continuing search for life in the universe will send human explorers and virtual explorers to Mars, possibly within the next twenty years.

Since long before Schiaparelli's time, people have stared at the blood-red disk of Mars with almost equal mixtures of wonder and dread. Could that world, our next-door neighbor in space, harbor intelligent life? The thought was thrilling and terrifying at the same time.

The "canals" intensified this ambivalent attitude. Lowell and his followers wanted to believe that Mars was a world populated by brilliant engineers, valiantly seeking to save their civilization from extinction. H.G. Wells seized on this idea and examined its darker side: intelligent Martians might be coldly calculating, eyeing our lush green world with desperate envy. They might invade the Earth and try to take it for their own, wiping out the human race in the process. Orson Welles' 1938 broadcast showed that there were plenty of people willing to believe that it could happen. Since then, science and science fiction have, in large part, been devoted to confronting this ambivalence, our mixture of terror and delight, at the prospect of life originating somewhere other than Earth.

Ben Bova

Bibliography

Anderson, Kevin J., ed. *War of the Worlds: Global Dispatches*. New York: Bantam Books, 1996.

Asimov, Isaac. Afterword to *The War of the Worlds*, by H.G. Wells. New York: Penguin Putnam, 1986.

Brady, Frank. *Citizen Welles: A Biography of Orson Welles*. New York: Charles Scribner's Sons, 1989.

Broun, Heywood. "It Seems to Me." *New York World-Telegram*, November 2, 1938, p. 25.

Bulgatz, Joseph. *Ponzi Schemes, Invaders from Mars and More Extraordinary Popular Delusions and the Madness of Crowds*. New York: Harmony Books, 1992.

Cameron, Gledhill. "Grovers Mill: A Trick That Was No Treat." *Trenton Evening Times*, October 30, 1968, p. 15.

Cantril, Hadley. *The Invasion from Mars*. Princeton, New Jersey: Princeton University Press, 1940.

Cimone, Marlene. "The Night the 'Martians' Landed." Los Angeles Times, October 30, 1979, sec. 5.

Clarke, Arthur C. Introduction to *The War of the Worlds*, by H.G. Wells. London: Everyman, 1993.

"Could 'Martian Invasion' Happen Today?" *Trenton Evening Times*, October 30, 1968, p. 15.

Delany, Don. "West Windsor Celebrates 'The War of the Worlds.'" Mercer Business, October 1988, p. 14.

Dixon, George. "Fake 'War' on Radio Spreads Panic Over U.S." *New York Daily News*, October 31, 1938, p. 2.

Dunlap, Orrin E. Jr. "Radio Challenges Playwrights to Try New Tricks." *New York Times*, October 30, 1938, sec. 9, p. 12.

Dunning, John. *On the Air: The Encyclopedia of Old-Time Radio*. New York: Oxford University Press, 1998.

"FCC Meets to Act on 'Mars Invasion.'" *New York World-Telegram*, November 1, 1938, p. 4.

Fedler, Fred. *Media Hoaxes*. Ames, Iowa: Iowa State University Press, 1989.

"Geologists at Princeton Hunt 'Meteor' in Vain." *New York Times* (October 31, 1938), p. 4.

Green, Michelle, Andrea Fine and Suzanne Adelson. "The Night the Martians Came to New Jersey." *People*, October 31, 1988.

Hansen, Harry. "The First Reader: H.G. Wells' Earlier 'War of the Worlds' Haunts His Latest, 'Apropos of Dolores.'" *New York World-Telegram*, October 31, 1938, p. 17.

Johnson, Hugh S. "'Mars Panic' Useful." *New York World-Telegram*, November 2, 1938, p. 25.

Klass, Philip. "Wells, Welles, and the Martians." *New York Times Book Review*, October 30, 1988.

Koch, Howard. *The Panic Broadcast: Portrait of an Event*. Boston: Little, Brown & Co., 1970.

Lamm, Jeffrey. "Scriptwriter Still Amazed at Effect." Trenton Times, October 27, 1988, p. F4.

Leaming, Barbara. *Orson Welles: A Biography*. New York: Viking, 1985.

Locke, Richard Adams. *The Moon Hoax*. New York: William Gowans, 1859.

MacAdam, Henry Innes. "Citizen Welles: Master Magician." *West Windsor News Eagle*, October 23, 1998, War of the Worlds section, p. 2.

MacAdam, Henry Innes. "War of the Worlds in the Media: A Short Guide for the Perplexed." West Windsor News Eagle, October 16, 1998.

"'Mars Raiders' Cause Quito Panic; Mob Burns Radio Plant, Kills Fifteen." New York Times (AP), February 14, 1949.

"The Night the Martians Landed." *New York Daily News*, October 30, 1988, Magazine section.

Oxford, Edward. "Night of the Martians." *American History Illustrated*, October 1988.

"Quito Hold Three for 'Mars' Script." *New York Times* (UP), February 16, 1949, p. 15.

"Radio Listeners in Panic, Taking War Drama as Fact." *New York Times*, October 31, 1938.

"Scare Analyzed by Psychologists." *New York World-Telegram*, October 31, 1938.

Smith, David C. *H.G. Wells: Desperately Mortal*. New Haven, Connecticut: Yale University Press, 1986.

Swanson, Glen E. "The War that Never Was." *Starlog*, December 1988.

Thompson, David. *Rosebud: The Story of Orson Welles*. Boston: Little, Brown & Co., 1996.

Thompson, Dorothy. "On the Record: Mr. Welles and Mass Delusion." *New York Herald-Tribune*, November 2, 1938.

"Twenty Dead in the Quito Riot." *New York Times* (UP), February 15, 1949, p. 5.

"U.S. Investigates Radio Drama of Invasion by Martians That Threw Nation into Panic." *New York World-Telegram*, October 31, 1938.

"U.S. Probing Radio Fantasy Which Terrorized Listeners." *Chicago Daily News* (AP), October 31, 1938, p. 4.

"War's Over: How U.S. Met Mars." *New York Daily News* (AP), October 31, 1938, p. 2.

Wells, H.G. The War of the Worlds. New York: Looking Glass Library, 1960.

West, Anthony. *H.G. Wells: Aspects of a Life*. New York: New American Library, 1984.

Television Programs

"Halloween 1938." *Our World*. Linda Ellerbee and Ray Gandolf, prods. and nars. ABC, October 30, 1986.

"The Night America Trembled." *Studio One*. Edward R. Murrow, nar. CBS, 1957.

Orson Welles Interview. *Tomorrow*. Tom Snyder interviewer. NBC, May 1, 1975.

Radio Programs

"Theatre of the Imagination." Special program on *The Mercury Theatre on the Air*, Leonard Maltin, nar. 1988.

Websites

http://helix.ucsd.edu/~aboese/moonhoax.html ("The Great Moon Hoax")

http://home.golden.net/~csp/reviews/waroftheworlds.htm (Review of *The War of the Worlds*)

http://hometown.aol.com/Battlecat0/WOW.html (War of the Worlds: "Mars Broadcast Causes Mass Hysteria as Listeners Panic")

http://members.aol.com/jeff1070/wotw.html (Radio's *War of the Worlds* Broadcast [1938])

http://members.tripod.com/~gwillick/obit/hgwellso.html ("H.G. Wells Dead in London at Seventy-nine; Forecast Atomic Age in 1914 Novel," *New York Times* obituary, August 16, 1946)

http://nssdc.gsfc.nasa.gov/planetary/viking.html (Viking Mission to Mars, NASA website)

http://waroftheworlds.org (The Official Grovers Mill War of the Worlds Home)

www.arches.uga.edu/~cmsgrisw/pease~1.htm ("I'll Take Martians Over Media Illiteracy" by Ted Pease, reprinted from the Logan, Utah, *Herald-Journal*, November 10, 1996)

www.bergen.com/region/war29199810297.htm ("NJ Town Has Last Laugh on Martians" by Wayne Parry, [AP], October 29, 1998)

www.best.com/~drzeus/wotw/wotw.html (War of the Worlds, a collection of cover art)

www.bway.net/~nipper/home.html (The Estate of Orson Welles Main Index)

www.csicop.org/si/9811/martian.html ("The Martian Panic Sixty Years Later: What Have We Learned?" by Robert E. Bartholomew)

www.forteantimes.com/artic/109/moon.html ("When Beavers Roamed the Moon: The Other Moon Hoax" by Brian Regal)

www.indiana.edu/~liblilly/guides/welles/orsonwelles.html (Guide to the Orson Welles Materials in the Lilly Library, Indiana University)

www.irdp.co.uk/hoax.htm ("The Psychological Power of Radio" by Tim Crook)

www.marsattacksfan.com/homepage.htm (Zelda's Mars Attacks! Home Page)

www.msss.com/education/facepage/face.html (The "Face" on Mars, NASA website)

www.otr.com/mystery2a.html (Radio Days—Mystery)

www.otr.com/sf.html (Science Fiction and Radio)

www.rdg.ac.uk/~lhsjamse/wells/wells.htm (The H.G. Wells Society)

www.rdg.ac.uk/~lhsjamse/fnd.htm (Foundation: The International Review of Science Fiction)

www.scifi.com/scifi.con/screen/invasion/essay2.html ("The Night the Martians Landed" by Anthony Tollin)

www.swl.net/patepluma/south/ecuador/martians.html ("Martians and Radio Quito: The Day the Martians Landed or Stories They Never Tell on HCJB" by Don Moore)

www.unknown.nu/mercury (The Mercury Theatre on the Air)

www.xtec.es/recursos/astronom/ask/refmoon.htm ("The Great Moon Hoax of 1835," from *Hoaxes in Journalism* by R. J. Brown)

Acknowledgments

Authors and editors routinely claim in their acknowledgments that the book you hold in your hands could not have happened without the invaluable contributions of others. In this case, it's abundantly true—the very idea for the book originally came from Dominique Raccah, our publisher. It was not only her inspiration and leadership that made this book possible, but the help of everybody at Sourcebooks that turned it into a reality. For their editorial guidance and valuable feedback, we owe a debt to Todd Stocke, Peter Lynch, Amy Baxter, Beth Hayslett, Jennifer Fusco, and John Cominos. For their wonderful design, hard work, and creative input, we thank Taylor Poole and Micah Taupule. Every department, however, including sales, publicity, marketing, editorial, and production, played a part in the final product.

This book and audio CD set would not have been what it is without the inimitable written contributions from Ray Bradbury and Ben Bova, or the authoritative voice of narrator John Callaway. We owe them our deepest gratitude.

For making this project possible, we thank Dennis Levin of Radio Spirits, Anne Koch, and Norman Rudman. For help in researching the figures, books, broadcasts, and other material relevant to this project, we gratefully acknowledge Susan Presnell and the staff of the Lilly Library at Indiana University for their help in navigating their exhaustive collection of Orson Welles material; Madeline Gibson and Gene Rinkel, at the University of Illinois' Rare Books and Special Collections Library, for their assistance in researching the life and works of H.G. Wells and in finding rare artwork for the book; Bob Koshinski, Jerry H. Stearns, and Tom Atkins for their help in investigating the 1968 WKBW broadcast; Brunella Bruni at KTSA in San Antonio, the station that recorded the only meeting between Wells and Welles in 1940; Eric Young and Fabiana Santana at Archive Films; Brett Gutride at Corbis Images; the Museum of Broadcasting Communications in Chicago; Dan Thomasson at Scripps-Howard, the publisher of the old *New York World-Telegram*; Asha Danierie at the Topps Trading Card Company, publisher of "Mars Attacks!"; Anne Slater at the Buffalo and Erie County Historical Society; Alex Boese for his help on the Moon Hoax; the West Windsor Library in New Jersey, for their comprehensive collection of "War of the Worlds" material; Catherine Shrope-Mok, the owner of the "Martian" water tower in Grovers Mill, who allowed one of us to traipse through her backyard to photograph the tower not once, but two times; and George and Alice Martch, whose research, knowledge of the West Windsor-Grovers Mill area, and willingness to act as chauffeur and guide can never be repaid and will always be remembered.

Photo & Audio Credits

Photo Credits

All credits listed by page number, in the order indicated on pages.

Every effort has been made to correctly attribute all the materials reproduced in this book. If any errors have been made, we will be happy to correct them in future editions.

Page ii Corbis-Bettmann. **Page viii** University of Illinois, Corbis-Bettmann. **I. Eve of Halloween** 2–6 Corbis-Bettmann; 7 Alex Lubertozzi, New York Daily News; 8 New York Daily News; 9 New York Times; 11 Scripps-Howard, Variety; 12 New York Times; 13 Corbis-Bettmann; 14 AP/Wide World Photos; 15–17 Corbis-Bettmann; 18 New York Daily News, Corbis-Bettmann; 19–20 Scripps-Howard; 21 University of Illinois, Scripps-Howard; 22 Corbis-Bettmann, Lilly Library/Indiana University; 23 Corbis-Bettmann; 24 Alex Lubertozzi, Trenton, New Jersey, Times; 25 Alex Lubertozzi. **The Radio Play** 26–27 Corbis-Bettmann. **Orson Welles** 56–57 AP/Wide World Photos; 58 Lilly Library/Indiana University; 59 Corbis-Bettmann; 60 Lilly Library/Indiana University; 61 Archive Photos; 62–65 Corbis-Bettmann; 66 Hulton-Deutsch Collection/Corbis. **II. Martians, Moon Men, and Other Close Encounters** 68–69 Topps Trading Card Co., Corbis-Bettmann; 71–75 Corbis-Bettmann; 76 Associated Press; 77 Buffalo and Erie County Historical Society; 80 Topps Trading Card Co.; 81 NASA, ©1989 Roger Ressmeyer/NASA/Corbis; 82 Twentieth Century Fox Film Corporation. **III. H.G. Wells** 84–90 University of Illinois; 91 University of Illinois, AP/Wide World Photos; 92 Corbis-Bettmann; 93 University of Illinois. **The War of the Worlds** 94 Corbis-Bettmann; 96–155 University of Illinois; 156 Corbis-Bettmann; 158–191 University of Illinois.

Audio Credits

Audio Engineering: Mark Ruff and Donovan Weyland, Chicago Recording Company.

"The War of the Worlds" on *The Mercury Theatre on the Air* under license by Radio Spirits, Inc. Schaumburg, Illinois © 1988 Howard Koch.

WKBW "War of the Worlds" program courtesy WWKB-Buffalo, Entercom Buffalo LLC.

Some audio segments have been edited for time and content. Archival audio provided by and copyright of:

Archive Films
NBC News Archives
Infinity Broadcasting Corporation and Station KTSA (AM)

Ray Bradbury is the author of more than thirty books. Among his best known works are *The Martian Chronicles, Fahrenheit 451, The Illustrated Man,* and *Something Wicked This Way Comes.*

He has written for the theater and cinema—including the screenplay of John Huston's acclaimed film adaptation of *Moby Dick*—and has been nominated for an Academy Award. He has adapted sixty-five of his short stories for television on *Ray Bradbury Theater* and won an Emmy for his teleplay of "The Halloween Tree."

Mr. Bradbury received the National Book Foundation's 2000 Medal for Distinguished Contribution to American letters. His next novel, *From the Dust Returned,* will be published by HarperCollins on October 31, 2001.

He lives in Los Angeles, California, with his wife.

Dr. Ben Bova has been writing award-winning science fiction, including *Moonrise* and *Mars,* and nonfiction, such as *Immortality* and *Space Flight* for more than fifty years. President emeritus of the National Space Society and a past president of Science Fiction and Fantasy Writers of America, Dr. Bova was elected a fellow of the American Association for the Advancement of Science in 2000. A former editorial director for *Omni magazine,* Dr. Bova's next work of nonfiction, *The Story of Light,* will be published by Sourcebooks in October 2001.

He lives in Naples, Florida, with his wife, Barbara.

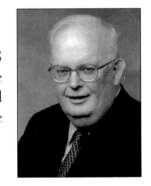

John Callaway has been a broadcast journalist for more than forty-three years, working for CBS Radio in Chicago and New York and WBBM-TV, CBS Chicago, before becoming the long-time host of *Chicago Tonight* on WTTW, Chicago's Public Television station. He is now the host and senior editor of *Chicago Stories,* the weekly documentary and interview program on WTTW. He is the author of *The Thing of It Is.* Mr. Callaway lives in Chicago with his wife, Sandy.

Brian Holmsten is a project editor with Sourcebooks. He is the coauthor of the forthcoming *How a Book Is Made* and has written numerous magazine articles as well as television and video scripts. He also teaches communications at the College of DuPage in Glen Ellyn, Illinois. He lives in Elmhurst, Illinois, with his wife, Lenora, and their two children, Michelle and Sean.

Alex Lubertozzi has made a living as a writer and editor for the past ten years. After five years running a small press that he helped start as a division of a nonprofit foundation, he joined Sourcebooks as an editor. Having earned a master's degree in advertising from the University of Illinois, he once considered going into the field, but eventually realized he didn't like advertising. He has written articles for *Screen, Small Press,* and was a contributing editor for the highly praised, but ultimately doomed, twentysomething, pop-culture magazine, *Pure.* This is his first book. A native of Chicago, he now lives in Oak Park, Illinois, with his wife, Helen.